THE
LEFT
SIDE
OF
REALITY

THE
LEFT
SIDE
OF
REALITY

a novel by

ROBERT J. SMITH

ISBN: 0985810351
ISBN-13: 978-0985810351

Published by Freeze Time Media
Cover design: Di Freeze
Illustration: Andrea Parks

Dedicated to my wife, Barbara, and our family.

PROLOGUE

In every life a major crossroad is encountered, a time when we, as think-ing, feeling beings, must determine the ultimate path our lives shall take. Once that path is resolved, we find ourselves committed along a narrow, winding road toward our own destiny. But are we to believe that the direction chosen is the only exploration? Is it possible that a part of us, a separate, distinct fragment of our own immortality, disassociates itself to follow that other road, the one that leads to the left side of reality?

Author Unknown

On the evening of July 14, 1885, a young French doctor, Pierre Genet, sat down at his desk and began a letter in which he would relate a story so incredible even he found it impossible to believe. For days he had relived the events of the last five months and each time he reached the same conclusion. What had happened to Claude Frontierre must be told. But, in doing so, he would have to take the greatest of care in choosing the proper person to take into his confidence. Many of his colleagues would consider him a lunatic and his practice would be in jeopardy. More than once he had seated himself at the little desk, writing instrument in hand, and more than once he had replaced it in its holder without the first word written. But tonight he had vowed it would be different. With new resolve he had set his course. He would write down the strange facts of the last months and send them off to the only person he felt he could trust. If he was found to be demented, none other than his best friend and former roommate at the university,

Doctor Jacques Marseille, would make that decision. Though they rarely saw each other, they were still like brothers. Neither would seek to hurt the other. Even so, there was still some measure of uncertainty as Doctor Genet began the letter.

My dear friend Jacques,

It is with much trepidation that I begin this letter. I'm sure that by the time you have finished reading it, you will feel that I am in need of being committed. Now I must ask you to hear me out and, please, with an open mind, for I assure you I have thought myself a bit touched a number of times these last weeks. Still, I have wrestled with this enigma again and again. And, I have always arrived at my original conclusion. But wait. Let me begin at the beginning, at the accident.

As you know, when I left the University seven years ago, I began my practice in Toule, a small agricultural and cattle community in the south of France. Many small farms dot our countryside. It was on one of these farms that Claude Frontierre lived, and there that he suffered the accident that changed not only his life but also his wife's life and of course, mine.

Claude was a vigorous young man standing nearly two meters tall. Stout of chest, he had grown quite strong over the few years he had operated the small farm. He was finishing his morning chores just before noon on February 10th. The night before had seen a combination of sleet and snow cover the countryside. Treacherously low temperatures remained throughout the day. A slippery glaze had formed over the snow-covered ground. After haying the mule, Claude had started back across the fifty or so meters that separated the house from the barn. I'm sure, as we all do, Claude was moving faster than he should have on the frozen ground, consequently a short distance from the barn his feet deserted him. A fall in soft snow would normally have served only to irritate such a robust individual. But on this occasion something unforeseen happened. During the summer Claude had driven a small metal stake into the ground. It was meant to tether the goat. As Claude fell backward, his head struck the object and he was knocked senseless. A half hour, possibly longer, passed before his wife became concerned and went looking for him. She found him half frozen and near death. Knowing Claude needed immediate medical attention, this frail creature managed to drag a human twice her size over the remaining distance to the bed they shared. I shall never understand how.

She came for me immediately. The woman was in a terrible panic, hardly able to communicate. When finally I was able to discern her problem, I quickly gathered my instruments and accompanied her to the farm. At first glance I thought my trip was for naught. Then as I examined the man closely I found the weak pulse. Heartened, I set about at once to arouse him. And though his pulse became stronger, he did not stir. Very soon I realized he was caught up in the deep sleep, the coma. I worked over the man for some time before it was evident that Claude would wake at his own appointed time. I had done my best for this day and so I took my leave, promising the distraught woman I would return the next evening and also stressing the importance that she should send for me immediately should any change in Claude's condition occur.

And so I did. Day after day I returned to the farm. And day after day I found his young wife sitting dutifully by his side. Many times the evidence of tears was fresh on her cheeks. But she persevered. Together we worked over Claude, massaging muscles, working limbs, turning his body to guard against the sores. But the man remained in his dormant state. Only his steady breathing assured me that he was still very much alive. Two weeks passed and I was beginning to doubt that he would return to a conscious state again.

Then, on the seventeenth day after the accident, as I was checking his pulse, I noticed movement in the fingers of his left hand. I took heart as did Daphne. With her help we continued massaging his muscles, now with renewed vigor. This change in Claude's condition became even more evident in Daphne's demeanor. The girl, who had worked tirelessly before, had become obsessed to the point of needing little or no rest at all. And all the while Claude was showing more signs of motion in his fingers and then other extremities. All of a sudden, I felt most assuredly that Claude would now recover from the coma. And recover he did, but slowly. It was at the end of the third week before his eyes opened, and *then only to flicker momentarily before falling back into a fitful sleep.*

It was the following day before Claude opened his eyes the second time and gazed up into Daphne's smiling face. I had arrived only moments before and stood on the other side of the bed. Claude stared first at Daphne; then, without moving his head, he cut his eyes toward me. His mouth opened but no sound emerged. Long days of inactivity had so weakened him that he could only mouth his words. For several moments he looked from one to the other of us as we quietly tried to reassure him. At the time I thought nothing of it, but as I look back now I realize there was no recognition on his part. He knew neither Daphne nor myself.

After a moment of searching our faces, his mouth opened again and I bent close to his lips, hoping to catch any word that he might be able to say. But it was hopeless and finally he became exhausted and closed his eyes. He slept quietly now and I knew his strength was increasing with each breath. It would only be a matter of time before he spoke.

The next day was much the same as the preceding day. Claude experienced moments of consciousness, but he still was unable to utter a discernible sound.

It was the middle of the fourth week when Daphne met me at the door with the telltale signs of tears still evident in her eyes and on her cheeks. To my knowledge she had not wept for some time now, possibly since we had first noticed movement in Claude's fingers. And now the tears were flowing again. I was fearful that Claude might have suffered a reversal.

"He cried out in his sleep," she whispered.

"Wonderful," I replied. "Wonderful."

But there seemed to be no happiness in the girl's face. Her eyes refused to meet mine now and her manner communicated a despair she had not exhibited since shortly after the accident. I was, of course, perplexed by this overnight change in attitude.

"What is it, Daphne? What troubles you, girl?"

"It is nothing," she insisted. I knew it was not the truth. The girl was holding back. Something was very wrong. At least in her mind it was. I did not pursue the question but followed her to their bedroom.

As we started through the door, she paused and allowed me pass into the room alone. I thought it odd. Her Claude had spoken, and now she seemed to separate herself from him. She lingered in the doorway a moment and then quietly departed to another part of the small dwelling.

Since I had been spending a goodly portion of my time at the Frontierre home recently, word had been left on my office door where I could be reached in case of an emergency. Now I sat patiently beside the bed, waiting for Claude to wake and open his eyes. It was perhaps a half hour or longer before he finally did. All this time the wife did not reappear. When finally Claude did open his eyes, he gazed around the small room as if he had never seen it before. Of course he had. He had awakened on several occasions in my presence. But I now realized his eyes were searching diligently for something familiar. Finally our eyes met and his face wrinkled in a questioning demeanor.

"Where is Stephanie?"

The voice was weak but clearly audible for the first time since the accident. I dismissed the strange name immediately, knowing the confusion he must be experiencing after so many days in the coma. I gave him no time to repeat the question but rose, went to the door and summoned his wife who was still in another part of the house.

"Daphne," I called and a moment later the girl came hesitantly into view. "Come quickly. Your husband is awake and speaking."

She came and knelt beside the bed, but with a hesitation I did not understand. The girl took Claude's massive hand in hers and pressed it against her face in a show of her love for the man. I watched as she did this and noticed as their eyes met. You could see the tenderness, the love in her eyes. But in Claude's there was no emotion, only the blank stare of a man who was truly mystified by his surroundings and the woman who sat beside him. I now know of a certainty that he neither knew his wife nor recognized where he was.

After a moment he turned his attention back to me and began to speak. In that weakened voice, he asked. "Where is Stephanie? I wish to see my wife."

At once the girl loosed Claude's hand and began sobbing. Her eyes sought out mine and silently screamed for help. I was at a loss.

"Here is Daphne," I said motioning to the girl. "Here is the wife that has nursed you back to life. Do you not know her, man?"

But he rejected my overtures and impatiently shook his head.

"No. No. My wife. My Stephanie. Where is she?" The voice was suddenly stronger.

It was at this outburst that Daphne rose from her chair and fled the room. I watched her go, the sobs growing louder as she disappeared into the next room. When I returned my attention to Claude, it was as if the girl had never been present. I found him searching my own eyes, awaiting an explanation I could not give.

He spoke first and his voice was strong, more authoritative. "Where am I? Why am I here? If I am ill or injured, why am I not in the hospital?"

"You are home, Claude. You had an accident, a fall, and you are here in your own bed so that your health might be restored. And I might add, that young woman you seem not to know is the reason you live today."

Claude glanced toward the door where Daphne had disappeared only moments before and addressed me again. His voice was much softer now. "I am thankful for her attendance to my injuries, but I neither know her nor this place you refer to as my home." He paused a moment. "Neither do I know you."

I was speechless until my stupidity slapped me in the face. Of course, I reasoned now in my mind. The man was suffering from a loss of memory, a malady I had studied but had never witnessed. The amnesias, as it was called, would explain his strange behavior.

But, I reasoned, the problem must be approached cautiously so as not to aggravate a situation that could drive the man into a deeper state of confusion.

I sought to calm Claude with a few questions. "My good man, you have had an accident. It has left you in a state of confusion. You will begin to remember details of your life soon. But for now, can you tell me if you remember anything about what happened to you, anything about your accident?"

His face contorted and there was a sting in his reply. "Of course, I remember. I remember everything." His eyes were suddenly alert. He

was measuring me now. "I have forgotten nothing. Who are you?"
he snapped.

"I am Doctor Genet. I have been tending your wounds since
the accident."

He studied me closely for several seconds. I did not disturb him but
let his eyes wander about my being. Finally he spoke again. "I thought
I knew every physician in Paris. Are you new to the city?"

I was dumbfounded by the question but managed to respond quietly.
"Why do you speak of Paris?" I could feel Daphne's presence behind me
and saw Claude glance up dispassionately. I knew that the girl must
be terrified by our conversation, unable to understand what was amiss
with her loved one. I did not turn to acknowledge her but kept my
attention focused on Claude.

"Why not Paris?" Claude continued. "That is my home. It is there
that I work. Why would I be elsewhere? Why would I not think I am
in Paris?"

The displeasure of a few moments ago was now replaced by concern
as he peered over my shoulder to Daphne. "Young woman, I understand
you have been nursing me to health. For that I thank you and will be
eternally grateful. But I do not know you. I do not know this place.
And I can only surmise at what madness has brought me here."

I held up my hand, aware of the emotional shock this insensitive
statement must have had on his faithful wife. At this time I felt that
to press on with Claude might further damage his fragile mind. "You
need rest. You must sleep now."

"No." He made a feeble effort at grasping my wrist. "I must have
answers."

I started to rise from my chair. "You're exhausted, Man. Your mind
will be clear tomorrow. We will talk then."

He shook his head vigorously. "Until you answer my questions,
there can be no rest." His head lifted slightly from the bed and fell back
quickly. "Please. Do not leave."

I thought better than to agitate him further and settled back in
my chair. "As you wish, Claude. But first you must answer a few of
my questions."

He started to protest but I held up my hand. "If you wish answers you must first give them."

He sighed and nodded his head. "Agreed," he answered reluctantly.

"We shall start with your name. Do you know it?"

"Of course. I am Claude Frontierre." He was not hesitant. And suddenly I questioned my original diagnosis. If there was memory loss it was only partial. Something else lay under the surface, something I found mystifying. This was not the same Claude I had known before the accident. Perhaps a few other questions would help explain what was happening.

"Of course you are Claude Frontierre." I hesitated before continuing. "What is your occupation?"

He was measuring me again. I think at this time he was becoming increasingly suspicious that we were playing some kind of devious trick on him. Still, he answered. "The same as you claim to be. I am a doctor of medicine, teaching and practicing at the Sorbonne."

I'm sure if the teeth in my mouth had not been my own, they would have surely dislodged and fell heavily on the floor. Evidently the man was in a greater state of confusion than I first believed. Either that or he was lying. But for what purpose? It was then that I saw something in Claude's eyes, something that caused me to realize that he truly believed what he was saying. This shocked me.

Still, I pressed on. I had to find an answer. "You teach and practice medicine in Paris. Who is professor of chemistry at the Sorbonne?"

"Louis Pasteur. He has been these last eighteen years. I know him well."

Again the answer came back without hesitation. But Pasteur had found a modicum of fame. Even a farmer from Toule could know of him. But could that farmer know how long he had been at the Sorbonne? I resolved to investigate that portion of his answer later. Now I got to the main question. Did Claude really remember how he came to be disabled?

I reached to the back of his head and pressed gently. Even then he winced. "This swelling at the back of your head. How did it happen?"

His eyes clouded and I could tell his mind was traveling back in time. He slowly ran his right hand up past his ear and gently massaged the knot that was still evident just above the base of his skull. "I was riding. My mount was spooked and threw me." He fingered the knot again and seemed to be gathering his thoughts. "The way my head feels, I must have sustained a severe blow to the occipital area of the skull." His answer came back as if it were something he had cause to observe on a regular basis. He had arrived at much the same conclusion as I had on my first examination.

I got up and walked around the bed to gaze out the window, pondering Claude's last statement. Outside, a light blanket of snow was beginning to cover the ground.

"When did this accident, this fall from the horse as you say, occur?" As I waited for his answer I continued to watch as the flakes began to intensify and gain in size. The snow of a few weeks ago had melted and now more was beginning to cover the ground. At the rate it was falling a white sheet would cover the ground very soon.

Claude was speaking again. "It must have been the eighth..." he said after a few moments of thought, "no, the tenth of February," he corrected himself. "It was shortly before noon. I was riding near my home on my way to lunch with Stephanie."

I noted the time. It was very close to the time that Daphne had told me she began to be concerned about Claude that very morning. I also noted that at the mere mention of the name Stephanie, Daphne would gasp. Claude seemed totally unaware of the hurt that he was heaping on her. If he was, he did not indicate such. The man was totally ignorant of his situation.

Suddenly, he blurted out. "Enough of your questions. I have some of my own."

I nodded and moved back toward my chair. Daphne was still in the room, resting her back against the door facing at the far side. The eyes that had been so radiant during the times that she spoke of Claude before he regained his voice were now dull and listless. She was truly suffering. I felt agony for her. I took my eyes from her and sat heavily in the chair again.

"I shall answer your questions to the best of my knowledge." I leaned forward in the chair and gave him my full attention.

He looked at me sternly. "Where is this place, this town, if it is not Paris?"

"A farm near Toule in the south of France." I did not say it was his. I'm not sure just why but I did not.

His head came several inches off the bed as he responded. "Toule!" He looked incredulous. "I have not been in Toule in more than fifteen years." His eyes narrowed, giving evidence of pain caused by his sudden movement on the bed.

I put my hand on his shoulder, and he gradually rested his head back on the pillow. "You are all right?" I questioned.

He nodded without speaking.

"Then you know the place?"

His eyes had lost the pained expression when he answered. "Most assuredly, I know the place. I was born here, grew to manhood here." He paused to regain his breath before continuing. "And left here when I was still very young, only twenty. I have never returned to Toule, at least of my own free will." He paused and eyed me accusingly. "Why have I been brought here now?"

"You are here now because you live here," I answered. "You are here of your own free will. No one has brought you here."

He took his eyes from me and stared up at the ceiling. "This is surely a joke and in very poor taste, I must say."

I was suddenly on the defensive. "I promise you, it is no joke."

He grasped my wrist again, this time quite firmly. "Someone must get word to the university, to Stephanie. They must know I am alive and recuperating. If I am not a prisoner, will you do that for me?" His grip and his intense expression communicated an urgency that was quite startling to me. For someone who had been so near death only a short time before, Claude Frontierre was suddenly quite strong.

I patted his hand and gently released it from my wrist. "You can be certain that I will do whatever is necessary to alleviate the fears of anyone associated with you."

"You will notify them!" Claude pressed. It was more statement than question.

"I will write letters immediately. Yes, I will write them." I promised

this more for his comfort than anything else. For Claude was beginning to get quite agitated. I felt it better to appease him than to let him think no one would act on his behalf. At this time I felt his mind was temporarily disordered, probably by the amnesia.

"You have made me a promise," he said matter-of-factly. "Are you a man of your word, Doctor Genet?"

"I would hope so."

He seemed relieved at my answer. "I believe you, doctor." He closed his eyes but they were open again almost immediately. "I must ask you again. How did I get to Toule?" Exhaustion had set in, for Claude did not wait for an answer to this question but closed his eyes and dropped off to sleep without another word.

As you can see my good friend, Jacques, the man was acting and talking like no normal human being. I could only conclude that he was suffering from some form of psychosis brought on by the fall and what seemed to be a partial memory loss. I was now convinced beyond any doubt that he believed everything he had told me.

During the next weeks and because of Claude's continued insistence, I wrote and received replies from a number of citizens of Paris, people he insisted were his very good friends and acquaintances. He provided their addresses without a moments hesitation. How would he know this, I wondered? But alas, I had no answer.

But, back to the people I wrote. Several stand out in my mind. One was a Doctor Thomas Diderot. Claude insisted they were friends and acquaintances and spent time together. Surprisingly, Diderot did exist. And he did remember Claude. He remembered a young man named Claude Frontierre from his early days at the University. But the young man he remembered had become disillusioned and dropped out of his classes. Diderot had neither seen nor heard from him during those nearly fifteen years.

After receiving his letter, I checked with some of the older citizens in and around our small community. It seems that Claude did leave Toule for a short time hoping to pursue a degree in medicine. But he had returned home shortly thereafter, bought the small farm where he now resided and settled down to the life of a farmer.

Perhaps a year later a new family moved to Toule. The daughter, Daphne, who was only eighteen and Claude, who was now in his middle twenties, met and fell in love. In less than a year they were married.

I spoke not only to Daphne but to a number of his friends around our small community. All swore that Claude had never ventured more than a horseback ride from Toule again in all those years.

The second letter and the most baffling was from a Charles Manchester, an Englishman and an unknown artist. Claude insisted the man was a close friend and had been a frequent visitor in his Paris home over the past four years. He described a painting that Manchester had done that the both of them referred to as the Iron Mistress. It portrayed a stern-faced Englishwoman sitting atop a magnificent carriage. With whip raised high above her head, she was staring down at several small waifs as they leapt out of the way of her charging stallions. According to Claude, he and Manchester had named the painting shortly after Manchester finished it. In my letter, I mentioned the painting to Manchester. His reply was most disturbing. He did not know Claude but the painting did exist. Manchester had finished the work only six months earlier. As of yet the painting had no name. But Manchester noted that the name I related fit the painting. His thought was that he would most likely name the painting exactly what I had mentioned in my letter. He also swears that no other eyes have witnessed the painting except his fiancee, a young woman by the name of Stephanie Bardot. But Claude, who had not been more than a day's horseback ride from Toule in ten years, knew of the painting and who had painted it. I spoke discreetly to Daphne, thinking the girl could shed some light on this mystery. She could not. Manchester's name had never been mentioned in her presence. Yet Claude knew the man, knew how to contact him, knew his work. The mystery deepened. It left me at a loss.

I wrote even to Pasteur only to receive a curt note in reply. He had never heard of Claude. I made an effort to contact the woman, Stephanie Bardot, thinking she might know Claude. It seemed quite a coincidence that Manchester should be betrothed to a woman with the same given name that our Claude had been raving about. But the woman did not know him and had never heard of him. Of this, I was not surprised.

I sent off numerous other letters. With the exception of Diderot there was no other recollection of Claude Frontierre. I immediately made Claude aware of each reply, with one exception. I did not tell him about the Manchester letter. Until I ascertained whether the Bardot woman was the one that Claude remembered as his wife, I felt it would be unwise to remind him of the name Stephanie.

When I inquired at a later date about the Stephanie he remembered, the maiden name he related to me was not Bardot. It was at that point I allowed him to read the Manchester letter. Upon reading these replies from Parisians he swore were his friends and associates, he angrily wadded the letters up and threw them across the room. I feel it was then that Claude made his decision. He knew it was only a matter of time before he would regain his strength and then he would find his own answers.

As I expected, when his strength continued to return, Claude announced his intention to travel, as he swore, home to Paris. He would settle this mystery himself. I think, in the hidden recesses of his mind, he still was not convinced that some type of hoax had not been perpetrated on him. The accident, he insisted, had occurred while he was horseback riding in Paris and not as both Daphne and I knew it had. We could not convince him otherwise.

He set his time of departure just a few weeks hence when he was sure he would be back at full strength. But something quite strange happened a short time before he was to leave us. I was called a half-day's buggy ride away to deliver a child. A great deal of stormy weather had moved through our area in the last few days; and as I left that morning, I could see new clouds gathering in the west. That afternoon the storm hit. Creeks and branches, calm during the morning, became impassable by nightfall and the storm continued to rage. Once the child was delivered and the mother out of danger, I made an effort to return home. But I found it impossible to cross the swollen creeks. Unhappily, I was committed to stay the night.

It was during this night that something happened to further convince me that a truly strange phenomenon had actually taken place in the life of Claude Frontierre.

A new family had moved into the area a few weeks before. Having never made their acquaintance, they neither knew me nor I them. Their son, a frail nine year old, began experiencing severe lower abdominal pains. At the height of the storm the father came looking for a doctor. Of course, I was not to be found in my lodgings. In his distress, the father began inquiring as to my whereabouts and learned that I had been spending a great deal of time at the Frontierre farm. There, the frantic father went looking for me and there the father gained Claude's sympathetic ear.

Without hesitation, and without revealing that he was not the doctor, Claude accompanied the man back to his home. By the time they arrived, from the man's description of the child's symptoms, Claude was already convinced of the problem. Only a hasty examination was needed. The child's appendix was in need of extraction.

Again, without relating that he was not the doctor they thought he was, Claude impressed on both the mother and father the urgency of immediate action. The boy, he said, could die if not operated on immediately. His seeming professionalism convinced both father and mother of the urgency of the situation and they quickly agreed that Claude should do everything possible for their son, still unaware that they were not dealing with me.

Claude instructed the woman in the preparations for the operation, then borrowed the man's wagon and drove to my home where he forced entry and confiscated the needed instruments. Within the hour he was operating on the child. All the while, I was some miles away captured by the swollen waters of the creek.

In short, my good friend Jacques, the operation was a complete success. The boy's life was spared. The next day when I was able to negotiate the creek and return home, I learned what had happened. Fearful, I went immediately to the child's home, fully expecting to find dire circumstances. It was not so. Upon examination, I found what I considered to be a very competent appendectomy. Everything seemed to be in order. The child's fever, which I learned had been at 104 degrees the previous evening, was very nearly normal. Already, he was sitting up in bed and seemed quite comfortable. It goes without saying that the child made a complete recovery.

    I was now baffled but also determined that Claude should not repeat events of the past night. The results could most certainly be disastrous the next time. When I approached him, he was unperturbed by my scolding and again insisted that he was a trained physician, fully capable of performing the most delicate of operations. I could not at this time find fault with the man. He had probably saved the child's life but it still left me shaken. I went so far as to ask him to relate the steps he had taken the night before to remove the appendix. He described each step in detail. His method was flawless from the first knife thrust until the last stitch was tied off.

    I gained a new appreciation for Claude's abilities. Though I still could not understand how this farmer could perform such an operation, I did now believe he had some knowledge of the practice of medicine; possibly, I reasoned, he had received some training during that time some fifteen years earlier when he had ventured out to pursue the practice.

    I questioned him further about other aspects of medicine, about other medical procedures. His knowledge was vast, even greater than my own. He described in detail a number of delicate operations. Even then I pressed on. I gave symptoms of several well-known maladies. He diagnosed each the same as I would under the circumstances.

    I then described other less-known diseases, thinking he would be at a loss. Some were diseases that had only recently been discovered. In every case, Claude diagnosed the illness as I would, told me whether or not there was a cure and what it was. More proof that a miracle had happened in the man's life. Something unexplainable had happened to Claude Frontierre. He was the same man and yet he was not. Physically, there was no difference. But in mind, spirit and personality he was a changed man.

    Two weeks later Claude hugged Daphne, possibly his only show of affection to the girl who still felt she was his wife, and boarded a coach for Paris. I stood next to the small open window, looking up at the man and wondering what strange spirit had invaded his body.

    He smiled down just before the coach pulled out and spoke his last to us. "Perhaps, my good friend, we shall meet again." He paused for a moment and his eyes took a faraway look, one I had observed on several occasions during the last months. It was as if he no longer occupied the body. A short moment and he was back with us. "In that other reality," he continued, almost to himself.

Then his eyes fell on Daphne. The girl was clinging to my arm and sobbing quietly. "I thank you, Daphne. You have nursed me back to health and for that I will be eternally grateful." He then paused and that faraway look invaded his eyes again. "But you must forget me," he said softly. "The man you knew no longer exists. You must forget Claude Frontierre."

It was the last he spoke to us, for the whip cracked and the coach leapt away, leaving the girl clinging steadfastly to my arm. A few moments later it disappeared around a corner of the street and was gone forever. The girl was now beside herself. Up until that moment, I think she must have felt that all would eventually work itself out. But, alas, it did not and would not. Afterward, it took some time to calm the poor child. It was as if death had transpired in her family and I wonder now if that was not the case on that dreary April morning.

I had determined when I was sure Claude would most certainly leave us that I would soon after follow him to Paris. Rest would not come to any of us until the riddle of Claude Frontierre was solved. But it was not to be.

Word reached us only a week after he left, forever altering my plans. It seems only a day out of Paris Claude's coach was set upon by highwaymen and all aboard were killed.

So, my good friend, it seems that the mystery has died with Claude. Yet, I wonder, Jacques. Did Claude, the Claude that loved Daphne, die on that coach or did he die on that cold February morning when he fell and struck his head on the tethering stake?

I have left this last mystery to the end. It is something that Claude revealed that last week before he left. Because of this last revelation and the events that were made known this last week, I finally felt I must write this letter.

As I mentioned earlier, Claude was convinced that he and the great Pasteur were working together. He spoke of the great strides that men *like Pasteur were making. I shall never forget his words.*

"I must return to Paris," he stated. "A great breakthrough will occur very soon in the fight against hydrophobia. I have been working closely with Doctor Pasteur on this research and I'm sure he must need me."

I listened patiently to his words; but as I had with many other things he told me, I dismissed them quickly. Alas, too quickly. For as we all now know, a great breakthrough has occurred. Word reached our small community only a few days ago. I now know that on the sixth of this past month, a week after Claude's death, Louis Pasteur inoculated and saved the life of a child bitten by a rabid dog. The cure that Claude had so accurately predicted has become a reality. I was totally unaware that such a cure was in the offing. And, yet, Claude knew. How? Did he in some way actually know and work with the great Pasteur? In his letter, Pasteur swore he did not know Claude. Would he lie about such a thing? I find it inconceivable. What reason would a man like Pasteur have for denying such knowledge?

Well, my friend, I have laid bare my innermost thoughts in few pages. I pray you do not think me daft, for I have truly been witness to a most astounding phenomenon. Perhaps I shall never know the riddle of Claude Frontierre, the physician, or Claude Frontierre, the farmer. I'm not certain I would understand should the explanation come. But of one thing I am certain. I shall always be mystified by the man who came to us from "the left side of reality."

Your devoted friend and colleague,
Pierre Genet

~ ~ ~

Doctor Genet slipped the letter in an envelope and sent it away the following day. Whether he received a reply from his friend is not known.

But the Genet letter appeared again in 1953. It was discovered by Jacques Marseille's granddaughter in a packet of the old doctor's private papers. Intrigued, she read it and showed it to friends.

One was a young doctor of psychology named Carl Savage. To all but Savage, the letter brought smiles and some mild laughter. Intrigued by the prospect of what the letter suggested, Doctor Savage requested a copy. In a show of generosity, the young woman offered Savage the original and he gladly accepted. It became the first piece of evidence in his lifelong quest of the unknown. The letter would haunt him throughout his professional life and ultimately lead to his untimely death.

CHAPTER 1

STEVE PEARCE ROLLED OVER in the king-size bed and blinked at the luminous numbers on the clock radio. Habit woke him this morning, not the alarm. It was fifteen minutes overdue. He reached for the button on the side of the radio and found it in the "off" position. Then he remembered. He hadn't set it last night. Today was Saturday, December twenty-third, just two days before Christmas. The kid in him still felt a tingle of excitement at the thought. But it wasn't just the holidays that buoyed his spirits as he lay there. It was the idea of spending the next week with Kathy and Tommy. No work. He would have nothing to do but relax and enjoy his family. Then the income taxes and monthly reports. The real world would come rushing back after January first. Three and a half months of early mornings and late nights. But he could put it on the back burner a while longer. He was going to enjoy this next week.

Kathy stirred and he rolled on his back and glanced toward her. In the half light he could barely see her. She was wadded up in her usual tight little ball with only the top of her brown hair showing above the covers. Even with the electric blanket she was probably still cold. Steve smiled and turned back to the clock. Six forty. By now Kathy was usually downstairs with the coffee pot perking. She would normally be into her second cup. His would be poured and waiting when he came down around seven fifteen. This morning he would return the favor.

Outside, the wind was howling. Steve turned on his left side and tried to focus his eyes on the heavy drapes that covered the sliding door a few feet away. A high-pitched whistling sound from behind the drapes told him the wind was working itself around the loose weatherstripping. He had spent two hours the last week taping the inside and outside of the door but it hadn't seemed to work. That guy, what was his name, Carl, he thought. A call was in order. The man was supposed to be the best at making a house as airtight as possible.

As his eyes adjusted to the light, he could see the heavy coverings flutter slightly. He could imagine how the sliding door track must look. On Thursday night the temperature had dropped to five above zero, and the wind chill factor had brought it down still further to nearly ten below. Ice had formed in the tracks during the night and he had resorted to Kathy's hair dryer to melt it, wiping moisture all the while as he did. If that wasn't enough, the inside bottom of all the metal windows was solid with half an inch of ice.

This isn't a normal December in Arkansas, he thought then. Maybe January or February, but not December. After he left for the office that morning, Kathy had spent two hours cleaning the ice and water off the frames. Last night they had made the decision. Storm windows would go up soon after the holidays.

"Ice age," Steve whispered under his breath. Maybe it isn't a thousand years off, he thought. Maybe, like the novel he had read a number of years ago predicted, it could happen any time. If the last two winters were any indication and now this cold before Christmas... He let the thought drift into nowhere.

Kathy had moved next to him and snuggled against his back. She was breathing evenly, still asleep. He started to turn over and slip his arm around her but thought better of it. After Tommy had fallen asleep, they were up until twelve thirty wrapping packages. She needed the rest.

~ ~ ~

He lay there for another half hour before he slipped his solid six-foot frame quietly out of bed and tucked the covers close around his wife. His slippers were not beside the bed, and in the half-light he couldn't locate them underneath. Finally, he gave up the search and tiptoed across the carpeted floor to the bathroom.

As he made contact with the cold ceramic tile surface, the shock sent a shudder throughout his body. It was if he had stepped from a warm, grassy, summer meadow directly onto a frozen winter pond. One quick hop and he was on the thick woolen rug that Kathy kept beside the tub. Seconds later he was stripped and under a warm shower.

By seven forty-five he had showered, shaved and brushed his teeth. Kathy was still asleep as he slipped on his pants and shirt. Quietly, he exited the bedroom, closing the door softly behind him.

Tommy's room was next to theirs and he took a quick look inside. The active six year old was resting comfortably, snuggled up next to the big gold and black striped cat. They had bought their son two Garfields, one small to sleep with and another larger one to sit in a corner of his bedroom. But Tommy had insisted on sleeping with the big one. In his double bed the cat took up more room than Tommy.

Steve shook his head and quietly shut the door. Out in the hall, he glanced wistfully at the third bedroom door, closed and shut off so that it didn't need to be heated. He and Kathy had thought to have a little girl tucked away in that room by now but after the miscarriage last year... Like other unpleasant thoughts, he let this one die and started down to the kitchen to get the coffee brewing.

As he descended the stairs, he could feel the temperature begin to drop. The thermostat in the breakfast nook read sixty-four. It felt more like forty-four. The first winter they were in the house they had kept the temperature in the high seventies. But no more. After they got their first January utility bill, the thermostat was reset to seventy. And Kathy began wearing long sleeves and a sweater in the house.

She was money-conscious, even more than he was. More than once he had caught her turning down the thermostat after he had turned it up. Steve's accounting practice was beginning to grow, but they still had to watch their spending and one way they were aware of money or the lack of it was when they got their utility bills. Amazing how those OPEC boys could affect your lifestyle.

Steve turned the thermostat up to seventy and wrapped his arms around himself. Chill bumps were forming as he went down the five steps from the nook to the den. He was thankful now that Kathy had insisted on the woodbox next to the fireplace. Because of her insistence he had instructed the builder to frame a three foot by three foot space to accommodate enough wood for a day's use. He was able to put wood in from the outside of the house and retrieve it on the inside.

Last night, before the temperatures and wind became almost unbearable, he had filled the box. He didn't like to admit it but it saved him on days like this. Count one for Kathy, he thought and, as he did, a grin spread across his face. In ten minutes, fed by hot coals from the night before, he had a roaring blaze going in the big stone fireplace. He closed the metal screen and partially covered the opening with the glass doors. Satisfied with his handiwork, he went back up to the kitchen and poured himself a cup of coffee.

He was sitting at the breakfast table finishing the first cup when he heard Tommy's door open, then close quietly. A moment later Kathy was coming down the stairs.

Steve looked up and smiled. "Morning."

"Good morning." She had been up long enough to pull her long, brown hair into a bun on the top of her head. The heavy, blue robe, the one he hated, was wrapped tightly around her. It made her slender, well-proportioned, five-foot-four inch body look like one shapeless blob, but he knew she liked it because it kept her warm.

"You slipped out of bed and I got cold," she said. "It's freezing down here."

Steve motioned toward the fire. "Got you a good one going."

"I know," she said. "I could hear it crackling. I want some coffee, then just stretch out in front of the fire."

He motioned toward the fire again. "You go on down. I'll bring the coffee."

"You sure?"

"You go and I'll be right behind you."

She bent to kiss him and laced her fingers in his thick, blond hair. "A cup of coffee, a warm fire, and someone to love me. What else could I ask for?"

"Ummm. In what order?" He turned her around gently and she dropped onto his lap. Their lips were about to meet when an upstairs door closed not so quietly.

"Mommy."

At the sound of their son's voice, they both jumped. She came out of his lap, feeling her heart skip a beat as she did. Her sudden movement almost caused Steve to tip over backward in the chair.

"Mommy, I'm cold." The boy, still wearing his red and white Razorback pajamas, was coming down the stairs, the back of his hand moving slowly back and forth across his half-closed eyes.

As she slipped out of his lap and moved toward her son, Kathy heard Steve take a deep breath. Tommy had stopped halfway down and was looking pleadingly toward his mother.

"I know, honey. I know. Mommy'll tuck you back in bed and cover you up real good."

"Okay," he said. Then, as he turned to retrace his steps, he had a thought. "Will you lie down with me, Mommy?" The words came more as a whimper than a question.   Kathy looked back at Steve, and he smiled and shrugged. "For a few minutes, until you get warm," she said.

At eight forty-five Kathy was still upstairs. Steve picked up the phone and dialed. Always three rings, he thought, and always Susan on the other end. Never Ray. Doctors, at least Ray Philpot, were insulated from the outside world, insulated by their wives, by their secretaries and nurses, and by their answering services. It was always the same when he called him at home. Never two rings, never four. Always on the third ring if they were home. And always Susan. There were times when Steve thought that Ray must have a phone in every room including the bathrooms. And he never answered them. Now, he counted the rings and smiled when the phone was lifted immediately after the third ring.

"Hello." The woman's voice was reserved, aloof.

"Susan. Steve."

The tone in her voice changed immediately. "Oh, hi, Steve." It was like going from that cold ceramic floor back to the warm rug. She could excite a man with her voice if she had a mind. The thought made Steve feel guilty, and as if he thought Kathy might be watching him from the top of the landing, he closed his eyes and tried to concentrate on what he had called for in the first place.

"Is Ray available?"

"Sure, hang on." Then as an afterthought she added. "You guys goin' handballin' in this weather?"

"Sure. Why not?"

"Not for me," she said. "Bad out there. Gonna snow later. I'm gonna snuggle here. May not get out of my pj's all day." Her voice turned a touch sultry as she said it.

Steve could feel his face turn a shade crimson. He gathered his thoughts and answered. "Guess we'll venture out for a little while. Probably get your man back to you before lunch."

"Okay. I'll see if I can get him on the phone." Without another word Steve heard her set the phone down. She was gone for half a minute, then back. "He'll be right here. By the way, how's Kathy?"

"Fine. She's upstairs with Tommy. Want to talk to her when Ray and I finish?"

Susan Philpot answered a little too quickly. "Oh, no. I don't want to bother her." She paused a moment. "Here's Ray." She seemed eager to get rid of him now, and he guessed it was because of his offer to put Kathy on the phone. Unlike Ray and himself, the girls had never been that close. They were friendly when the two couples visited each other, but they were never tight. Ray and Susan were childless, and the times they had gotten together, it seemed as if she was uncomfortable around Tommy.

Ray's husky voice broke Steve's train of thought. "Mornin', Steve."

"Hey, Buddy. You on call this morning?"

"Yeah, but I got the ever-present beeper in case of emergency. I told Sandy not to bother me unless it's life or death. And Paul Harrington is covering for me at the hospital this morning. So I'm set."

"Great. I'll pick you up at nine thirty," Steve said as Kathy came up behind him. She rested her hands on his shoulders and bent and kissed him lightly on the neck. As she did, he wrapped his hand over the speaker end of the phone and looked over his shoulder at her smile.

"Tommy's asleep again," she whispered. "Put Ray off till later." She blew softly on the back of his neck for emphasis and squeezed his shoulders.

Steve started to shake his head at Kathy until she kissed him again on the neck. "Uh, Ray, if you want I can make it a little later." He winked at Kathy and smiled.

"Rather not, Steve. I've got a tight schedule after lunch. The sooner, the better for me. Besides, they'll give our court away if we aren't there by ten."

Steve glanced quickly at his watch. It was nine o'clock. He shrugged at Kathy and turned his attention back to the phone. "You're right. I'll be there at nine thirty." He hung up as Kathy planted herself in his lap. "Sorry, hon. We lose the court if we're not there by ten."

Kathy's lips puckered as she wrapped her arms around his neck. She had let her hair down, and it fell loosely around her shoulders, just the way he liked it. He loved the clean scent of her long hair. Not only that but the fragrance of her perfume still lingered from the night before. She had taken off the heavy robe and he could see and feel the soft curves of her body.

"You sure you have to go so soon?" She kissed him softly, brushing her lips back and forth across his.

"Hey, don't do that," he scolded and slapped her on the hip. "You don't play fair."

"You'll be sorry," she said seductively as she slid out of his lap. She crossed to the table and picked up the half-empty cup of coffee that Steve had been drinking. Staring over the cup into his eyes she repeated the threat. "You'll be sorry."

"I'm already sorry," Steve grunted. He got up and headed for the stairs. As he started up, he could hear her giggling. "You know how to torture a guy."

He stopped at his son's bedroom door and peered in. Tommy was sleeping, the big Garfield taking the place Kathy had occupied a short time ago. He went into his bathroom and ran a comb through his thick hair, dropping his eyes to his waistline as he finished. He was satisfied with what he saw. The extra two inches from last winter were gone, and he was back to thirty-two in the waist. Plenty of golf and tennis during the summer was responsible for that. But the handball was keeping him fit this winter. Maybe he had found the combination, he thought. Steve dropped the comb back in the drawer.

Kathy was filling the dishwasher as he descended the stairs. "Honey, it'll be noon or later before I get home. What's your schedule?"

She turned to face him. The seductive look of a few minutes ago was gone. "I'm not sure. I've got a few last minute things to pick up downtown. Can you fix yourself something for lunch if I'm not back?"

Steve feigned displeasure. "Gosh, I don't know," he joked. "I'm not sure I can handle it." When she frowned and put her hands on her hips, Steve got the message that the playfulness of a few minutes before had evaporated. "Sure, hon. You have a good time. I can make out fine."

She held the frown. "In that case I may not be back in time to fix dinner either."

"Hey," he said and moved across the kitchen toward her. "I can't make out that well," he said as he reached for her.

"That's better," she said. Instead of melting into his arms as he expected, she took his shoulders and twisted them toward the back door. "You don't want to lose your court. Go and have your game and keep that beautiful hunk of a body in shape."

He turned just long enough to plant a kiss on her lips. "Tonight," he whispered.

"Go," she said but there was a twinkle in her eyes.

~ ~ ~

At thirty-five, Ray Philpot had not achieved the same results with his waistline that his handball partner had. His exercise routine during the summer had been totally without rhyme or reason. Not very good, he thought. But a doctor's schedule, he rationalized, was much more difficult to arrange than an accountant's. And it was especially so when the doctor lived more for work than play.

He had thought the weekly handball games would help, but they hadn't. His legs were rubbery and sore for days afterward, and his stomach still lapped over his belt. At six-foot-four he was several inches taller and four inches bigger in the waist than Steve. A doctor ought to know how to keep the weight off better than an accountant. And he did. But he hadn't taken the same advice he gave others.

Now, as bad as he hated to admit it, he was going to have to restrict his eating habits. It would not be a diet, as such, he thought. He didn't believe in strict diets and he didn't recommend them for his patients. But he did believe in pushing away from the table a little quicker. And he did believe in eating the right food. It was hard but he would have to make the effort. He would do it, but not until Christmas was behind him. Too much good food, too much turkey and dressing would be on the table. He would restrict his eating after Christmas. But right now he would enjoy the holidays. Christmas only came once a year.

Ray went into the bathroom and spread shaving cream on his face. The phone rang as he was reaching for his razor. He hesitated, waiting until he was sure Susan had answered. She always did. Long ago he had learned never to answer himself unless it was absolutely necessary. Susan had become accustomed to screening his calls, involving him only when the situation merited. She had the knack to know when she should or shouldn't. It came from being a doctor's wife. But people were getting more and more paranoid every day. Cancer, heart problems, HIV, a new flu virus every few years all kept everyone on edge.

Susan came to the door and leaned against the facing. "Who?" He asked as he pulled the razor down the right side of his face.

"The same woman that's called the last two nights."

"Janice Parsons." It wasn't a question but an acknowledgment. The woman had become a pest, calling him at home at all hours and the office several times a day. Her son was getting better every day but she wasn't satisfied. Her complaints about the hospital staff were about to get the best of him. The afternoon before she had followed him down the hall, raising the roof about one of the nurses. She had become so irate that she had not noticed which door he had stepped through. It was only after she heard a toilet flush in one of the stalls that she stopped short and beat a hasty retreat from the men's room. She wasn't outside the restroom door when he came out a few minutes later. Ray had not seen her again that day. Now it seemed she had shaken off the embarrassment and was at it again.

"Is she still on the phone?"

Susan only shook her head.

"What did she want?"

"To know whether you'd be at the hospital this morning."

Ray finished the last razor stroke and toweled off the excess cream. "And what did you tell her?"

"I said you'd be making your rounds sometime after lunch and to call Doctor Harrington if she needed someone before then."

"Good. Thanks, hon."

"She said she would wait and talk with you whenever you came by."

Ray was about to drop the towel beside the sink. Instead, he pitched it roughly toward the tray of cologne and perfume that Susan had stacked neatly at one end of the long vanity. The bottles took a tumble and clattered loudly. "Great," he grumbled.

"Ray," Susan scolded. "Be careful." She scurried past him and began re-stacking the scattered bottles. "At least nothing is broken."

Ray shook his head and went into the bedroom without another word. He glanced at his watch and muttered just loud enough for Susan to hear. "I have to hurry. Steve will be here any minute."

"Please don't keep him waiting. That would be the crime of the century." Her words were laced with a bit of sarcasm.

"What's got your wagon turned upside down?"

She sat heavily on the bed and looked up at him wistfully with her deep blue eyes. "Nothing. I guess I'm just bored."

"Why don't you call Kathy and go shopping or something. You two always seem to get along fine."

Susan ran the fingers of her right hand through her shoulder-length blonde hair and shook her head. "She's always got Tommy along and it isn't much fun. Besides, it'll be a madhouse downtown today." Her voice perked up a bit . "Ray, let's plan a trip for right after the holidays, just the two of us. We could go to Colorado and ski for a week. Or we might go to the Bahamas. Either place would be fun, just like a second honeymoon." She paused and her voice took on a soft tone. "Remember our first one?"

Ray ran a comb through his thinning hair and smiled. He remembered very well. "Sounds like fun," he said. "We'll talk about it later."

She was enthusiastic now, her blue eyes sparkling as she got up from the bed and slid her arms around him. "Can we plan it tonight?" She asked and looked up into the eyes of the husband, who was a good foot taller than her. "Please?" Her voice was downright sensuous now.

Ray bent and kissed her lightly on the forehead. "Maybe. If something doesn't come up we'll talk about it at dinner."

Something in the tone of his voice sent a chill through her. She released her hold on him and sat down on the bed again. "You'll never think of it or mention it unless I do. And even then you won't do anything about it," she whimpered. "We've been through this a hundred times. You always have some kind of excuse, some patient only you can save." The sarcasm was back. "It looks like you'd enjoy getting away once in a while and spending some of that money you work so hard for. I certainly would like to spend some of it before we get too old to enjoy it."

A horn sounded outside and Ray breathed a sigh of relief. They were getting dangerously close to the same argument. He was ignoring her, not spending enough time or money on her. A doctor, she insisted, made an embarrassing amount of money and then spent it like poverty was skulking in the bushes, just waiting to pounce on the poor, unsuspecting victim.

Ray went to the window and glanced out. Steve's '67 Corvette was idling in the driveway, a steady wisp of smoke slipping out of the muffler. It was his escape, although he really meant to plan that trip tonight. The thought of some time alone with Susan really did excite him. But not cold Colorado. He opted for the Bahamas.

"I have to go," he finally said. "Will you be here at lunch?"

"I don't know. Maybe." She had turned her back on him. She was pouting.

Ray stopped at the foot of the bed and put a hand on her shoulder. "We will talk about the trip tonight. That's a promise, a number one priority. It really does sound like fun. Okay?"

She looked up at him and he saw just the hint of moisture in her eyes. "Really?" Her voice was subdued, almost pleading. "You aren't just saying that."

"I really do promise. We'll make plans tonight. No matter what comes up." Their eyes locked for several seconds and then she smiled. When she did, Phil stooped and planted a kiss on her forehead. "I'll see you in a few hours." With that he turned and slipped out of the room.

~ ~ ~

The inside of the Corvette was just beginning to get warm. Fog was forming with every exhaled breath. It was twenty-one degrees on the thermometer when Steve left the house a few minutes earlier and not likely to get much warmer, maybe even go lower. The weatherman on television last night had predicted a high of twenty-eight, but that had been revised down to twenty-five on the morning weather report. On the way to Ray's he had noticed a low smooth overcast but dismissed the possibility of snow. The weatherman had only mentioned it in passing and then said there was only a 20 percent chance. Still, it always seemed when snow wasn't forecast, that's when it was likely to happen in Hot Springs.

"Come on, Ray," Steve muttered and the fog formed in front of his face again. He glanced toward the huge, colonial style house that Ray and Susan had moved into just six months earlier and shook his head. Just two years ago he and Kathy had built their dream home for less than $200,000 and thought it was really something. Then along came Ray and built this: sunken tub in a bathroom that was larger than Steve's master bedroom, inside swimming pool, a hidden bar—Ray and Susan didn't even drink—that appeared at the touch of a button, three fireplaces, five lavishly furnished bedrooms—without children—and four extra baths larger than any of his.

But the kitchen...when Kathy saw it she couldn't believe her eyes. It had everything: two ovens, a microwave, more fancy cabinets than Susan would ever use, a refrigerator/freezer and a second stand-up freezer that happened to be filled with all kinds of meat, a built-in counter in the middle of the big kitchen. Everything was top of the line. Steve knew Kathy was swept away. She couldn't help but talk about it for days after Ray and Susan had asked them over for dinner. It was much more than an accountant could afford. Had to cost three times as much as their house.

~ ~ ~

Steve stroked his chin and sighed as Ray came out of the house and started down the slippery walk. The big man was moving briskly, seemingly unaware of the moisture that had collected on the concrete during the morning. Halfway to the car his feet hit a thin sheet of ice and his arms flew above his head. A moment later he hit the icy concrete on his rear.

If he hadn't had the motor going and the windows up Steve could have heard the roar as Ray hit. He was about to roll down the window and check to see if he was hurt, but the doctor quickly picked himself up and stepped over onto the grass. As he regained his feet, Steve saw his lips move up and down rapidly. It was good that the window was closed, and he couldn't hear what Ray was saying. Still, he had to contain the grin that wanted to spread across his face as he watched his friend moving much slower across the grass.

A moment of guilt swept Steve. Ray was still moving gingerly as he reached out and grabbed the door handle. He was rubbing his backside as he tried to maneuver his big body into the Corvette. "When you gonna trade this matchbox in for a real car?" Ray growled as he physically pulled his right leg through the opening.

Steve laughed. Ray had a habit of razzing him about the size of his car. In the past he had always ignored the jabs leveled at the Corvette. But this morning it was different and Steve could feel it. "You okay?"

"I was until thirty seconds ago. Now, I'm not too sure. Maybe I'll know by the time I unfold out of this toy." The fall had taken the humor out of the doctor, and he was rolling his shoulders and rubbing his right hip. His narrowed eyes revealed obvious discomfort.

"You want to pass on the handball today?"

"Not on your life. Get this museum piece going," Ray growled. "All I need is to trounce you on the court. That'll cure all my aches and pains, physical and mental."

"You got it," Steve said and pulled out of Ray's circular drive. Five minutes later they turned off Belaire onto Malvern Avenue, headed into town. A light mist the night before had not only settled on Ray's sidewalk but the road had become slippery in several spots. The speed limit was forty, but Steve wasn't used to holding it down on the wide road and he pushed up to fifty despite the danger. Only when he got close to the Indiandale Shopping Center where the radar trap was usually set did he slow back to forty. He glanced down a side street where he had seen the police car a few nights before but none was visible. Still, he held the speed to forty. In another block the limit dropped to thirty.

"I suppose you're taking next week off." It was the first Ray had said since they left his house. Steve had noticed as they drove that he was still rubbing his hip.

"Yep. The grind begins in earnest after the first of the year."

"Grind." Ray chuckled. "What would you accountants do if you had the same kind of grind a doctor has and that's not for just three or four months a year but the whole twelve?"

Steve measured his friend and grinned before he answered. "Probably clear another hundred thousand a year."

Ray slapped his right leg. "You, too."

Steve glanced sideways at Ray. The usual combative smile was not there. It wasn't just the fall a few minutes before that was eating at Ray.

Almost as if he knew what Steve was thinking, Ray shifted in his cramped quarters and glanced toward his friend. "Susan thinks it's immoral to make as much money as I do and not spend it just as fast. She's on a vacation kick again. Been on it for several months. Wants to go to Colorado and ski or the Bahamas and lie in the sun. I've been able to hold her off, but I'm afraid I'm losing the battle." He brushed his hand across a lock of hair that had slipped down from his receding hairline. "Can't you see me on skis. I can't even negotiate a sidewalk."

He paused but Steve remained silent. He glanced toward his friend and realized that Steve was not ready to respond. "Forget it," he finally said. "Forget everything I said. I think I want to get away as bad as she does. But not Colorado. I'm tired of cold weather. I'm gonna vote for the Bahamas. I think Susan and I could have a high old time down there."

He paused again. They were getting close to the old football field where he had played nearly twenty years ago. A new library had been built on the site, and there was no longer any sign of the field where he had been a star lineman. It wasn't right. Everything he remembered from his childhood was changing. It wasn't right and the thought depressed him.

"I had an idea something besides that fall had bent your personality this morning."

Ray grunted. He was working on the stray lock again, trying to force it to stay in place on his partially bald spot.

"Might not be a bad idea though," Steve said.

"What?" Ray abandoned the hair and was massaging his hip again.

"The trip. You and Susan need to get away."

Ray laid his head back against the headrest. "Yeah. She's really right. This last year or two we haven't seen as much of each other as we should. I owe her the trip," he said quietly. Then he continued. "I owe myself the trip. We need to get reacquainted, a second honeymoon."

Steve nodded and glanced toward Ray. A glint had appeared in his friend's eyes when he mentioned the second honeymoon. "You're right. You owe it to yourself," Steve agreed.

They were in the city proper now. To the right was the new library where the old football field had been. Good memories flooded his mind. His last game as a Trojan had been played there. They had won the state championship on that field in that game. He could still remember everything that happened on that forty-yard pass on the last play of the game. The coach had called a post route for the split end and a crossing route for the tight end. When Steve made his cut and streaked across the middle, he was wide open. With his hands high in the air, he saw the pass coming directly toward him. To his consternation it soared over his head and he screamed in frustration. Then he turned, expecting it to fall harmlessly to the ground. Instead he saw Mike leap high at the goal line and pull the ball in. When he came down in the end zone, it was all over but the shouting. Ten seconds remained on the clock. Just enough time to kickoff. The championship was theirs. Yep, good memories even if he didn't catch that last pass.

Steve slowed to thirty-five, still a few miles above the limit. After another half-mile they turned north onto East Grand Avenue. They passed a few motels and restaurants that had sprung up since the theme park opened in 1979. Those first few years the park had not lived up to expectations and had been sold and reopened several times. For that reason a couple of the motels had never been completed and some of the restaurants were just barely able to stay in business. Now it seemed to be growing, even flourishing.

The town had not grown in this direction as it had to the south, along Central Avenue and out past the racetrack. Like so many other ventures of the seventies and eighties, the timing had been bad. The biggest culprit turned out to be the energy crisis. While the park should have been an adequate answer to the larger and more lavish parks in surrounding states, until the last few years the crowds just never seemed to materialize in numbers that would keep it out of financial straits.

They were on the highway, passing the theme park now. "You take the boy out to the park before it closed this year?" Ray asked.

"Once," Steve answered.

"I took Susan one night in September. Got inside the gate and the beeper went off before we could take a dozen steps. Had to go to the hospital. By the time I was finished, the park was closed. Needless to say, she hasn't let me forget that."

"Hey, Buddy," Steve said and reached over to gently tap his friend's arm. "I didn't mean to offend you. The remark about money, I mean."

They were getting close to the turnoff for the handball facility. Ray straightened up and squared his shoulders. When he did, his head touched the cloth padding of the roof, and he stooped over and reached to move his hair back in place. "No offense taken. Just gave me a chance to let off a little steam at you. Maybe even psyched me up for the match."

Steve pulled into the parking lot and glanced toward Ray again. He could see that his friend was already trying to decide just how he was going to extricate himself from the Corvette.

"Let's do it," Steve said as he watched Ray open his door and lift his leg through the opening. In his mind, Steve decided he would bring Kathy's car the next time. He did not enjoy seeing his friend in such obvious discomfort.

CHAPTER 2

IT WAS TEN-THIRTY when Kathy went to the foot of the stairs and looked up toward the empty hall. "Tommy, are you ready to go?"

Silence answered her.

"Tommy, do you hear mother?"

"Yes, Mommy."

"Let's go then, honey. Mommy has a lot to do."

The boy came out of his bedroom and looked down toward Kathy. "Are we going to see Santa, Mommy?"

Kathy smiled and nodded. "I'll bet we can find him somewhere in town. Do you need to talk to him?"

"Yes, Mommy. I want to ask him to bring me something."

"Well, I'm sure we'll see him."

Tommy was holding a replica of the world globe in his hands. It was about the size of a soccer ball. In reality it was a bank that Steve had gotten Tommy for his fourth birthday. One of the boy's evening rituals was to invade his father's coin collection when Steve emptied his pockets. Steve had agreed that any change Tommy found was his for the bank. By now the bank had grown quite heavy, even though Tommy had occasionally slipped out a few quarters or dimes now and then. Now he held it out toward his mother.

"Can I buy something with some of my money?"

Kathy smiled but shook her head. "Not today, honey. Remember, Santa is coming tomorrow night. Let's wait and see what he brings. Okay?"

His disappointment was evident but he didn't argue. Instead, he retreated to his room and a moment later was coming down the stairs, pulling on his coat as he did.

At ten forty, Kathy backed out of the carport and headed down the winding drive. As she turned onto Shady Grove Road, she glanced up at the smooth, gray mass of clouds that covered the entire sky. She had heard no mention of snow, but it looked like the sky could open any minute. An eerie tremor moved through her body, a premonition of danger. Earlier that morning when Steve left for the handball court, she had experienced the same feeling. She had shaken it off then. Now it was back.

Steve stripped out of the sweaty shorts and shirt, kicked off the yellow and green gym shoes and headed for the shower.

~ ~ ~

The last hour and a half had sapped him, especially the legs. Professional athletes always said it was the legs that went first and he knew they were right. Not too long ago he could have run all day and still felt a lot better than he did now. But those days were long gone. Still, he was in better shape than Ray. The doctor was prone on a bench in front of his locker, soaked with perspiration, his breath just returning to normal. He still hadn't shed any of his clothes. As Steve started for the showers, Ray pulled himself into a sitting position and began fumbling with his shirt.

The shower was empty and Steve went down halfway, stood to the side and turned on the water. When he had the temperature adjusted, he braced his hands against the wall and leaned into the warm spray, letting it beat down against the top of his head and upper torso. It was like a hundred fingers massaging and caressing his aching muscles. He was aware of nothing else until he heard the sound of Ray's shower a few feet away. He glanced up and saw his friend working to get the water temperature right. After a moment he slid under the stream and braced his hands against the wall much as Steve had a few moments before. Steve could see the exhaustion in the big man's face. It seemed Ray could hardly move.

"You okay, old buddy?"

Ray only grunted and began turning his body from side to side under the cascading water. Steve settled in under his own shower. From the look of it, Ray would be awhile.

~ ~ ~

Sunshine Road was about ten miles southwest of Hot Springs. At eleven thirty Evelyn Bradley was sitting in Margaret Ramsey's living room. The Ramseys had a small farm five miles down Sunshine Road. At seven o'clock the night before Evelyn had received a call that John Ramsey had died of a heart attack just after five in the afternoon. The two women were in the same Sunday school class at the Baptist church on Highway 270.

Two years earlier when Evelyn's husband had been in the hospital for two weeks, the Sunday school class had provided food for her. Margaret had been in charge, coordinating the women and seeing to it that Evelyn had plenty to eat while Mike was ill. As much as she had hated to make such a long drive alone, it was time for her to return the favor, so she prepared a pot of stew and struck out at nine thirty that morning. She had arrived at the Ramsey house at ten fifteen. Her intention had been to pay her condolences and be on her way in a half hour. She would be home before eleven thirty. Mike would have a fire going, and she could begin making that pumpkin pie he wanted for Christmas dinner.

But the half hour had stretched into nearly an hour and a half, and as she slipped on her coat and started out the front door the first snowflakes of winter were beginning to fall. If Evelyn had looked closely she would have noticed that tiny grains of sleet were mixed with the snow. The flakes were small at first, hardly noticeable on the dirt driveway. But by the time she had said her goodbyes and was planted behind the wheel, the flakes were nearly twice the size of the first ones and sleet was still mixed in.

As Evelyn slid the key into the ignition, she thought about

calling Mike. But that thought lasted for only a few seconds. He would think her silly and he would probably be right. Besides, he would gripe about having to drive so far just to get her. And what would they do with an extra car? Still, driving by herself in the snow was extremely uncomfortable.

Evelyn sighed, turned the key and shook her head at her own foolishness. Only light patches of white were visible on the grass and it was only thirty minutes or so home. And Sunshine Road looked no different than it did when she arrived. She backed down the dirt drive and turned onto the narrow highway. If Evelyn had known that snow had been falling for nearly half an hour all along her route, she would not have hesitated to call Mike.

~ ~ ~

For Lester Weatherspoon, the snow that began falling shortly after eleven was a welcome sight. He was cutting firewood ten miles northwest of Hot Springs in an area the local lumber company had set aside for free cutting. When the snow began, he pulled his woolen cap down over his ears and shut off the chainsaw. A full truckload of red oak was piled on the ground, and he knew it would take at least a half hour to load. Some of the roads in this area were narrow and already muddy, and he had no desire to get stuck out here. The snow would be a good excuse to quit. And besides, the kid in him still loved the snow.

At twenty-two he still looked forward to all the adventures that went along with the first snowfall. Marcie had surprised him with a sled last Christmas and in January, when there was six inches of snow on the ground, they had slipped onto the local country club grounds and had a ball. The sled had performed magnificently on the steep hills and they had mentioned it several times in the last month.

That night, last year, they had gone home, built a fire, made hot chocolate and roasted marshmallows. Afterward they had slept next to the wood stove. Although it wasn't as nice as a real fireplace, it had been a special evening for both of them.

As he loaded the last of the logs, he realized he had more than he first thought. The top row had covered half of the back window of the truck and would be a hindrance if he needed to look out the main rearview mirror. Still, he had the side mirrors, he reasoned. He just had to be careful about slamming on the brakes. A log hurtling through his back window would be no fun. Satisfied that the load was safe enough, he slammed the tailgate shut.

Lester was already making plans for the night. Snow had been falling heavily for more than a half hour by the time he slid behind the wheel of the 1995 Ford pickup. It had been in the low twenties for the last few days, and the snow was beginning to stick to everything it touched, turning the surrounding countryside into a winter wonderland. More than a half-inch of snow was already on the ground, and now he realized that a mixture of sleet was interspersed with the snow. Lester started the engine and felt a measure of relief when the old truck roared to life. He shoved the gear lever into drive and began to move slowly down the old logging road.

~ ~ ~

Kathy was standing in the doorway of Swenson's Shoe Store when she noticed the first flakes begin to fall. On the way into town the radio announcer had mentioned snow in the Russellville area, but he went on to say that it would most likely move north of Hot Springs. At the time she had felt sorry for Tommy, but relief for herself. Well, so much for weather reporting, she thought. Still, it could be only a dusting of snow here. Many times it went just north of them and blanketed the Benton/Bryant area without hitting Hot Springs. If they were lucky that would be the case this year.

But then there was last year. There had been no forecast or hint of snow until the middle of January, then with very little warning, eight to fourteen inches all over the state. Temperatures had stayed unseasonably low, not climbing out of the teens and twenties for nearly a week. The ground was white for nearly two weeks. It was not good in a state that was ill-prepared for winter's worst. An early snow could be an omen.

The thought made her shiver and brought back the feeling of danger she had managed to put behind her for the last hour. It was Tommy's squeal that brought her back to the present. He had grabbed her hand and was pointing excitedly toward the rapidly growing flakes.

"Mommy, look at the snow. Is it going to snow a lot? Can we make a snowman, Mommy?"

"I see it, honey. Yes, Mommy sees it." Her voice did not hold the same excitement as her son's, but the boy was too excited to notice his mother's anxiety.

Kathy felt someone's presence behind her and turned to see the saleslady who had sold her the shoes a few moments earlier. The tall, gray-haired woman had her arms folded on her chest and was staring out the glass doors. She shook her head slowly and sighed.

"Our manager just heard it on the radio," she said.

"What?"

"The low pressure area didn't go the way it was supposed to. They've changed the forecast again. We're going to get the weather they were predicting for Northwest Arkansas."

Kathy shuddered. That feeling of danger was all over her.

"Six inches," the woman continued, "maybe more."

"You have to be kidding." Kathy's voice seemed to be pleading.

"I wish, Missus," the woman said, brushing a twig of gray back into place on her forehead. "I live all the way out to Pearcy. If they wait very long to close the store, I'll have to spend the night in town at my sister's house."

Kathy was only half-listening to the woman. She was watching Tommy but, at this moment, not sharing his excitement. He was mesmerized by the snowflakes, which seemed to be growing in size and intensity with every passing minute. "Honey, I think we better start for home before the streets get too slick." She was still unaware of the small particles of sleet that were mixed with the snow.

"But, Mommy, we haven't seen Santa Claus yet."

Oh, my, Kathy thought. She had promised him. But now it was too dangerous to go all the way out Central to the mall. "Honey, I think Santa will have to go home too. He needs to get everything ready for tomorrow night."

Tommy was silent, his eyes questioning his mother. Finally, he nodded and looked back at the snow. "Then can we make a snowman when we get home?"

When Daddy gets there and if the snow is deep enough, I'll bet he'll go out with you."

"Okay," Tommy said. "Let's go home."

Kathy looked back to the saleslady now who was smiling down at her son. "Good luck and Merry Christmas. I hope you make it home."

"And Merry Christmas to you, Missus," the woman offered as Kathy pushed the big glass doors open and pulled Tommy out into the cold air. The flakes were huge now, some almost half the size of golf balls.

An hour ago there had been no wind. Now, as they turned north up Central Avenue, they found it driving large puffs into their face and hair. When one slithered past the protection of Kathy's heavy coat and slid down her neck, she cried out in surprise and slapped at her chest.

"What's wrong, Mommy?"

"Some snow went down Mommy's neck. Come on, let's hurry. It's getting worse."

They were crossing Central just south of Wheatley Plaza. A half block away she could barely see the statue of the man the plaza had been built to honor. She had a fleeting thought of Steve and wished he were here. Driving in the snow was one of her greatest fears. Her father had been seriously injured in a snow-related accident. Now, every time it snowed she remembered him and how it had affected her whole family, especially her mother. It had been a cold December morning, much like this one, when her father's accident had occurred. Could that have been the reason she had felt the way she had all morning?

"Mommy, will Daddy be home when we get there?" Tommy's voice jarred her thoughts back to the present, and she realized that he must have been screaming at her through the wind for several seconds.

"I don't know, honey. Maybe." I certainly hope so, she thought.

"Can we build a snowman if he is?"

"We'll see. Let's talk about it when we get in the car. Mommy's freezing."

The sharp wind made talking difficult and her lower jaw was quivering as she spoke. For the first time she took note of the small ice crystals that were falling along with the snow. The sleet was already clinging to the concrete walk and Kathy slowed down to keep from falling.

By the time they traveled the three blocks to the car, a full ten minutes had passed since they left the shoe store. The slick sidewalks had forced them to make sure of every step they took. Kathy could imagine how the streets and highways must be getting. Sleet mixed with snow could be a deadly combination, she thought. "Steve, where are you when I need you?" Kathy whispered under her breath as she slipped into the car. With Tommy safely buckled in, she pushed the key into the ignition and breathed a sigh of relief when the engine roared to life.

She moved out into traffic and proceeded south on Broadway until she reached Malvern Avenue. Traffic, still moving on the street, was moving much slower than normal. As Kathy turned off Broadway onto Malvern, she searched the street ahead. Already, the asphalt was turning a bright white. When Steve bought the car last year, he had insisted on front wheel drive. She breathed a quiet prayer of thanks for his foresight.

Even as she did, she felt the back end of the Buick fishtail slightly, then, after a moment, regain traction. Steve had told her when the wheels began to slide into a turn to always turn the wheel into the turn. That had saved her now. Even as she regained control, she found that her heart was in her throat for just that instant. Dropping her speed down to fifteen miles an hour, she moved slowly along Malvern Avenue.

It took her twenty agonizingly tense minutes to reach the highway. Traffic here, with the exception of a few cars, was moving carefully. But on the four-lane road they were still moving a little faster than she wanted to go. As she moved closer to her turn-off, she began to realize just how hard the storm had already hit their part of town. Everything was covered white. She glanced quickly at her dashboard clock and found that it was already twelve twenty-five. Kathy realized the snow must have started out here soon after she left home. If only she had known, she thought.

Golf Links Road and the country club were on her right now and the Belair subdivision where Ray and Susan lived were on the left. A blanket of snow covered the fairways. No golf today, she thought. A quarter of a mile before she got there, she began slowing for her turn onto Carpenter Dam Road. As she did, she noticed a blue pickup truck pull over to the right side of the road just ahead of her. It was loaded with firewood and it made her think of home and Steve. He should be there by now and would have the fire blazing away in the fireplace.

Kathy shuddered with anticipation and glanced in her rear-view mirror at Tommy. Thankfully, he had fallen asleep back on Malvern Avenue and still lay with his head over against the side of the back door. Kathy smiled and concentrated again on the highway. She was moving past the blue pickup now, giving it a wide berth as she went by. In her rearview mirror she noticed a young man open his truck door and step gingerly onto the frozen shoulder of the road. He was moving toward the back of the truck and pushing at the logs that were piled high in the truck bed. A moment later Kathy turned onto Carpenter Dam Road and down the shallow hill toward home and that warm fire that she envisioned.

Over a half-inch of snow was on the ground when Steve and

Ray departed the sports facility.

~ ~ ~

Steve glanced at his watch. It was already twelve ten. They were a little later than usual but it didn't matter except to Ray. He had rounds to make at the hospital this afternoon. It wouldn't take long to get him home and then he could get home to Kathy and Tommy. By now the huge puffs of snow were extremely thick, making it impossible to see the mountain and the tower only a mile to the south.

"It wasn't supposed to do this," he shouted above the wind to Ray.

"That's when we get our worst ones," Ray answered. "When we aren't supposed to."

They crawled into the Corvette and Steve flipped on the radio. The weather news was already in progress.

"....with accumulations of six inches by midnight. Snow is expected to continue until the early morning hours with temperatures dipping into the low to mid teens in the Central Arkansas area. The current temperature in downtown Hot Springs is twenty-six degrees with a heavy mixture of snow and sleet. Streets in the downtown area are already getting slick. Hot Springs police are working two fender-benders, one on Highway 270 east just a half-mile west of the Bull Bayou bridge. The other is on Central Avenue, a mile south of Oaklawn Park. It's getting dangerous out there, Folks. Drive carefully if you're out. If you don't have to go anywhere, cuddle up in front of a warm fire and read a good book. 'Cause it looks like we're in for it."

Steve flipped off the radio and pulled onto the access road that paralleled the freeway into the city. He went several hundred feet, cut left and felt the rear end of the Corvette slip left then straighten up as he entered the main road.

"Already pretty slick," Ray said as he reached out and grabbed the door handle to keep from falling against Steve.

"A bit," Steve answered casually. Snow had never been something he feared. On the contrary, when he was a teenager he and his brother had taken his old junker out on the back roads around their farm and skidded their way back and forth in private. Once or twice they had nearly turned the old Chevy over. But they became masters of the game, and whenever it snowed enough, they headed for back pasture. Good times, he remembered. Good memories until he thought about Jim and Mona. How long, he wondered? How long had Jim and Mona been dead? The thought, as always, depressed him and he forced himself to think of something besides his late brother and sister-in-law.

They were on Belaire, half a block from Ray's house, before his passenger spoke again. "Hope you won't hold today against me," he said and glanced toward Steve.

Ray's voice snapped Steve back to the present and he ventured a quick look at his friend. "What you talkin' about?"

Ray's focus remained on the road as Steve turned into his driveway. "My mood. It's lousy, I know. Guess I really need that vacation Susan's harping about. I promised her we'd talk about it tonight." He seemed to be talking to himself now. "I haven't had a decent night's sleep since Monday. I'm worn out. Susan's bored. The trip would be good, good for both of us," he said with emphasis.

Steve stopped the Corvette in the circular driveway and looked at his friend. Ray was still staring straight ahead, unaware the car was no longer moving.

"I think it's a good idea, Ray."

"What?"

"The trip," Steve answered. "You and Susan need to get away now and then."

Ray looked embarrassed. "I guess I was thinking out loud. Didn't mean to involve you in our problems." He opened the door, worked his large frame out and bent over to peer back at Steve. "Next time I'll take you." He managed a weak grin and closed the door.

Steve held his breath as Ray moved slowly up the walk toward the front door. At the door, he stopped and raised his hand in Steve's direction. A moment later he disappeared into the house.

~ ~ ~

Steve glanced at his watch, saw it was twelve twenty-five and gunned the car down Belaire toward Malvern. The snow and sleet, he estimated, were already an inch or more thick. He hoped Kathy had plenty of food in the house. From the look of the sky, they were in for a pretty good storm. He and Tommy, and Kathy if she had a mind to, would have a ball in the snow. It was time for snowmen, snow ice cream and hot chocolate.

A block from the intersection of Belaire and Malvern Road, he thought he saw Kathy's Buick go by. In the snow he couldn't be sure, but instinctively he increased his speed slightly. If it was Kathy, he might catch her by the time she reached the Carpenter Dam turnoff.

He began braking a hundred feet before he reached the highway and was about to turn east on Malvern when an old Chrysler topped the hill just to the left and started down. Knowing the car might not be front-wheel drive he waited patiently, watched the old car pass him, then turned the Corvette onto the highway. The Buick he thought he had seen was nowhere in sight. If it was Kathy, there would be no catching her now.

~ ~ ~

Evelyn Bradley had been fighting the car all the way. When she turned off Sunshine Road onto Highway 70, heading back toward Hot Springs, she realized what she was in for. The road was extremely slick. Several cars were already in the ditch along the main highway. One, at the junction of Marion Anderson Road and Highway 70, had spun completely around and was headed back in her direction, its left side planted firmly against a light pole.

More than once, in the next mile, she thought about pulling

over somewhere and calling Mike to come get her. If she had been able to see the wreck on the other side of the Highway 70 bridge, she might not have hesitated. But it was hidden from view and by the time she reached the summit of the new bridge it was too late. What she saw sent shivers up and down her spine.

Evelyn was crawling along just under twenty miles an hour as she started down the opposite side of the bridge. She couldn't stop. A car was dangerously close to her back bumper and if she tried to stop, it could slide into her. Thankfully, the bridge was new and four-lane. When the highway department built it, they also widened the road where the bridge and the regular road met.

It was the widened road that allowed Evelyn to slip safely to the right of the two cars. They were seemingly locked together in the middle of the road, straddling both the south and north bound lanes. Evelyn thought about stopping to help, but several other cars had already pulled over and a couple of men were walking toward the damaged vehicles. Sweat was pouring down her back and she knew if she stopped she might never have the nerve to continue.

With a final glance in her mirror, she turned her attention back to the road ahead. After negotiating the wreck, Evelyn had silently vowed to make it home without calling Mike. She followed the road to Highway 88 and turned up 88 toward Central Avenue.

She had successfully negotiated what she felt was the worst part of the trip. She was nearly home. From Central she turned onto Winans Avenue. Even though she was closing in on home, she was still tense from so long behind the wheel. Her fingers were aching from the pressure she was exerting on the steering wheel. Every few minutes she would let go of the wheel and wring her hands to relieve the tension. But in seconds she was gripping the wheel so tightly that the ache would just return.

She kept telling herself that the worst part of the trip was behind her. As she approached the Malvern Road intersection, she glanced quickly at the clock on the dashboard. It was nearly twelve twenty-five. Though she was sweating profusely, she was beginning to relax. Home was only minutes away. And then she would have a long talk with Mike. If she had anything to do with it, they were going home to southern Florida. Let somebody else experience the four seasons. Give her the warm Florida sun three hundred sixty five days a year. She never wanted to have another experience like this as long as she lived.

~ ~ ~

Lester Weatherspoon was like a kid with a new toy. He pulled the pickup onto the shoulder at the intersection of Golf Links and Malvern. It was the second time he had stopped to check the load. He tramped around the truck, pushing at the hastily loaded wood until he was satisfied. It was riding just like he had loaded it. No reason to worry. It wasn't going anywhere. A grin spread across his face as he glanced skyward.

The snow was heavier and from all indications it would be around for a day or so. He was eager to get home and find out what the weatherman on television said. The old radio in the truck hadn't been working for several months. When he got home, he reasoned, they would soap the runners on the sled. Skiers did it. He had seen it in the Olympics.

His body tingled with excitement as he worked his way around to the passenger side of the truck. As he started around the front, Evelyn Bradley's gold Mercury had already started down the slick incline that dead-ended into Malvern Road. Lester stopped to watch.

~ ~ ~

The muscles that had relaxed a few minutes before became taut as Evelyn turned the shallow curve and started down the last hundred yards before the Malvern intersection. It was just a couple of miles to her house, and she reached up to dab at the dampness on her forehead. When she did, her left hand turned the wheel just slightly to the right. The slight motion of the wheel caused the rear end of the Mercury to move quickly to the left. She didn't lose it completely until her foot slammed down onto the brake.

That was her first major mistake. On the incline it only served to aggravate the slide. The car was sideways in the road and she began fighting the wheel as the momentum of the car increased on the snow and sleet-covered road. From somewhere she thought she heard a scream but quickly forgot it as she saw herself sliding sideways toward the highway. The car was completely out of her control, and for an instant she thought it might flip over.

Then, as the incline began to shallow, she felt the Mercury's momentum begin to slow. But there was no stopping short of the highway. She hit the brake again, hoping to regain control. The nose of the vehicle, as it began to slow even more, began to move back to the left. It moved past the median that separated traffic entering and leaving Golf Links Road. As it did, she twirled the wheel to the left and the car began to respond. Now she slammed on the brake again. Just like that, it shuddered to a stop, crossways, straddling both lanes of southbound traffic.

Just then she caught movement out of the right corner of her eye. Two cars, moving north and side by side on the four-lane road, were only yards away. Just as she was about to panic again she realized they were in the northbound lanes and would pass her with room to spare. As they were going by, she let her head drop to the steering wheel and breathed a sigh of relief. But it was short-lived. Something caused her to glance to her left. Horror-struck, she watched as a small sports car hurtled toward her in the lanes she was straddling. The scream stuck in her throat for an instant, then came out like the wail of some lost soul who has just fallen from some great height and knows life will be snuffed out in seconds.

~ ~ ~

Steve was a hundred feet from the intersection when he saw the gold car slide into his path. Inadvertently, in his haste to catch Kathy, he had let his speed climb to forty, a fatal mistake on a highway of ice and snow. He was not on a back road today, not a place where he was insulated from harm. He knew immediately that he couldn't stop before he hit the gold car.

From here he could see the terrified expression on the woman's face. His first reaction was to swing left and pass the gold car in one of the opposite lanes. But, two cars occupied those lanes, moving toward him. His next reaction was to go around the right side of the stalled car. There would be room in the outside lane and on the shoulder of the road. He saw Lester Weatherspoon's old truck too late. His last alternative was the brakes he knew would fail him. But it was all he had.

The Corvette went out of control, hurtling the left side of the car sideways toward the truck. He saw a flash of blue, something that looked like logs rushing toward him, and a glimpse of someone running from the truck. He jerked at the wheel. Nothing happened. In that last instant his left arm jerked up automatically to cover his face and he tried to throw himself over toward the passenger side. But it was too late.

The last sound he heard was the meshing of plastic, glass and steel. The last thing he saw was the twenty-pound piece of oak firewood that had become a projectile. It was only a blur as it came crashing through the side window and windshield. Steve felt terrible pain as the wood drove his arm back into his head. The warm taste of blood filled his mouth and a vision of Kathy and Tommy swept over him. It was his last conscious thought.

CHAPTER 3

FROM THE ASHES OF the morning fire, Kathy found
enough hot coals to rekindle a roaring blaze. Unlike some of her
friends, Susan Philpot especially, she enjoyed a fire that filled the
big fireplace. She had mentioned to Steve two weeks earlier, when
they had been invited to the Philpot's for dinner, that Susan would
only lay two or three small sticks in her fireplace. The blaze was so
small that even though Kathy had snuggled right up to the opening, she could barely feel the heat. Steve's only comment had been
that Susan's fire was cosmetic, not meant for warmth but for effect.

Now as Kathy stood back and admired her handiwork she
wondered about Steve. He should have been home before her and
she was becoming concerned. During the next thirty minutes she
made half a dozen trips to the double windows in the playroom.
From here she could see half a mile down Shady Grove Road and
all the way up to the new rest home. But there was no Steve.

Finally, she decided that watching would not get him home any
sooner so she went back to the kitchen and took out some frozen
hamburger patties. Kathy turned the electric burner on low and
placed the patties in a skillet. She glanced toward the den where
Tommy had the television going a little too loud.

"Want a hamburger for lunch?" she asked as she moved to the
railing that overlooked the large den.

Tommy had his eyes glued to the weekly wrestling show.
"Now?"

"When Daddy gets home. He should be here any minute." As

she said it she felt an eerie sensation sweep over her. She shook it off nearly as soon as she felt it and spoke to her son again. "How about it? A hamburger?"

Tommy nodded without looking up. As usual, he was mesmerized by the action on the screen.

She watched her son for several seconds, unable to understand the fascination that he felt for the violent sport. Ever since he had been old enough to crawl, wrestling programs had drawn him like a magnet. When he was smaller, he would throw a fit whenever the show was over. Steve finally broke him from that habit by restricting his privilege to watch for a month. The fits had stopped.

Kathy climbed the steps to her bedroom, slipped out of the pants and sweater and into a comfortable blouse and jeans. Then she went to the bathroom window and searched, for at least the seventh time, along Shady Grove Road. The Corvette was not in sight. That strange feeling she had been having all morning swept over her again and she felt her body shudder for just an instant. It stopped immediately but the feeling was still there.

Snow was still falling heavily but the flakes were a little smaller now. Still, she knew that they could get larger again in a matter of moments. An inch and a half of snow, mixed with sleet, was already on the ground. And it had only been ninety minutes since it started. She left the window and went back downstairs. Tommy was still hypnotized by the wrestling show but she knew it would go off in just a few minutes and he would probably be up in the kitchen looking for his father. He wouldn't know it but she was beginning to get very concerned.

Kathy opened a can of pork and beans, poured them in a skillet and mixed a half-cup of brown sugar in along with some ketchup. She stirred the ingredients together and glanced again at the clock. It was nearly one thirty. It was not like Steve to be this late without calling. Unless something had... She dismissed that thought and felt a shudder run through her body again. After she turned the fire down low under the beans she picked up the kitchen phone and began dialing.

After the third ring, "Doctor Philpot's residence."

"Susan... Hi, this is Kathy."

"Oh, hi, Kat. What's up?"

"Are those guys of ours gonna spend all day on the handball court. I expected Steve back an hour ago."

There was an uncommon silence from the other end of the phone line. When Susan didn't answer immediately it sent a chill through Kathy that was much worse than before.

"Ray isn't back yet, is he?" Her voice had an edge to it as she pressed the question.

After another moment's hesitation Susan came back. "He got back about an hour ago, Kathy. Isn't Steve home yet?"

"No." She felt her voice quiver a bit as she picked up a pencil and began doodling on the desk calendar. It was a habit she had when she was nervous and right now she was not only nervous, she was scared. "Ask Ray if Steve mentioned going anywhere else before he came home."

"Hon, I'm sorry, but Ray grabbed a bite and ran for the hospital. He's been gone fifteen minutes or more. If you like I can call his cell phone and leave word for him to call. He'll get back to you as soon as he can."

"Oh, no. Don't do that, Susan. Steve'll be here any minute. I'm just being a worrywart. He may have gone into the office for something." She said it but didn't believe it herself. Deep down she knew something was wrong. He would have called. He always called when he was going to be late. Unlike herself he had always been that way. She was caught up in her own thoughts when she realized Susan was speaking again.

"Kathy, you still there?"

"I'm sorry, Susan. What were you saying?"

"I just wondered if there was anything I could do."

"Oh, no thanks. I'm sure he'll be home soon. Thanks a bunch. I'll talk to you later."

She replaced the phone in its cradle before Susan replied and turned her attention back to the beans. She was cold now even though the house was warm. She pulled the sweater close around her and picked up the big spoon to stir the beans. As she was pulling the spoon back and forth she heard the sound of a car engine outside. It would be Steve. Where had he been? Why hadn't he called? She ran to the side window and glared through the falling snow toward a white car that was moving slowly up the drive toward the house. All of a sudden the chill and the shudder became uncontrollable. Once before she had seen a car like that pull into her driveway, only then it had been to tell her mother that her father had been in a terrible accident.

~ ~ ~

The frigid temperature was not the only reason Carl Ryan was shaking under the heavy blue coat. Of all the jobs he hated about being a policeman, this one he hated most. In three years it had been his responsibility to tell three women that their husbands or children had been seriously injured or killed in an accident. He would have to do it again today.

Now, as he rolled up the driveway, he wished he had not offered to take Packer's shift. He could have been home with Molly right now. Packer would have been here. Packer would have had to tell this woman about her husband. Carl swallowed deeply as he stopped the police cruiser just short of the carport. As he sat there gathering his courage, he thought he saw movement at a back window. The curtain was moving slightly. It was the woman. He was sure of it. She had already seen him. Reluctantly, he pushed open the car door and stepped into the snow. It was cold, colder than it should have been.

When the knock came, Kathy could hardly bring herself to open the door. The sight of the patrol car sitting behind her Buick caused her to go limp. Her whole body seemed strangely disassociated from her mind. She knew what waited for her on the other side of the door before she even opened it. It struck her. Maybe she shouldn't open it. She could ignore it and the policeman would go away. Then she could go back into the den and sit by the fire. Steve would be home. He would be there anytime now and they could laugh about her crazy fears. That's what they were, crazy.

But to her dismay, the knock came again and shocked her back to reality. She grabbed the knob and turned it quickly. It didn't release. The lock had been sticking for nearly a week now and Steve had promised to fix it. In her confusion now she began pulling frantically on the door. All of a sudden it released and she pulled it open to stare into the grim face of the young policeman.

She felt immediately as if she should apologize. "I'm sorry. I couldn't get the door open. My husband is going to fix it." She wasn't sure why she was going on about the door. Perhaps, she thought, if she talked he wouldn't. Maybe he was here to sell tickets to the policeman's ball. If he was she would buy some. She would buy anything right now if Steve would just come home. Maybe, even, this sad looking man was at the wrong house. Maybe he was looking for the Madden house next door. She could direct him there. Then he would go away and just let her get back to her beans. Perhaps he would just turn and walk away. Perhaps...

Instead, the young policeman touched his cap bill and nodded. The expression on Carl Ryan's face, which on a normal day would have been pleasant, continued to be grim.

"Mrs. Pearce?"

"Yes." Strange, she thought. I sound like I'm a mile away.

"Mrs. Pearce, does your husband own a blue Corvette, license number..."

Kathy clutched at her chest. He was still talking but she wasn't hearing him. Steve had been killed. He was dead. It was all she could think. Her knees buckled but she caught herself.

"Mrs. Pearce. Are you all right?"

She had caught hold of the doorknob and it was supporting her weakened knees. "My husband isn't here," she stammered. Even as she said it she knew this young man standing just a few feet away already knew that. After a moment she asked the question she hoped beyond hope she would never have to ask. "Has something happened to him?"

The young man persisted. "Was your husband driving the Corvette this morning?"

"Yes." She gasped.

Officer Carl Ryan took a deep breath and let it out slowly. "I'm sorry, Mrs. Pearce. There's been an accident and Mr. Pearce has been taken to the hospital. St. Josephs." Even Kathy noted that the pronouncement had nearly expended the young man's entire energy supply.

"Is he..."

Carl Ryan was shaking his head before Kathy could finish her question. "He's alive. I'm here to take you to the hospital."

Kathy pulled the sweater tightly around her body. "How badly was he hurt?" She was shaking uncontrollably again.

"I'm not sure, Mrs. Pearce. I got to the scene just after the ambulance left. I'm to take you to the hospital," he repeated.

Carl's words had not registered yet with Kathy. "I don't know if I can drive in the snow. Steve always drives when the roads are dangerous."

"Mrs. Pearce, it's very slick and you don't have chains on your car. I'll drive you."

This time Kathy understood and nodded. "Thank you. I have to get my son and take care of the fire. I'll only be a couple of minutes." She closed the door without waiting for an answer, then opened it again quickly. "I'm sorry. Please, come in and wait where it's warm."

Carl Ryan touched his cap again. "Thank you, but I'll wait in the car until you're ready." Without hesitation, he turned and carefully made his way back to the white patrol car.

Kathy shut the door and collapsed against it. For the first time the tears began to flow, partly because she was so thankful that Steve was still alive and partly because she didn't know how bad he was. At least he was still alive. As long as there was life there was hope. If God had not let him die in the accident, God would not take him now. At that thought she pushed herself away from the door, wiped the tears away quickly and went into the kitchen. She turned off the burner under the beans and went to the railing overlooking the den.

"Tommy." Her voice still seemed foreign.

"Yes, Mommy."

"Get your coat on, honey." Kathy was having trouble controlling her voice and she knew now was the one time she needed to be strong. She didn't want to upset her son any more than was necessary.

"Are we going out and make a snowman?"

"No, honey. We're..." Her voice broke for a second. "Please, honey. Don't ask Mommy any questions right now. Just do as I say very quickly."

She turned away from her son, trying to hide the fresh tears that were beginning to well up in her eyes. She hurried down into the den, separated the logs in the fireplace and closed the glass doors, leaving just enough opening so that the heat could escape into the room. Satisfied that the fire would eventually burn itself out, she climbed the steps back to the foyer. Tommy had come down from his room and was standing at the foot of the stairs, zipping up the red jacket.

His eyes clouded perceptively. "Why are you crying, Mommy?"

Kathy dabbed at the tears with the back of her hand and knelt in front of her son. She gathered him into her arms and pulled him tight against her. After a few seconds she released him and held him at arm's length.

"Honey." She hesitated, searching for the right words. Finally, she took a deep breath and exhaled. No words could ever be right at a time like this, she decided. "Honey, Daddy has been in an accident. You and Mommy are going to the hospital and see how he is. Do you understand?" Kathy could feel the tears again and she pulled Tommy tightly against her and fought to control her body.

She was still fighting her emotions when she felt two small hands grasp the sides of her face and push their bodies gently apart. Their faces were only inches apart and Tommy was staring solemnly into her eyes.

"Mommy, is my Daddy going to go live with Jesus?"

Kathy felt as if she was going to choke. Her insides seemed to be rising in her throat, suffocating her. If she had not been holding tightly to Tommy, she would have toppled over. But when she answered her voice was strangely calm.

"He will someday, Tommy. We all will someday. But right now Jesus isn't ready for him. Daddy's going to come home very soon. He's going to be fine. You'll see. But right now we have to be brave and show Daddy just how big we are. Okay?" For the first time in more than an hour Kathy seemed calm and in control. For Tommy she had to be. She released her son and began working on his shirt collar, forcing a smile as she finished and zipped up his jacket.

"Tommy, a policeman is outside. He's going to take us to the hospital in his car. You'll like that, riding in a police car, won't you?"

Tommy shrugged his shoulders and looked up at his mother. The first tear began its journey down his cheek. Halfway down, Tommy reached up with his sleeve and wiped it away. Then, with his hands stuffed into his jacket pockets, he started toward the back door. Kathy took a handkerchief out of her coat pocket, blew her nose and followed.

~ ~ ~

Carl Ryan watched as the woman and boy came out the back door, then remembered the Timex on the seat beside him. Impact had torn it off the man's wrist. Ryan had picked it up off the Corvette seat and placed it in the patrol car, meaning to send it along to the hospital. But the ambulance had gotten away too soon. The young policeman picked it up now, studied the hands frozen at twelve thirty and closed it away in the pocket of the car. He would turn it in at the station when he completed his shift. There would be a better time for returning the watch. And, he thought, someone better qualified to do it.

CHAPTER 4

THE PAIN IN STEVE'S left side seemed more unbearable with every breath. He wasn't sure how long he had been out but ever since he had regained consciousness, only a few seconds earlier, every breath had been pure agony. Everything was a blur and, as hard as he tried, his eyes refused to focus.

He began to reach slowly across his body with his right hand. The area that hurt the most was the left side of his rib cage. But the slightest movement sent sharp pains through his arm and hand. It hurt too much for him to even move it to his rib cage so, with his left hand supporting his right wrist, he let his right arm down slowly onto his right leg.

His vision was slowly beginning to improve and for the first time he could see his right arm and wrist more clearly. It was a solid mass of red from his hand to his elbow. Strangely enough, his left arm didn't seem to be injured. That couldn't be right, he thought. The log, or at least he thought it was a log, had crashed through the side window and windshield and he had caught the brunt of the blow with his left arm. That, he could remember.

With his eyes, he began to study both arms. No blood on the left. The right arm was a mess. Something was wrong, very wrong. Dismissing that momentarily, he took his left hand and carefully turned his right arm over until his hand was palm up. The underside of the sleeve was ripped from just above the wrist to the elbow, revealing a deep gash more than six inches long on his forearm. The sight sickened him and he turned the arm back to its original position.

The crystal on his watch was smashed with hands stuck at twelve thirty. And that was odd. The watch was on his right wrist. He hadn't worn it that way in years. Kathy had kidded him about wearing it on his right wrist soon after they got married and he had changed it just to satisfy her. Now, it was on his right wrist again. Had he done it without thinking when he had gotten dressed after the handball game?

But something else was amiss. This watch was not his. Kathy had bought him an expensive Timex—at least expensive for a Timex—last Christmas. The watch on his wrist was an old Bulova, much like the one his parents had given him when he graduated high school. He had worn it until last Christmas when Kathy gave him the new one. In fact, this one looked exactly like his old watch.

With his left hand, he reached over and twisted the flexible band until he could see the underside of the watch. Just that little bit of pressure on his wrist sent excruciating pain through his entire arm. It brought tears to his eyes and until he could clear them, he couldn't see anything on the underside. Then as his eyes cleared of the tears, he saw it. It was dim now because of the years. The inscription read "To Steve from Mom and Dad." It was his old watch, the one Kathy had tucked away in her jewelry box last Christmas.

As he stared at it in bewilderment, he felt the car shift. For the first time he realized he was on his left side, resting heavily against the door. Something else began to bother him. It was strangely quiet, no one talking, no one trying to get him out of the car. He paused and listened and for the first time let his eyes wander around his surroundings.

He seemed to be locked in place, unable to move his body. It was as if something was holding him firmly against his seat and pressing him against the driver's side door. With his left hand he reached down and located what it was. A seat belt was cutting into the lower part of his abdomen. But that was impossible. The Corvette belt on the driver's side was broken and had been since the week before Thanksgiving. Had Kathy gotten it fixed for him without telling him? And had he fastened it without thinking when he got into the car at the sports facility?

Now he began a slow examination of the interior of the car. Everything was a mess. The car had to be totaled. But then he looked closer. What he was beginning to see made absolutely no sense. What he was seeing clearly now was not the interior of the Corvette. The instrument panel, while slightly familiar, was not his instrument panel. What he was looking at could not be. He was staring in disbelief at the instrument panel of an airplane, a small Cessna. And he knew it was a small Cessna because he had taken private lessons the year before he married Kathy. He had even soloed twice. Then he met Kathy and everything changed. He was hallucinating. He had to be.

Steve closed his eyes, shook his head slowly and opened them again. Nothing had changed. He was still hallucinating. He opened his mouth to express his anguish, felt something huge and rough in his throat and clamped his lips back together without uttering a sound.

With his left hand, he reached up and felt his throat. It was swollen and he could feel dry blood just under his chin. He wanted to scream but would have to do it without opening his mouth. He let that thought die quickly and turned his attention back to the interior of what he now knew was an airplane. He had definitely been here before or in a plane uncommonly similar. What he thought he was looking at was the interior of a Cessna 172, probably ten or fifteen years old.

Steve shuddered, half from the apprehension of what he was experiencing and half from the numbing cold he was beginning to feel. He had been conscious only a few minutes and it seemed the shock was beginning to wear off and the elements were invading his body. It had been snowing and the temperature was in the 20's when he got out of the handball facility. At least that was the way it was before the accident. He could freeze to death if someone didn't get him out of here and it didn't seem anyone was around.

The windshield above the instrument panel was gone and the

wind was whipping around his body. A short time ago, when he thought the car was shifting, he expected he was on solid ground. Now he realized his predicament. Outside of the cockpit window, he could see that the plane was a good ten feet off the ground. All that was keeping it from falling was the stub of the left wing. It looked like the tip had broken off some ten feet from where he was trapped. The main body of the plane had to be resting against a tree or a big rock or something substantial. Otherwise it would be resting on the ground.

He still couldn't understand what was going on. This had to be a nightmare, he thought. I'll wake up in a few minutes and everything will be back to normal. It couldn't be real unless someone was pulling some gigantic hoax. When he felt the pain in his side and arm he knew better. No one in their right mind would do something like this to him.

Steve closed his eyes and turned his head to the right. The swelling under his chin and the lump he felt in his throat were beginning to hurt more with every breath. He opened his eyes slightly and found himself looking up at the underside of the Cessna's right wing. It was resting against the trunk of a tall pine tree. That was why the plane seemed suspended on the left wing.

Without thinking, he opened his mouth and muttered, "I don't believe this." It was a mistake he wouldn't make again for some time. The pain that exploded in his throat was excruciating. This was not a nightmare. He was hurting too much. You didn't experience this kind of pain in a dream or a nightmare.

He closed his eyes and turned his head slowly back to the front. Nausea was setting in. It was suddenly impossible to open his eyes. It was panic time now and he desperately tried to fight off the dark cloud that was enveloping him. But it was hopeless and he slipped away into a black void.

~ ~ ~

In all her twenty-two years, Lisa Carter had known this kind of fear and dread only once before, only when her mother had gotten sick and then died unexpectedly. They had been best friends and the loss was overwhelming. Her dad was still there and he had tried his best to fill the void. But he couldn't. Lisa loved him dearly, but her mother could not be replaced.

And neither could Steve, she thought, and a wave of guilt swept over her. She closed her eyes and rested her elbows on the desk, dropping her head in the palms of her hands. The long auburn hair slid over her shoulders and rested against her forearms. She had been sitting behind the desk for what seemed to be an eternity, her hand resting on or near the red Razorback phone. In that time she had probably checked her watch more than thirty times.

The phone had rung only twice in the last two hours, once when Nora called to see if there was any word on the search, and again when the Civil Air Patrol called to report that Steve's plane was still missing. Off and on, in the quiet of the little office, she had cried until her black mascara was smeared down both cheeks. She knew her face was a mess. But she could have cared less. Until there was word one way or another, she was not moving away from the phone.

Everything else was on the back burner, even her Christmas plans. It had been her intention to pick up her father's Christmas present today. But that would have to wait. She glanced at her watch again and saw that it had moved only five minutes since the last time. It was four o'clock, over three and a half hours since Steve's mayday call.

Now, for the first time in more than an hour, she got up from the wooden swivel chair and walked over to glare out the window. Snow was still falling, though not quite as heavy as it had been an hour ago. The entire parking lot was white and most of the cars were covered so much that she could hardly make out her own.

Across the way, toward the main terminal, a couple of CAP automobiles were still evident outside the main terminal. There was no visible activity anywhere. Most of the men and women were in the air. Lisa felt helpless sitting here manning the radio and waiting for a phone call. Air traffic, except for her father's plane, which landed twenty minutes earlier, and the few rescue planes that were in the search pattern had been terminated more than an hour ago. No flights were going in or out of Hot Springs Memorial unless it was an emergency.

Lisa longed to be involved in the search and rescue operations but she was stuck here. She had even offered this office to the CAP but the officer in charge, Colonel Hardage, had declined, saying the team needed more room than Carter Flying Service could provide. And he was right. Her reasons had been selfish. She wanted to be in the middle of the search and if Hardage's people were in here, she could be out there flying. But she knew she would be the first to know when they found Steve. The colonel had promised and he was a man of his word. He was also an eternal optimist and she wished she had just a small measure of his optimism right now.

Lisa focused on the window, just inches in front of her face. Her reflection was clear and she knew she looked terrible. She looked even worse than she imagined. The streaks of black mascara made her look like those football players she saw on Saturdays and Sundays. Only she looked worse. Theirs was neat and served a purpose. Hers looked ugly. She turned and started for the desk and the box of tissues just as the phone rang. She swept her vanity aside and pounced on the phone before it rang a second time.

"Carter Flying Service," she hurriedly said.

"Miss Carter, Colonel Hardage here. We've found your pilot. His plane went down about ten miles west of Mountain Pine. Pretty close to where he reported on his mayday."

Lisa was impatient. "How is he?"

"Young fella's banged up pretty good but he's alive. My men are transporting him out as we speak. Be taking him over to St. Josephs. Will you pass that word along to your father?"

"Yes. Yes, I will tell him." Lisa was trembling as she started to replace the phone in its cradle. Then, remembering, she lifted it back to her lips and called excitedly. "Thank you, Colonel. Thank you." But Bill Hardage had already hung up.

~ ~ ~

Jake Carter was standing on a stool beside a green and white Cessna 150. The cowling was open and he was feeding a quart of oil into the crankcase. The squat, little man had taken a paying customer to Shreveport during the morning and had only gotten back a half hour ago. Lisa had called him just a short time before he left Shreveport to tell him that Steve's plane was missing and now he was about to refuel this Cessna and go looking.

Now, as he watched the last drop of oil drain into the motor, he cursed his luck, he cursed the snow, but most of all he cursed the fact that it was Steve Pearce who was missing. The man was admittedly his best pilot. All that bothered Jake now was whether Steve was under the influence. As far as he knew, Steve had never gone up when he was drinking, especially if customers were involved. It was one of the sacred rules that all pilots were sworn to abide by. And he didn't think Steve would break that rule. If the man was anything, he was conscientious.

Jake didn't like to admit it but Steve was an even better pilot than he was. The man was a natural. But he hadn't been the same the last year or two. Before Ed joined the company, Steve never drank. Something had changed in that last year or two, something that Steve kept to himself. And the drinking was a by-product.

Jake had seen Steve when he could smell alcohol on the young man's breath. But that had been on his days off, never when he was on duty. Even so, Jake was afraid it would only be a matter of time before he did go up under the influence. Now he was missing and Jake could see the headlines in the paper tomorrow. If he was drinking and had been killed, it would be his, Jake Carter's responsibility. He would be hung out to dry.

But that wasn't important now. Even though he knew it could all come back to haunt him, it was Steve he was concerned for, not himself. Jake closed the cowling and locked it in place. His mind wandered back to his last serious talk with Pearce, just a week ago. Steve had promised him he had not taken a drink for more than three months. He made the promise in Lisa's presence and for some reason Jake believed him. He believed him because he knew Lisa wanted him to.

He shook his head sadly at the thought of his daughter. She was hopelessly in love with Pearce, in love with a married man. Her mother had raised her better. Jake clamped down on the ever-present cigar stub that protruded from the corner of his mouth. If not for her, he thought, he wouldn't be going out in this storm again.

Before he finished the thought he shook his head and sighed. He would be out there no matter who was down. And especially for Steve. As bad as he hated to admit it the young man was one of his favorite people and without a doubt the best pilot who ever flew for him. Yes, he would be going out and he wouldn't be back until Steve's plane was located or he ran low on fuel.

Jake was about to open the door on the pilot's side when he heard the sound of running feet. The maze of planes made it impossible to see who was hurrying toward him but he knew who it was without seeing her. He took the unlit cigar stub out of his mouth and spit a stream of tobacco juice on the concrete floor just as Lisa emerged from the other side of a twin-engine Piper.

"Daddy, they've found him!"

Jake took his hand from the door handle and stuck the cigar into the left side of his mouth. The news sent a chill through his body. He pulled an oil rag from his back pocket and began wiping his hands. It was the only way he could keep them from shaking.

"Alive, from the looks of you."

"Yes, Daddy. But he's hurt. They're taking him to the hospital. Are you going?" Her legs were putting on the brakes now as Jake moved quickly past her toward the office.

"Where did they find him?" Jake shot the question back over his shoulder without slowing his pace. Lisa had turned and was running to keep up with her father.

"Ten miles west of Mountain Pine."

Jake thought about it for a moment. Steve had taken a charter to Fort Smith this morning. It had been a one-way trip and for that Jake was thankful. Steve was flying alone. "He was on course. That's good." Then as an afterthought, "Anybody let Nora know?"

Lisa stopped short. "I never thought to."

Jake bit deeper into his cigar and shook his head. "Woman's his wife." He started to say more about Nora Pearce, then thought better of it. "Never mind. Hardage will call her. It's part of his checklist. And I'll get in touch with her as soon as I check on Steve's condition."

Lisa nodded, relieved. She wasn't too excited about calling Nora Pearce. It had been evident for a long time that Steve's drinking problem had a lot to do with his wife. She believed that Nora's escapades were the reason he drank. She was a little too free with herself. Lisa and Jake both suspected it. In the privacy of the little office they had discussed Ed Nelson and Nora Pearce.

Once when Steve was on a charter to Atlanta and Ed was on his day off, Lisa had seen Nora's car in front of Ed's apartment. And Ed was a little too braggadocios. Whether Steve knew about Nora and Ed was a good question. If he did then that could have contributed to the drinking. Ed had been with them for about two years and it was soon after that when they noticed Steve drinking. On his days off, when he would drop by the office, Lisa could smell some on his breath. It was never overwhelming. But it was there.

But now she was convinced that Steve wasn't drinking anymore. He was clean. She was sure of it. She forced herself to put thoughts of Ed and Nora behind and concentrate on Steve.

"Are you going to the hospital, Daddy?"

They were in the office now and Jake was hanging the keys to the Cessna back on the rack. "Yeah." He eyed his daughter, surveyed the black streaks on her cheeks and motioned toward the tissue box on the desk. "Clean your face. You're a mess."

Lisa pulled out a tissue, went to the small mirror next to the door and began working on the black smear. She could see her father's eyes. He was watching her intently. Was it anger or concern she saw in those eyes?

"What is it, Daddy?"

"I'll take you home first, honey. I don't want you driving in this. Then I'll go to the hospital."

Lisa started to protest, then thought better of it. She wanted to go and see how Steve was for herself. She wanted badly to go. But Nora would probably be there and she wasn't anxious to see the woman. And knowing Steve's wife, she would be an infrequent visitor of his. Lisa would have her chance at a later time. "Will you call me as soon as you know something?"

Jake was surprised. He expected an argument. He was relieved when it didn't happen. "You'll be the first to know," he grunted. It was hard to be angry with the only person in his life. But he couldn't stand to see her suffer and she was suffering. No good could ever come of her feelings for the man. But she was a grown woman now and had a right to make her own mistakes. He just hoped it didn't destroy her in the end. "Now, get your coat on and I'll take you home."

"No, Daddy. There's no need for you to do that. Walt put chains on my car and your truck. I'll be fine. Besides, when this stuff is over I'll need transportation. You go along to the hospital." She paused and studied her face in the mirror. Satisfied, she tossed the tissue in the waste basket and turned to face her father. "And don't you dare forget to call me as soon as you know something."

Jake started to say something about her obsession with Steve but didn't. He still had not asked the question that had been uppermost on his mind since she had told him they found the plane. Finally, he cleared his throat and spat out the words.

"Did they say anything about Steve's..." He paused then finished his thought. "Condition."

"Just that he was hurt but alive."

"That ain't what I mean, Girl." When he was impatient with her he always referred to her as girl.

Lisa frowned and placed her hands on her hips in a defiant gesture. She knew what her father was getting at but deep down she wished he would trust Steve. "I know what you mean, Daddy. But, no, they didn't mention anything about liquor." For a moment it seemed the tears were about to flow again but she quickly regained her composure. "You know he promised us he wouldn't drink again. And I believed him then. I still do now and will until somebody proves otherwise."

Jake's countenance softened considerably. For all his tough exterior, his daughter was his soft spot. Sometimes she could get under his skin and make him feel lower than the underside of a turtle's belly. "Okay, baby, okay. I hope you're right." He paused and softened even more. "I know you're right. You read people a whole lot better than me."

Lisa sat down at the desk and looked up at her father with just a glint of dampness in her eyes. "I am, Daddy. I know I am. You'll see." I pray I am, she thought, then felt guilty for even doubting it.

Jake walked behind the desk and placed a dirty hand on Lisa's shoulder. "Close up and go home, honey. Nothin' more to do here. I'll call you soon as I see him." He stooped and planted a light kiss on the top of her head, then went out into the snow.

The wind was blowing straight out of the north and the snow was already nearly four inches deep in the parking lot. Jake was suddenly thankful for old Walt and the chains that adorned the old Ford truck. He was oblivious of the cold as he trudged across the thirty yards to the truck. Once there he realized that he had bitten the cigar cleanly in half. The stub was too short to keep and, as he opened the door, he spit it out quickly and reached into his pocket for another. He clamped the fresh cigar between his teeth and climbed behind the wheel.

Jake's mind was torn between Lisa and Steve Pearce as he stared unseeingly at the white windshield in front of him. In his heart he knew Pearce had not led his daughter on. At least, he better not. Possibly, Steve didn't even know how Lisa felt. Although that seemed unlikely. Lisa had been taken with Steve from the first, even before she graduated from high school. And while he knew nothing could ever come of her love, it pained him deeply knowing how she must be feeling.

Jake turned the key in the ignition and for the first time was aware of the white blur in front of him. He flicked on the wipers and they started slowly, laboriously, wiping away a little snow at a time. He watched it disappear, then shoved the gear lever into drive and pulled carefully out of the parking lot.

CHAPTER 5

IT WAS THE STRANGEST sensation. Steve found himself suspended above the bed, staring down at his own body. Wires, bottles, tubes were everywhere. He was a mass of bandages. Even though he knew it was his own body, he felt strangely disassociated, like a spirit hovering over its former tabernacle. And yet, he knew this was a dream. What else could it be? It wasn't real. He had read about this kind of experience, about people who swore they had died and, while dead, been allowed to view their remains. Then, by some miracle, they had regained life and returned to their body.

But this was not happening to him. He was in a dream, no a nightmare. The plane was a nightmare. He would wake up and Kathy would be there and so would Tommy. This was a nightmare. Or was it? Was it really them standing beside his motionless body. Not Kathy crying and Tommy looking from his mother to the lifeless form in the bed. Poor little guy. He could not perceive what was happening.

Who was that behind Kathy? He was in the shadows, somebody in a white shirt. His hand was resting on Tommy's shoulder. It was Ray. Paunchy, tired Ray. He wants to go home to Susan and I'm not letting him. No vacation yet, Ray. If that's really me. Got to put me together again. Got to put Humpty Dumpty together again.

Steve's thoughts seemed rational. He could see everything but he could not hear or reach out to the people in the room. And then Ray took Kathy's arm and led her and Tommy out of the room. Steve struggled to reach down and touch them, but just as quickly as the vision appeared, it began to disappear, leaving him flailing his way through a long, black tunnel. It was like the dreams he had when he was a child. He would be falling through what seemed miles and miles of endless space until he finally woke up in a sweat. He always woke up before he hit the ground and he would this time.

Voices were at the end of this tunnel. He seemed to be on the small end of a huge megaphone that stretched as far as his eyes could see. Someone was standing at the far end shouting at him against the wind. Little by little, as he fell through the void, the megaphone began to change its shape until his end became large and the far end became small. The wind had stopped and the person shouting into the small end was trying to break his eardrums.

"He's waking up, doctor." It was a woman's voice, not Kathy's.

Steve opened his eyes and tried to focus. The room was dimly lit. All he could see was a blur of white hovering over him. A distorted face was attached. He caught movement off to the right and the bed moved slightly. Someone had brushed against it. Steve licked his lips and tried to speak, but the huge lump he had noticed before was still there. It was there when he woke up in the plane. The plane, Steve thought. That was part of the nightmare. The nightmare had to be over. This was reality. This was where Kathy and Tommy were.

It was a man's voice this time but not so loud. "Mr. Pearce. Can you hear me? If you can, don't try to speak. You received a blow to your throat. It isn't serious but I don't want you to try to talk until we've had a chance to examine it further."

Steve's eyes were beginning to clear a little more. The white mass he had first seen he could now identify as the upper body of a big, red-headed nurse. She was standing just to the left of the bed, bending over him doing something to some wires or tubes that were attached somewhere above his waist. He could make out her face now. It wasn't distorted at all. It was just plump. But where was the man who had spoken?

"Mr. Pearce, I'm Doctor Banks. Can you hear me? If you can, just blink your eyes. I don't want you to talk or move about any more than possible."

It was painful for Steve to even shift his head slightly to the right. That's where the man's voice was coming from. And now he could see him.

"Mr. Pearce, if you can hear me blink your eyes."

Steve did. No pain there.

"Good. We have you stabilized, Mr. Pearce. I know you are experiencing some pain and we're going to give you something for that. But you're going to be fine. None of your injuries are life-threatening. So I want to assure you that we have everything under control. If you're understanding me just blink your eyes once."

Steve did.

"Good. Now, the reason I don't want you to talk right now is because you have sustained a very heavy blow just under your chin that has caused quite a bit of swelling to your neck and also some damage inside your mouth and into your throat. Do you still understand what I'm saying?"

Steve blinked.

His eyes were searching the small room. Kathy and Tommy should be here somewhere but he couldn't see them. And where was Ray? Who was this Dr. Banks? He shifted his eyes back to the doctor. The man looked short and thin, in his fifties or sixties. His voice came in a slow drawl that reminded him of an old doctor his mother had taken him to as a small child.

There was another face in the room, a woman, a blonde woman. She was standing several feet behind the doctor, peering at Steve. She looked familiar. Maybe she was a nurse, he thought. Maybe she worked in Ray's office. Where was Ray? He was in the dream or whatever it was a few minutes ago. Kathy and Tommy were there too.

Ted Banks saw his patient's eyes shift to a spot behind him. He stood to the side and took the woman's arm. "You can speak to him but just for a few minutes. I want him to rest."

The doctor turned back to Steve.

"I know you'd rather hear your wife's voice than mine. We'll have time enough later to talk about your injuries. Be assured you're in good hands, Mr. Pearce."

Steve's eyes began to search the small hospital room. Kathy was here. She was here somewhere. The doctor said she was. But where? He could not find her.

Doctor Banks walked to the foot of his bed and put his head next to the nurse's. They were speaking quietly and she was writing something on what Steve presumed was his medical chart. He assumed the doctor was telling the nurse to let Kathy come in.

He watched the two of them for a moment; then the doctor left the room. In the half-light Steve continued to search for Kathy. She was not in the room. Only the nurse and the blonde woman were there. He could see the other woman more clearly now. She was not wearing a uniform. There were plain-clothes policemen, Steve thought. Maybe she was a plain-clothes nurse. That didn't sound right to him. Now the blonde had come close and was bending over him. The odor of tobacco and just a hint of alcohol was on her breath. Steve turned his head slightly to the left so that the odor didn't flow directly into his nostrils.

"Darling, you had us worried."

Steve's eyes darted back to the woman. She had called him darling and now she was kissing him on his lips. Her lips were dry and hard. As she pulled away, Steve had a faint recollection. She was a face from his past, someone he once knew.

"We thought we had lost you, Steve. You have to stop worrying us like that." As she spoke, Steve noticed that she was cutting her eyes up toward the big nurse.

Now he could smell the odor of cheap perfume mixed with sweat. And he could taste the tobacco from her lips. The churning in his stomach, from the smells and tastes he was experiencing, told him this was not a nightmare. This was reality. Yet, how could it be happening? The plane, the watch, now this woman trying to take Kathy's place. Surely he was caught up in some kind of nightmare.

Someone was moving behind the blonde. The doctor was back

and he was speaking to the big nurse. After a moment he came up beside the blonde woman and whispered something in her ear. On the other side of the bed, he felt something cold being rubbed on his arm. A moment later he felt the prick. And suddenly the blonde woman was gone and the doctor was bending over him.

"Mr. Pearce, we've given you something for the pain and to help you sleep. When you wake up maybe we'll be able to talk then." He patted Steve on the shoulder and straightened up. "Now, don't worry. You're going to be fine in a few days. You'll see."

The doctor's voice was fading quickly. His face was hazy, swimming. First it was close to Steve's, then moving rapidly away from him. Steve wanted to laugh. The man's teeth were huge, even bigger than that peanut farmer's, the one who was president. President who? Steve couldn't remember the man's name. Now someone was laughing. He tried to see who it was but everything was a blur. His eyelids were very heavy. They were closing and now he was falling again, falling through the black void into endless space.

Ted Banks took Steve's wrist and stared down at his watch. The rhythm was steady. Satisfied, he turned to the blond woman.

"Your husband will sleep now, Mrs. Pearce."

"How is he, doctor. Really, I mean?"

Doctor Banks puckered his lips and brushed several strands of gray hair back onto his forehead.

"Quite lucky. The x-rays show three cracked ribs on the left side. We were concerned that there might have been a punctured lung but we've ruled that out." He reached down and turned Steve's right arm over, revealing a bandage that stretched from his hand to his elbow. "He has a deep gash on his right forearm that stretches from his wrist nearly to his elbow. We removed quite a bit of glass. I was told that the plane's windshield had shattered and that's probably what caused this. It isn't serious but it'll take a while for it to heal." He paused for effect. "But it will in time." He paused again. "The only other thing we can find is this."

Banks reached down and lifted Steve's chin slightly. He ran his fingers gingerly across the swelling around the area of Steve's

Adam's apple. His neck was already turning a deep purple. "You can see the swelling. He took a tremendous blow up under his chin. We don't know what hit him but something blunt caused this. It's going to be difficult for him to speak or swallow for a while." He paused and ran his fingers across Steve's throat again. "I'm not sure I've ever seen swelling like this in the area of the throat."

Nora had lost interest in the doctor's medical analysis, especially when he showed her Steve's neck. It was grotesque. She wanted to turn away and not even look but that red-headed nurse was leering at her. So she feigned interest as long as she could. Finally, she could keep her impatience in check no longer. "Is it necessary for me to stay with him tonight?"

The question surprised Doctor Banks. He looked quickly at the nurse, then pursed his lips and replied. "Not particularly. The nurses will keep a close eye on him."

Nora tried to hide her relief but when she looked toward the nurse she saw the smirk. But she didn't care what the nurse thought. The doctor had given her an out and she was determined to press her advantage. "I am more than willing to stay if you think I should but I do have a small daughter staying with a neighbor. I should get home to her."

Ted Banks shook his head. "No need for you to stay. Just leave your phone number at the nurse's station. If anything unforeseen should happen they'll contact you immediately."

"Of course." Nora took another look at Steve, then bent and kissed him lightly on the cheek. Satisfied that she had fulfilled her wifely duties, she turned to give the doctor a parting smile. But he had turned away and was whispering again to the nurse.

Nora slipped out and closed the door behind her. It was an ordeal for her to play the loving wife and she was exhausted. She collapsed against the cold gray wall of the hospital corridor and dug in her purse for the silver case. Her hand was shaking as she fumbled to open it and extract a cigarette.

~ ~ ~

Jake stepped from the elevator half a minute after Nora exited Steve's room. He was halfway down the long hallway before he saw her. She was resting her head against the cold plaster and her eyes were shut. A cigarette was protruding out of the left side of her mouth and smoke was already wafting toward the ceiling.

"How is he, Nora?"

Startled, Nora turned her head in Jake's direction and, as she did, the cigarette in her mouth fell harmlessly to the floor and the case slipped from her hand and several filter tips went rolling across the wide hall.

"Don't do that to me, Jake," she snapped. "I'm nervous enough without you sneaking up on me like that." Her words were sharp and her eyes bore into him. She glared at him for several seconds, then dropped to her knees and began retrieving the unlit cigarettes.

Jake ignored her tone and knelt to pick up two that had rolled close to him. Then he picked up her lit cigarette. He was helping Nora to her feet when two nurses came down the hall. The older nurse frowned and stopped beside Jake and Nora. She held out her hand and nodded to the cigarette Jake had just picked up.

"Sir, if you wish to smoke you will have to do it at one of the approved areas outside the hospital." She nodded again at the cigarette. "I'll dispose of that for you."

Jake handed it to her.

Then she pointed toward his mouth and the ever-present cigar stub. "A cigarette and a cigar, all at the same time. Really, sir."

Jake grabbed it out of his mouth and quickly stuck it in his pocket. "Ain't lit," he muttered. The older nurse only shook her head and struck off down the hall in pursuit of the other nurse. "Weren't mine," Jake muttered again toward the retreating nurse. But she did not acknowledge him. A moment later both nurses disappeared around a corner, leaving Jake and Nora in their wake.

When he turned to face Nora, she was leaning against the wall, another cigarette lit and protruding from her over-red lips. A swirl of smoke was rising toward the ceiling. She had just a hint of a smile working around the corners of her mouth.

"Why didn't you tell her it was your smoke?"

Nora ignored him. "To answer your original question, Jake, he has three broken ribs, a swollen neck and an ugly gash on his right forearm. The doctor says he'll be just fine with some rest. No doubt, he'll be back up in the wild blue yonder before you know it," she said sarcastically. She raised the cigarette to her lips, exhibiting a slight tremor in her hand as she did. It was for effect but it did not fool Jake. He knew her too well.

"I want to see him."

"No, he's asleep. Come back another time," Nora snapped.

"You gonna stay up here with him?"

"No, the doctor said I don't..." She was going to say 'have to' but caught herself. "The doctor wanted me to go home and get some rest. I'll be back tomorrow."

Jake was about to say something he shouldn't have when the door to Steve's room opened and Doctor Banks came out. Jake recognized him immediately. The man had operated on a private pilot who had been injured the year before while trying to hand prop a small Piper. The pilot had not been quick enough when the engine caught and the propeller had nearly severed the man's left arm. Ultimately, the limb had been lost but Banks had made a valiant effort to save the man's arm.

"Doc." Jake said as he reached into his pocket. He was about to pull out the cigar stub and stick it back in his mouth when he thought better of it. "Jake Carter, Doc. From out at the airport. Pearce is one of my guys. What's the word on him?" Jake was studying the doctor's eyes for any telltale signs. As much as he was concerned about Steve, he was also concerned about his pilot's condition before the accident.

Doctor Banks studied Jake's face for a moment, then turned to Nora. "I'm sorry, Mrs. Pearce, but you'll have to put the cigarette out. They've clamped down on smoking in the hospital. You'll need to go outside to smoke." He turned back to Jake and noticed the little man had a strange smirk on his face and was staring at Nora Pearce. "I do remember you, Mr. Carter. The pilot with the severed arm last year."

With his fingers parted slightly, Ted ran a hand through the silver/gray hair that insisted on falling over his forehead. "As I was telling Mrs. Pearce," the doctor continued, turning back to Nora who had now dispensed with the cigarette, "Mr. Pearce is a lucky man. Right now we think his main problem is the broken ribs. Otherwise, a few minor injuries to his throat and arm. A lot of bruises. We'll monitor him closely tonight and should know more tomorrow."

"Any chance of me slipping into the room just to see him a minute?"

"Not tonight, Mr. Carter. Tomorrow, maybe."

"Sure, Doc. I understand." He understood but was still disappointed. Instinctively he pulled the cigar stub out of his pocket and stuck it in the left side of his mouth. Before Ted Banks could say anything, Jake pulled the brown stub out and replaced it in his pocket. "Sorry, Doc. I don't smoke 'um. I just chew 'um."

Ted Banks grinned and started off down the hall. Before he got ten feet, Jake called after him. "Okay if I bother you about Steve tomorrow, Doc? The boy's pretty special to me."

"Make it after three," Ted Banks called over his shoulder.

As Jake turned back toward Steve's door, Nora brushed past him without a goodbye and headed in the direction of the elevators.

Jake took a long look at Steve's closed door, thought about peeking in, then grunted and followed Nora down the hall. Halfway down, he ducked through a door marked "STAIRS" and descended the three flights on foot. Nora was exiting the front door of the hospital when he came out of the stairway door on the first floor. He hesitated until she was gone, then found a phone booth and dialed Lisa's number. The phone rang for nearly a minute before he heard the click.

"Hello." Jake could hear heavy breathing on the other end. "You okay, Baby?"

"Oh, hi, Daddy. Yes, I'm fine."

"Where were you?"

"In the shower. How's Steve?"

"Gonna be okay. A few broken ribs and some cuts and bruises. He got off lucky. Doc said he'll be fit soon enough."

"How about the," she paused, " you know..." She had lowered her voice as if someone would hear them.

"Don't know. Wouldn't let me in the room." Jake was fingering the stub in his pocket. He pulled it out once more and stuck it in the corner of his mouth.

"Are you okay, Dad?"

"Fine."

"You sure?" Lisa was concerned about him because she knew how worried he was. As much as she believed in Steve, she still felt for her father.

"Yeah. I'm okay." He paused, waiting for her to say something. When she didn't, he said, "Nora was here. Left when I did. Didn't seem none too worried."

"At least she came," Lisa said.

"Yeah. I'd like to tell the little..."

Lisa cut in before Jake could finish. "Daddy, behave."

"Unh-unh."

"Daddy."

"Yeah, yeah. Okay."

Lisa's voice softened. "Come by the apartment and I'll fix you something to eat."

"Nah, think I'll go down on Albert Pike and get some barbecue. Kinda cravin' somethin' spicy."

"I got a ham when I was up on Petty Jean Mountain a couple of days ago. I'll fix you some homemade biscuits with ham gravy."

Jake was tempted but he shook his head as if Lisa could see him. "Take a rain check on that, honey. How about tomorrow night?"

"It's a date, Daddy. Daddy, when do you think we can visit Steve?"

Jake hesitated a moment. He knew this would be coming. "Don't know, Lisa. Doc said I could check with him after three tomorrow afternoon."

"Don't think we might be able to get in tomorrow evening?"

"Let's wait and talk to the doctor tomorrow. See what he says."

"Okay, Daddy." Jake could hear the disappointment in Lisa's voice.

"Night, baby."

"Night, Daddy. And, Daddy, please be careful. It's pretty slick out there."

"I will." He paused a moment. Honey, don't come in tomorrow unless I call you. Probably won't be any flying for a couple of days."

"Okay. I'll wait till I hear from you."

Jake replaced the phone in its cradle and slid the cigar stub from one side of his mouth to the other with his tongue. Tonight, he realized, would be no different than any other. They had all been much the same since Marge died three years ago. Lisa had moved into her own apartment six months after that. It seemed they had made a pact to desert him, Marge in her way and Lisa in hers. The big house was too empty, too hard to adjust to. It was for that reason that he waited until the last minute to go home every night. A one-room apartment would serve him just as well but he couldn't stand the thought of parting with Marge's things.

A hard lump formed in Jake's throat and he felt the same burning sensation in his eyes that he had on so many occasions these last few years. He gritted his teeth, nearly biting through the stub as he had earlier. Then he started for the front door of the hospital. The snow was still coming down hard and he estimated there were already five or six inches on the ground and nearly that much on the roads.

A few feet short of the electric eye on the swinging door, he paused and pulled on the heavy, woolen gloves. As he advanced toward the door, he adjusted the jacket collar around his neck. The cold air slapped at his face the moment he stepped outside, running its icy fingers around the collar and down his neck. Jake dropped his chin until the cigar stub rested in the "v" of his jacket collar, then stepped into the snowy night.

name? Was it Doctor Banks?

And who was the strange blonde woman? She was strange but somewhere in the back of his mind he knew that he had known her sometime in the past. But it was the distant past. He was sure of that. It would come to him. He would remember her if she was real. If she wasn't, sooner or later she would fade away. If he was patient, he would wake up and Kathy would be there in his room. Just like in the dream. He would tell her about this and they would have a good laugh. Maybe what he was living now was the dream. But right now he was finding it hard to separate dreams from reality.

Steve let himself down gently onto the bed and stared up at the ceiling. His ribs were beginning to ease but his throat was still burning. To take his mind off the pain, he began to study the little room. There was no overhead light. The drapes over the window were closed but he still knew it was snowing outside. It was snowing in the dream and for some reason he knew it would be snowing here. He also knew, without having to look, that it was nighttime. It was in the dream. It must be here.

Without turning his head very much, his eyes moved to the opposite side of the room. His door was partially open and a narrow shaft of light from the outside hall slipped in. He was mesmerized by it for several seconds, then he heard footsteps. They got louder until a shadow passed by the door, then disappeared and the footsteps receded. He realized now he had been holding his breath for several seconds. He was afraid and he didn't know why.

Steve turned his attention back to himself. Bandages covered his upper torso all the way from his navel to just below his arms and shoulders. With his left hand, he moved his fingers back and forth across the bandages on his chest. Something didn't feel right. He dropped his hand to his stomach and pressed gently against the bandages. He felt swelling. His normally flat stomach was misshapen, fat. Body fluids from the accident must have built up and caused this change. As he got better the fluids and his stomach would return to normal. But it bothered him, this feeling of excess flesh. He thought it could be something as simple as the way his body was resting in the bed. As painlessly as he could, he tried several different positions. It made no difference. His stomach remained several inches larger than before. It had to be fluids, he reasoned.

~ ~ ~

A buzzer was attached to his pillow and he pressed it three times. He suddenly realized he was sweating profusely. His hospital gown was soaked around his neck and he could feel beads of sweat popping out all over him. Even the bandages around his stomach were soaked. His whole body seemed to be rigid. It seemed to be impossible to relax.

Slowly, he let his head sink down into the thin pillow, let his fingers relax and, as he did, he could feel his stomach muscles loosen. Steve brought his hands up in front of his face and studied them. They seemed normal. They looked like his hands. But now something else was wrong. He had not noticed it until now. His ring, the one Kathy had placed on his finger at their marriage ceremony, was gone. His left ring finger looked as if there had never been a ring on it. The one Kathy had given him fit tight and would have left an impression. It had not been off his finger since their wedding, not for any reason. But it was gone now and there was no indication it had ever been there.

"Mr. Pearce."

In his anguish over his condition and the missing ring, Steve was unaware that anyone entered the room. The big, red-headed nurse from before was bending over him, leering into his face.

"You rang the buzzer, Mr. Pearce. Are you feeling alright?" As she spoke, she remembered the injury to his neck and throat and raised her index finger to her lips. "I'm sorry. Don't try to talk. We don't want you to injure your throat any more. You just rest while I straighten these covers and we'll find a way to communicate when I finish. My, my. It looks like you've been thrashing around."

She ran her hand under the sheet and around his upper body.

"No wonder. This bed is soaked. You poor man. I'm sorry. I'll have someone change these sheets." She paused and ran her hand over his chest again. "And your gown. You're wet all over. We'll get you dry right away." She bent over him until her face was only inches above his and he could smell the coffee stench from her breath. "Now, don't say anything. We'll do it the same way Doctor Banks did. Blink once for yes and twice for no. Is there anything else I can do for you?"

Yes, Steve thought. You can get me out of this nightmare. You can bring me Kathy and Tommy. He wanted to scream that to this big woman. Instead he blinked twice, hoping she would, at least, move her face out of his.

"Good." The nurse straightened up and was about to turn toward the door when Steve reached up with his left hand and caught her arm. She stopped and bent over him again. Before she could stop him, he opened his mouth and mouthed a word. It was inaudible.

"You must not talk, Mr. Pearce."

Steve wasn't listening. He pulled her down closer so that her face was right next to his. Then he tried to mouth the word a little louder. It was painful, but this time the woman understood.

"Mirror. You want me to bring you a mirror?"

Steve nodded and blinked at the same time.

"Well, I don't see anything wrong with that. Now, mind you, you may not be too happy with what you see."

Steve nodded and she patted him on the arm and disappeared out the door. A few minutes later she was back with the mirror. She snapped on the light and held the mirror over him.

"Want me to hold it for you?"

Steve shook his head and grasped it in his left hand. He could make out his face. It was his, the same eyes, nose and mouth. That hadn't changed. His teeth didn't look quite as white as he remembered. But when he pulled down his lower lip he could see the chip on the right middle tooth. His brother had given him that present when he was in the eighth grade. They had been playing football on the concrete slab next to their house. Steve had been trying to run past Jim and their feet tangled and he had hit the surface face first. He could still feel the pain and hear the crack when his teeth met the pavement. He shuddered at the memory.

His eyes moved to his hair. A touch of gray was visible around his temples. That wasn't normal. And his cheeks were puffy. Everything about him pointed to a man twenty or thirty pounds heavier than he knew he was. His body was more like Ray's than his own.

Steve dropped the mirror on his stomach and began making writing motions to the nurse. She tilted her head to the side, reminding him of the little Boston Terrier, Pickles, that he had bought Kathy soon after they were married. It would sit at Kathy's feet and look up at her with those knowing eyes, and when Kathy would say something the dog would cock its head as if it were taking in everything she said. A year after he bought Pickles she was killed crossing Shady Grove Road. He remembered how Kathy had cried. They had buried the little dog under the big oak tree beside their bedroom window.

"You want something to write on," she said, acknowledging his actions. When he blinked she pulled a small notepad and pencil out of her pocket and handed them to Steve.

As best as he could with his left hand, he scrawled, "What day?"

She thought about it for a moment. "Saturday, the twenty-third. Two days before Christmas." She paused a moment.

Steve closed his eyes and thought about it. The same day or night now. No days lost. The accident was only hours ago, less than twelve. He opened his eyes, nodded and drew a line under his question. Then he slowly began writing again.

"Where is my wife?"

The nurse smiled. "She was here a little while ago. Doctor Banks told her to go home. I'm sure she'll be back first thing in the morning." She reached for the notepad but Steve drew it away from her. "Mr. Pearce, you must get some rest."

He shook his head a little too vigorously and the pain in his throat intensified. He ignored it and began writing again. It took him several minutes to scribble the words. "Blonde woman. Not my wife. Where Kathy?"

The nurse shook her head and frowned. "I don't understand, Mr. Pearce. The woman who was here said her name was Nora Pearce." She managed to relieve Steve of the notepad. "Now you must rest. You're worn out and confused. That's normal after an accident like you had. Don't you fret now. Everything is going to be just fine. You'll see."

She paused and it looked as if Steve was about to say something else. But the nurse put her finger to her lips again and shook her head. "Someone will be in here to change your bed clothing and you'll be able to go to sleep in no time. And tomorrow when you wake up everything will be much clearer."

Steve opened his mouth to protest but she bent over and, this time, placed her finger over his lips. "Hush, now. It's time for rest." Without another word, she flipped off the overhead light and left Steve in the semidarkness.

Elaine Wright thought very little about her encounter with the patient in room 310. It wasn't unusual for an accident victim to be confused. Many thought they were someone else and couldn't or wouldn't recognize a husband or wife. Some, she had come to the conclusion, did not want to remember their spouse. Based on her first impression of Nora Pearce, this man might be one of those.

The head nurse, Sally Blaylock, looked up as Elaine came around behind the nurse's desk. "Everything all right with Mr. Pearce?"

"Just a little confused."

Sally watched as Elaine picked up Steve's chart. "What do you mean?"

Elaine stuck a wad of gum in her mouth. "Says the woman who was in earlier isn't his wife. Says his wife's name is Kathy."

"What is his wife's name?"

"Nora. Nora Pearce."

Sally nodded. "Note what he said on his chart."

Elaine nodded. "Oh, and we need to get Jennifer down to change his linens and gown. Poor man's been sweatin' somethin' terrible."

"She's in 325 right now with old Mrs. Wilkerson. She should be back in a few minutes. I'll send her down when she gets back."

"Good." Elaine placed Steve's chart back in the rack. "It's about time for his shot. I'm gonna check on 315 and then I'll fix it." Elaine started off down the hall. When she was out of sight, Sally picked up the chart, read it and put it back in the rack. Like Elaine, she knew it was not unusual for an accident victim to be confused. Still, she wanted to be sure Ted Banks was aware of the situation. He could deal with it tomorrow.

~ ~ ~

Kathy pulled the blanket even tighter around her and sat down again beside the bed. Steve had not moved now in the more than twelve hours since the accident. Ray had stopped by the room again before leaving the hospital and checked for vital signs. They were unchanged from the time her husband had been admitted. As banged up as Steve was, it had not been necessary to operate. It seemed that Ray was more concerned about the damage around Steve's throat than anywhere else. Now, they were just waiting for him to wake up. The oxygen was just a precautionary measure to be sure Steve didn't have any trouble breathing.

Kathy felt a shudder move through her body. The strange chill that seemed to invade the room had happened once before earlier in the day. When she and Tommy had gone out into the hall, it was much warmer out there than in the room. Now the chill was back. The room was cold, downright cold. But, strangely, during the first cold moments earlier in the day, she had seemed to be much closer to Steve. It was like he was there with her trying to console her. Consciously, she loosed Steve's hand and pulled the covers up close around his neck, careful not to touch the terrible looking bruise and swelling. She touched his face with the back of her hand. Unlike hers, it was warm to the touch.

She stood and moved to the door that led into the hall. As she approached the door, warm air began to flow into the room.

It was as if someone had suddenly turned the temperature up ten degrees. She pulled the blanket off and dropped it into a chair next to the door. Somehow, she didn't feel Steve's presence like she had a moment before. Quietly, she sat down next to the bed, took his hand again and held it close against her cheek. As she did, a single tear worked itself down to bury itself between her cheek and his hand.

CHAPTER 7

EIGHT-YEAR-OLD SARAH had been working at the small chalkboard in the middle bedroom on Dickson Drive for the last hour. The note was important and she wanted it to be perfect. Twice now she had wadded up a piece of paper and tossed it into the trashcan at the foot of her single bed. The third version was showing signs of promise.

Now and then a blonde curl would slip down across her brow and eye and, as Sarah had seen her mother do countless times before, she stuck out her bottom lip and blew the sprig back onto her forehead. She stopped writing and thought back to the morning. It had started uneventfully. She was half asleep when her father slipped into her room before daylight and kissed her lightly on the cheek. He said something but she either didn't hear him or couldn't remember what he said. Right now she wished she knew what it was. It might have been important.

He was flying today. Last night one of her parents, she wasn't sure which one, told her he was due back around lunch. It was probably her father who told her that. But she had been so absorbed in a television show that she didn't remember for sure.

This morning when it all started she was in her room coloring. When the doorbell rang her mother yelled at her to answer it. It was a man in an official looking car. He wouldn't talk to her so she had gone to get her mother. It was then that she learned that her father's plane was missing.

Sarah went to her room, shut the door and didn't leave for the next three hours, not until she heard the doorbell again and saw the same man standing there. He told them that they had found her father alive. Back in her room, she had cried tears of relief. She was still crying when, moments after the man left, she was bundled up and sent across the street to Mrs. Peterson's house. She was to stay with Mrs. Peterson while her mother went to the hospital to find out about her father.

No amount of begging could persuade her mother to take her along. Children, she was told, weren't allowed. If that was really the truth, Sarah reasoned, then children weren't allowed to do a lot of things. So now she had to wait until her mother got home.

But Sarah was not a patient child. It was boring at Mrs. Peterson's. The woman did not have a television set so she had taken a book with her. The book lasted all of ten pages and she was then bored with the book. She couldn't think of anything but her father and how bad he might be hurt.

Finally, she found a chair in front of the big picture window and sat back to wait until her mother came home. Snow had been falling all during the afternoon. She wondered if the snow had made her father's plane fall. If it had she hated it. She hated anything that could hurt her father. But she sat and watched it, watched it cover up the tracks she had made when she crossed the street, watched into the cold December night.

When the lights of the gold Montego entered the far end of the street, she was still watching. She yelled at Mrs. Peterson and was out the door and across the street before her mother could get out of the car. The news was good and Sarah was elated. But she was told she still wasn't allowed to go see her father. She thought about the telephone but was told he had an injury that wouldn't allow him to talk. So Sarah had resorted to the letter. Her mother assured her that he could read.

Sarah closed the note with the words Love and Kisses. Then she made five x's and signed her name, Sarah Pearce. She took off her small, brown-rimmed glasses and placed them on top of the chalkboard. A pink envelope was on her dresser and she folded the note neatly and slid it into the envelope. On the outside she printed "DADDY" in capital letters.

For several seconds Sarah sat immobile, staring at the envelope. Then she sealed it and placed it next to her glasses. The girl missed her father, missed him terribly. All the time she had been waiting for them to find him, she imagined what it would be like without him. Terrible images had swept through her little mind. Now, as she sat thinking about the day, she didn't hear her bedroom door open. Nora's sharp voice jarred Sarah from her trance.

"Sarah, you are supposed to be in bed by eight forty-five. You have just one minute to get in, young lady."

Sarah turned quickly and looked up at her mother. Nora was standing some five feet behind her, hands on hips and framed in the doorway.

"I'm ready, Mommy. I was just finishing a letter to Daddy." She took the envelope and handed it to her mother. "Will you give it to Daddy tomorrow?"

Nora took the note, glanced at it indifferently and dropped it on the dresser. She eyed her daughter suspiciously. "Are you writing again without your glasses on? You know Doctor Evans said you were to wear them anytime you were reading or writing. Do you want to end up blind so that I'll have to take care of you for the rest of my life? I ought to tan your hide, as many times as you've been told."

Sarah pointed to her glasses on the chalkboard. "I was using them, Mommy. I just took them off a minute ago." She had learned at an early age that it did no good to reason with her mother. Nora did not believe in sympathy or forgiveness and very seldom used the words "I'm sorry." They were signs of weakness.

Sarah was used to the sudden fits of temper that characterized Nora Pearce's personality. And the fits were not reserved just for Sarah. Her father had experienced his share. She had witnessed the arguments between her parents, had seen the hurt in her father's eyes when her mother had said something especially hateful. And though she ached for her mother's love, she loved her father without reservation and knew that he loved her in the same way. And she didn't want to find out what it would be like without him.

Now, as she pulled the covers back and slipped into bed, she was fighting back the tears. Sarah pulled the covers tight around her chin, smiled up at Nora, and asked timidly, "You won't forget Daddy's letter will you, Mommy?"

"No, I won't forget the letter. I'll take it tomorrow." Nora picked up the envelope and, without so much as a goodnight, flipped off the light. "Go to sleep now." Nora started to shut the door but Sarah's voice cut through the darkness.

"Mommy, won't you let me go with you to see Daddy?"

Nora pivoted toward the child. "I told you not an hour ago. They won't let kids your age on his floor. Now, go to sleep. I'm tired," she snapped.

Sarah pulled the covers even tighter around her neck as Nora closed the door. In the darkness she allowed the first of a number of tears to flow freely down her cheeks onto the cool sheets.

Back in the den, Nora flipped the envelope toward the coffee table and watched it flutter to the floor underneath. Then she kicked off her shoes, picked up the newspaper and settled down on the couch. She was just getting comfortable when the phone rang. The insistent ring aggravated her. Nora was not anxious to deal with anyone or anything right now.

Her first thought was of the hospital. It would be them, she thought. Why couldn't they just take care of him and leave her in peace? Quickly, she ran a string of excuses through her mind. By the time she crossed the small den and was about to lift the phone from its cradle, she knew what she would tell them. She couldn't come back to the hospital tonight because her small daughter was already asleep and there was no one to stay with her. Surely, they could understand that. On the fourth ring Nora picked up.

"Yes."

"Nora." A man's voice greeted her.

"Oh, it's you," Nora growled. "I was afraid it was the hospital."

"Now is that any way to greet a very close friend?" The word "very" was overemphasized.

"I'm not in the mood for small talk, Ed. I just got Sarah in bed and I'm tired. What do you want?"

"I'm just checking. How's everybody's favorite pilot?" Ed Banning made no special effort to hide his disdain for Steve Pearce. He was aware that he was a distant second in Jake Carter's eyes when it came to flying. His way of showing his contempt for his rival was to have an affair with the man's wife. And her way to punish her husband without him knowing was to be Ed Banning's willing confederate. At least she didn't think Steve knew. But, if he did, she really didn't care. Her husband was too soft to do anything about it.

"They say he'll be all right," she said.

"Do I detect a twinge of regret?" Banning chuckled.

As if it would affect the tone of Ed's conversation, Nora whispered into the phone. "I hope you aren't drunk in some bar where everyone can hear you. I don't want the whole world to know about us."

Again Ed chuckled and now Nora could hear the faint sound of music and laughter in the background.

"You are in a bar," she growled.

"How 'bout me comin' over? You got the kid bedded down, ain't you? No chance of the husband walkin' in on us."

"No. There's no telling who's sneaking around after what happened today."

Nora could hear the squeak of a door from the other end of the line and the music and laughter got a little louder. For the first time the sound of a woman's voice, up close to the phone, came through the line.

"Hey, Handsome, I need my drink freshened. You comin'?"

"Yeah, Sweet Thing. You traipse on over to the bar and I'll be right there. Go on now, you hear." There was silence for perhaps fifteen seconds.

Nora was about to hang up when Ed's voice came back. "Hear that? I'm missed. You better get me while I'm available and my lips are still sealed. A few more beers and no telling what could slip out."

It was a veiled threat. As much as Nora wanted to hang up in the big cowboy's ear, she couldn't bring herself to do it. This was not the night to let Ed Banning go unchecked. So she relented.

"All right, Ed. Shut up and come on over. But park down by the school and come through the old field. And for the love of Pete, don't let anyone see you."

"I knew my girl would come through. See you in about fifteen minutes."

Nora waited until he had hung up, then slammed the phone angrily into its cradle. Her hands were shaking as she fumbled in her black purse for the cigarette case. Ed Banning was a mistake, one in a long line of bad mistakes. He had been from the beginning but she had been slowly drawn into the trap by his outward charm and her growing indifference for Steve.

Eight years was a long time to live with someone you didn't love, someone who didn't love you. That had been one of her first mistakes. She blamed that on Sarah. If not for her... Nora let the thought die as she lit the cigarette and plopped down of the couch to wait.

No sooner was she down, than she let the memories of those first years run through her mind again. Steve had been a pushover when he saw Sarah for the first time. Nora had not even suggested marriage, even though it was the reason she had made the drive from Texarkana to Hot Springs that day. He was gullible and she knew when she confronted him with his daughter, a daughter he had no prior knowledge of, that he would be quick to take responsibility. And he had. The child had to have a father, he had insisted.

And so he arranged for the private ceremony in the judge's office. Right up to the "I do's," she continued to insist that he didn't have to marry her. Her argument was just strong enough to make him think he wasn't being pushed but not strong enough to change his mind. She was smart, smarter than him, smarter than his family who would have it no other way when they saw Sarah. And in less than a week they were man and wife.

Steve had promptly dropped out of college. He had a family to support and somebody told him there was an opening at the airport for a mechanic. He had grown up working on old cars around his farm. So he applied and got the job.

The first year or two had been good. Not long after Steve started the job he came home raving about his love for the planes and flying. He began working extra hours without pay. He traded those extra hours for flight lessons. His senior year in high school he had gone up with a friend who had been flying for about a year. That was when flying got into his blood. He purchased a few lessons but couldn't afford to continue when he started college.

Now, since he had found a way to get back in the air, he seemed content. And Jake Carter, his new boss, allowed him to build his hours flying right seat on long charters. Within a year and a half Steve had his commercial license, an instrument rating, and a multi-engine license. The flight instructor's license was next. He was flying more than he was working on the ground. The pay was better. His life was more fulfilling.

By the end of the second year he had enough hours in the air to qualify to fly regular charters. His job description changed from mechanic to pilot and Steve was off and running. During those two years very little trouble had cropped up between him and Nora. But because of his intense love for little Sarah, Nora soon became jealous. He spent more time with Sarah when he was home and less with Nora. And time away on long flights was beginning to wear on his wife. She was growing weary of motherhood. The child was cutting into her free time. Sometimes he was away several days at a time flying people all over the country and she was left to take care of a child who was becoming an ever-increasing burden.

As Steve's reputation as a pilot grew during that third year of marriage and into the fourth, so did Nora's displeasure with her situation. By their third anniversary, Nora was drinking heavily. The squabbles were more frequent and more intense. To punish Steve, Nora began drinking more heavily than ever. And it began to rub off on Steve. Though he was very careful to drink only on his days off, he was still being pulled into the trap.

The more they fought, the more Nora drank. She couldn't wait for Steve to leave the house and Sarah couldn't wait for him to come home. Nora became more and more jealous, now of her daughter's evident love for her father. For Steve it was a no-win situation. He was uncomfortable around Nora but he wanted to be with Sarah. When he wasn't flying or taking an occasional drink, he and Sarah were at the bowling alley or the miniature golf course. They both wanted to be away from Nora. He knew she was getting very little love from her mother and he tried to fill in the gap.

All this was playing through Nora's head as she lounged on the couch. She blew a smoke ring through her lips and watched it rise lazily toward the ceiling. It would have been better, she thought, if the plane crash had ended their misery. The thought caused a brief moment of guilt to sweep through her. But as quickly as it came, she dismissed it and decided she was just being honest. And honest was what it was all about, she decided. Steve, she rationalized, would probably have agreed with her if he thought about it for a while.

"Instead I'm playing the role of loving wife again," she said aloud. Nora grimaced at the words. Her thoughts turned suddenly to the grimy little man at the hospital. He had seen through her tonight. But she didn't care what Jake Carter thought. He smelled of stale tobacco and oily sweat. He didn't mean beans to her. "Jake Carter, you can go..."

The knock on the carport door caused her to pause in mid-sentence. She knew who it was. Once Nora had been excited to know he was just on the other side of the door. Now, it only reminded her that the indiscretions of the past become the pitfalls of the present. Nora sighed and rose wearily from the couch. She crossed the den, into the small kitchen and opened the door to a leering Ed Banning.

CHAPTER 8

ON MONDAY MORNING, CHRISTMAS day, Steve sat up in bed for the first time since the dream two nights before. That night he had found himself sitting upright with his arms outstretched. The pain had been unbearable. Today he was sitting with a minimum of pain. The broken ribs seemed to be better, the swelling in his neck and throat was going down and his arm was healing nicely, though nurse Elaine had told him the bandage would have to stay on for at least another week or two.

Gray clouds still hung over the city. But the snow had stopped sometime Sunday evening. According to nurse Elaine, eight inches covered the ground. Tommy's white Christmas would be a reality this year.

Reality. The word echoed through Steve's mind. What is reality? Two days had passed and still no Kathy or Tommy, only a vision of them in the dream. Where were they and where was Ray? A strange doctor was tending his injuries. A strange woman was claiming to be his wife. But, he had to admit she was not altogether strange. He had been right. She was from his past.

The name Nora had sparked a recollection. He remembered her as Nora Stephens. They had dated a few times in college. At one time he even thought about asking her to marry him. And because of that, they had gotten a little closer than he wanted to admit. Sometime around the end of their sophomore year they had broken up. And he was glad they did.

After their split Nora had gone from boy to boy those last months of school. Her reputation became tarnished and after school let out that semester, she dropped out and he heard she was transferring to the University of Arkansas. That was the last he had heard of her. That was eight years ago and now here she was claiming to be his wife.

Steve opened his mouth and whispered Kathy's name. He did it very slowly and carefully. It didn't hurt as much as it had last night. What would it be like if he spoke normally?

He tested it a little further. "Kathy." Even though the pain increased the louder he spoke, just saying her name made him feel better. She was real. He knew that. And he knew somehow he would find her. He said her name again and realized his voice seemed much deeper, not like his voice at all. The swelling, he thought.

The door to the hall was open and he looked to see if anyone might have heard him. Activity beyond the open door seemed normal. No footsteps hurrying this way. His voice had evidently fallen on deaf ears.

The burning sensation was back in his throat, but not nearly so bad as before. Steve reached up and began massaging his swollen neck. His fingers move gingerly back and forth over the spot just below his Adam's apple. A good bit of the swelling had receded in just the last eight or nine hours. Last night it had felt like he had two Adam's apples, one soft and pliable and the other hard and protruding farther than he remembered. Now he could feel his real Adam's apple.

He was still puzzled by the layer of fat just below his chin. It seemed to be no different than last night. He still had the mirror the nurse brought him on Saturday night and he held it up to study his neck and head. The gray around his temples had not gone away. Last night he had taken a wet cloth and tried to wash it off. It didn't work. His two-day old beard even showed signs of graying. The beard, along with the heaviness in his face and neck, made him look older than he was.

He had a lot to sort out. Ever since he had regained consciousness the doctor and nurses had been in so much that he couldn't think straight. Today he had to try to think things through. He had come to the conclusion that one of three things had happened to him. He had either been involved in some strange supernatural event, gone absolutely crazy, or someone was playing some monstrous practical joke on him.

He wasn't crazy and the only thing supernatural that he believed in was God. He knew God was real. His faith was real. God was still here. That left only one thing that could be happening to him. Someone was playing some cruel joke. But why? What did they hope to accomplish? Were they trying to make him think he was crazy?

He wasn't anyone important, just a day-to-day accountant. He wasn't even a CPA. Things like this happened to people who led shadowy lives. Steve let his mind move back through everything that had taken place in the last few weeks. Nothing strange or important had happened to him that he could remember. He was at a loss. This was beyond comprehension. And the plane. What was the purpose of having him found in a plane? Nothing made sense. And the dream. What did that mean? Maybe he was crazy. Maybe he was hallucinating. Maybe none of this was really happening.

Steve let his eyes drift toward the window. From here only the skyline was visible; no buildings, no trees or birds, nothing except a shifting cloud pattern. He closed his eyes and tried to concentrate. It was like some fantastic story right out of someone's mind. Things like this happened to James Bond types, government agents who flitted from page one to page four hundred in a suspense novel. This didn't happen to people like him.

There were voices in the hall, moving in his direction. It was a man and woman. He recognized the man's voice immediately. It was Ray, Ray Philpot. Finally, someone familiar was coming to see him.

In a moment he saw them, a tall skinny nurse that reminded him of Popeye's girl friend, Olive Oyl, and Ray. Same old Ray, Steve thought. Now he would get some answers. But as suddenly as they appeared, they passed by the door and continued down the hall. Ray had not even bothered to look his way. Could it be possible that his friend didn't know he was here? It was more than Steve could take. Without thinking about his throat, he instinctively raised his good arm and called out.

"Ray. Ray Philpot. In here." The pain stabbed like a hot poker. Even so, he was prepared to call again if he got no response. But the footsteps suddenly stopped. He heard muffled voices, then the footsteps started up again. They were back. Ray had heard him. Steve found himself leaning toward the door with anticipation. Everything would be fine now. Ray would get it all straightened out. A moment later Ray Philpot turned the corner and stood framed in the doorway.

"Did I hear you call my name?" The question was impersonal, the way a person might greet a perfect stranger.

"Of course, I yelled at you. It's me, Ray. It's Steve Pearce."

Ray looked at him quizzically.

"Steve Pearce, your handball partner, the one who waxed you just two days ago."

The doctor moved slowly into the room, leaving Olive Oyl hanging in the doorway. "Are you sure you have the right person, Mr. ...?." Ray paused as if trying to remember Steve's name. Then he said. "I believe you said your name was Pearce."

Steve caught his breath. He couldn't believe his ears. Without actually saying the words, Ray was telling him that he didn't know him. And yet they were best friends. They had been playing golf in the summer and handball in the winter for years now. They went to church together. Steve taught the Sunday school class the Philpots attended. They visited in each others homes.

Steve wanted to shout at Ray, call him a liar, even shout a few obscenities. Why would he do this? What could cause a man to deny a five-year friendship? Then he noticed the skinny nurse. She was watching both of them, measuring them. Ray had to be acting the part for her benefit. Something is wrong, terribly wrong.

Steve found himself in a strain and realized his ribs were

beginning to hurt again. He let himself down onto the pillow and stared past Ray to the nurse. Olive Oyl was still watching both of them. Who was she? Now, along with the pain in his side, his throat was burning again. It had been several hours since he had pressed the pain button on his pillow and he reached up now and pressed it twice. The he closed his eyes for a moment. When he opened them Ray was bending over him.

"Are you all right, Mr. Pearce? Would you like me to call your nurse?"

Steve shook his head. "I'm fine." The medicine had not kicked in yet. "I guess I got you mixed up with someone else." He shifted his eyes toward the door and saw that the nurse had retreated into the hall and was talking with another nurse. Despite the pain, he took Ray's arm and pulled him down close to his mouth. "Kathy and Tommy, are they all right?" He whispered the words just loud enough for Ray to hear and received a blank stare in return.

"I'm sorry. I don't know a Kathy or Tommy."

Steve glanced toward the door. His watchdog was back.

"I understand," Steve whispered and loosened his grip on Ray's arm.

Ray Philpot stood up and looked over his shoulder toward the nurse. "Miss Riley, who is Mr. Pearce's doctor?"

She stepped out into the hall and read the card next to the door. "Doctor Banks."

"Olive Oyl Riley," Steve muttered. If Ray heard him he did not respond.

He patted Steve gently on the shoulder. "Doctor Banks is a fine doctor. He'll have you back on your feet in no time." Ray smiled down at Steve, then turned toward the door and followed the skinny nurse on down the hall.

Steve listened as the footsteps receded. As silence set in, he became more aware of the pain in his throat. It was hard to think about Ray now, hard to think about anything until the pain receded. Unlike the first night in the hospital, the acute pain didn't last as long. In less than a minute Steve was able to relax and take his mind off his throat. When he did, his thoughts turned back to Ray. He would be back. He knew where Steve was now and he would find a way to get back and let him know what was going on. Until then, Steve had to be patient.

And, yet, when the nurse had been away from the door, Ray could have shown some sign of recognition. He had looked at Steve as if he had never seen him before. Ray could have winked, could have even cut his eyes in the nurse's direction. But he had done nothing. Steve found his body rigid again and, without realizing it, his head had raised several inches off the pillow. He dropped his head back on the pillow and tried to relax again. It seemed he was telling himself to relax every few seconds. But it was impossible to stay relaxed. Everybody he knew and loved, except for his brief encounter with Ray, were gone.

Telling himself over and over to relax, he let his eyes drift around the small room. There was a cross on the far wall, one with Jesus nailed to it. He had seen one just like it in the local Catholic hospital in Hot Springs. Evidently, they were trying to convince him that he was there. The room was a drab gray. A picture hung on the wall to his left just beside the hallway door. To his right was a window and in the corner just to the left of the window, a television was sitting on a wall stand near the ceiling.

Just to the right of his shoulder and up close to the head of the bed was a table complete with telephone, a plastic pitcher that he knew had water in it, some magazines, a box of tissues, the mirror the nurse had left two nights before, and a pencil. Two chairs were in the room. One was to the right of the window and across from the table. The other was right under the television. A closed door was to the left of the hall door. That would be the bathroom. He looked back at the little table and studied the phone. It looked real enough. But it wouldn't be hooked up, he decided. They wouldn't let him have access to the outside world.

He reached across his body with his good hand and arm and lifted it from its cradle. The steady buzz that greeted his ear was unexpected. It was alive or at least it seemed to be. He replaced it and looked around the room to see if he had missed anything. The only other thing was the vanity and sink. A glass was to the right of the sink with a toothbrush sticking out.

Gently, he turned on his right side and reached across to pull the table drawer open. Inside were a comb, more tissues, a handkerchief, a pair of sunglasses with a small crack in one of the lenses, a paper clip, and a telephone book. It was the Hot Springs directory. His keys and wallet were not there. They had relieved him of all links to the past, except, he thought, Ray. His pictures, his licenses. They were all gone.

He closed the drawer and his eyes fell on a newspaper. He hadn't noticed it before because it had evidently fallen off the table or bed and gotten stuck between the two. Steve unfolded it. It was the local paper, the same one he had been reading for years. It was dated December twenty-fourth. The headlines across the top of the front page jumped out at him. It was yesterday's news and it was all about him. His name was on the first line and all of a sudden he remembered. Someone had given it to him the day before and he had read it. But everything had still been a blur and he wasn't thinking clearly. Now he forced himself to concentrate on the article. The headline read:

Private Plane Crashes Near Mt. Pine; Pilot Alive But Seriously Injured

Steve Pearce, commercial pilot for Carter Flying Service, was seriously injured when the Cessna 172 he was flying crashed in the mountains near Mt. Pine. Pearce was pulled from the wreckage nearly four hours after search operations began. As of this writing, cause of the crash has not been determined. The head of Civil Air Patrol said officials of the National Transportation Safety Board (NTSB) were flying in today to examine the wreckage and that...

Steve let the paper slip through his hands and flutter to the floor.

"No," he said through clinched teeth. There was very little pain. Maybe that's the key, he thought. Keep your teeth together and it won't hurt nearly so much. He concentrated again on what he had read. "I don't believe it. I was in an auto accident," he whispered.

"No one can convince me otherwise."

Still very little pain, he thought. That was the key. Keep your teeth together. He closed his eyes and he could still see the log hurtling at him through the windshield of the car. Even now the memory caused him to flinch and duck. He could still feel the thing ripping into his left arm and head. He had shielded his head with his arm and felt the arm crash back against his face. Maybe it hadn't done as much damage as he thought.

His eyes opened now and he reached for the mirror on the table. He held it up with his left hand and studied each feature of his face carefully. There was no apparent damage. All the damage was beneath his chin. But he distinctly remembered the force against his arm. Then he remembered the dream.

The man whose hand Kathy had been holding did have some damage to his face. There were bandages on the left side of that person's face. Why was he thinking that way? He was that person in the dream. He was the one lying in that hospital room with Kathy holding his right hand. That's the way it should have been.

Steve dropped the mirror and looked at his two arms. His left arm caught the log, not his right, because the car was sliding nearly sideways with the driver's side moving toward the old truck. His right arm was away from the collision. His mind switched back to the dream and what he remembered of it. Was the dream real? Was it something that had happened in the past, a month ago, two months ago? If so, that could explain the excess weight and the gray hair. Only time could change a man's body that much. That would mean that the accident had occurred more than two days ago. A lot more, he thought.

"You awake this time?"

Steve had been looking toward the window and was unaware that someone was standing next to the bed. He thought he recognized the gruff voice from yesterday. The man was small with a crew cut, something a friend of his had been wearing since high school. His friend's wife and kids and grandkids had seen Burr no other way for the last fifty years. Steve wasn't sure why he thought about his old friend now unless it was because of the hair.

"I was here yesterday, me and Lisa, and you were asleep. They treatin' you okay?"

Without waiting for Steve to answer, the man pulled the chair from under the television and sat down. He poked an unlit cigar stub in his mouth and leaned forward with his elbows on his knees.

"Still ain't doin' no talkin', I take it. They said you was hit along the throat and shouldn't be talkin' too much for a time." Jake Carter rested an oil-stained hand on Steve's good arm and eyed him earnestly. "You ain't to worry none about Nora and the girl. I'm goin' to see to it that they're taken care of while you're in here. You and me can square later."

Jake moved even closer now and his voice dropped to a whisper. "I ain't been able to sleep since the crash. Them NTSB boys is pokin' around the crash, examinin' everything. I just want to hear it from you, then we won't talk about it no more." He paused and looked back over his shoulder toward the open door. "You gotta tell me the truth. Ain't nothin' been said about it, mind you, but I gotta know before they come a questionin' me or Lisa." Jake's eyes narrowed and he glanced back again to see if anyone had slipped into the room. Without hesitation, he blurted it out. "You wasn't drinkin', were you?"

It seemed to be a question, asked as this strange little man asked it, that demanded a negative answer. It was an easy question to answer. Steve had taken his last drink in high school so he shook his head. The little man was pleased and he smiled and leaned back in the chair.

Steve was mystified. The man was a complete stranger. Who was he and what was he talking about? Why was the man trying to make him think he was a drinker? What would that accomplish? All of a sudden, as he looked at the man, he had the strangest notion. He wanted to reach up and rub his hand over the short, prickly hair. And he might have if the man was still bent over him.

The man was talking again. "You don't need to worry none about the plane. The CAP boys said you done one sweet job of bringin' it down where you did. Course it's totaled. But that ain't important now. I had it insured." He changed thoughts. "I'm gonna take a run out there first chance I get and see for myself."

Jake sat there eyeing Steve and chewing on the cigar stub. Finally, he stood up and reached down. He grasped the bandages on Steve's bad arm and squeezed just enough to cause Steve to grimace. The arm, which had been pretty pain free for the last few hours, began aching again. It was the big, red-headed nurse that rescued him.

"Here now. What are you doing in here?" Steve recognized Elaine's voice before he saw her. The crew-cut man released Steve's arm and turned toward the nurse. "You'll have to leave unless you're a member of the family."

"Same as," Jake protested. "Pearce works for me. I'm just checkin' on him."

Elaine advanced into the room shaking her head and motioning him toward the door as she did. 'Unh-unh. You'll have to come back later. Mr. Pearce isn't allowed visitors yet. You can call the third floor desk later and find out his condition."

Jake shifted the cigar stub from one side of his mouth to the other and glared at Elaine Wright. The woman just stood there with her hands on her hips. Her eyes never wavered. Jake shifted the stub back where he had it originally and started to turn back to say something to Steve. He was in mid-turn when Elaine growled at him.

"You know better than that," she squealed. "Get rid of that foul-smelling thing or I will. Smoking is definitely against hospital rules."

Jake started to protest but thought better of it. The big woman was planted squarely between him and the door and Jake knew he would have to go around her to get out. She was bigger than him and he was not about to test her. There was a time, Jake thought, when he would have. But not today, not with this woman, he thought. Obediently, he pulled the stub out of his mouth and stuck it in his jacket pocket.

"I'll be back when we can talk," he said over his shoulder as he

THE LEFT SIDE OF REALITY

gave the woman a wide berth and disappeared into the hall.

Steve watched the door until he was out of sight. He couldn't explain it but, in spite of the man's rough exterior, there was something about him that he liked. And yet, could he like any of these people? They were all involved and he had no clue about what was going on.

Once the man was gone, Elaine Wright walked to the foot of the bed and held up a flowerpot with a poinsettia growing out. "Now, isn't this just the prettiest thing you've ever seen." An envelope was attached to the flower. "Do you want it on the table next to the bed or on the window ledge?"

Steve turned his attention back to Elaine as he nodded toward the little table. Now that the other man was gone, the ready smile was back on her face. She sat the flower next to the bed, disengaged the envelope that was pinned to the stem and handed it to Steve.

He was sure the woman could see the excitement in his eyes as he worked to get the card out. It was exactly what Kathy would have sent him. She was a nut for red poinsettias, such a nut that he had adopted them himself. When Tommy was born, he had showered the hospital room with flowers. His fingers worked clumsily now as he tore at the small envelope.

"This surely does brighten up your room," Elaine was saying as he opened the card and began reading the message:

Big Brother, just got into Lincoln last night. Devastated by the accident, but excited to hear that you're going to be fine. Weather permitting, we'll see you sometime Monday. Take care. All our love, Jim and Mona.

This was crazy and getting crazier by the minute. The first two words had sent an uncontrollable spasm through Steve's muscles. When they were younger and Steve was still in college, it was all Jim ever called him. And the poinsettia. Jim and Mona had also sent poinsettias to Kathy when Tommy was born. They knew Poinsettias were Kathy's favorite flower. They also knew Steve loved them. Someone had done their homework when they hatched this plot, or whatever it was, Steve thought.

He glanced at Elaine. She was watching him, measuring his reaction to the card and who had sent it. "From your wife I bet."

He dropped the note on his chest and shook his head gently. If they were playing games, then he would too. Whatever they had done to him he must make them think they had been successful. Otherwise there was no telling what else they might do.

"Well, whoever sent it, it sure is beautiful. I just love poinsettias, don't you?" She walked around to the left side of the bed, took hold of his wrist and studied her watch for maybe a half minute. Then she nodded and smiled his way. "Buzz if you need anything," she said, and pointed to the beige instrument pinned to the pillow next to his left ear.

Steve nodded and waited patiently as she turned and disappeared into the hall. Several seconds later the sound of her footsteps on the tile floor receded. Normal hospital sounds were back. It had been all he could do, ever since he read the note, to keep from reaching out and wringing the truth out of the big woman. Using Jim was inexcusable. These people had to be sick.

Steve's fear had turned to anger now. He had to think. He had to figure out what was happening. The day before he had not been thinking clearly. At least he thought it was the day before. He couldn't be sure of anything now. Whatever was going on, he was sure he would not be able to reach any of his friends, especially Kathy. They would have made sure of that. Otherwise he would not have access to the phone. Still, he had to try. He had to do something. He couldn't just lie in the bed and wish. Steve glared at the phone for perhaps a minute, then picked it up and dialed his number.

"Hello." The answer came back quickly, almost too quickly. It wasn't Kathy. The voice was feminine, but younger, a teenager maybe. If he spoke they would be on him. Then it occurred to him. The phone would be monitored. They would already know he was calling and where he was calling. He threw caution to the wind and pressed on.

"I'd like to speak to Kathy," he said and felt the terrible pain.

He had forgotten to keep his teeth clenched.

"Who?"

"Kathy Pearce. Isn't this the Pearce residence?" This time his teeth were together.

"No, it isn't."

"What number have I reached?"

The girl repeated his number. Suddenly heavy beads of sweat spread across his neck and chest and there was a clammy dampness under both arms. His gown was soaked again.

"I'm sorry. Please forgive the intrusion." He broke the connection before the girl could respond.

His finger was still holding the button down and the phone was pressed to his ear. He finally released it and let it slide down his chest to rest in his lap. Everything on him was wet. Someone could have sprayed him with a garden hose and he would have been no wetter. And there was a strange odor about his body. Somewhere he had read that you could smell the fear of a cornered animal. Well, he was cornered. And now he could relate to those animals.

The card, resting beside the phone in his lap, caught his eye again. The handwriting was certainly not Jim's. Of course, it wouldn't be. The poinsettia would have come directly from the local florist. And the note would have been written locally.

Of course, he thought, he would be listed in the phone book. He opened the table drawer and pulled out the book. Only one Steve Pearce was listed, a city address that he didn't recognize. It was a 624 prefix. His prefix had been 262 ever since Fred had built the house on the hill for him. His mind was doing strange things, thinking strange thoughts. He was hearing strange noises. Suddenly he knew what it was. It was the intermittent buzzing of the phone. How long had it been doing that? In his state, he wasn't sure. It was still resting in his lap. He pressed the button, got a dial tone and punched in the 624 number. It rang twice before he heard the click.

"Hello." The voice was feminine again but this time much younger, a small child. Steve cleared his throat and made an effort to speak as clearly as possible through clenched teeth. Even clearing his throat was painful but he was convinced it was necessary.

"Can I speak to your father or mother?"

"My daddy is in the hospital. But Mommy is here. Would you like to speak to her?"

Now children, he thought. Finally, he asked. "What's your name, little girl?"

The child was silent for several seconds. When she didn't answer in what Steve thought was a reasonable time, he asked again.

"Are you there, little girl?"

The little voice came back quickly this time? "Daddy," she squealed. "Is that you, Daddy?"

The shock was more than Steve could deal with. He hung up quickly and sat staring at the phone. Just that few moments had completely drained him. For ten minutes he sat on the bed trembling, the phone clutched in his hand. He was in a nightmare and he didn't know how to get out. Finally, he got control of his emotions. Did he dare dial the number again? If he wanted to get to the bottom of this, he had to. He punched in the numbers and waited three rings.

This time it was a woman's voice. It was unmistakeable. She had been here the first night and then again yesterday and into the night. It was the woman who claimed to be his wife.

"Nora," he quietly said.

"Is that you, Steve?"

He didn't answer.

"Steve, answer me."

He braced his body and spoke into the phone. "I know who you are. You were Nora Stephens in college at Ouachita. Am I right?"

Now there was silence on the other end of the line for perhaps thirty seconds. He could imagine that she was trying to decide how to answer his question. Finally, she came back. "What is wrong with you? You know good and well what my name was before we were married and you know what it is now." She paused to catch her breath. "Was that you on the phone a few minutes ago?"

It was her. He remembered now, remembered why he had unpleasant memories of her. She was the same Nora after these eight years. Snappy, cross, sarcastic. Always ready to argue but never able to make up or say she was sorry. It was why they had broken up during his sophomore year. It was why he was glad they had never gotten back together. But then it struck him. They were together now. If you wanted to believe this crazy, mixed up mess, they were together now. For the first time since he was a child, he felt like crying.

"Are you listening to me? I asked if you called a few minutes ago. Sarah swears it was you."

Steve hunched his shoulders and tried to pull himself together. "Yes, I called. We got disconnected," he lied.

"Why did you wait so long to call back?" She hesitated momentarily, seemingly uninterested in whether he answered or not. She changed the subject and shocked him again. "By the way, I tried to get through to Jim and Mona Saturday night and all day Sunday. I finally got them late last night. They've been out of town, but said they would catch a plane out as soon as possible. It seems the snowstorm has closed the airport. They've had quite a time out there." Her voice trailed off before continuing. "I told them they could stay with us while they're here." Steve could tell by the tone of her voice that she hadn't wanted to do that.

Suddenly, he could take it no more and the words gushed forth before he could stop them. It might cost him, but they would know his fury. It probably wasn't smart but he couldn't control his anger and frustration any longer.

"I don't know what you people are up to. But whatever it is, it won't work. Tell your sick friends that."

Before Nora could answer, Steve slammed the phone back in its cradle. His whole body was shaking and he wasn't sure now whether it was more from fear or anger. He was feeling both emotions. Anger had taken control of him a few moments ago, but it was fear he was experiencing now, fear and pain from the shock his throat had experienced from his sudden outburst.

Now his ears were sensitive to every sound in the hall. If they were listening they would be after him. He couldn't move, much less run. This time they would fit him with a straitjacket. He should have kept his wits and kept his mouth shut, continued to play dumb. He wasn't cut out for this kind of life. If it hadn't been for the card. If they hadn't used Jim and Mona.

He picked up the card and read it again. How long had it been? Six years. Six years since they died. Six years since the fire. It was still as vivid as the day it happened. Jim and Mona were on the way home after Tommy's birth. They had stopped for the night in an old motel on the outskirts of Oklahoma City and never left. At three thirty in the morning it caught on fire and fifteen people died. Jim and Mona had been two of the fifteen.

Steve crushed the card in his hand and dropped it beside the bed. He listened again for any sounds that shouldn't be there but there didn't seem to be any unusual activity in the hall. No one had come. No one seemed to be coming. He didn't know why. Maybe it was one of those other alternatives he had thought about earlier. Maybe he was crazy.

He brushed a tear off his cheek and let his head sink deep into the pillow. He closed his eyes and Jim's face, sometimes dimmed by the years, flashed into his mind. They had used a dead man. And that dead man was his brother. It irked him that they would use his dead brother and sister-in-law. Who would be next? Would they bring back his parents? He didn't know what to do or think, but he was determined they, whoever they were, would not get away with it.

~ ~ ~

On Dickson Drive, Nora Pearce replaced the phone in its cradle and stared at it in disbelief. She could not imagine what had set Steve off unless he knew about Ed. She thought about it for a minute, shrugged her shoulders indifferently and looked across the room at her daughter.

"Was that Daddy?"

Nora rose abruptly from the kitchen chair and shoved it roughly against the table.

"Yes," Nora grunted. "The man's crazy as a loon.

CHAPTER 9

LISA TRIED AS BEST she could to concentrate on the paperback novel. Except for the brief hour on Sunday when Jake had picked her up and taken her to the hospital the book had been her only escape. It was difficult to focus on anything. She found herself reading but not digesting the story. The last hour was a blur. She had no idea what she had read.

It had been that way for two days. All she had been able to think about was Steve. She was obsessed with him and that wasn't healthy. Somehow she had to get him off her mind. Maybe if he hadn't been asleep on her visit it would have been better. She wanted to talk to him, make sure he was okay. The nurse had assured her he was doing fine but that didn't help. He looked so vulnerable lying there in the bed. His left hand was dangling over the edge of the bed, and when she lifted it and placed it beside him her own hand had lingered longer than necessary and her father had grunted and frowned his disapproval.

She fingered the pages of her novel and thought about calling the third floor nurse's station to see if everything was still the same. But she had thought about doing that half a dozen times during the morning and discarded the idea each time. If she did, would they give her an honest answer? It would be the standard response and she wouldn't know any more than she did now.

Jake might know something by now but she didn't want to seem too anxious. It was a dilemma. The book in her lap no longer held her interest and she flipped it on the coffee table and slid across the couch toward the phone. Her father might scold her for being too forward, but she had to know. She dialed his number.

"Yeah," came the quick reply.

"Daddy."

"Oh, hi, baby."

"Merry Christmas, Daddy. Have you opened your present yet?"

"Yeah, sugar. Right after I got up this morning. Been meanin' to call and thank you for the cigars and shirts."

"You're welcome, Daddy. And thank you for the perfume and underwear." A wide grin spread across Lisa's face. She could imagine how embarrassed he must have been buying the panties and slips. Still, he invariably came up with the same present every year. He was a creature of habit. That last Christmas before her mother died they had both kidded Jake unmercifully about his annual gift. The sudden memory of her mother brought an ache to Lisa's heart and she closed her eyes and tried to visualize what her best friend had looked like. The years have a strange way of erasing faces, she thought. Jake's voice shocked her back to the present.

"You still there, Lisa?"

"I'm here, Daddy. Have you talked to anyone at the hospital today?"

"Yep."

A moment of uncomfortable silence ensued while Lisa waited for her father to report on what he knew. When he did not, she sighed and pressed on.

"Is anything wrong, Daddy?"

"He's okay. Can't talk yet. Seems to be okay except..." Jake let his voice trail off.

"Except what, Daddy?"

"Nothin' probably. Maybe I'm just imaginin'. He just acted a bit strange. Didn't act like he knew me there for a bit."

"You think it was because of the accident?"

"Maybe," Jake answered.

"He wasn't in any pain was he?"

"Didn't seem to be. I'd of been able to talk to him a little longer if that big, red-headed nurse hadn't run me out."

Lisa could feel her father's frustration through the phone line. Jake Carter had always been in control. When he wasn't, he could be a cantankerous man. He would not have surrendered to the big nurse without a struggle. But the way he had spoken about the woman, Lisa knew who had won the battle. Now, as she waited for him to continue, she could hear him working the ever-present cigar back and forth in his mouth.

"Why did she run you out?"

"Visitin' hours. I thought they done away with them."

Lisa laughed at her father's mimic of the nurse's voice when he said 'visitin' hours'. "Did you tell Steve we came to see him yesterday?"

"I did." Jake growled. "Baby, don't you forget Nora."

A charge of electricity worked through her body. Jake had found a way to tell her to back off without really saying it.

"I just wondered. I'm glad he's doing well." She tried to sound nonchalant but it didn't work. It didn't fool Jake and she knew it.

"Yeah, okay," Jake grunted. "Just remember he's got a wife and kid."

"I know, Daddy." It was time for her to change the subject. "You coming by for our ritual Christmas Dinner at five?"

Lisa's mother had been a great cook. Every Thanksgiving and Christmas, since she could remember, the table had been set with turkey, dressing, mashed potatoes, gravy and all the trimmings. It had been such a special time. Now, since her death, Lisa and Jake had been forced to settle for ham, baked beans and corn bread. The one thing Lisa knew she couldn't do was compete with her mother and she hadn't tried. It suited Jake and they shared the seasons, just the two of them. There was silence on the other end of the line. She could hear her father breathing but he wasn't talking.

"You okay, Daddy."

"Yeah, baby. Just thinkin' and rememberin'."

"I know, Daddy." She waited and he was silent again. "I've got the ham in the oven. I don't want to eat it alone."

"I'll be there. I may not be the best of company though."

Jake's voice was cracking just a bit and Lisa imagined that the tough, little man was probably wiping away a tear. He was definitely having a hard time controlling his emotions.

"Daddy, I don't know anyone I'd rather be with tonight than you."

"Me, too, baby. Me too." There was a click on the other end and Lisa sat listening to the silence for several seconds. Finally, she replaced the phone and leaned her head back against the couch. Like her father's, Lisa's eyes welled up with tears. She closed them and there was her mother smiling just like she always had.

~ ~ ~

It had been two hours since Steve's call. Nora was still baffled by his outburst. Her first fear was that he had found out about her affair. But there had been no mention of Ed. The more Nora thought about it, the more convinced she was that his anger had nothing to do with Ed. But what? That was what she couldn't understand.

Sarah had been hustled off to the Peterson house a few minutes before. As she pulled the red coat on, she spotted the envelope Sarah had given her on Saturday evening. The child had found it under the table where Nora dropped it and picked it up and laid it on Nora's purse. It was her way of reprimanding her mother. Nora frowned, started to drop it again on the table, then, after a moment, slipped it in the outer pocket of her purse and started toward the door that led to the carport. At the wall phone she stopped, lifted the receiver and dialed. After three rings the connection was completed.

"Hello."

"Ed."

"Hey, babe. Whatcha doin'?"

"I talked to Doctor Banks this morning. He said Steve might be able to come home by the weekend. But I'm worried. His throat must be a lot better because he called this morning and was talking crazy. He accused me of being involved in some plot. He was talking really weird." She swallowed deeply. "He sounded like some nut."

"Not to worry, sweet thing. He's just confused. He'll snap out of it in no time and be the same adorable Steve he's always been."

"I'm serious, Ed. He sounded crazy. It kinda scared me."

"Aw, come on, Nora."

"You haven't told anyone about us, have you?"

"Now, Nora, you know me better than that. It's Steve that's crazy. Remember? Not good old Ed." He waited for a response. When it didn't come, he continued, "Why don't I come over tonight? We'll have a beer and ..."

She didn't let him finish. "That's another thing. I don't want you over here anytime soon. Steve's brother and sister-in-law are flying in from Colorado. Unfortunately, they'll be staying here. So we'll have to keep clear of each other until they leave. I've got to play the devoted wife and an extra lover banging on the back door may not sit too well."

Ed howled. "The devoted wife," he cackled.

"Shut up, Ed."

He was still chuckling when he suggested, "Maybe we could meet somewhere else."

"No, I said we have to cool it. So don't call, don't show up. Don't even breathe in this direction. Do you hear what I'm saying?"

"Okay, okay. Whatever you say."

"That's what I say." She checked the wall clock. "I have to go. Remember what I said. No phone calls, not even to check on Steve, and by the way, you're supposed to be a friend of his. Have you been to see him yet?"

"Tonight, baby. Tonight I visit my good buddy."

Nora hung up and glanced toward the fireplace. The last embers of her morning fire were dying away.

~ ~ ~

The snow was turning to slush, the worst part of a snowfall. Nora guided the car onto Albert Pike, then down Hobson and was about to turn left on third street before she turned her thoughts back to Steve and his wild accusations. Something was terribly wrong. She could feel it and she felt like she had no control over whatever it was.

Thinking about it now, she was convinced that Steve's anger had nothing to do with Ed. In ten minutes she would be in Steve's room and she needed to be ready with answers. Based on his outburst this morning, he might say anything, ask anything. How would she handle it? If he did know about Ed, she didn't want to be backed into a corner. Nora decided not to let him get her on the defensive. If he attacked then she would counterattack. Wasn't that little hussy, Lisa Carter, sweet on Steve? Ed had mentioned that she had goo-goo eyes every time he came into the flight office. Who was to say that he hadn't returned her feelings? Nora nodded and smiled. Yes, who was to say?

~ ~ ~

Doctor Banks had been in the hospital less than an hour when he approached the third floor nurses' station. Only four more patients on this floor and he could go home and spend a normal Christmas afternoon with his wife. As was his custom, he made rounds every day whether he went to his office or not. Today, being Christmas, he had not gone to the office.

People around the hospital said he was the closest thing to the old television doctor, Marcus Welby, that Hot Springs had to offer. He was even known to make an occasional house call. Some of his colleagues had frowned on the practice and one or two had unofficially reprimanded him. But he chose to ignore them and continue to practice medicine the way his father had for so many years. It was also the way he thought it should be practiced. Though his patients adored him, he had not won any popularity contests with his peers.

Ted Banks was at Elaine Wright's shoulder before the pudgy nurse realized he was about. "Afternoon Miss Wright. Can I see Mr. Pearce's chart, please?"

She looked up quickly. "I'm sorry, doctor. I didn't hear you come down the hall."

"I'm part Apache. I walk softly in my moccasins."

A grin spread across the big nurse's face. Ted Banks was one of her favorite doctors, if not her favorite. "Yes, sir." She handed him the chart. "Mrs. Shelton just stepped down the hall. Would you like me to accompany you on your rounds?"

"Not necessary," he said as he studied the chart. "If she should get back in the next few minutes, have her meet me in Mr. Pearce's room."

"Very well, doctor."

Ted Banks was still engrossed in Steve's chart when he entered the room. Because of the calls he had made earlier, Steve was expecting someone to come. When they didn't early on, he decided they must be letting him stew. The thing that bothered him the most was the phone. Why would they let him have access to a phone? That was a link to the outside world.

Several times since he talked to Nora, he had picked up and listened to the steady buzz. Once he had dialed the number of his church and got an answer. He hung up quickly when the person on the other end of the line identified herself. He didn't know why but he had found himself afraid to talk. Perhaps it had been the outburst at Nora. Whatever it was, he had not been willing to identify himself. But, of course, they knew he was calling. Now this strange doctor was back.

Doctor Banks had Steve's chart in one hand and a pen in the other. He acknowledged Steve with a smile and a quick greeting. "Good afternoon and merry Christmas, Mr. Pearce."

"Doctor," Steve said through clenched teeth, "did my..." He paused. He was about to say wife but couldn't bring himself to. "Did Nora report on me?"

"Oh, you're able to speak. How is it? Does it hurt?" Ted grasped Steve's wrist before he could answer and began counting pulse beats. After a few seconds he released the wrist. "I spoke to Mrs. Pearce this morning, but she didn't mention anything about the two of you talking."

He raised Steve's chin and ran his fingers slowly across Steve's neck. "Much better. Most of the swelling is gone. You still have a little discoloration but that'll go away in time." He took out a small flashlight. "Open your mouth wide and let me take a quick look inside." He took out a tongue depressor and gently pressed down on Steve's tongue as he shined the light inside Steve's mouth. After a moment he flipped off the light and stuck it back in his pocket. "Looks better. Not hurting as much, I trust."

Steve shook his head. It doesn't when I don't talk, he thought.

"Let's take a look at the ribs. Are they hurting much?"

Steve shook his head.

Ted Banks pulled the sheet back and ran his fingers slowly across the bandages. "Does that hurt?" He looked at Steve, then back to his chest.

Steve shook his head again.

The doctor continued to put pressure around the area where the ribs were damaged. After a few minutes he pulled the sheet up and smiled. "Seems to be getting better."

Steve nodded this time. He was still wondering when the doctor was going to get down to the real question. When was he going to clamp a straitjacket on him?

"How about the arm. Been bothering you much?" Doctor Banks lifted Steve's arm and gently turned it over palm up. "Needs to be changed," he said, nodding to the bandage. "I'll have the nurse replace this with a fresh bandage."

Steve remained baffled. But if they wanted him to, he would play along until something happened or someone told him what was going on. "How long will I be in here, Doctor?" Wasn't that the standard question most patients asked?

Banks was engrossed in the chart again, his pen working its way across the page. He held up his hand for a second and then continued writing.

Steve was mystified. Surely Nora would have told them by now. But this doctor, if he really was a doctor, seemed ignorant of the tirade he had loosed on his.... Steve stopped in mid-thought. They even had him thinking of Nora as his wife. But she wasn't. She was only a former girlfriend, never his wife. Nothing more. They were trying to brainwash Kathy and Tommy out of his mind and Nora in. They could never do that. Not while he had any sense at all, he thought.

Banks finished writing and turned back to Steve. "You asked me about going home. I told Mrs. Pearce that I expect to release you around the end of the week. We want to be sure there aren't any complications. Don't want something cropping up that we haven't thought about." He paused a moment. "Any other questions I can answer for you?"

Steve shook his head.

"Good man." He paused again to see if Steve might say something. When he didn't, the doctor smiled. "I'll see you tomorrow, Mr. Pearce." Without another word, Ted Banks turned and disappeared into the hall.

~ ~ ~

Steve placed his hands together, intertwining the fingers and rested them on his chest. So they weren't ready to clamp him in irons yet. But they would sooner or later. Of this he had no doubt. His eyes moved to the window again. He had to find out. He had to know what was outside that window. It would not be downtown Hot Springs. The scene outside would not be familiar, of that he was sure.

He decided it was time to see. Using his good left arm and hand he moved his body slowly to the right side of the narrow bed. His next move would be to lower his legs to the floor. But he wasn't sure whether he could handle the pain. He had to be careful. If he fell, he could damage his ribs further, maybe hurt his arm and get it bleeding again.

But he couldn't stand the thought of not knowing. He would do it. He had to do it, and so he braced himself and began to carefully work his legs over the edge. It was an effort and it was painful, just as he expected, but his legs finally slid off the edge of the bed. Then with his good left hand he pushed his body into a sitting position.

Steve's feet were touching the floor now. He had not yet put any weight on them and found himself hesitant to do so. Very gently, he pushed his bottom off the bed until he had his full weight on the balls of his feet. His legs were like rubber and he thought they might give way. Steve was forced to lean back and rest against the bed for more than a minute.

When he finally decided that he could keep himself erect, he stepped out with his left foot. A sharp pain raced through his right side. He wanted to fall back against the bed again but he was committed. Three painful steps later, Steve collapsed against the windowsill, puffing like a seventy-year-old man.

After he regained his breath, his eyes focused on the landscape below. What he saw should have shocked him nearly as much as the accident. But it didn't. For some reason, even though he had swore it wouldn't be that way, he was not surprised. What he was looking at was downtown Hot Springs. The cars, the people, they were all there. Just below and to his left was the fountain at the intersection of Park, Central and Whittington Avenues. It was just as he remembered.

In the distance he could see the Arlington Hotel and farther on to the south the old Army-Navy Hospital. In recent years it had been converted into a rehabilitation center. It was the place he and some of his friends had gone to play basketball when none of the gymnasiums were open. All the familiar landmarks were right where they should be. It was Hot Springs, but somehow it wasn't his Hot Springs. What was different? Why couldn't he put his finger on it?

Then he remembered. This was the old St. Joseph's Hospital. The new one had been built on the south side of the city several years ago. Something was terribly wrong. He searched for another couple of minutes. Except for the fact that this hospital had been abandoned years ago, everything was in its place. Now he was really depressed. And for the first time he questioned his sanity. Steve shook his head and retreated the same painful steps to the bed. He was just working his way back onto the mattress when he heard the click of a woman's shoes on the tile floor. For a fleeting instant he thought of Kathy. But he quickly knew. It wasn't Kathy's familiar walk. It was Nora. His depression deepened even further as she came through the doorway.

CHAPTER 10

THE WINTER STORM THAT had hit Hot Springs on Saturday was light in comparison to the storm that inundated the Denver area. It began moving through western Colorado early Saturday night, and by noon on Sunday over two feet of new snow covered the ground. Power lines, overloaded with massive amounts of ice, had begun falling by Sunday morning. By mid-afternoon, power officials estimated that two hundred thousand customers in central Colorado were without electricity. The temperature had fallen below zero, causing those homeowners without fireplaces to either take refuge at friends or neighbors or to huddle together as family units under mounds of blankets. It would be an unforgettable Christmas for many. For some older residents who either couldn't or wouldn't seek adequate shelter, it would be their last.

At Stapleton International Airport, drifts fed by high winds and heavy snow averaged four and five feet deep. The big snow-plows had been working furiously throughout the night to clear runways. Though the snow had diminished somewhat by midnight, Christmas Eve, it would be at least morning before service could be resumed at the facility. Travelers, stranded by the storm, were squeezed together in every corner and cubbyhole of the terminal building. Many were college students getting a late start home for the holidays. They sprawled everywhere, cluttering walkways, benches and even restrooms with their bodies and baggage.

By noon on Christmas day, more than a little irritation prevailed among the travelers. But as brief patches of blue began to peek through the low clouds, the anxiety of the past twenty-four hours began to fade. At one fifteen, the announcement came that service would resume within the hour. Relief spread quickly through the masses and people began gathering belongings and moving slowly toward their boarding stations.

The slender, blonde woman looked up from her magazine as her husband came down the wide corridor and through the entrance to the waiting room.

"Honey, I just got word. Our flight will be boarding soon."

"Praise be," she said, as she got up and stretched her five-foot-four frame. About thirty passengers were scattered around the small waiting area, some asleep, some reading, as she had been doing; one particular foursome she had been watching had pulled two chairs together and were playing cards. In a corner of the waiting room a young couple, probably in their late teens or early twenties, were embraced and kissing. The woman noted the embrace and remembered the same couple had been in much the same position a half hour before. She tugged at her husband's arm and motioned toward them.

"Remind you of anyone?"

He smiled and nodded. "Another world, another time."

"A happier time?" There was just a hint of anxiety in her question.

"Never. This is my happy time."

The woman smiled and squeezed her husband's arm.

He spied a pretty stewardess as she came through the gate and started across the waiting room. "Miss."

"Yes, sir." The young woman paused and flashed a ready smile.

"Flight six forty-seven, will it be boarding soon?"

The stewardess glanced at her watch. "About twenty minutes. But it could be some time before we get off the ground. A number of flights will be boarding at the same time." She glanced behind her and nodded toward a young man in uniform. "He'll be issuing boarding passes very shortly."

The man nodded his thanks to the stewardess and took his wife's hand. They moved behind the uniformed man as he crossed the room and were the first in line at the desk. Here, they found themselves in a direct draft from the tunnel that led to their plane. The woman felt the sudden chill and moved tightly against her husband. They watched as the young attendant arranged several sheets on a clipboard. After a few minutes he looked up and acknowledged the couple.

"Names, please."

"Pearce. James and Mona Pearce."

CHAPTER 11

NORA WASN'T QUITE SURE what to expect as she marched down the hall toward Steve's room. His display of temper had left her at a loss and had even frightened her. If it happened again, she wasn't sure what her reaction might be. She had already made the decision that Steve would not back her into a corner. If he knew about Ed, then she would go on the offensive. Knowing her straight-laced husband, any accusation she might bring against him probably wouldn't be true. But she could still use that snippet of a girl, Lisa Carter, to deflect any of his accusations. And she would do it if necessary. But she was certainly unprepared for the smile and cordial greeting from her husband.

"Good morning, Nora."

She became suspicious at once. Like a fighter backed into a corner, her guard came up immediately.

"Steve." She advanced to the bed and gave him a quick peck on the cheek. "How do you feel?"

"Much better." He took her hand as she started to move away from the bed. "I want to apologize for this morning. I've been feeling pretty rough and I guess I just got confused and said some things I shouldn't have. Will you forgive me?"

"Sure, forget it."

Now she was really suspicious. She loosed her hand and retreated to a chair at the opposite side of the bed. Steve's friendly attitude had to be an act. For the next hour Nora did not budge from the chair. Occasional small talk passed between them but much of the time was spent in silence. During that hour he seemed to be measuring her as if he knew her innermost secrets.

An uneasy feeling permeated her body and more than once she had trouble meeting Steve's constant stare. She must have crossed and uncrossed her legs a dozen times. When it was time to leave, Nora realized she could remember very little of what had transpired in the little room.

Unlike Nora, Steve was very aware of everything. For the first time since the accident, his mind was functioning perfectly. He still didn't know what was going on, just that he wasn't crazy. Someone or something was trying to destroy his life and his family. That would not happen if he had anything to say about it.

But from this moment forward great care had to be taken. Like a basketball player trying to get involved in the offense, he had to bide his time and let the game come to him. Eventually it would and when it did, he would have to determine how to attack the problem.

Steve was so engrossed in his own thoughts that he didn't realize Nora had gotten up and moved next to the bed. "I'll be back tomorrow. I hope you get a good night's sleep." She bent and touched his lips lightly. "Good night, Steve." She turned without another word and was at the door when she paused and opened her purse. "I nearly forgot. Sarah wrote you this on Saturday afternoon. She'll give me the third degree if I forget to give it to you." She retraced her steps and handed the envelope to him.

It was simply addressed "DADDY." He opened it and looked up to ask Nora about the child. But she was already gone. Steve unfolded the note and began reading.

Daddy

I love you. I miss you very much. When are you coming home? Mommy won't let me come see you. I miss you very much. Mommy doesn't read me a bedtime story like you do. Hurry and get well. I love you.

Sarah

Steve studied the paper carefully. It was definitely a child's uneven scribbling. And, if he hadn't known better, he would have sworn a child had composed it. But someone else had composed it. It was part of their carefully devised plan. He folded it carefully and replaced it in the envelope. As he reached across his body to lay the note on the table, he felt a twinge of pain in his rib cage. Resting his head back against the flat pillow he tried to ignore the pain, but little by little over the next quarter hour it began to intensify. He finally gave in and pressed the button that would release the medication into his body. Now he would just have to wait and be patient. The medicine would work in its own time.

Steve rolled carefully onto his left side, found no relief, then back to his right side to see if that would alleviate some of the pain. It seemed to help and he stayed in that position holding the side of the bed with his left hand. In less than ten minutes the medicine was beginning to kick in and he was finding some measure of relief. He closed his eyes and tried to block out the dull ache in his side. His eyes were beginning to feel heavy. His last conscious thought was that the medicine was doing its job. Twenty minutes after he had pressed the pain button he was asleep.

~ ~ ~

It was sometime after dark when something woke him. He wasn't sure what it was, but it seemed that a familiar voice had called his name. It was a voice from the past. In the semidarkness he momentarily forgot where he was. His eyes were unaccustomed to the dark, and as he tried to focus on his surroundings he thought he saw a figure standing just at the foot of the bed. He knew where he was now.

A shaft of light was peeking through a small crack in the door and he recognized the sights and sounds of the hospital. Steve turned his attention back toward the shadowy figure at the foot of the bed. Whoever or whatever it was had disappeared. Then he felt a gentle touch on his shoulder and he jumped.

"Big brother." It was the voice that had wakened him. His body became rigid as the shadowy figure bent over him. "Steve, it's me, Jim."

Oblivious to pain, Steve began groping for the cord that operated the bed lamp. After a second he located it and pulled. The room exploded in light. For a moment his eyes were blinded and he blinked to focus. The face that the voice came from was just a foot above his own.

"How you feeling, Steve?"

He was staring into the face of someone who looked exactly like his dead brother. The sight took his breath away. Speechless, he could only stare up at this man. The features were the same. Everything was the same. Then he remembered the ear. Very few people knew about the ear. When they were kids, their father had taken them fishing one Saturday in April. Steve was just learning to cast and, as kids will invariably do, they become careless. His fishing lure had caught Jim's ear, and after much screaming and working to remove the lure, they had been forced to visit the doctor to get it removed. The episode had left a notch in his brother's left ear lobe. Now, Steve reached up and tilted the man's face to the right. The scar was there. Steve took his forefinger and thumb and ran them back and forth along the old wound. It looked and felt the same as he remembered.

Two hands grasped his shoulders and squeezed gently. "Snap out of it, brother. It's me. It's Jim."

Forgetting about the pain in his right arm, Steve reached up and took Jim's face in his hands. Tears were streaming down his face. "Is it really you, Jim?"

"Yeah. It's me. Who did you think it was? You didn't think I wouldn't come, did you?" He paused and searched Steve's face. "Didn't Nora tell you we would be here?"

Steve let his head sink back into the pillow. If they could change his body and wipe out his family, why couldn't they reproduce a dead brother? He reached up and touched the scar again. His fingertips told him it was real. But he had to know. He had to be sure. There were things only he and Jim knew. He would ask this man questions that he could not answer unless he was real.

"I need to ask you a question."

"Shoot, big brother."

Steve thought about it for a moment. The man would not know this. "How long has it been since you've seen Bitsy?"

Jim's face clouded and Steve thought he saw confusion in the other man's eyes. This man, if he was not his brother, could not know the answer Steve wanted.

"That's a funny question, Steve."

"How so?"

"You know the answer to that as well as I do."

"How long?" Steve insisted.

"She's dead and buried."

"Who's dead and buried?" Steve persisted.

"Mom. Darn, Steve. What's wrong with you anyway? You're acting crazy. Have they got you on something?"

So they knew about his mother. They knew what his dad had called his mom since Steve and Jim were children. They could have learned that. Someone could have told them. He dug deeper in his memory. Something happened to them when they were children, something no one knew but the family.

"One more question."

"Come on, Steve. This is crazy."

"One more question, Jim." He called the man by his brother's name.

"Okay. But this is the last one. Okay?"

Steve nodded. "Do you remember that old refrigerator we had out in the barn, the one Mom finally had dad sink in the pond?"

"Yes, I remember."

"Do you remember what the name of the dog was that you shut up in that old 'fridge?

Jim's face went blank.

"You were nine and you caught the dog and shut him up in the refrigerator because Dad said you couldn't keep it."

A light suddenly appeared in Jim's eyes. He shook his head. "It wasn't a dog. It was a cat—a cat we named Bambi. And Mom talked Dad into letting me keep it after you rescued it." Jim's face suddenly grew dark. "What is this, Steve? What is this third degree? I didn't come all the way from Denver to play twenty questions."

Tears were building in Steve's eyes. He had to find out and he had. His brother was alive. "Dear Lord," he whispered prayerfully. "You're alive. You aren't dead."

Jim chuckled, then his face turned serious. "Is that what's wrong with you? You thought I was dead. When was I supposed to have died? How did I die in that crazy, mixed up mind of yours?"

Steve's head sank further into the pillow as he tried to focus on his brother. He couldn't find the words.

Jim bent over him again. "You okay?"

"Yes. I'm just…just overwhelmed."

"You want me to go and let you get some rest?"

Steve reached out quickly and grabbed his brother's arm. "No. You're here and I don't want to lose you again."

"Okay. I'm not going anywhere. Do you want to tell me why you thought I was dead?"

Steve nodded and for the first time realized he had been talking without pain. He hadn't done that since the accident. "I'll tell you. But you may not like it."

"Just tell me."

Again he nodded. "I was told there was a fire, a fire in a motel. They told Kathy and me that you and Mona were dead. They had your remains, which we later buried. They checked your dental records, everything. They were positive it was you and Mona."

"Wait a minute, wait a minute. You've lost me. What fire are you talking about?"

"The motel in Oklahoma City, the one you stayed in on your way home after Tommy was born. After Kathy got out of the…"

"Okay, hold it." Jim rested his hand on Steve's shoulder and shook his head.

Steve stopped and watched Jim's other hand snake through his thinning hair.

"This Kathy and Tommy that you're talking about. Who are they?"

Steve's mind was racing again. His brother, his flesh and blood, was denying the wife and son he knew he had. Someone had gotten to him. But how could they get to Jim? What could they be holding over him that he would deny even knowing Kathy and Tommy? Suddenly, the hall door opened and a slender woman slipped into the room. He was looking directly into the outer light and couldn't immediately make out the face.

"Hi, Steve."

The voice was unmistakeable. Mona Pearce came immediately to the bed, bent over and kissed him on the cheek. "Ugh, you need a shave," she said rubbing her lips.

"Mona?" He was looking at another ghost. He should have realized if Jim was alive, Mona was too.

"In the flesh."

Mona settled in the chair under the television and for more than a half hour they talked. When they were finished, Steve was even more sure than ever. This was his brother and sister-in-law. They were about to get up and leave when Steve felt he had to ask the question.

"Jim, do you and Mona remember Kathy?"

"There's that name again," Jim grunted.

"Who's Kathy?" Mona asked as she pulled her hair out from under her coat collar.

"Kathy Wilson. She was a sophomore the year I graduated."

"I should remember her," Jim said. "I think I knew most of the girls in my sophomore year in high school." He winked at Steve and glanced toward Mona.

"You knew every girl in your sophomore year," Mona offered facetiously.

Steve shook his head quickly. "Not high school, Jim. She was a sophomore at Ouachita the year I graduated college."

Jim had one arm in his overcoat, but when Steve said what he did, he drew it out and dropped the coat back on the chair. Steve glanced from Jim to Mona and saw uncertainty on both their faces.

It was Jim who spoke first. "Hon, how about waiting for me out in the hall. I'll just be a minute." Jim jerked his head toward the hallway.

Mona looked first to her husband, then to Steve. "Sure," she said pleasantly. She moved up beside the bed and bent over to place a kiss on Steve's cheek. "We're gonna have to do something about that face." She smiled and patted her brother-in-law on the shoulder. "Sleep well. We'll see you tomorrow."

"Sure, Mona. You don't know how good it is to see you after so long and..." He caught himself before saying thinking you were dead.

Jim followed her to the door and shut it quietly. Then he came back to the bed and pulled a chair close.

"We need to talk, Steve. You need to tell me exactly what you've been talking about. I don't know any Kathy or Tommy."

"You don't remember Kathy Wilson? I met her my senior year at Ouachita."

Jim shook his head and leaned back in his chair.

"What's wrong?"

"Steve, you couldn't have met her in your senior year in college."

"Why not?"

"Steve, I don't know what's going on. But, I spent half the night sitting up at the airport and most of today running around the terminal trying to find out when we could get a flight. It took us eight hours and three transfers because of the weather. I'm beat. So, please don't play games with me."

Steve was getting frustrated. "I'm not playing games, Jim. I don't know what I said that was wrong. But, believe me, I'm not playing games."

Jim leaned forward and placed the palms of his hands against the edge of the bed. "You keep talking about college and graduating. You can't be serious."

"About what?"

Jim got up and pulled his coat on. "Graduating," he said. "How could you graduate? You quit to marry Nora after your sophomore year." Jim stopped at the foot of the bed and studied his brother's face. Nora had said over the phone that he had been talking crazy. Jim hadn't wanted to believe that. He really didn't want to believe much that Nora said because she very seldom said anything good. But it looked like she was right this time. Something had happened to Steve in that accident, something bad and Jim had every reason to be concerned.

"Are you saying I didn't graduate?"

"That's what I'm saying."

"And you're saying I quit to marry Nora."

"Yep."

"But, why would I do that?"

Jim took a few steps toward the door. "Because of Sarah. When Nora told you she was pregnant with Sarah, you wouldn't have it any other way. Nothing Dad and Mom could say would change your mind."

Steve closed his eyes and tried to remember. Nothing Jim was saying made sense.

"Get some sleep, big brother. I'll be back in the morning and we'll talk. Okay."

Steve nodded as Jim reached for the knob. When his brother was gone, he reached up and pulled off the overhead light, sending the room into semidarkness, much as his mind now seemed to be.

CHAPTER 12

ON FRIDAY MORNING, DECEMBER twenty-ninth, six days after the accident, Steve awoke with mixed emotions. The night before, Doctor Banks had told him he could go home the next noon. He had lain awake until the early morning hours running the word home back and forth through his mind. A common fear now permeated all his thoughts.

Would he ever really go home again? Would he ever find Kathy and Tommy? Were they even real? And if they were real, then what was this? And why couldn't he remember the child Jim insisted was his own, the little girl, Sarah?

And Jim. It was Jim. It was his brother, reborn and not dead. He was sure of that, sure that he had his brother back. But in the process had he lost Kathy and Tommy forever? All these and other questions ate at him until he wasn't sure what to think or what to do.

There were times during the last few nights when he had questioned his sanity. Had his subconscious manufactured that other life? But how could he manufacture something like that in such a short time? There was a whole other life out there somewhere, a life with two people he loved dearly.

As soon as he had those thoughts, he knew the answer. Kathy and Tommy were just as real as he was. He could feel them in his heart. They were real. They had to be and he would find them. The dream that he had on that first night after the accident had recurred twice since Jim's arrival—once on Christmas night and again on Wednesday. And it was so real, not like most dreams with unrealistic fragments that didn't seem to mesh. It flowed.

Kathy was always there beside the bed. But Tommy had been missing the last two times. And always something just outside his vision, something that looked like an apparition, something he couldn't quite make out in the darkened room of his dream. Had something supernatural happened to him in that accident? For the life of him, he couldn't understand what it could be.

He picked up the mirror that Elaine Wright had left that first night and checked his face again. The bluish bruise on his throat was still visible. The swelling was gone but the discoloration, while not as vivid, still lingered. Something puzzled him. In the first dream on the night of the accident, he hadn't noticed the man's throat, the man who looked more like he remembered himself. But in the last two dreams he had and the blue mark and the swelling were visible on the man. The swelling was in the same place as his, just under the chin around the Adam's apple.

In his dream the swelling on the body in the bed had not gone down. And he had noticed no movement from the man. It was as if the person in the dream was not getting any better. And, based on his vision of Kathy in the dream, she seemed very concerned. In the last dream she was alone with the man and she was crying.

Steve wondered why he kept thinking about the other man in such strange terms. That other man was himself. Of that he was sure. Nothing else made sense. Maybe that body in the other hospital room was about to die. He didn't want to think about that. That had to be his body. If that body, his body, died, then he had surely lost Kathy forever. The realization caused an uncontrollable shudder to flow through him.

Steve walked to the window and looked down at the intersection of the three streets, Whittington to his right, Park to his left and Central straight ahead. The snow had melted several days ago and the low pressure area that had brought it had shifted to the east. Someone said the jet stream had made its way back up north and the weather they were getting now was coming from the west and not out of Canada. It was supposed to be sixty degrees today and even warmer tomorrow. He was glad for that.

Footsteps sounded outside his door. Someone passed and kept moving down the hall. His mind drifted back to something someone had told him or something he had read about many years ago. Ever since the last dream it had been rattling around in his brain. He just couldn't put his finger on it. But there was something that he needed to remember, something that might reveal what was happening. It was in his head, trying to get out.

What would Jim think about all those dreams, about what he remembered and knew was real. They had already spoken about some of it that first night. But since then, Steve had been careful not to mention it again. Only yesterday, Jim said that Steve was finally beginning to get his head back on straight. He didn't want to destroy that. Even Nora seemed friendlier. But Steve felt that was an act for Jim and Mona's benefit. The last four days all of them had come to see him as a group. On two occasions Jim had visited alone.

"Good morning."

Steve turned to see Doctor Banks enter the room.

"Morning, doctor."

Ted Banks glanced at his watch. "Looks like you're dressed and ready to go home. How do you feel?"

"Great," Steve lied.

"Good. How about sitting down on the bed and unbuttoning your shirt? I want to poke around on you one more time before I let you go."

Steve did as the doctor asked and the man began moving his fingers slowly across the thin bandages. At one spot his fingers dug in a little heavier and Steve winced.

"A little tender there?"

"A little."

The doctor made no comment but continued to probe. After a couple of minutes, he nodded. "You can button up. Let's take a look at the throat." He lifted Steve's chin and moved his fingers gently over the blue mark. "Any pain?"

"Not really."

"Open wide." Doctor Banks took a tongue depressor and held Steve's tongue down for several seconds. Finally, he removed it and smiled. "Looks much better. How's the pain when you talk?"

"Gone." Steve said.

"Good. One more thing. Let's take a look at the arm." Ted Banks unwrapped the bandage and examined the damaged arm. "Healing nicely. I'm going to get the nurse to put on a fresh bandage before you leave. We ought to be able to take it off in about a week. Do you take a bath or shower?"

"Shower."

"You'll want to put a plastic bag over the lower part of your arm and tape it above the elbow to keep from getting the bandage wet. I'm also going to have her take off these bandages around your stomach. I want you to keep the bandage on your arm until I see it again. If it should get dirty or wet or just a little bloody, call the office and my nurse will make a time for you to come in and get it changed. Okay? And no physical work yet." Doctor Banks got up and looked down at Steve. "I want to see you next Friday. Call my receptionist and make an appointment when you get home. Okay?"

"Can I drive, doctor?"

"Hmm. Yes, I guess that'll be okay but don't overdo it."

Steve nodded and the doctor turned to leave.

"Doctor."

"Yes," he said as he turned back.

Steve touched the marks under his chin. "These marks and the damage I had to my throat. Is there anything significant about it?"

"Significant in what way?"

"I mean, was something vital..." Steve stopped. He was beginning to feel foolish.

"You said you weren't having any discomfort around the area."

"No. But you seemed concerned about it on several occasions and I wondered if there was any particular reason."

"No, nothing other than the bruise and the swelling and, of

course, your inability to speak at the beginning. I wanted to be sure that there was no internal injury and I'm satisfied now that there wasn't."

"I see. Well thank you, doctor, for everything."

Ted Banks smiled. "Surely. I'll see you next week. Now, don't forget to call."

A moment later the doctor was gone and Steve was alone in the room, his question still unanswered. Finally, he sighed, picked up the phone and dialed. On the fourth ring someone lifted at the other end.

"Hello."

"Jim, Steve. They released me. How about picking me up at the front door of the hospital."

"Will do, brother."

Steve dropped the phone back in its cradle and sat back down on the bed as the nurse came through the door. Once the bandages were taken care of he could get out of this place and go wherever home was supposed to be. The rumble in his stomach reminded him that he had not eaten since last night. He was hungry but would not miss hospital food.

CHAPTER 13

KATHY PEARCE WAS CURLED up in the hospital chair where she had been for the last week. Ray had told her more than once to go home and get some rest, but she refused to budge, not until Steve woke up or something else happened. She didn't want to think about something else happening. He would wake up.

Ray said Steve's injuries were healing nicely. But somewhere in his head he was not stirring. His brain was asleep. The coma, Ray said, could last a week, a month, even longer. As gently as possible, he finally told her it might never go away. He had told her that on Wednesday night and she had cried and held Steve's hand. And she had prayed. Their whole church was praying night and day and she knew God answered prayers. He would answer this one. He would give Steve back to her and Tommy.

Her mother had been a godsend. If not for her, she would have had to find a babysitter. But she had come as soon as Kathy called her and she would stay as long as necessary. Kathy thought back through the events of the last week, possibly the most miserable she had ever endured. During those long nights she had the weird feeling that Steve was trying to reach out to her from the coma. But he never moved or gave any physical indication that he knew she was there.

Ray told her to talk to him and she did. Sometimes, Ray said, when people talk to a person in a coma it helps. It helps the person in the coma and it helps the person talking. Some medical people, Ray continued, believed that a person in a coma was able to hear the person talking to them.

So she had tried to keep up a constant banter, taking a rest several times a day when her voice seemed to be wearing out. It was like that last night. The night had been long. It was one of those nights like she had experienced lately, when the room had felt uncommonly cold. But when she had gotten up and slipped out into the hall it felt like the temperature was ten degrees warmer.

Kathy hadn't slept but an hour or two, and now as she curled up on the uncomfortable chair and tucked her legs under, she closed her eyes and tried to remember everything about the last time they had been together before the accident. If only she had known then. If only. Kathy was aware she was drifting toward sleep and she tried to fight it. She needed to stay awake in case Steve needed her, but she couldn't and her head drooped to her chest and she dozed.

CHAPTER 14

THE BROWN AND TAN car pulled into the hospital drive. Jim stopped and searched the double doors. Steve was sitting in a wheelchair just inside, his bag on the floor next to him and a male nurse leaning against the chair handles. His brother looked normal enough, and Jim was beginning to think that Steve was snapping out of those first confusing days after the accident.

Each time Jim had been to the hospital, Steve had shown steady improvement. While he could tell Steve was reluctant to do so, he had finally admitted that he didn't really believe Jim and Mona had been killed in a motel fire. If Steve had not been his own brother, the matter might have been laughable, especially now that it wasn't an issue any more. But it was not laughable and, deep down, Jim really wasn't sure that Steve was convinced. Every time they talked he had the feeling Steve wanted to confide in him, but his big brother just wouldn't break loose and tell him what was bothering him.

Jim gave a short blast on the horn and Steve looked toward the doors and waved. A few seconds later the nurse pushed him outside, opened the car door and helped Steve into the front passenger seat.

The young man patted Steve on the shoulder and smiled. "Good luck, Mr. Pearce. Hope everything works out."

"It will, Eddie. It will. Thanks again." Steve reached across his body with his left hand and the two men clasped hands. They exchanged glances and Eddie closed the door and stepped back.

"Ready to go home?"

"Ready as I'll ever be. Thanks for picking me up." Steve touched his brother's arm just to reassure himself once more that Jim was really there.

"My pleasure."

"Feels great to be out of there."

"What did the Doc say?"

"Not much. Seems I'm a quick healer. Wants to see me next week. Can't do anything physical in the meantime. Can't see how going into the..." He cut himself short before he said the office.

In his mind he was still that accountant he knew he had always been. It was nearly January first and, as it had in years past, his mind was already focusing on income taxes. But that was not to be. Everyone had assured him that he was now a pilot, and for right now he would play that role. At least he would until they tried to get him in the air.

But if he wasn't an accountant, he reasoned, then how was it that he could recite many of the income tax regulations by memory. Jim and everyone else pictured the left seat of an airplane as Steve's office. It was crazy. His only memory of an airplane was the few lessons he had taken as a teenager. He hadn't even flown enough to solo.

"What were you about to say?" Jim questioned.

Steve snapped back to the present. "Nothing really. I was just thinking about going out to the airport and helping around their office. I don't see how that could hurt me."

"I agree. I just don't think your doctor wants you to go up until you get a clean bill of health."

"I guess so. Anyway, you can bet I won't go near an airplane until he okays it." And not even then, Steve thought.

~ ~ ~

They were on Central Avenue passing the Arlington Hotel and Bathhouse Row. Steve's logic said they should be entering the eastbound lane to go out Malvern Avenue. But his logic didn't hold true anymore. Instead, Jim was maneuvering the car into the right lane. They were about to head up Ouachita toward South

Hot Springs. It was just another reminder that he was not going home to Kathy and Tommy. He had to get his mind off them, at least right now. If he grieved about them, he wouldn't have the energy or the sense he needed to find them.

"How long will you be here, Jim?" Steve glanced to his right as they passed the new bank that had been built where the old Como Bath House once stood.

"Gotta catch an early flight Wednesday morning," Jim said, "but we'll have a few days to visit."

"Great." Even though his heart ached for Kathy and Tommy, it would be great to spend some time with a brother he thought was dead. Who knew when Jim might be snatched from him again? The only way he could stand to lose his brother again was to find his family, his real family. They were out there somewhere and he knew he would find them.

~ ~ ~

His eyes took in every facet of the landscape. It was his town, his Hot Springs. Familiar streets, familiar eating places. They left Ouachita Avenue and started west on Grand. The Dairy Queen was right where it always was. Five blocks down they turned south on Summer and then back to the west on Albert Pike. It was all there, just like he remembered. They passed McClards, the best barbeque restaurant in Arkansas, maybe the best in the country. He had been raised on that barbeque since he was a kid and right now it sounded better than anything he could think of. He'd even found himself craving it in the hospital.

But Jim moved on past and out toward the 70/270 junction. They took the right fork and started out the Mt. Ida Highway. After about a half mile, Jim put on the turn signal and turned left onto a street called Dickson Drive. Steve remembered the street from the phone book when he had called and given Nora a verbal thrashing. He remembered the street for another reason too.

Several years ago he had been on the street delivering a set of books to a client who had since died. There were several houses on the block that he didn't remember. They could have been there before but he wasn't sure. It was one continuous street about three hundred yards long, without cross streets. The houses were nice, but not extravagant. At the far end a fence stretched across the street and a large field was on the other side. Jim maneuvered the car down the street and turned into the last driveway on the right. They hadn't spoken for nearly five minutes but now Jim pointed toward the front yard of the red brick house.

"Someone's been waiting for you all day."

Steve saw her for the first time. She was blonde, possibly a little taller than Tommy. She was jumping up and down and waving wildly as the car turned into the driveway and pulled under the carport. He confirmed two things very quickly. First, the little girl was not acting. That was plain to see. She was truly excited. And second, she was a complete stranger. He had never seen her before. This had to be Sarah, the child that was supposed to be his and Nora's, the child that had sent him the note in the hospital. She added another dimension to the mystery. By the time the car stopped, Sarah was beating on the window.

"Daddy, Daddy!" Steve was hardly out of the car before she flung herself into his arms. He felt a twinge of pain shoot through his ribs, but it was quickly gone. Her blue eyes were shining as she threw her arms around him and began kissing him. "I was so scared. I thought you might die, Daddy. I love you so much."

Steve held her against him, ignoring the pain he was again experiencing in his rib cage. This was a strange sensation, this little girl. So many times he had held Tommy like this and took him for granted. Now as he held this child, Sarah, he longed for the feel of his son against his chest. This child was a stranger. Yet, somehow, he knew she had been in these same arms, the arms of this Steve Pearce, a thousand times.

And he didn't know how any of this was possible. But the strange thing was that in only a few short minutes he had begun to feel an overwhelming affection for the girl. No one could ever take Tommy's place, but he suddenly realized he had feelings for this little girl and the guilt was overwhelming. It was as if he was rejecting his son in favor of this child who was clinging to him. But he knew he couldn't hurt her. She was innocent. She believed in him. As he held her, his mind raced back to that day over six months ago when he had come home from the convention in Chicago and Tommy had given him just such a welcome. But he wasn't holding Tommy now. Steve knelt on one knee and let her to the ground. He gently removed her arms from around his neck and placed a light kiss on her forehead.

"Daddy's all right now. You don't have to worry anymore. Okay?"

"I won't, Daddy. I love you."

Before he could answer her, the carport door opened and Mona bounded down the stairs. Steve got up and watched her come around the car, then glanced toward the door. Nora was standing just inside the glass storm door. He wasn't sure whether her face held a smile or a smirk. But when he studied her eyes he knew she wasn't smiling.

"Welcome home, Steve." Mona threw her arms around her brother-in-law and planted a light kiss on his cheek. "Are you feeling better?"

"Almost like my old self," he lied.

"Wonderful," she said.

"I want to thank you and Jim for staying here with Nora and Sarah while I was laid up."

"We were happy to. It's been fun."

Steve felt like Mona was being just a little less than truthful now but he kept his tongue. Nora was the last to greet him, and she put one arm around him and kissed him lightly on the lips. Steve could sense the same chill he had observed every time she visited him in the hospital. "You look good," she said.

"I feel good."

Jim brushed by him with his bag. "I'll put this in your bedroom."

"Thanks, Jim. Hey, I'll go with you."

As he turned to go, Sarah let go of his hand and ran toward the front yard. Steve watched her for a moment, then turned and started to follow Jim into the house.

"Have you eaten anything, Steve? We can fix you something." It was Mona who made the offer.

"I am hungry. Give me a few minutes and I'll be ready."

He followed Jim through the kitchen and den to a hall that stretched from what Steve assumed was the front bedroom to the back bedroom. There was a middle bedroom straight across from the door that led from the den to the hall. From the looks of the bed and dresser on the left wall, that would be Sarah's room. He looked down the hall to the right. Jim had set his suitcase down and was framed in the bedroom doorway.

"Want to lie down awhile?"

"Been doing that number for a week now. Feels too good to be on my feet."

"Okay. But don't overdo it. Get off your feet if you get tired."

"You got my word on that."

There was a tap on the bedroom door. Sarah was peering in. "Can I come in, Daddy?"

"Of course you can." He sat down on the bed and instinctively held out his arms. He wasn't sure why but it seemed the right thing to do under the circumstances. The girl was not timid. She crawled into his lap and slid her arms around his neck. Surprisingly, the pressure on his neck didn't hurt, didn't cause any discomfort for his throat.

"What's this, Daddy?"

"What, hon…" He caught himself. It didn't feel right to call her honey, at least not yet.

She didn't seem to notice the catch in his voice. "This, Daddy." She touched his neck again and ran her fingers along the spot that was still discolored.

Steve reached up and touched the spot himself. "Something hit me in the throat when I had the accident. It was swollen and blue. Now, it isn't swollen anymore. But it's still blue. The doctor said that'll go away soon."

"Does it hurt?"

"Not anymore."

Jim was still standing next to the bed and he nodded to Steve. "I'll be in the den." He touched Steve's shoulder and squeezed gently. It was vintage Jim.

How many times over the years had he felt those strong hands just when he needed them most. And now his brother was here again.

"Thanks, Jim. Thanks for being here."

Without another word, Jim Pearce turned and disappeared down the hall. Steve and Sarah were alone and now, for the first time, he looked into her eyes and realized she had been crying.

"What's wrong, Sarah?"

Her bottom lip was quivering. "I was so scared, Daddy. I talked to Jesus every night and asked him to make you well. I wanted to come see you but Mommy said little children couldn't go into the hospital." She hesitated and ran her fingers over the blue mark on his neck again. "Daddy, what happens to little children if they get sick? They aren't allowed in the hospital."

Steve drew her close to his chest and pressed his lips against her forehead. He held them there for nearly thirty seconds. "You don't have to worry, honey." He said the word and felt no guilt at all, no disloyalty to Tommy or to Kathy. This child, even though he had never known she existed, was his. She was from his body. "Little children can go to the hospital. Mommy just didn't want you to see daddy when he was so..." he hesitated, "...banged up."

She didn't move in his arms and Steve knew she was digesting what he said and what had happened. When she drew back and looked up in his eyes, more tears were beginning to form. "You won't ever die, will you, Daddy? I don't ever want you to die."

Steve lifted her chin and kissed her on the lips. "I love you, Sarah. Daddy won't leave you, not for a very, very long time. That's a promise." All of a sudden he knew that what he was saying was the truth. He did love the little girl and knew he had for a long time.

CHAPTER 15

JUST BEFORE FIVE ON Friday afternoon, Jake taxied the blue and white Cessna 150 across the apron and into the huge hangar. Ten yards short of a red Cessna 207, turned sideways in front of him, he chopped the throttle and applied brake pressure. The 150 sat over on its nose wheel and rocked to a stop. Jake flipped off the key and settled back in the seat, his mind reviewing the short flight.

An hour earlier he'd lifted off with the idea of landing in the clearing where Steve had crashed six days earlier. It hadn't been hard to find the crash site but when he checked it out from the air he was amazed. It was narrow and short, almost too short, he thought for even a 150 to make an emergency landing. But he had come to see just how hard it really was and he was determined to give it a try. He lined up from west to east, into the wind, and began his approach at normal landing speed. Holding just fifty feet above the trees, he took dead aim at the little clearing. Once he cleared the trees, he dropped the nose and pointed the Cessna toward the ground. It didn't take him long to make his decision. Twenty feet above the ground and nearly halfway to the end of the clearing he applied full throttle and climbed out. He would never have made it.

The second time, with half flaps and holding his speed to just ten knots above stall speed, he thought he might get in but again he was forced to abort. He had gotten lower but he was still using up the clearing too fast. Determined to pull out all stops, Jake lined up for a third try. This time he dropped the flaps all the way. The plane immediately felt sluggish, like it might stall at any moment. But he persisted. He was no more than ten feet above the first of the trees when the clearing came into view. As soon as he cleared the trees, he cut power and dropped the nose. The Cessna dropped quickly toward the ground. It only took a moment to decide. He could make it, he was certain of that.

Fifteen feet above the ground, he applied full throttle and lifted the nose slightly. For a split second he thought he had waited too long. Then the plane slowly began to climb. At the far end he cleared the trees with about twenty feet to spare. It was then that he noticed that he had bit the cigar clean in half. The stub was still in his mouth, but the rest was in his lap. Even with his experience it had been a hairy ride. He could imagine what kind of ride it had been for Steve with little visibility and a bigger airplane and a higher landing speed. His pilot had done some job of getting the big plane down without blasting into the trees at the far end of the field and killing himself.

As he climbed out, Jake caught a glimpse of the 172. It was canted on its side against a tall pine tree. The left wing seemed to be supporting the rest of the plane. Bad weather and impossible conditions had slowed the removal process. But the NTSB would have the plane disassembled and transported back to the airport in the next day or two. They would be able to examine it more thoroughly there.

Now, as Jake sat in the little Cessna chewing on the dormant cigar stub and staring at the big, red airplane in front of him, he wondered how Steve could have ever gotten the plane down. Even in the 150 it would have been touch and go. And he had perfect visibility and the confidence he could apply throttle and pull out at any time. Steve didn't have that luxury. He had one chance to get down in one piece. And he did it. Not many would have walked away from the 172. Strange as it seemed, Jake felt a certain elation at his discovery. A pilot on the sauce could never have pulled it off, no matter how skilled they were. Jake nodded his head and smiled. His pilot was sober. Of that, he was now certain.

CHAPTER 16

STEVE HAD BEEN TRYING to slip off to the telephone in the back bedroom all afternoon. Now, with both women in the kitchen preparing supper and Sarah engrossed in an old rerun of the Andy Griffith Show, he excused himself and slipped down the hall. He'd never thought of himself as a nervous person, but the muscles in his arms and legs were trembling. He didn't know why but he had the terrible fear that he was moving farther and farther away from Kathy and Tommy and if he didn't do something to slow the process, it might never be reversed. Yet, he had no idea what the process was or how it came about, much less how to reverse it. All he knew was that it was happening and he seemed powerless to stop it.

Earlier in the day he'd ventured into the dining room and located the bookshelves in a waist high cabinet that separated the dining and living rooms. On one side of the cabinet, facing the dining room, Nora had a set of crystal and a few pictures. On the other side, facing the living room area, Steve found the bookshelves and located, what appeared to be, his sophomore yearbook from Ouachita. He had taken it from the shelf and carried it with him to the bedroom. Now, for the first time, he had a chance to examine it.

As he thumbed through the book, it seemed to be the same. The signatures were the same. Faces were the same. Even the remarks that his friends had made looked remarkably familiar. It had to be the same yearbook. Halfway through, close to the end of the sophomore class pictures, he saw a familiar face smiling up at him. The name at the side of the picture brought back memories.

The girl had graduated with him from high school. They had both gone on to Ouachita that next fall. Steve dropped the book on the bed and went back to the den.

"Jim, do you remember Cindy Vickers? She graduated high school with me."

His brother looked up from the evening news on television. "Cindy Vickers." He looked toward the ceiling and wrapped his teeth around his bottom lip as he concentrated. "I remember a Ron Vickers. I think he had an older sister about your age."

"That's her. Whatever happened to her?"

"Who knows. You know we haven't lived in Arkansas for several years. Hold on. Let me ask Mona if she knows anything about her." Jim looked toward the kitchen. "Honey, do you remember a Cindy Vickers?"

Mona came into the den wiping her hands on a dishtowel. She reached up and pushed a wisp of blonde hair out of her eyes and back onto her forehead.

"Sure. We were in the same social club. Why do you ask?"

"What happened to her?" Steve asked quickly—almost too quickly. He noticed Nora give him a questioning look.

"I think she married a teacher. The last I heard she was right here in Hot Springs."

"Who?"

Mona looked puzzled.

"Who was the teacher?" Steve asked impatiently.

Mona got that faraway look in her eyes. She rested her hand on her hip and stared at the ceiling. "Wagner or Warner. Something like that."

"Lou Werner," Steve said quickly. The man had been a grade school principal in the Hot Springs system for several years. Steve had met him once a couple of years ago when his accounting firm had been hired to do an independent audit of the system. He never placed the man with little Cindy Vickers.

"That's him. Lou Werner. He was quite a bit older than Cindy. I think she met him at Ouachita when he was working on his master's."

Steve walked over and gave Mona a light peck on the cheek. "Thanks, Mona. You're a lifesaver."

Steve was halfway to the hall door before Mona could respond. She raised her eyebrows toward Jim and shrugged her shoulders. He acknowledged her questioning look and turned his attention back to the evening news.

"What was that all about?"

Jim shook his head. "You got me."

Back in the bedroom, Steve thumbed quickly through the telephone directory, found the name and dialed. After the third ring a woman's voice came on the line.

"Hello."

"Cindy Vickers, uh, I mean Cindy Werner." The slip of the tongue was on purpose. He wanted to be sure the woman was the Cindy he needed to talk to.

"Yes, this is Cindy Werner. And who is this?" She was friendly but cautious.

"Cindy, I'm not sure you'd remember me. We graduated from high school the same year. Steve Pearce."

"Steve, of course I remember you. You've been all over the news for the last week, the crash and all. How are you?" The voice was soft and quiet, relaxed now. She sounded much the same as he remembered, a quiet, shy girl who dated very little.

"I'm home and fine now, Cindy. Thanks for asking." It seemed strange saying he was home when he really wasn't.

"I'm so glad. I meant to send a card, but you know how that is. I feel terrible about it now."

"Hey, I understand." Steve changed the subject quickly. "Cindy, I know you went to Ouachita when I did. I'm trying to locate someone that was down there at the same time, a girl I used to know." Steve sat back on the bed, trying to find a way to get comfortable with the extra pounds around his midsection. "Her name was Kathy Wilson. I thought you might remember her."

There was no response from Cindy.

167

"You still there, Cindy?"

"Yes, I'm still here. I was just trying to think. I knew a Kathy Summers in my senior year. Then there was a Jeanette Wilson. Her first name wouldn't have been Jeanette by any chance, would it?"

"No, I'm afraid not. I know for certain that it was Kathy. Maybe..." He hesitated, feeling he might be intruding. "Maybe, if it isn't too much trouble, you could check your senior yearbook. She might be in there."

"No trouble at all, Steve. Hold on a minute while I get it."

The minute stretched into what seemed a half hour but was really only five minutes. When she finally returned, Steve was sweating profusely around his neck and stomach.

"Still there?"

"Still here."

"Okay, I got it. What class would she have been in?"

She would have been a year behind you if you finished in four years."

"I'm looking at the junior class pictures. Wilkens, Winston, a Carl Wilson, and then it jumps to Roy Wilson. Sorry, Steve. No Kathy."

Steve was not ready to give up just yet. "One more thing," he said. "Would you check the index in case she didn't get her picture in the book." He knew before he asked that it would be futile. Her picture was in his book.

"Just a second." He could hear her flipping pages and then it stopped. "Still a big fat zero. I'm sorry."

Steve's spirit sagged to shoe top level. "Well, we tried. Thanks anyway, Cindy."

He was about to hang up when her voice cut across the phone line.

"Steve, wait a minute. Why don't you call the registrar at OBU? They keep records of every student that passes through the system. They should be able to look her up for you."

"Hey, I bet they could. That's a great idea. Thanks, Cindy."

"Anytime, Steve. And, hey, don't be a stranger. Drop by and

see me sometime. I'd love to have you meet my husband."

"I'd like that, Cindy. Thanks for the invite."

They exchanged goodbyes. After he hung up, Steve sat looking at the phone for several minutes. He was about to call information for the OBU number when he heard a small plane. Steve walked to the window and pulled back the curtain. It was about a thousand feet high and looked like it would go directly over the house. We must be directly in the flight path, he thought. He watched until it disappeared above the house, then closed the curtains and retraced his steps to the bed and picked up the phone again. It took only a few seconds to get long distance information.

"What city?"

"Arkadelphia, Arkansas."

"What's the name?"

"Ouachita Baptist University."

Steve listened and wrote the number down in the front of the phone book. He thanked the operator and pressed the button on the phone to break the connection. A moment later he had the Ouachita phone ringing.

"Ouachita Baptist University." The voice was feminine and young, most likely a student working for her tuition.

"Registrar, please."

"I'm sorry. That office is closed for the Christmas holidays."

"Is there anyone I could talk to? I'm trying to locate a student that attended there between six and ten years ago."

"Sir, I don't think anyone is there." Steve could hear the sound of male laughter in the background. The girl's attention was evidently elsewhere.

"I'm sure you're right. But would you ring the office anyway?"

"Certainly. Just a moment."

The phone began ringing immediately. After the sixth ring, Steve was about to hang up when someone lifted the phone.

"Yes."

Steve's heart skipped a beat at his unexpected luck. He sat straight up as if his appearance might affect the conversation.

"Hello. I'm sorry to bother you, but I'm trying to obtain some information about a former student. I wonder if you might help me? It's really an emergency." Steve didn't feel he was lying in this case. To him, this was an emergency of the highest order.

"I'm just passing through the office on the way to dinner." The man seemed impatient and it was obvious he wished he had never answered the phone. "Can it wait until Monday?"

"I don't think so. I'll just be in the state until Sunday." It was a lie but at this point in time he felt it necessary. "I'll be gone for some time. I would really appreciate the help."

"I guess I've got a few minutes. What's the student's name and what years did they attend Ouachita?"

Steve cleared his throat and leaned forward. "The name is Kathy Wilson and she began in the fall of '98. She was a junior transfer from Tulsa University."

"Kathy Wilson, Fall of '98," the man repeated. "Hold on. It'll take a few minutes, Mr...."

"Pearce, Steve Pearce. And thank you."

"Hold on, Mr. Pearce. I'll see if I can help you."

Several minutes passed before Steve heard activity on the other end of the line.

"You still there, Mr. Pearce?"

"Yes. I am." Steve held his breath as he waited for the man to continue. If he told him there was no Kathy Wilson it would drive his spirits even lower.

"We had a Kathy Wilson who entered in August of 1998. Like you said, she transferred from Tulsa University. Our records show that she withdrew on October twenty-third, same year, and transferred back to Tulsa. Must not have liked us. Sound like your friend?"

Steve's mind was already computing the information. Less than two months and she was gone. But she was real. She existed. His whole body shivered with excitement.

"That's her."

"Anything else I can help you with?"

"Just one more thing. Is her home address listed as 2243 Hibridge in Van Buren? And are her parents Mr. and Mrs. Henry Wilson?"

"One and the same."

Steve was on a high. It was like he had just swallowed a lethal dose of narcotics.

"You don't know what you've done for me, sir? Can I send you something for your trouble?"

"I'm glad to be of service. Hope you're able to get in touch with your friend."

Steve thanked the man again and dropped the phone back in its cradle. He sat on the bed for several minutes digesting what he had just heard. How many dinners had he eaten at the Hibridge address? He wasn't sure. But he was sure that he was on the right track.

Henry Wilson had died the year after Kathy graduated from college. Now, as he thought about it, Henry might still be alive. In this crazy, mixed up world, anything could have taken place. And maybe both Henry and Ann were dead. That was a possibility. And then they could be alive and might have moved. The phone number could have been disconnected. He reached for the phone again, part of the elation subdued by these new possibilities. He recalled the Wilson number and was about to lift the phone from its cradle.

"What are you doing back here?" In his excitement and lost in his thoughts, he hadn't heard the bedroom door open. Nora was standing in the doorway. "What in the world are you doing, Steve? You're brother is sitting in the den by himself twiddling his thumbs."

"I'm sorry. I was just calling a few people, catching up on what had been going on since the crash."

"Well, come and be a good host to your brother. Heaven knows, I'm doing my part with Mona." With that, Nora turned and walked away down the hall.

Steve watched until she disappeared into the den, then took a long look at the phone and got up. There would be time, he decided, time for the call after supper.

CHAPTER 17

LISA FLIPPED THE CHEESE sandwich over on the grill. She had been home long enough to shower before coming into the small kitchen and starting the grill. The apartment was warm. It stayed that way during the winter. Like her mother before her, she always seemed to be cold. Because of that, she kept the thermostat set at seventy-four degrees. Now, as she poured a soft drink into a glass filled with ice, she was clad only in a sheer white gown. When the doorbell sounded, she jumped and nearly spilled the drink.

"Who can that be?" As she asked herself the question, she thought she already knew. She set the drink on the cabinet and started toward the bedroom for her robe. Halfway down the small hall, she stopped and retraced her steps to lift the cheese sandwich off the grill. Then she went back for the robe. Before she could slip it on, the bell rang again.

"Coming," she called.

She stopped in front of the small mirror over the couch and examined the front of the robe. Satisfied, she cracked the door open as far as the chain would allow and peered through. The end of Jake's cigar was the first thing she saw.

"Daddy, what are you doing here?" Lisa released the chain and opened the door.

Jake looked his daughter over. "Didn't mean to get you outa the shower."

"You didn't. I was in the kitchen fixing a sandwich. Can I fix you one?"

"Took you long enough to get to the door."

Lisa blushed. "I didn't have much on, Daddy."

Jake looked toward the window that opened high over the street. "You runnin' around in the altogether? Taught you better than that."

Lisa laughed. In some ways her father was very straitlaced. In others he was loose as a goose. When it came to her he was far from loose. "I wasn't naked, Daddy, just not presentable."

But Jake was not satisfied. "No tellin' what kinda nutcase is just sittin' out there pantin' for a chance to see a pretty girl half dressed."

Lisa ignored him and started back for the kitchen. "You didn't answer my question."

"What was that?"

"Do you want a grilled cheese sandwich?"

"Yeah. With hot peppers. You got any peppers to put on it?"

"You're going to burn your stomach up."

They were in the kitchen and Jake was peering into the refrigerator. "Okay if I have a beer while I wait?"

"Help yourself. You know I don't drink the foul things. I just keep them for you, and I've just about decided if I didn't keep them you might quit."

"Not drinkin', that's one smart thing I taught you." His eyes seemed to take a faraway look. "Really, your mama taught you that, I guess." He paused and looked at the can in his hand. "Need to quit them myself one of these days."

Lisa put her half toasted sandwich back on the grill and buttered two more pieces of bread. While they were toasting on the buttered side, she sat down on the stool and studied her father. He was working to get the easy opening top off the can. She started to lecture him again about the evils of drinking, then thought better of it. He would quit one day on his own. That would be better than her bugging him about it. He had to want to, not for her, but for himself. If she knew her dad, if he ever quit it would be for good.

She finally said. "I saw you fly off by yourself this afternoon. Where'd you go?"

Jake took a sip of the beer and made a sour face. "Don't know why I drink this stuff. I swear I don't."

She couldn't resist. "You have a choice about what you put in your body."

He seemed to ignore her and took another swallow. "Flew up to the crash site. I wanted to see it for myself."

Lisa got up and flipped her sandwich onto a plate. Then she took Jake's bread off and spread mayonnaise on the toasted side before she put two slices of American cheese on, buttered the top and bottom and dropped it back on the grill. "And what did you find?"

Jake hesitated and seemed to be measuring his words. "Steve did a fine job of getting it down. I'll have to give him that. I'm not sure I could have got the 150 stopped short of the trees."

"Now that wasn't so hard was it?" Lisa turned the sandwich over.

"What's that?"

"Admitting that he's a darn fine pilot."

"He's okay, I guess." Jake took another swig of his beer. "Pretty tight little spot even for a 150 to get in."

"You didn't try to land, did you?"

"Just got it down close enough for a touch and go."

"You touched down," she squealed.

"Naw. Got down to about ten feet off the ground. Just wanted to see if I could get it in."

"Daddy, you could have been killed."

Jake looked up at her and frowned. "You sayin' he's better'n me, sayin' he can get it into a tight spot when I can't?"

This time she ignored his question. She took the sandwich off the grill, slid it onto a plate and handed it to him.

"What about the peppers?" Jake asked.

"They aren't good for your ulcers." She handed him a half full bag of potato chips. "Eat these instead of the peppers."

Jake grunted his dissatisfaction. But even so, he was glad he had someone to worry about him. "Need to use your phone." He took the beer and sandwich into the living room and dialed. In a few seconds Lisa heard him call Steve's name. She listened intently but could only catch bits and pieces of the conversation. Finally, she turned her attention back to the sandwich and what her father had told her about the crash site. It was quite a revelation for Jake to admit that Steve had done a good job, even though she knew Jake thought he was a top pilot. They had both known for a long time that Steve was the best around. But, stubborn as Jake was, getting him to admit it was like pulling teeth. Lisa felt that was partly her fault. If she hadn't been stuck on the big pilot, her father might have been more objective toward him. He feared that her attraction to Steve would lead to trouble and had naturally held the young man at arm's length. But it seemed Jake was beginning to mellow toward him.

Five minutes went by before Jake came back into the kitchen. He set the plate on the counter and took another gulp of beer.

"Want another sandwich?"

Jake put his fist to his mouth and belched. "Nope."

"What was the phone call about?"

"Just called to let Steve know I flew up to the crash site."

Lisa took a sip of her cold drink. "Were you nice?"

"Sure. Didn't have no reason not to be." He took a last swallow of his beer and dropped the can in the trash can. "You're old daddy ain't no ogre."

She laughed. "Only now and then."

"I gotta go." Then he stopped and Lisa could tell his mind was off on another tangent.

"What's wrong?"

"Steve. He don't seem just right."

"What's not right?"

"Ever since the accident, he ain't called me Jake once. It's Mr. Carter this or Mr. Carter that. He ain't called me mister since the first week I hired him." He took the cigar stub out of his jacket pocket and stuck it in the side of his mouth. "Ain't such a bad idea though."

"What, Daddy?"

"Callin' me Mr. Carter. Shows proper respect." With that, he pulled the stub out of his mouth and bent over to plant a kiss on

Lisa's forehead. "You lock the door and fasten the chain when I'm gone." He looked toward the window. "Ain't no tellin' who's out there with binoculars."

"Oh, Daddy."

"You do what I say, you hear?"

He pulled the front door open and was gone.

"

CHAPTER 18

JUST BEFORE EIGHT IN the evening, Steve slipped away from Jim and made his way to the back bedroom. This time, to insure privacy, he set the lock on the bedroom door and shook it. If anyone came looking at least he would have a warning. In seconds the long distance operator was on the line.

"What city?"

"Van Buren, Arkansas."

There was a sound as the operator transferred the call to another exchange in the northwest part of the state.

"What city?" This one was young and spoke with a deep southern accent.

"Van Buren."

"What name, please?"

"Henry Wilson, 2243 Hibridge."

"Thank you."

A moment later the recording came on and called out the number. It was the same as he remembered. He disconnected and dialed quickly. His breathing was labored and he was sweating profusely again. He wasn't sure whether to put it down to the excess weight or nerves.

After what seemed an eternity but was probably only fifteen or twenty seconds, the phone began ringing. Six times, nine, then a dozen times it rang. He was holding his breath, praying that Ann Wilson would pick up on the other end. When she didn't, he pressed the button to disconnect and dialed again. The results were the same and after countless rings he replaced the phone in its cradle. No answering machine, he thought. That was just like Kathy's parents.

Steve had worked himself into a state of nervous exhaustion by now. His whole body was soaked with perspiration. Even his socks were damp. He walked into the little three-quarter bath at the foot of the bed and found a towel. His neck was damp and when he wiped off with the towel it left a sticky sensation. It was all he could do to keep from stripping his clothes off and slipping into the shower. He glanced at the bandage on his right arm. The nurse had given him some special bags to wrap the arm in when he did take a shower. If not for having to deal with the bag he might just get in right now.

Steve examined his body for what seemed to be the hundredth time. "How could I, how could anybody let themselves get in this miserable condition?" He cut his eyes to the clock on the night-stand. Fifteen minutes had passed since he left the den. They would miss him and come looking. He put the small piece of paper with Ann Wilson's number in his pocket and unlocked the bedroom door. Then he stopped and retreated to the bathroom. He took out the paper and tore it up. Ann Wilson's number had been imbedded in his mind for years. That was more proof that something unbelievable was happening to him. He glanced around the room to be sure no signs remained of what he had been up to, then went back into the den and joined the others.

Jim was on his feet, twirling a metal key chain around his right index finger. When Steve came into the room, he stopped twirling and pitched it toward his brother.

"Those are yours." He pointed toward the keys just as Steve caught them. "One thing. Don't you think you ought to keep Mom's wedding ring in a safer place. I'd hate to see it get lost for another fourteen or fifteen years."

Steve's face went blank. But as he searched his brother's eyes he saw the younger man staring toward the set of keys. He glanced down at the half dozen or so unfamiliar keys that he held. All he saw were keys until he moved a large silver key to the side. A small gold band was underneath. It was a ring he had not seen for fifteen years. But he remembered it like yesterday. On the inside there was a small nick where the jeweler had cut it down to fit his mother's tiny finger, then failed to smooth it properly. Steve turned it over in his hand. Had it been fifteen years or fifteen days, he wondered. Nothing made sense anymore. All he could remember was that his mother had lost it all those years ago and they never found it. Now here it was, another mystery to be solved. But he couldn't let Jim or Mona know that he didn't know where the ring had come from.

"I really think you should put it up, maybe in Nora's jewelry box." Jim's voice cut into Steve's thoughts.

Steve looked up and nodded. "I agree. We don't want to lose it again. I'll take care of it." He stuck the key ring in his pocket and patted it against his leg.

Sarah came out of the hall toward him.

"You still up, honey?" The words in reference to Sarah were getting easier now. It hadn't taken him long to realize he loved her.

"Mama said I could stay up until eight thirty." She took hold of his hand. "Will you tell me the doggy story when you tuck me in?"

The doggy story was new to Steve but he smiled. "Tell you what. I know a passel of good stories better than the doggy story. How about me telling you one of those and we'll save the doggy story for another night. Okay?"

"All right, Daddy. I'll go and get my jammies on."

Steve reached down and patted her bottom as she turned and ran from the room. "I'll be back in a few minutes, Jim."

"Sure."

Jim sat back down in the recliner and turned his attention to the television program that had been on since eight. Steve took a quick look toward the women. Both were on the couch talking and seemed oblivious to his presence. They would not miss him, probably wouldn't even know he had come and gone.

After he tucked Sarah in and told her one of Tommy's favorite stories, he slipped back to the bedroom and dialed Ann Wilson's number again. There was still no answer. His mother-in-law wasn't one to be away from home during the holidays unless there was an emergency. At least, the Ann Wilson he knew wouldn't have been gone. And Kathy always went up to Van Buren for a couple of days to celebrate the season again with her mother. Steve found it hard to believe that she wasn't home now.

But Kathy was not his wife and this Ann Wilson's priorities might be altogether different. He was dealing with a mystery that he might never solve and the thought scared him. Strange as it seemed, the only contact he had with the reality he knew were the dreams, dreams of himself in that hospital room and Kathy there with him. Kathy was real. She was real and he had to find her. He had to get her back. Steve got up off the bed and lumbered back to the den.

Nora and Mona were alone in the den. "Where's Jim?"

Mona glanced back over her shoulder. "He went to bed. Said he'd see you in the morning."

Steve stretched and patted his mouth. "Think I'll follow suit. See you both in the morning."

"Goodnight, Steve," Mona said. Nora nodded and turned her attention back to her sister-in-law.

Steve watched them for several seconds, then slipped down the hall to the bedroom. He dialed Ann Wilson's number again and listened as it rang a dozen times. There was still no answer.

As he slipped off his pants, the jingle of keys reminded him of his mother's ring. In the privacy of the bedroom he examined the ring more closely. There was a bit of green tarnish on the inside. It didn't scratch off and he assumed it was embedded in the metal. The band, originally nearly twice as thick, had worn thin over the years. As he rolled it back and forth in his fingers, he thought of his mother, dead now for nearly two years. His father had been gone for three. And now her ring had shown up here.

He slipped the ring off the key chain and looked around the room for a safe place. To the left of the bed were some built-in drawers. When he opened them he found only clothes, nothing to hold a ring. He did the same with the dresser. There was a small pink box that looked like it might be Nora's jewelry case but it was locked. Finally, he gave up and returned the ring to the key chain, convinced it was safest with him.

In the bathroom, he turned on the shower and adjusted the water. Two cups marked his and hers were on the vanity with a toothbrush sticking out of each. He brushed his teeth quickly and stripped. All he could think of as he stepped into the shower was Kathy and Tommy and the dream. Would he experience it again? It was the only contact he had with them. And now he longed for that contact. Just before midnight, and after another failed call to the Wilson residence, he slipped into bed and fell quickly asleep.

When Nora came into the bedroom, Steve had been asleep for nearly an hour. She started to wake him and tell him to move to his own side of the bed, but she didn't for fear it might lead to a confrontation she wasn't up to. Ever since her affair with Ed had begun, she found it extremely difficult to respond to Steve. She was thankful now that he had made no movement toward her since the accident.

As she flipped off the light and pulled the covers up over her shoulders, Steve turned onto his back and his leg flopped against hers. She drew back instinctively, unaware that a dream was beginning in his subconscious mind.

~ ~ ~

It was strange how the dream seemed. In most dreams there was a bit of fantasy, many things in the light of day that seemed unreal, things that couldn't or wouldn't happen. But the hospital room was so real. He could even hear the drip, drip, drip from the bottle that hung above the right shoulder, his right shoulder. It was his body in the hospital bed, the body he kept in top condition. A dim light was seeping through a nearly closed door that had to be the bathroom. The man on the bed, his body, had his eyes closed. How aware he was.

Somehow, he knew he was in the house on Dickson Drive but he also knew that he was dreaming. He was in the room with this motionless body. All was still. There was no movement from anything. Then he saw something in the shadows. Something was there in the corner, something that seemed to be watching him. He still couldn't make it out. But it was there. He was sure of it. He just didn't know what it was. In the dream he looked back toward the bed. The man was still motionless. When he looked back to the shadows, the apparition was gone.

A new movement in the darkness at the foot of the bed caught his eye. A shapeless form moved toward the shaft of light at the side of the bed. It was Kathy. She bent and kissed the man's silent lips. But he felt no sensation. She was kissing him, his face, his lips, but he felt no sensation. Steve reached out to touch her and again she eluded him. His hands seemed to pass through her body as if she didn't exist. It was her that was real. He was the ghost.

He watched as Kathy, his wife, pulled her sweater tightly around her. She seemed to be cold all of a sudden, like a cold wind had suddenly swept across the room. And, not only did she seem cold, she seemed afraid. He reached for her again, only to see her draw back and move quickly toward the door that led to the outside hall. And then, as quickly as it came, the dream dissolved.

~ ~ ~

Kathy was at the doorway that led from Steve's hospital room into the hallway. That strange chill she had experienced before had returned. The room was freezing and she couldn't find relief except in the warmth of the hall. It seemed the cold was only in the room and only happened at night. The last time it happened she had felt of Steve's arm and found that it was warm. She evidently was the only one it affected.

Now, in the empty hall she leaned against the wall and tried to understand the strange sensation. Even in the chilling cold she had felt, it was as if Steve was trying to reach out to her. Somehow, she felt closer to him, like he was there with her, trying to contact her. She had shaken it off before, but the feeling was there again. She pushed away from the wall and walked to the open doorway. When she stepped inside, the room was warm, just as it should have been. Kathy went around to the far side of the bed and touched her husband's arm. It was warm. He was warm. She sat back in her chair, still holding his arm, and bowed her head until it rested on his good arm.

~ ~ ~

Steve woke with a start and realized where he was. He was at that other house. And he was in that strange bed. The bed belonged to the man whose body he was sharing and to Nora. She was breathing steadily just inches to his right. He was not with Kathy now. Just being with Nora this way gave him a terrible sense of guilt. He moved slightly away from her and realized he was lying in a puddle of his own perspiration. It would have been a welcome relief to slip out of bed and put on dry underwear and pajamas. But he didn't. Instead he lay there in the wet, drying off slowly until sometime after three in the morning when he dropped off to sleep again.

CHAPTER 19

JIM AWOKE JUST BEFORE six. It seemed uncommonly cold in the dark bedroom. The first rays of the morning sun were still nearly an hour away. He turned onto his right side and reached out in the darkness for Mona. She was resting on her side facing away from him. She stirred at his touch and he pulled his hand away to keep from waking her. Mona wasn't a morning person and never had taken too kindly to being awakened early, especially on a morning such as this.

Somewhere toward the hall he heard the creak of settling timbers. The sound rekindled memories of his childhood. The old farmhouse where he and Steve had grown up was fairly new when they were small and many nights he could have sworn someone other than Steve had been in the room with him. It always seemed that way until he reached up and flipped on the light that hung over the double bed he shared with his brother. The room was always empty.

And though Steve, more than once, must have become irritated with his childish behavior, he never scolded like one would think a big brother might. It was that recollection that warmed Jim now. Steve had displayed patience with a little brother during those early days. Now it was time to be patient with a big brother. But something was bothering Steve. There were too many signs. Unconsciously, Steve had reached out to touch him several times during the ride home from the hospital. It was as if he was trying to be sure that Jim was really there. The way he talked those first days in the hospital and then the ring incident yesterday had him concerned. It was evident, even though Steve had tried to hide it, that the ring on the key chain had taken him completely by surprise.

Now that his eyes had adjusted to the dark, Jim slipped out of bed and into his robe. Halfway down the hall he switched on the light and checked the thermostat. It was set at seventy-two degrees. He glanced down the hall toward Steve's closed door, then turned off the hall light and went into the kitchen to start the coffee.

~ ~ ~

Steve woke with a start. Something, some unusual sound, had jogged him awake. Nora was gone. But not for long, because the bed was still warm where she had been. The bathroom door was open but the light was off and he could hear no movement from there. He turned back on his left side and checked the bedside clock. It was after nine. With the heavy drapes pulled tight it was hard to tell that it was even daytime.

His first thought was the phone. Ann Wilson was an early riser and he had her phone ringing in seconds. With each buzz, Steve beat his fist softly on the bedside table. After a dozen rings he replaced the phone and slumped on the bed. She was not home. She had not been home last night. She was not home today. To him, that could mean only one thing. She was out of town, gone for who knows how long. The thought smothered him with depression. If he couldn't get in touch with her, how would he be able to find Kathy? He bent over on the side of the bed and buried his face in his hands.

Several soft raps on the door startled him and he cleared his throat and stood up.

"Come in."

Jim stuck his head around the edge of the door. "Morning."

His brother's face lifted a bit of the depression. "Good morning, Jim."

"Feel better this morning?"

"Better."

"How did you sleep?"

"Great," Steve lied.

"Feel like a ride after breakfast?" Before Steve could answer, Jim continued. "I thought we might drive out to the farm and see how things look. Give us a chance to talk. You game?"

"That sounds great. I need to get out. Tell you what. Let me get some clothes on. Oh, what's the weather like?"

"Not bad. In the fifties. Not much wind. Really beautiful day."

"Good. I'll be there in a few minutes."

"Mona's in the kitchen. What do you want her to fix you for breakfast?"

Steve shook his head. "Just coffee to take with me."

"You sure?"

"Yeah, just coffee."

Fifteen minutes later they were traveling east on Albert Pike. Steve was sipping the black coffee and nibbling on the donut Mona insisted he take with him. He glanced toward Jim and wondered if his brother was beginning to wonder about him. It had been hard to cover his surprise at the ring. Jim was perceptive. Was he beginning to think Steve was losing it?

The next question took Steve completely by surprise. "When did you start taking your coffee black?"

"Since college," he said quickly. As soon as he did he knew it was a mistake.

Jim took his eyes from the road for a second and stared at his brother. For three years or more, Steve had mixed both cream and sugar in his coffee. Nora fussed at him continually, saying that the cream and sugar contributed to his weight problem. But Jim let the comment go and concentrated on the road again.

"Any place special you want to go while we're out?"

"Just the farm. It's been a good while since I've been there."

"How long?" Jim questioned.

Steve wasn't sure how to answer. His last memory of the farm was last February when the ice storm hit and he went to check for damage. "Not sure," he finally said and hoped that would be sufficient.

But Jim was sure. He took a long look at Steve this time and saw that his brother was looking out the side window. Jim had received a letter from Steve just two weeks ago saying he had met with the plumber at the farm. They had met the day before the letter was written to inspect the plumber's work and give him a check. It was the last thing they had to do before putting the farm in the hands of a realtor. Steve should have remembered that.

They drove without talking for the next ten minutes, out Central Avenue past Oaklawn Park to Winans Avenue. By the time they turned east on Winans, Steve had made up his mind.

"Jim, I have to talk to you." He turned to face his brother. "In confidence, with the promise that you won't repeat what I'm going to say."

Jim was silent.

"Will you promise me?"

"I'm here. Talk to me."

They passed the retirement home on Golf Links Road and the street straightened for about a half mile. Before they reached the end of the straight stretch, Steve leaned forward and pointed to a road that cut off at an angle to the right.

"Turn right on Shady Grove Road."

"The farm is closer this way," Jim said, nodding in the direction they were moving.

"I know it is, Jim, but turn on Shady Grove. I have something I want to check on."

Jim did and they followed the road for about a quarter mile to where the blacktop had been torn up during the fall. The street department was to resurface a portion of Shady Grove but winter caught them before they could. Less than a week and a half ago, he'd driven the Corvette over this same stretch of road. It was all potholes and dirt ruts just before the snowfall that had begun the day of the accident. Now it was resurfaced with asphalt. And the resurfacing was not recent. It was another thing that he found glaringly different.

After about a mile they came to the intersection of Carpenter Dam Road and Shady Grove Road. From here, he should be able to see the house, his and Kathy's sitting on Hi-Lo Drive. It was not there. His eyes moved back and forth over an empty three-acre hill. It looked exactly like it had when they had bought it five years ago.

"Where to now?" Jim asked.

Steve pointed straight ahead. "Keep going down Shady Grove."

As they crossed Carpenter Dam Road, Steve searched the surrounding area. The old farmhouse and barn were the same. The woman that lived there owned the three acres they had built on. About a hundred yards east of the hill, the yellow brick house where Bill and Sandra Mahoney lived was just as he remembered. They were already living there when he and Kathy bought. The only thing missing was his home—his home and his family.

"Pull over, Jim."

"Where?"

"In that driveway where it says Hi-Lo Drive."

Steve felt Jim's look and knew his brother was about to let loose a barrage of questions his way. "I know you're wondering what's going on. Give me some time and I promise I'll tell you everything I can. But you've got to be patient just a little longer."

Jim nodded, pulled into the driveway and stopped. Steve got out and looked up the hill toward the Mahoney house. It looked the same. The two-car garage was there, out to the side and unattached. If everything was the same, there would be a new tennis court on the back side of the hill. Bill had built it because his oldest daughter was big into tennis.

He let his eyes drift over the three acres where his house should be standing. For just an instant, he could even visualize Tommy playing in the massive yard, Kathy on her knees in front of the big stone and cedar house digging in the flowerbed and himself riding back and forth on the little red mower they had purchased at Wal-Mart. He stared at the hill until the image slowly faded away, then he stuffed his hands deep in his jacket pockets and got in the car. Jim was still sitting behind the wheel where Steve had left him. "Let's go." If he didn't know better, even he would have thought that he was crazy.

"Where to now?"

"The farm," Steve said.

"You ready to talk yet?"

Steve shook his head. "I will, Jim. Just a little longer."

Jim backed out on the road and turned back up Shady Grove toward Carpenter Dam Road. Five minutes later they were on the Malvern Highway, moving southeast toward Westinghouse Drive and the farm.

Steve's eyes fell on the key ring dangling from the car's ignition. His mother's ring was attached. He reached over and fingered the ring. "Where'd you find it, Jim?"

"The ring?" Jim stared at him for several seconds. "You really don't remember, do you?"

Steve was silent again, his eyes turned back to the surrounding countryside. How would he be able to tell his brother what he suspected, no, what he knew had to have happened. Finally, he took a deep breath and let it out slowly.

"No, I don't remember. I wasn't there when you found it."

They passed Lakeside School and turned left on Westinghouse. "You mean you can't remember being there?"

"No, that's not what I mean. I mean I wasn't there."

"We were both there," Jim insisted. He looked at his brother but Steve was staring straight ahead. For the time being he let it drop and concentrated on the road. They turned off Westinghouse onto a narrow asphalt road. Then about a half mile further on, they turned left onto a dirt road that led to the old farmhouse. It had been nearly a year since Steve was out here, yet the road looked well traveled. The brush and tree limbs that scraped the Corvette the last time he was here had been cut back to allow traffic to pass without damaging a car.

"I need you to tell me about the ring," Steve said.

"Are you serious. You really don't think you were there?"

"Trust me, Jim. I have no idea how the ring was found."

Jim licked his lips and shook his head. "I'll show you when we get to the house."

They were quiet for the next few minutes, driving slowly along the narrow path. After about a quarter mile, they broke into the familiar clearing that stretched out two hundred yards in every direction from the house. At first Steve couldn't see the changes, but as they moved closer it became evident. The faded paint he remembered was a bright white with the morning sun beating down on the front of the frame building. Several loose boards that Steve had noticed the last time had been replaced on the left sidewall, and when he looked at the roof he could see new shingles. Jim stopped next to the front porch and Steve could see that the wooden steps were now concrete.

He stepped out of the car and looked the house up and down. Steve could imagine his father standing just inside the door smiling down at him as he came home from college. He could even seem to smell the fried chicken that would invariably be on the table every Sunday after church. And somewhere, in the back of his memory, he could hear his mother humming a tune as she put the finishing touches on the Sunday meal. Out across the pasture, the family milk cow would be grazing. It didn't seem right that she wasn't.

"Let's go in," Jim said.

"Yes."

Jim unlocked the door with a key from Steve's key chain and stepped inside to let his brother pass. The first thing Steve noticed were the floors. They were new hardwood. The old flowery wallpaper his father had put up was gone and sheetrock, painted and off-white, was in its place. Steve took it all in as he moved slowly across the living room and into the kitchen. A new double sink had been installed where his mother's old stained one had been. He took his left hand out of his jacket pocket and ran it back and forth over the shiny porcelain. The cabinets, once white, plain and ill-fitting, were new and stained oak.

"Mother would have liked this."

"You bet," Jim said.

Jim touched Steve's arm and pointed to the window just above the sink. "We found it there."

"What?"

"The ring. We found it under the old windowsill. When they tore the wood window out last summer the ring was wedged under the sill. You remember how Mama used to take the ring off and lay it on the sill. She was always afraid it would slip off her finger and go down the drain.

"I remember."

Jim walked over to the sink and rested his hand on the new sill. "Somehow, it must have gotten knocked to the outside and pushed up under a crack where the outside of the sill didn't fit down tight. From in here we couldn't see the crack. Last summer when we bought the new custom-built aluminum windows and the man and his wife came out to install them, he had to tear the rotten sill out and put this new one in. And there it was as pretty as you please, wedged back in one corner."

Jim found the ring on the chain and showed it to Steve. "You see this slight bend in the metal? The window man must have caught it under his crowbar when he was prying the old sill off." Jim studied Steve's face. "You still don't remember?"

"No."

"We were both standing right over there when the man found it." Jim pointed toward the door that led back into the living room.

Steve just shook his head.

Jim watched him for a moment, then leaned back against the kitchen cabinets and folded his arms. "I've been very patient, big brother. You said you wanted to talk to me. I know something's wrong. I've known since that first night in the hospital. Something happened to you in that accident. You need to tell me about it."

Steve retreated to the living room door and stood staring at nothing in particular. "I need to tell someone. But you'll think I'm crazy."

"Talk to me, Steve. Whatever it is, you know I'm on your side."

Steve crossed to the kitchen window and stared out across the pasture. Finally, he turned to face his brother. "Okay. Here it is." He took a deep breath and began. "Everything you've told me since we got to the farm is totally foreign to me." Jim had the key chain in his hand and Steve reached out and took it from him. "I've never seen any of these keys before. I've never seen that car that brought us out here. The last time I saw this farm, it was about to fall down." He motioned around the room. "All this, totally new. I've never seen it before."

Jim started to say something but Steve held up his hand. "No, Jim. Let me finish before I chicken out."

He turned away from Jim and stared unseeingly out the kitchen window. "Something is wrong, something I don't really understand. I'm not sure what happened to me during or after the accident. But something happened, something unnatural."

Now he turned back and met his brother's questioning eyes. "I'm not the Steve you know." He searched his brother's eyes and saw nothing but questions. "You may think I'm crazy when I tell you the rest of this, but, I promise you, Jim; I'm not. I know everything I'm about to tell you is true."

His eyes seemed to be boring into his brother's now, looking for understanding. "You made me a promise earlier. You promised you wouldn't mention what I'm going to say to anyone."

"I meant what I said," Jim answered.

"Okay. Then here goes."

Steve turned back to the window and for the next thirty minutes told Jim everything. He told him about his life with Kathy and Tommy, about their marriage in the old Baptist church at Fourth and Garland, about the birth of Tommy. The only thing he left out about Tommy's birth was the fire that had taken Jim and Mona when they were on their way back home. That, he decided, might be something Jim would find too far out to accept. But, he thought, everything he was telling him was too far out to believe. Still, he held back about the fire.

Steve told him about his accounting practice and his complete ignorance when it came to flying an airplane. The last thing he told him about was the dreams he was having and everything he saw in them. In short, Steve laid bare his soul and prayed Jim would keep an open mind. All the while, he stood at the kitchen sink staring across the pasture he and Jim had played in when they were kids. When he finished he turned and looked into his brother's eyes. What he saw was doubt and disbelief.

"You think I'm crazy?"

Jim had pulled up an old paint can, covered it with a newspaper, and sat down. "What about Nora and Sarah? What do you remember about them?"

Steve turned and looked back across the pasture. He was still fingering the ring on his key chain. "Not much about Nora and nothing about Sarah. The last time I saw Nora was during my sophomore year in college. We had a few dates during the fall semester. Just after the spring semester started, she just disappeared from school. We had already broken up a couple of months or so before Christmas, so I didn't really miss her until one of her friends told me she had dropped out of school and gone home to Texarkana. That was it really. There's nothing else to tell. Nothing except…"

Suddenly he was struggling with his voice. The guilt he had felt for all those years seemed to swallow him. He wanted to tell Jim but it was difficult to admit his indiscretion. Finally, he cleared his throat and continued. "We got too close one night early in the fall semester. Things went too far. What happened never should have. I regretted it almost immediately. But I regretted it even more once I met Kathy." He hesitated and looked back at Jim. "I regretted it, that is, until I met Sarah yesterday. Until the accident I had no idea she existed."

"How do you feel now?"

"About Sarah?"

"Yes."

Steve turned back toward Jim. His eyes clouded over when he thought about the little girl he and Nora had brought into the world. "She's my daughter and I love her. There's no way I could ever deny that."

"How do you know she's yours?"

Steve ran his fingers through his hair and leaned back against the sink. "I know, Jim. I just know. Things like that you just know. I would never, could never deny Sarah."

Jim got up from the paint can and crossed the kitchen to where Steve still leaned against the sink. His eyes roamed the pasture outside the kitchen window. After a few seconds, he turned and put his arm around his brother's shoulders. "You asked me if I thought you were crazy. You're not crazy. Except for Nora..."

He paused, wondering if it was Nora or this phantom Kathy who knew his brother best. But he had to deal with reality as he knew it. "Except for Nora, I probably know you better than anyone. And I know you aren't crazy. Something happened to you during the accident, something that thoroughly confused you. You've admitted as much. But that doesn't mean you're crazy. Confused, yes. Crazy, no. But you have to realize, what you've told me could not have happened except in your mind. Remember your dream. Kathy and..." Jim hesitated a moment, "Tommy were in your dreams. They're a result of your subconscious. They aren't real. They exist only in your dreams. You've got to accept that and try to forget them."

"But there is..." Steve stopped himself before he continued. Even though he had already proven to himself that Kathy existed, nothing would make sense to Jim until he actually found her.

"But what?" Jim asked.

Steve was suddenly very tired. And he knew he was making no headway with his brother. He suddenly wanted to get back to the house on Dickson Drive. Sarah was suddenly uppermost on his mind. "Nothing. Not important. If we're through here, let's go back." Except for Sarah, he found it extremely difficult to refer to the Dickson Drive address as home.

"I'm ready," Jim said, and they went through the kitchen and front room. Steve locked the door behind them and took one last look around the front of the house. The transformation was amazing. But in his reality it had not yet happened.

They were in the car and back on the Malvern Highway before either one spoke. Steve broke the silence.

"Jim, tell me about Nora. Did I marry her because of Sarah?"

"You really don't remember?"

"No. I really don't remember but I have to know."

Jim leaned back in the seat and locked his elbows as the car moved past Lakeside School. After a moment, he began. "Nora came to Hot Springs that summer, just a week before you were to begin your junior year at Ouachita. You were working your last day at that window screen shop on Hobson Avenue. She drove up in the yard one Friday about the middle of the afternoon. Cutest little baby girl you ever saw was in the backseat asleep. Nora said she came to see you. Didn't tell anyone why she was there, just that she needed to talk to you. Mom and Dad had met her sometime before you broke up and they invited her in. You were due home shortly and Nora took Sarah out of the car and came into the house. Of course, you know how Mom was about babies. She fell in love with Sarah immediately. Dad was taken with her, too. You know what happened when you got home."

He stopped and shook his head as he realized what he said. "I guess you don't know what happened." He paused again and looked toward Steve. "Anyway, when you got home she proceeded to tell you in front of Mom and Dad that you were Sarah's father. You were twenty years old and already half packed for school. All of a sudden your life was turned upside down. All our lives were. Well, maybe not me so much. But it hit Mom and Dad like a ton of bricks, to say the least. You too. But you, good old Steve, insisted on doing the right thing." He paused and touched Steve's knee. "And it was the right thing. We all knew that. The ceremony was held a week later at the farm with just family. So ended your college. Simple as that."

"Simple as that," Steve repeated. "And I don't remember any of it." In his own mind he knew why. He was not a party to any of it.

"Look, Steve. I've been thinking. You know I love you. You're my brother and, except for Mona, there's no one I care about more.

But you need help. You need to tell the doctor everything you've told me. He'll know how to get you some counseling, get you back on track."

Steve ran his hand back and forth across his eyes. "I know you want me to do what's best for me. But I'm not ready to talk to a shrink. I just need you to keep this to yourself for a while."

"Steve, for your own good, I can't. I..."

Steve straightened in his seat. They were coming up on the spot where his Corvette had slammed into the old truck. In his mind he could still see the log flying through the air and crashing into his arm and head. "It happened right over there, Jim." He pointed toward the Shell station at the intersection. Then it dawned on him what Jim had said. "Jim, you made me a promise. You promised you would keep our conversation to yourself. I'm going to hold you to that promise."

"But..."

"You have to, Jim. I need two weeks, maybe less, to work this out. If I can't or don't, I'll do whatever you say. Agreed?" Steve grasped his brother's right wrist.

"Steve, I don't know."

"Two weeks, Jim. Then I'll go see the doctor if you still want me to."

"But I'll be gone before two weeks, really in just a few days. How do I know you'll follow through?"

"Have I ever lied to you?" As soon as he asked the question he realized even he didn't know the answer. He was relieved when he saw Jim shake his head.

"No." The younger man glanced to his right and saw his brother's eyes searching his. "Two weeks, no more. No longer. Don't let this go any longer than that."

Steve let go of Jim's wrist and leaned back in the seat. For the first time he realized he was sweating profusely. "Two weeks. Thanks, Jim. Thanks."

CHAPTER 20

STEVE WAS BEGINNING TO run out of excuses for his frequent trips to the bedroom. Each time he got up, Nora gave him a questioning look that seemed to be tinged with a bit of anger. But he was determined to keep trying the number until he got an answer. Every half hour, religiously, he would make the trek and every half hour he would get no answer. This time he listened through three, then four rings and was about to hang up just after the fifth when he heard a click from the other end of the line.

ther and I thought I might touch base and see how she was doing."

"Oh, I just know she'd love to hear from you, but I'm sorry to say that Kathy and her husband are living in Dallas now. In fact, I just got home from there a little while ago. I spend Christmas with them every year."

"She's married then." There was a definite change in the tone of Steve's voice. His heart sank and he slumped back against the headboard. It was hard to think of her as another man's wife.

"Oh, my yes. For some time now. As a matter of fact, Gerald drove me home this afternoon. I won't fly and they wouldn't hear of me riding a bus or driving myself. They've become quite protective of me these last few years."

Steve was trying to think while Ann Wilson talked. Married or not, he had every intention of hearing Kathy's voice and without Ann Wilson's help it would be nearly impossible to locate her. He cleared his throat and felt a slight tingle from the raw spot that was

Robert J. Smith

not completely healed.

"That is a coincidence, Mrs. Wilson. I have to be in Dallas on business next week. Do you suppose she would mind if I gave her a call just to say hello?"

"Oh, I'm sure she would be most happy to talk to you."

Steve waited a few seconds, hoping she would offer the phone number. When she didn't, he asked.

"Who did Kathy marry, Mrs. Wilson?"

"A fine gentleman. His name is Gerald Southerland. He's a Baptist minister. They met during Kathy's senior year at Tulsa, fell in love and were married right after she graduated." Her voice became more guarded as she continued. "Of course, Gerald was a widower and is a good deal older, not much younger that me, really. But he's such a fine man and Kathy is quite lucky."

Steve scribbled the name on a sheet of paper and repeated it. When she confirmed he had it right, he thanked her and hung up.

In less than five minutes he had secured the number of Reverend Gerald Southerland from Dallas information. Then, holding the number in his hand, he sat on the edge of the bed staring at the phone and trying to get up the courage to make the call. It was nearly ten minutes before he could dial. It rang half a dozen times before there was an answer.

"Hello." The voice was a child's, a girl, very young.

"Whose place is this?" Steve asked.

"My mommy's and daddy's."

Even in the predicament he was in, Steve still found it difficult not to smile at the child's answer.

"What's your name?"

"Missy."

"Missy who?"

"Missy Southerland. What's yours?"

"I'm Steve." There was the sound of a voice in the background and the girl answered.

"It's Steve, Mommy." There was only a moment's hesitation before Missy spoke again. "Steve, here's my mommy."

Steve froze and waited for the voice he expected.

"Hello."

It was her. There was no denying it now. She was real and he had found her. But now that she was found, would he be able to see her, talk to her?

He cleared his throat again. "Whose residence is this?" He managed.

"This is the Southerland residence. Who were you trying to reach?"

Steve took a deep breath and closed his eyes. She was right there on the other end of the line, yet he was totally powerless to do or say anything. But he knew he had to respond. He didn't want to scare her by remaining silent.

"I think I've reached the wrong number. I was trying to reach..." He went blank, then said the only thing he could think of. "The Pearce residence."

"Oh, yes. You did get the wrong number. I'm so sorry."

"No, I'm the one that's sorry. I hope you'll forgive the intrusion."

"That's quite all right. I hope you find your party."

She would hang up any second and he didn't want to break the connection just yet. He had to say something, anything, or she would be gone. "I'm really sorry to have disturbed you."

"Really, that's okay.

There was a click on the other end and after a moment the monotonous buzz came across all those miles. She was gone before he was ready. It was only then that he realized his teeth were clinched tightly together and the muscles in his legs were tensed to such a degree that he thought they might cramp at any second.

Unconsciously, he brushed some dampness from the corner of his eyes with the back of his hand. He dropped the phone back in its cradle and leaned back against the headboard again. She was found only to be lost again. And maybe for all time. And Tommy. There would be no Tommy. For the first time he realized it. Tommy was not of this world, not this alien world he found himself trapped in. He existed somewhere else. He could never exist here. All of a sudden Steve was wiped out. His arms and legs felt like jello and he didn't want to move.

The sudden jangling of the phone startled him and, instinctively, he reached for it to silence the roar.

"Hello."

"Hello. Is this the Pearce residence?"

"Yes, it is. This is Steve Pearce. Can I help you?"

"Mr. Pearce, I'm Betty Morrison, your brother's secretary, in Denver. I wonder if I might speak to him, please?"

"Of course. Hold on and I'll get him."

Steve dropped the phone on the bed and hurried down the hall to the den. "Jim, you've got a call from Denver. A Betty Morrison. Says she's your secretary." Steve glanced at the television, saw it was too loud and motioned to Jim. "Why don't you take it in my bedroom. You'll be able to hear better in there."

Jim got up quickly and followed Steve down the hall. At the door, Steve started to excuse himself but Jim motioned for him to stay. The younger man sat down on the bed and picked up the phone.

"Betty, Jim. What's up?"

Jim listened for several seconds as his face clouded. His lips tightened and a frown spread across his countenance.

"When did it happen?"

There was another pause as Jim listened to the woman. "How are Judy and the kids?"

He listened again, then got up from the bed and turned away from Steve. "When's the funeral?"

He glanced at his watch. "No way we can get out of here tonight. I'll start checking as soon as I hang up. We should be able to catch something in the morning and get home sometime tomorrow afternoon or night. Hopefully, it won't be as bad as it was a few days ago." He listened again. "Will you take care of the flowers?"

After another moment. "Thanks. Just sign them, 'With all our love, Jim and Mona. And Betty, make sure it's something nice—not gaudy, but nice. Phil wasn't pretentious. Okay?"

There was silence for nearly a minute. "Thanks again, Betty. I'll call as soon as we're on the ground in Denver. See you soon." He hung up and dropped back onto the bed with the phone still in his hands.

"What is it, Jim?"

"Phillip Dane, my boss and one of my best friends. He had a heart attack this morning, a massive coronary. He died before they could get him to the hospital. Left a wife and three small kids. We're gonna have to leave first thing in the morning if I can get a flight." He reached for the phone book. "They think the funeral will be day after tomorrow. I'd better start calling the airlines."

CHAPTER 21

KATHY DISMISSED THE MAN'S call quickly and went back into the family room where Missy was busy coloring in the book she had gotten for Christmas. When the phone rang a few minutes later she glanced at Missy, who was about to get up and run to answer it.

"Mother will get it this time, Missy."

She crossed the family room to the phone on the hall table and answered it just after the third ring.

"Hello." In the back of her mind, and for some reason she could not explain, she half-expected to hear the man's voice again.

"Kathy."

"Mother." Her first thought was that something had happened to her husband. "Is everything all right."

"Oh, I've frightened you, dear. I didn't mean to do that. Yes, everything is fine. I just thought I'd call and let you know I'd arrived safely and I've sent your Gerald back to you. He thought he'd arrive sometime after midnight."

Kathy breathed a sigh of relief and sat down on a chair next to the telephone.

"I'm sorry I scared you, dear."

"You really didn't, Mother," she lied. "I guess I'm a little jumpy, what with the calls I've been getting. I didn't expect to hear from you and, when I did, I jumped to the wrong conclusion. I'm really glad you called."

There were several seconds of uncomfortable silence before Ann

Wilson spoke again. "Honey, I really phoned because of a call I got right after I got home. I hope I didn't do something I shouldn't have. After I hung up, I got to thinking about the trouble you've been having for the last few months."

Kathy's pulse sped up every time there was a mention of the phantom caller. Even though it had been nearly two weeks since the last call, her heart still skipped a beat each time the phone rang.

"I know it's silly of me, but I thought maybe I'd done the wrong thing by telling the man your name. I didn't give him your phone number though," Ann said.

"What man, Mother?"

"A nice-sounding young man. He called maybe a little over a half hour ago. I'm sure he was exactly what he said he was."

"Who was he, Mother? What did he want?" Kathy was on her guard now. She looked toward the front door. The safety chain was unhooked. The other two outside doors were probably unchained also.

Ann Wilson was still talking. "He said he'd gone to college with you at that Baptist college in Arkadelphia. He had a class with you and just wanted to say hello. I told him you were living in Dallas and married to Gerald." She stopped to gather her thoughts. "Strange, I thought. I had the impression he was surprised and upset when I told him you were married."

Kathy went cold. "Did he tell you his name?"

"Yes, I believe he did. Said it was Parks or Pearcy. No, Pearce. That's it. He said his name was Steve Pearce."

Steve, Kathy thought. She glanced back toward the family room where Missy was still coloring. The man had told Missy his name was Steve. But Pearce, why did that ring a bell?

"Do you think I did the wrong thing, dear?" Ann Wilson seemed distraught now.

Kathy wanted to get her mother off the phone. She could imagine that every door was unlocked. "No, Mother. I'm sure everything is fine. I don't remember the man, but then I was at Ouachita only a few weeks." She was trying to remember if she had locked the door leading into the garage and whether she had lowered the garage door when they got back from the grocery store a little while ago. She could feel her heart pounding and sweat beginning to roll down the small of her back.

Ann Wilson was still talking and Kathy was not sure of everything she had said. "I'm sure you're right." Her mother's voice was more cheerful. "Now, I must go. You take care and write soon and thanks again for a wonderful Christmas."

Kathy managed a cheerful goodbye, then, without hesitation, hurried into the kitchen. The door leading to the garage was locked and the chain fastened. That gave her a measure of relief. One by one, she checked each window in the house. All were locked. The only door that had been unchained was the front and she had secured it quickly. Once she finished checking the house, she began to breathe easier.

Her next chore was the old Ouachita yearbook. It was tucked in the bookshelf along with the four she had received from Tulsa. After leaving the Arkadelphia school, she had forgotten the annual was paid for. But promptly, the next fall, it had arrived at her mother's house in Van Buren. Even though her picture was not in it, she still displayed it alongside her others. Thumbing through it now, she could find no mention of a Steve Pearce. There was only one Pearce, a James A. Pearce, a freshman from Hot Springs. He was good-looking but unfamiliar.

For some reason the name Pearce was still striking a chord. She had heard the name recently. But where? She returned to the family room and glanced toward the phone. Something about the phone, she thought. What was it? And then she knew. The man had said he was trying to reach the Pearce residence. The name Steve, the Pearce residence. Both names had come from the man during the phone call, only not together. She glanced again toward the front door. The chain was still in place.

"Missy."

"Yes, Mommy."

Kathy knelt beside her daughter and smiled down at the image of Bugs Bunny that Missy was working so hard on.

"The man who called a little while ago. When I came to the phone, what did you say his name was?"

"What man?"

"When you answered the phone for mommy a little while ago. You told me the man's name. Do you remember what it was?"

"Oh. Yes, Mommy. It was Steve."

Kathy had the temperature close to 75 degrees but she was still shaking. "Did he tell you what his last name was?"

Missy shook her head without looking up. "No, Mommy."

Kathy ran her hand through the girl's long brown hair, then got to her feet and sank down on one end of the couch. The man had said his name was Steve and that he was trying to call the Pearce residence. It was all too much of a coincidence. Now she was really frightened. The woman's magazine she'd been so engrossed in a short time ago seemed unimportant now. She flipped it to the other end of the couch and looked at the clock.

She was downright cold and she pulled her sweater tightly around her. Gerald would not be home for hours, an eternity, Kathy thought. She pulled her feet and legs up under her on the couch and made herself into as small a ball as she could. They would not go to bed, not leave the room until Gerald got home. She had heard somewhere there was strength in numbers and they were two.

CHAPTER 22

IT WAS NEARLY TEN thirty when Doctor Ray Philpot finally pulled into his garage and switched off the ignition. He had spent the last hour with Kathy at the hospital as he had done nearly every night for the last week and he was beat. After he lowered the garage door he just sat there with his head against the headrest. Finally, he opened the car door, slid out and slipped into the kitchen. A note on the cabinet from Susan reminded him of the cold chicken in the refrigerator. A "ps" at the bottom told him she would be on the couch in the den and to wake her when he got home.

The chicken was on the top shelf of the refrigerator covered with a clear sheet of plastic wrap. Susan had cooked it last night and he had gotten home too late to eat it hot. It would be cold again tonight. Thankfully, he liked cold chicken. Ray grabbed a chicken leg and bit off a chunk. He loosened his tie and went through the dining room to the family room. Just as the note said, Susan was curled up on the couch with a paperback novel resting beside her head. Ray reached down and touched her lightly on the shoulder.

"Susie."

She didn't stir.

"Hey, Susie. Wake up."

This time she opened her eyes just enough to see him. "What time is it?"

Nearly ten thirty. Why aren't you in bed?"

She rubbed the back of her hand across her eyes and sat up. "I don't know. I've just had a feeling all day about Steve. How is he?"

"Not much change. Physically, he's improving every day. Mentally..." Ray shrugged his shoulders and took another bite out of the chicken leg. "He just won't wake up."

"How's Kathy holding up?"

Ray sat down on the couch and studied the chicken leg. "I'm concerned about her. She won't leave the hospital. She won't even leave his room except for the bathroom. She's wearing herself out. Doesn't eat half of what they bring her."

Susan leaned her head against her husband's shoulder. "Is Steve going to make it?"

Ray dropped the half-eaten chicken leg on a copy of the Hot Springs paper and leaned back on the couch. He ran his hands back and forth over his face and head and closed his eyes. That had been the question on his mind for several days. Steve was fortunate to survive the car wreck. Something was holding his mind prisoner. Something wouldn't let him wake up. His mind seemed to be stagnant while his body was getting stronger. Would he make it?

Ray shook his head and kissed Susan lightly on the forehead. "I don't know, hon. I just don't know. If he'd wake up from the coma, yes. He'd make it." He worked his hands over his face and head again. "I'm praying he will."

~ ~ ~

Kathy got up from the uncomfortable hospital chair for what seemed like the twentieth time and bent down to feel Steve's breath. It was steady, not labored like it had been as recently as yesterday. The blue mark on his throat looked much better tonight. Maybe it was the light, but it wasn't as bright as it had been, at least it didn't seem so. She sat back down, took out another cheese cracker and took a bite. Like the last one, it didn't taste good and she deposited it in the trash can beside the bed.

She ached all over. Ray said she needed to go home for the night, get a good night's sleep in her own bed. But she couldn't.

She couldn't leave Steve. He would wake up soon and wonder where she was. She had to be there when he did. She needed him. Tommy needed him. He had to get well. Kathy got up, went to the head of the bed and looked down at his face.

"Steve. Please wake up. I need you. Tommy needs you. Please wake up." She watched for a reaction for more than a minute. When none came she went back to the chair and sat down. Her eyes were extremely heavy and she closed them. It was to be for just a few seconds. But in those few seconds she fell sound asleep.

CHAPTER 23

STEVE HAD SPENT MUCH of Saturday night staring at the dark ceiling, listening to Nora's steady breathing. Sometime around two in the morning he made his decision. The few minutes on the phone with Kathy were not enough. He had to see her face, touch her, be sure she was okay and was the same Kathy he knew. And yet, he knew even as the thought passed through his mind, she was not the same. She might look the same, sound the same, but she was not the same.

His Kathy was somewhere else, somewhere unreachable. She was in that recurring dream. Only the dream was real. What he saw in that dream was really happening. And he was on the outside looking in at his life and his real body. It was as if Kathy was just a reflection in the mirror. And even though she existed here, she could never be his. Still, he needed to see her. So, in that dark bedroom he made the decision. He would go to Dallas and he would go tomorrow.

A preacher's wife she was. A preacher's wife would likely be at church every time the doors opened. He would be there when they opened for evening services. Tomorrow, after Jim and Mona flew out, he would go. He would satisfy himself this one time. And then, whatever else might happen, he would have to leave her to her own life. And, Tommy, he was lost too. Steve felt a tear slip out of his eye and he reached up with his left hand and wiped it away. Then he closed his eyes and tried to sleep.

It was eight thirty the next morning when Steve rose and went into the shower. He pulled the protective bag over his arm and stood under the warm spray for nearly fifteen minutes before reaching for the washcloth. By the time he was finished and dressed it was nearly nine thirty. Jim and Mona had to be at the airport by ten thirty for their eleven-fifteen departure. That meant he should be able to get away from Hot Springs before noon. Dallas around five o'clock, he thought. He would have plenty of time to locate the church before evening services began.

It would be a long day. If he were able to see Kathy, it would be hard to drive away, knowing he might never see her again. And then when he got home, sometime after midnight, there would be excuses to make. But they were the least of his concern right now.

Nora was in the kitchen when he came through the den. "You certainly slept late this morning. You know they have to be at the airport in less than an hour." She motioned with her head toward the hall that led to the guest bedroom.

"I know. We'll make it." He poured himself a cup of coffee and peered over the rim at Nora. "You going with us?" He hoped she wasn't. That would let him escape Hot Springs a little earlier.

"I guess." She made a face and glanced toward the hall. Steve could tell she wasn't thrilled about going.

"You don't have to," he offered.

"I'll go," she snapped back hurriedly.

Steve nodded. "I'm going to bring you home afterward. I have some things to do." He hesitated to let that sink in. "And I probably won't be back till late."

Nora eyed him suspiciously. "What things?"

Steve was ready for her. "It has to do with the crash. The NTSB is in town investigating what happened and I need to drive out to the crash sight, look it over and get my bearings, see what I can remember. They'll have a lot of questions and I need to be able to answer them." Most of what he said was a lie but he needed an excuse and it was all he had been able to come up with in the shower. If Nora checked she would quickly realize it was a lie. But he was counting on her not checking.

"And what am I supposed to do all day, sit here and twiddle

my thumbs with no way to go anywhere?"

Steve tensed at the possibility of a confrontation. He didn't want anything to interfere with the trip.

"I'm sorry, Nora. But this is something I have to do."

She turned her back on him and refilled her coffee cup. He waited until she took her cup to the table and sat down, then he refilled his own.

~ ~ ~

The airport was a five-minute drive from the house. During the short time he had been out of the hospital, he noticed that the house lay directly under the approach to the short east-west runway that dead-ended into Highway 70. More than once, he'd pulled back the curtain and watched a small, single-engine turning on its final approach. Once he went to the mirror and looked at himself, wondering how many times this body had done just that. Time was running short for him. One day soon he would be expected to strap himself into a plane and resume a career he knew nothing about.

While he had answers for other things, he had none for that. Swimmers never forgot how to swim. Golfers never forgot how to swing the club. But could a body with a different mind, a different soul, remember how to fly a plane. He thought not. Muscle memory would not serve him in this case. The body might be capable, but to the mind it was foreign. The first time he tried, he would kill himself and possibly someone else.

Now, as he drove down the lane toward the terminal, he knew he could never strap himself into the left seat of a plane again.

His mind was wandering as he drove down the short drive that led from Highway 70 to the terminal building. Nora's voice startled him. "Let us out in front of the door, Steve. You can find a place to park and meet us inside."

"Right."

He pulled next to the curb, turned off the key and flipped the trunk lid release so Jim could retrieve the bags from the trunk. A few minutes later he drove alone to the parking lot. By the time he got inside, Jim was already paying for the tickets.

"We didn't have to be early after all," Jim said. "Looks like we're the only ones boarding here." He grasped Steve's arm. "We need to go somewhere and talk. Alone," he whispered.

"Sure." They looked across the terminal building and Steve spotted the men's room. "How about there?"

"Good idea." Jim nodded to Mona. "We're going to the men's room. Be back in a few minutes."

Once inside, Jim scanned the half dozen stalls until he was sure they were alone.

"Steve, I lay awake most of the night thinking about what we talked about yesterday and what I promised."

"You aren't going to back out on me?"

Jim shook his head. "No, but I want you to think very seriously about your situation. You've come through a pretty rough experience. It's very possible for a man to lose his memory and imagine all sorts of crazy things. That doesn't mean he's crazy. I want you to think about what's best for you and Nora and Sarah. I know I promised you two weeks, and I'm not backing down on that. I just wish you'd take it on yourself to go in tomorrow and see the doctor. Tell him what you told me. Let him be the judge as to what you should do next."

Steve turned on the water and ran his hands back and forth through the warm stream. "I'll think about it, Jim. I won't promise anything right now. But I will think about it."

"Then you'll make an appointment tomorrow?"

Steve dried his hands and turned to face his brother. "Maybe." He paused and shook his head. "Jim, I won't lie to you. I want that two weeks. I need it."

Jim let out his breath and sighed. "I promised it to you. I'll stand by my word. I'm not sure what you hope to accomplish though. Do you?"

Steve shrugged. "I don't know either. Maybe nothing. But, maybe..." He didn't finish.

"All right. But I'm going to call you every two or three days to see how you are. When I do, will you tell me the truth?"

"You have my word."

"That 's good enough for me."

Jim turned toward the exit door, but Steve caught his arm. He turned his brother around, and for the first time there were tears welling up in Steve's eyes. It was possible, he knew, that he might lose Jim a second time. He had no fear for Jim's safety, but for some reason he felt this short interlude might be their last time together.

"Take care, Jim." Steve put his arms around him and held him in a bear hug, completely unaware of the two men who had just entered the restroom. "I love you and I'm going to miss you."

"I'll be back," Jim whispered. "And things will be better then."

"Yeah, I know," Steve acknowledged. But will I be here, he wondered?

CHAPTER 24

STEVE'S ONLY REGRET WAS leaving Sarah. On the way home, she begged to go with him. But that was impossible. It was important that no one, not even Sarah, know where he was going. Leaving her behind wouldn't have been quite so bad if Nora's attitude had been different. But she ignored both Steve and Sarah on the way home. When she got out of the car, she grabbed Sarah's arm and pulled her roughly out of the car and into the house. When he last saw his daughter, she was standing inside the carport door, tears streaming down her face, as she watched him back out of the driveway. He was nearly to Hope on the I-30 freeway before he was able to erase that image from his mind.

Just after one fifteen, Steve pulled off the freeway onto State Line Avenue in Texarkana and stopped at a fast food restaurant on the Texas side of the street. By two o'clock, he was back on the road again. There was still a bit of discomfort around his damaged ribs and by midafternoon he had stopped twice at roadside parks to stretch and walk around. The stops were short, no more than ten minutes each. Just before dark, he turned onto the freeway loop that skirted Dallas, took the first exit and stopped at an all-night grocery. A phone booth stood conveniently at one corner of the brick building. To his dismay, when he began to search through the yellow pages of the thick Dallas phone book, he found several pages of Baptist churches. Only a few listed the minister's name in the advertisement.

Finding no Gerald Southerland, he dialed the first church on the list. There was no answer. The second was the same, but a young woman answered at the third.

"Hello."

Steve cleared his throat. "I wonder if I might trouble you for some information. I'm just in town for a short time and I understand a friend of mine is the pastor of one of the Baptist churches here in Dallas. I'm not sure just which one. Can you help me?"

"I'll try. What's his name?"

"Gerald Southerland."

"Oh, Doctor Southerland. Hold on a minute, sir." She was off the line for several seconds. "Sir, are you still there?"

"Yes."

"I thought I was right but I wanted to be sure. That would be Ridgeview Road Baptist."

"Ridgeview Road. Thank you. Thank you very much."

Steve hung up and went into the store. It was empty except for a tall, long-haired man behind the counter. He had a Dallas paper spread out in front of him and hardly gave Steve a glance when the door opened.

Steve walked over to the counter and the man glanced up. "I'm looking for Ridgeview Road Baptist Church. Can you help me?"

"Ain't never heard of it," the man said looking up from the paper. He held Steve's gaze for several seconds, then turned his attention back to the paper.

Steve reached in his billfold and pulled out a five-dollar bill. "I'm trying to find a friend. It's very important to me." He placed the bill on the counter next to the paper and left his hand on the money.

The man's attention switched from the paper. He reached under the counter and pulled out a worn map of the city. "Maybe I can help you. Let's take a look at the map."

~ ~ ~

Gerald Southerland came down the steps from the upstairs bedroom and stuck his head into the family room. He was a handsome man and looked much younger than his years. Running every morning before breakfast had helped him keep his weight down and his body in some degree of shape. Though with his six-foot-plus frame he'd never been excessively heavy. Only the touch of gray around his temples indicated the possibility of an age difference between him and his young wife.

"Kathy, I have to go now. The personnel committee meeting is scheduled for six." He glanced at his daughter on the floor in front of the television set and motioned toward her with his head. "How's she doing?"

"Much better, darling." Kathy pulled her legs out from under her and dropped her magazine on the couch as she got up.

"Think she's up to church?"

"Yes, I think so," Kathy said.

"Are you still worried about last night?"

She licked her lips and put her arms around his waist.

He didn't wait for her to speak. "You know that was probably just a coincidence," he continued. "You said the young man was polite and hung up as soon as you told him he had a wrong number."

"I know. I guess I'm just a fraidy cat. But I don't want to stay at home tonight and Missy is much better."

He bent and kissed her on the forehead. "I'll see you at church then."

Kathy went to the door and watched him pull out of the driveway, then went to the entrance of the family room and called her daughter.

"Missy, turn off the TV. It's time to get ready for church."

~ ~ ~

Only a few people were seated when Steve stepped through one of the two sets of double doors that separated the vestibule from the auditorium proper. It was dimly lit inside. Only half of the overhead lights were on and he had to squint to study the back of the people already seated. After a few minutes of searching he realized she was not there. He had the awful feeling that she might not come. She could be ill or the child, Missy, might be.

His stomach churned from the thought, and all of a sudden he felt sweat on the end of his nose. He moved from the doors to grip the back of one of the seats. For the first time he noticed that the entire auditorium was filled with theatre seats. It reminded him of the big church in Hot Springs, the one on Garland. They had put in theatre seats when it was first built and taken them out in favor of church pews some thirty years later. Why he thought of that at a time like this he wasn't quite sure. For whatever reason, it didn't calm his nerves.

There were doors on either side of the pulpit that probably led to Sunday school classes toward the back of the church. After several minutes of watching, they began to swing open regularly and members of the congregation began to pour into the big room. But, no Kathy.

And then, he saw her. She entered from the door to the left of the pulpit. A small girl was in tow. Except for the brown hair, the child looked very much like Sarah. She started up the aisle on the left but an old man stopped her and they talked for several minutes. Then she continued up the aisle to the sixth row and guided the child into the pew.

Steve tried to swallow but his throat seemed congested. She was there only yards away. He started to move in that direction when he felt the touch of a hand on his shoulder.

"Are you looking for anyone in particular?" The slender, red-haired man asked.

"Uh, no. I'm just letting my eyes get accustomed to the lighting."

"It is a little dark in here. They'll be turning up the lights soon now. You just visiting this evening?"

"Yes, just passing through town and thought I might stop for church."

"Glad to have you. I'm Red Lacey. If I can help you, just holler."

Steve nodded. "Thanks."

The man walked away and Steve took a deep breath. He told

himself he must remember not to stare at Kathy. Red walked to the opposite side of the church and immediately became engaged in conversation with a short, rather fat, bald-headed man. Steve wasted no time hurrying down the aisle. He seated himself four rows behind Kathy and the child, making sure he had her between him and the pulpit. He would not have to look to the side to see her. She was directly in line with his vision to the pulpit.

As much as he knew he shouldn't stare, it was difficult to take his eyes off her. The hair was shorter and seemed a touch lighter than his Kathy's. The voice was the same. From this distance he could hear fragments as she spoke an occasional word to passersby. They all seemed to like her. Nearly everyone stopped, leaned over and offered some word. Many asked about the girl, how she was feeling.

He was so engrossed in Kathy that he didn't realize when the service started. But when the name Southerland was mentioned he tore his eyes from Kathy and looked toward the pulpit. The man had rugged good looks, seemed to be slightly taller than Steve and, right now, much thinner. Unconsciously, Steve pulled in his stomach. It made his ribs hurt and he let out his breath.

"As pastor," the preacher began, "of Ridgeview Road Baptist Church, it's my privilege to recognize our guests and welcome them to our congregation. Our custom is to ask our visitors to remain seated while our members stand."

Out of the corner of his eye, Steve saw the red-haired man stride down the aisle and take his place at the front facing the congregation. Gerald Southerland was not finished. "The ushers will hand out visitor cards to those seated. So, if our members will stand at this time, we'll give our visitors a warm Ridgeview welcome." He held his arms in the air and everyone around Steve stood. Gerald Southerland was still not finished. "Now, members, greet all those around you."

Steve lost sight of Kathy immediately as a huge man moved into the pew in front of him and was leaning over offering his hand. The man said something and Steve responded, all the while trying to locate Kathy. When the man released his hand and moved away, a hand touched his shoulder from behind. An elderly lady who looked to be in her seventies or eighties was smiling down on him. She spoke to him for nearly a minute, before moving away to shake some other hand.

When he faced forward, Kathy was leaning over the pew where the big man had been only a minute before. Her hand was outstretched in his direction. It was all he could do to keep from standing and taking her in his arms. As their hands made contact he was aware that his were clammy and shaking. But her hand was warm and steady. It was her touch.

"Welcome to our church. I'm Mrs. Southerland, the pastor's wife. We're so glad to have you, Mister...."

Steve caught himself in time. "Stevens," he said carefully. "Ted Stevens." His voice was breaking up and he worried that she might recognize it from last night.

She smiled and made an effort to draw her hand away from his. For a moment it seemed as if their hands were locked together. He was having a hard time letting go. Her gentle effort to disengage his grip became a little more vigorous. The smile, warm and friendly a moment before, seemed not so congenial when she finally pulled away.

Almost immediately, another hand reached out and took his. People were all around him, speaking and smiling and saying all manner of things. He was invited to come back again. But he couldn't concentrate on anything but Kathy. She had resumed her seat four rows up and was facing forward with her arm around the girl. When the music began and the people finally sat down, he found a visitor's card in his left hand. He had the vague impression that the smiling, red-haired man, Red Lacey, had placed it there.

His focus was on Kathy again. But something was different. Her shoulders were rigid, where a few minutes before they had seemed relaxed. He could see the tension in her neck. He knew her. The same strain had been evident two years ago when Tommy fell and broke his left wrist. She was frightened then and frightened now. But what tore at him the most was the knowledge that it was because of him. He had frightened her. He closed his eyes and cursed himself under his breath. Why had he held onto her hand so long? She was scared of him now.

~ ~ ~

The music man was introducing a song and the congregation stood. When they did, Kathy turned her body and head just far enough to see his face. Their eyes met and lingered for several seconds. Steve was unable to look away. Perhaps if he had she might have relaxed, but he didn't and it seemed the strain in her eyes intensified. There was no hint of a smile on her face. He knew then what he had to do. He loved her too much to see her suffer any longer.

Halfway through the second verse, Steve slipped out and stole back up the aisle. Red Lacey was leering at him as he brushed past into the vestibule. He stopped outside the double doors and looked back through a small glass. She was facing forward again. Then, as if she knew he was there, she turned and looked directly toward the glass he was looking through. He moved aside but he knew she saw him. After a moment he looked through the glass again. She was bent over whispering something in her daughter's ear.

His car was parked in the lot across the street and he went to it and crawled in. It was not a big car, and all of a sudden he remembered Ray and the trouble he had getting into the Corvette. He thought about that for a moment, then settled back against the headrest and waited. Less than an hour later the people began pouring out of the church.

What he was about to do would be the hardest thing he would ever do. Crossing the street and climbing the front steps of the church, he nearly turned to run more than once. When she came out, the child was not with her. There were a few men conversing on the wide front steps but they were on the other side. It seemed she was looking for something. When their eyes met, it was evident she was looking for him. Without hesitating, she came directly toward him. The look on her face showed no signs of fear as it had inside the church.

Steve nodded as she approached. "Mrs. Southerland."

She stopped in front of him and met his gaze without speaking.

It was up to him. "I want to apologize. I know I frightened you inside. That's why I got up and left. But when I saw you in there... when I took your hand...." Steve looked deep into her eyes. He was having a terrible time finding the words he wanted to say. Finally, he said it. "You look enough like my wife to be her twin." He swallowed and watched her somber face. "I lost her not long ago."

So much of what he had been saying to so many others since the accident had been a lie. He would not lie to Kathy. "There was a car accident. When I saw you, I...." His voice broke and when it did she reached out and touched his hand. He wanted to grasp it again but he didn't. "I guess I got caught up in the moment. Please forgive me for frightening you."

She moved forward and did what he had wanted to do. She took his hand much as his Kathy had so many times and looked up into his eyes. "I understand. It wasn't you that frightened me. Some other things have been happening and I've been on edge. But I understand your grief."

The wrinkles in her forehead told him a story. He'd seen them before. That first time was when they got word that Jim and Mona had been killed in the fire. She'd put her arms around him then and they had cried together for a long time. He wished they could do that now. "I'm sorry for your loss. I know you must have loved your wife very much."

Yes, very much." She had taken her hand away a few moments before and he reached out and touched her arm. It was his physical way of saying goodbye for the last time. "Thank you for being understanding. I won't bother you again. Goodbye."

She smiled and he turned to cross the street. He had never been very emotional, but as he retreated down the steps with her final goodbye ringing in his ears, it was everything he could do to hold back the tears. Across the street he worked his way into the car and looked back at the church. Kathy was standing in the doorway, looking toward the car. She raised a hand and held it for just a moment, then disappeared back into the church. She was gone, maybe for good. And Tommy, too.

He felt empty, alone. But then he thought of Sarah. He had Sarah. And Jim and Mona were back. At least he had them. But could they replace Kathy and Tommy? It was as if they never existed, and maybe for him they never had. Maybe he was crazy. Maybe he did need to see that doctor. Whatever else, one thing was certain. Kathy and Tommy could never be replaced. Steve turned the key in the ignition and drove the car onto Ridgeview Road, turning northeast toward the interstate.

CHAPTER 25

THE PHONE WAS RINGING when Nora stepped from the shower. She draped a heavy towel around her and ran to the bedroom extension.

"Hello," she snapped.

"Steve there?"

She frowned and rolled her eyes toward the ceiling. "No, Jake, he isn't." The towel had slipped to reveal part of her upper body and she stuck the receiver between her head and shoulder and made an effort to cover herself. "I don't know where he is or when he'll be back. He brought me home at noon and just drove off."

"He able to drive by himself?"

"Yes, Jake. He is or he wouldn't have done it, would he?"

"Must be doin' better'n I thought."

"I guess," she said. Her patience was wearing thin. "What do you want, Jake?"

"I haven't seen him since he got out of the hospital," Jake said.

"Is that bad?"

Jake ignored the sarcasm. Nora Pearce had been that way since day one. He had wondered more than once what Pearce had seen in such a sullen person. At least he didn't have to deal with her on a regular basis. "Tell him to call me if he gets in before midnight."

"I'll most certainly do that." Without waiting for Jake to reply, Nora hung up and started back to the bathroom. At the foot of the bed the phone began ringing again. She stalked back and grabbed it before it could ring a second time.

"Jake, I wish you'd leave me alone. I was in the ...."

"Hey, baby. Hold on. If you run that pretty little motor too hot, you'll burn up a bearing."

Nora sat down on the bed and crossed her legs under the towel. "Oh, hello, Ed."

"Wow, now we don't sound too excited, do we?"

She lay over on her left side and braced her upper body on her elbow. "Sorry. It's just that I've been sitting here all afternoon with no transportation. I'm about crazy trying to be the loving and understanding wife, and then Jake called a few minutes ago and I didn't think I'd ever get rid of him. The man makes my skin crawl."

"Hold on there, baby. You're talkin' about Mr. Moneyman. Better be nice to the boss. He writes the checks."

"He can go to...."

"Hey, sugar. Cool down. Let's talk about something more interesting."

Sarah came out of her bedroom and started down the hall toward Nora. The towel was up over her knees and she pulled it down and sat up on the bed. "Sarah, go and play in your room. I'm busy." Nora thought for a moment then changed her mind. "No, Sarah. Take your clothes off and get in the tub. It's nearly bedtime." Before Sarah could reply, Nora got off the bed and closed the door in her daughter's face. She applied the lock and went back to the bed.

"It was just Sarah. I got rid of her." She rolled over on her stomach and hiked her legs straight up in the air. Now that the door was locked she was not nearly so careful with the towel. "Steve's gone, no telling where. What're you doin' tonight?"

~ ~ ~

Every house on the street was dark when Steve unlocked the carport door. Fatigue had set in on the way back, somewhere around Texarkana. On the way to Dallas his ribs had been uncomfortable and aching. Coming back he had been so tired he hadn't noticed them.

Along the way, before he got to Texarkana, he'd stopped and grabbed a barbeque sandwich. Now, he couldn't even remember for sure where that had been, maybe Mount Pleasant, Texas. It had long since evaporated in his stomach. He opened the refrigerator and spied a single piece of cherry pie that was left over from last night's supper. Mona knew it was his favorite and surprised him with it when he and Jim got back from the farm. Kathy never forgot how much he loved them. It would be on the table the third Friday of every month when he got home from the office. He retrieved the slice now and poured himself a glass of milk. When he sat down at the little round breakfast room table a two-word note greeted him. "Call Jake."

Steve shook his head and whispered, "Tomorrow, Jake. Tomorrow." He finished the snack quickly and put the dishes in the sink. In the hall, he paused at Sarah's door and glanced in. She was asleep with a stuffed animal hugged close under her chin. For Tommy, he thought, it would be Garfield. Sarah needed a Garfield, he decided as he quietly shut her door.

The door to the back bedroom was shut. He tried it and found it was locked. He was relieved. It would give him a good reason to move out of the master bedroom. Tomorrow he would move the clothes that belonged to him to the front bedroom. He had never been unfaithful to Kathy and he didn't mean to start now. And he was sure, knowing Nora and her attitude toward him, that she would be just as happy.

A thought struck him. Would he have to live a celibate life? Could he remain true to a wife he might never see again? It was too much for him to deal with, as tired as he was. He started back down the hall to the guest bathroom and paused to check the thermostat. It was set at seventy-four. He started to lower it a few degrees, then thought better of it. Who knew how warm they kept it. Before he started changing things around here to suit himself, he needed to learn a little about Nora and Sarah. At Sarah's door, he paused and listened. No sounds from inside.

Steve stepped into the guest bathroom and locked the door.

Luckily, he had slipped a protective bag for his arm in the cabinet under the sink. With that tied onto his damaged right arm, he stripped and turned on the water, adjusting the temperature before stepping into the tub and under the warm shower. The pulsating current soothed and massaged his tired, aching muscles. He leaned against the wall much as he had that day not so long ago in the showers at the handball court. That day he was a different person. Since then his life had taken a turn that he couldn't explain. It would be a miracle if anyone could.

Kathy had been on his mind all the way from Dallas. It seemed inconceivable that he knew her but she had never seen him. She just felt sorry for him and that disgusted him. He let her and that was wrong. He turned under the water and let the stream flow slowly down over his shoulders and back. The thought kept hammering at him that she should have known him. But this Kathy had never met him. She hadn't started at Ouachita until her junior year, the year this Steve did not return to school. The events in both their lives took different paths. But, how, he whispered? What am I missing? What is it I can't or won't remember?

Steve doubled his fist and banged it against the shower wall. "What in the name of all that's holy has happened to me?" He closed his eyes and leaned against the sidewall of the shower, water and tears mixing and flowing slowly down the drain. There had to be an answer and he had to find it. If he didn't, he would never get home.

CHAPTER 26

JAKE WAS SITTING ON the side of the bed in his boxer shorts, the phone pressed to his right ear. Percy Cole had called him twenty minutes ago. Percy, his good friend and long-time customer, had been given two tickets to the Sugar Bowl game , and now at five o'clock in the morning on the day of the game, he decided to use them. Being from Birmingham and a rabid Alabama fan, there was nothing else to do but be there in person. And Jake or one of his pilots was to fly him to New Orleans. It didn't matter to Jake that Percy was donating the second ticket to the lucky pilot that flew him there.

Jake was still irritated that Percy had intruded on his sound sleep. He wanted to ask Percy why he thought a rabid Razorback fan would want to fly to New Orleans to see the Tide play when he could cuddle up on the couch and watch his beloved Hogs in the Orange Bowl. But he was sure Percy could care less about his Arkansas Razorbacks.

Now, as he listened to the endless ringing of the phone, he could feel his neck and face getting redder by the second. Ed wasn't home. Where could he be at this time of night, Jake wondered? Out chasing some skirt, Jake surmised. After more than a dozen rings he hung up and sat there steaming. Steve couldn't fly yet. That left him or Lisa, and she was not about to go. Jake grunted and peered down to the floor between his legs. To top everything off, he couldn't find the cigar stub he had placed on the bedside table a few hours earlier.

"Ought to be asleep," he grumbled.

He dialed again. This time he got an answer on the fourth ring.

"Hello," came the sleepy voice.

"Have you seen Ed?" He knew it was a silly question when he asked it but he was still groggy and couldn't think of anything else to say.

"Daddy?"

"Of course it's me. Who'd you expect?"

"Nobody at this time of night." There was a pause. "It's five thirty in the morning, Daddy. Are you drunk?" She paused a second. "Why did you ask me if I had seen Ed?"

"Sorry about that. But I can't find him and now I've got to fly to New Orleans."

"To New Orleans in the middle of the night. Why?" All of a sudden there was a crash on Lisa's end of the phone. A moment later she came back on. "Sorry, Daddy. I knocked the phone off."

Jake had hardly noticed. "If you was a boy, it'd be you sittin' on the side of the bed in your skivvies tryin' to find your cigar."

Lisa squelched a giggle.

"I gotta take Percy Cole to the Sugar Bowl. I'm gonna transfer the office calls to your phone till I get back."

"How late will you be?"

"Dunno. Nine, ten, maybe midnight." His foot touched something familiar. "Maybe later," he added as he trapped the cigar stub between his toes and pulled it up to his hand.

"Be careful, Daddy."

"Hmff," he grunted and hung up. He stuck the stub in the corner of his mouth and wrinkled his nose. It tasted like dirty socks.

CHAPTER 27

IT WAS IMPOSSIBLE FOR Lisa to go back to sleep. Every position afforded only moments of drowsiness, before her eyes would be wide open again. At seven thirty she gave up and went into the kitchen to start the coffee. She was still in her housecoat when the phone rang an hour later.

"Hello."

"Ummm, you sound awfully good this morning, sugar."

Lisa frowned. "Good morning, Ed. What can I do for you?"

"You really want me to answer that?"

Lisa was disgusted. Ed was getting more and more bold every day. It was about time for her to talk to Jake about him, see if he couldn't put a stopper in the man's mouth. No, she decided, she would be the one to put the stopper in at the appropriate time. "What do you want, Ed?"

He realized he had gone a little too far. "Where's big Jake?"

"On a charter that you should have taken. Should I ask where you were at five thirty this morning when he was trying to call you?"

"Uh oh, was I being paged?"

"Daddy tried to reach you. Percy Cole decided at the last minute that he wanted to go to New Orleans to the Sugar Bowl. Daddy had to take him."

"Gosh, I hate that I missed that." Ed was being facetious. "When'll Jake be back?"

"Late tonight. Could be anywhere from nine till midnight." Lisa took a sip of coffee and set it back on the table.

"You goin' into the office today."

"No chance. I'm going to snuggle up right here on the couch and read."

"If you're feelin' chilly, I could come over and keep you company."

"Did you want something, Ed, or did you just call to annoy me?" She was poised to hang the phone up in his ear.

"Now don't get riled. I'm just horsin' around. I really called to see if the big boss cut them bonus checks. He said he was writin' them over the weekend."

"He did."

"And?"

"And they're in the safe where they'll stay until tomorrow."

Ed's voice got a touch softer. "I couldn't persuade you to take a drive out to the office and open that great big safe. I'll even pick you up and bring you right back to your cozy couch and book. Might even be persuaded to buy you lunch."

Lisa couldn't think of anything she would like to do less. "I'm sorry, Ed, but I'm here for the day. No side trips for me." The chance to turn him down delighted her.

"You sure about that now," Ed grunted, and his voice registered obvious disappointment.

"Very sure."

"Okay then. See you tomorrow."

~ ~ ~

When Steve got up that morning, the house was deserted. Sarah's bed had not been made and, from the den door, he could see that the bed in Nora's room was the same. The faint odor of ashes from the fireplace wafted lazily through the house. The odor had been there the night before but he was so tired from the drive back from Dallas that he hadn't put the smell and fireplace together.

The first thing he saw when he reached for the coffee pot was the note from Nora telling him to call Jake. On the bottom of that was another note that Nora had evidently written earlier in the morning. It read, "I have to go out until this afternoon. Sarah is at Mrs. Peterson's. She is going to her sister's this morning and Sarah is going with her." The note was unsigned.

Steve went to the dining room window and looked across at the house where Mrs. Peterson lived. Her car was not in the carport. The teakettle was singing and he went back into the kitchen and poured the hot water over the instant coffee. There was a list of phone numbers on the wall next to the phone. The day before he had noticed that Jake's was listed. He dialed and waited.

"Hello."

Steve was surprised by the woman's voice. "Is Mr. Carter there?"

There was a moment of silence before the girl answered. "Steve, is that you?"

"Yes." She knew him but he had no idea who she was.

"Oh, it's so good to hear your voice. I came to the hospital to see you but you were asleep. How are you now?"

"I'm good. Much better," he added. "I had a note to call Mr. Carter. Is he there?"

"No. Daddy had to take a charter to New Orleans. He didn't want to go but he couldn't find Ed and you aren't ready to fly yet."

Amen to that, Steve thought. Nor will I ever be.

"You should have heard him griping this morning."

"I should call him back later."

"Steve, are you all right? You don't sound like yourself." Her voice softened. "What's wrong?" She realized now what Jake had been trying to tell her about Steve. He really wasn't acting normal.

"Nothing." He was at a loss to know how he was supposed to act. But at least now he knew who the girl was, Jake's daughter, Lisa.

"Hey, it's me, Lisa. Talk to me, Steve."

"It's nothing," he hesitated for a moment before saying her name, "Lisa. I just haven't quite gotten things back together since the accident."

"You sure that's all?"

"Positive."

"All right, for now. But, I'll bet I know what Daddy called you about. He wrote the yearly bonus checks last night and left them in the safe. I'm sure he'd want you to have yours. If you'll meet me at the office, I'll get it for you."

"Sorry, but I'm without transportation. Nora's gone in the car and she won't be back until this afternoon."

"Is Sarah with you?"

"She's gone too."

"You're stuck there all by yourself?"

Steve wasn't sure what he read into her voice. "Afraid so."

"Then this would be a good time for you to get your check. I'll pick you up in thirty minutes. Be ready now."

"Wait a minute. I...." The phone was already disconnected from the other end.

~ ~ ~

For a few seconds he thought about redialing and stopping the girl before she could leave. But he thought better of that. At this point he needed to find out everything he could about Steve Pearce, this Steve Pearce. The girl and the place he was supposed to work might supply some answers. He was convinced that Nora would provide nothing but conflict.

Besides, this Lisa interested him. Her voice had been friendly and soft and even at one time in the conversation, sexy. She sounded no more than early to mid-twenties. For a fleeting second he wondered if he had more than a working relationship with her. The thought startled him, and for a second he actually felt guilty. Kathy was always there, just on the edge of every thought. There could be nothing between this girl and him. Of that he was sure.

Steve was still considering what possible connection he might have with Lisa Carter when the brown Corolla came racing down the street and turned quickly into the driveway. The engine was running when he stepped out the kitchen door and ambled toward the car. The inside of the car was warm and he settled beside the young woman and smiled.

"Hi," she said and touched his knee gently. "I've....we've

missed you."

Steve got the message. There was definite interest there. She was prettier than he imagined. And he thought, younger. No more than twenty-three or twenty-four. Her hand still rested lightly on his knee and he realized he had mixed emotions. The touch felt good but it also made him uncomfortable. It would be nice, he thought, if I knew how I was supposed to react now.

As if Lisa was reading his thoughts, she took her hand off his knee and grasped the steering wheel. A mixture of relief and regret engulfed him. The regret made him feel guilty again. It was as if Kathy were right there in the car with them.

"It's nice to be missed," he finally said.

More than you'll ever know, she thought. She put the car into reverse and backed into the street, then shoved the gear into drive and burned rubber up Dickson. At the highway, she stopped and looked toward Steve. His head was turned away from her, looking down the highway to the right. She was unaware that, while he was looking out the side window, his eyes were studying her reflection in the glass.

"How's Sarah?"

He turned back. "She's fine."

"I wanted to come see her, but Nora doesn't...." Nora Pearce didn't like her but she didn't want to say that to Steve. "I thought it best not to intrude," she finally said.

"I understand." And he really did. This short episode with Nora had been an unpleasant several days. Lisa turned left onto the highway, went a few hundred yards and turned left again on Gardner Lane. "How are you, Steve? Really, I mean?"

"The doctor says I'm going to be as good as new."

Ten minutes later they pulled into the parking lot next to the flight office. Lisa shook her head and pointed toward a lighted window.

"If Daddy had to write the utility checks himself, he'd be a little more conservative."

The front end of an old, yellow Nissan 280Z protruded from

the rear of the building. Steve took note of it and turned his attention back to Lisa.

"He never thinks about bills because he isn't involved in paying them. Ten years ago, he'd have bit his cigar into little pieces if someone had left a light on in the house. Believe me, I know from experience." She slipped out of the car and started toward the door where the light was visible. Steve noticed as he approached that the sign just above the door indicated that it was the pilot's lounge.

Inside he noticed that the next room, about twice the size of the lounge, was set up as a classroom. A dozen desks faced the back wall where a huge map of the United States hung. Circles on the map ran out every one hundred miles from Hot Springs. When they reached a thousand miles, the circles expanded to five hundred mile distances. A rolled-up movie screen hung above the map and a projector rested on a rolling table against the front wall. There was a chalkboard on the left wall that looked like it hadn't been washed in at least ten years. A bulletin board, with several aerial maps tacked to it, hung next to the chalkboard.

Lisa looked at Steve and smiled. "Daddy wants you to take over the ground school until you can get back in the air. You can make a little extra money and help him out too." She was still standing in the doorway that led from the classroom into the pilot's lounge.

Steve took in the lounge. An old, black leather couch was against one wall with a wooden magazine stand pushed against it at one end. Soft drink and candy machines sat side by side in one corner with a plugged in coffee pot on a windowsill to the left. A table and three straight chairs were in the middle of the room. There was a half-filled coffee cup on the table and, when Steve first saw it, he could have sworn steam was rising from it.

He started to mention it to Lisa but she had retrieved a sheet of paper off the floor and was tacking it up on the bulletin board. While she was doing that, he crossed to the table and felt the cup. It was warm.

"When did you say your father left?"

"Probably got in the air around seven or seven-thirty. Why?"

He nodded toward the cup. "This is still hot. Someone else have keys to the office?" He knew when he asked the question that it was a mistake. If he was the hot pilot they all thought he was, he would know the answer to that question already. He probably had a key himself.

Lisa gave him a quizzical look and glanced at her watch. "Over three hours. Not possible. Ed must have come by but I didn't see his car anywhere."

"A yellow 280Z?" It was the only car anywhere close to the building and only a guess.

"Did you see it?"

"It's parked behind the building."

She relaxed and stuck her hands into the pockets of her long leather coat. "He's probably in the hangar or up flying."

"Probably."

"Come on. Let's go into Daddy's office and get your check before Ed comes back." She seemed to be in a hurry now as she went through the classroom and into a smaller office. The room was windowless. They were halfway across the small office when Steve caught her arm. He put an index finger to his lips and they stopped and listened. Muffled laughter came from behind the door they were about to enter. Both of them glanced toward the bottom of the door where a faint light could be seen.

"Someone's in there," Steve whispered.

"It's Ed. I recognize his laugh," she whispered back.

"Maybe we better come back another time."

There was anger in Lisa's eyes. "What are they doing in Daddy's office? If they're...." She didn't finish but looked at Steve. "We need to go, Steve," she whispered. "Come on." She turned and caught his arm and began pulling him back toward the other room. As they passed into the classroom, the door to Jake's office opened. Nora, with a surprised Ed peering over her shoulder, was framed in the opening. The four of them stared wordlessly at each other for several seconds. It was Lisa who acted first. She closed the door between the classroom and the small office and looked up at

Steve with a somber expression.

"I didn't know, Steve. I'm sorry."

"I know you didn't. Come on. Let's go."

In the car and back on the highway, she reached over and put her hand on his leg just as she had earlier. This time she held it there and it rested heavier than before. "Do you want to come to my place for a little while?"

He shook his head. "Sarah will be home soon. I need to be there."

"We could pick her up and go get something to eat."

"And compound the problem. No, Lisa. Thanks, but I think I better go home now."

The drive back took longer than going. When Lisa pulled into the driveway and killed the engine, she turned toward him and laid her hands in her lap. He didn't make a move to get out and after a minute she put her hand on his. It was time to bare her soul.

"If I don't say this, I never will. And Daddy will probably kill me for doing it." He was still looking out the front window but when she spoke, he turned his head and looked into her eyes. "You have to know how I feel about you. I probably haven't hid it very well. Daddy says I should be ashamed and maybe I should. But nothing can change the way I feel. I think I've loved you from the first time I saw you." There were tears in her eyes.

"Lisa, don't." This was not the time he reasoned in his heart. There was too much Kathy in him. "There are things you don't know, things I don't know right now. And there's Sarah and my obligation to her."

"I know, but I had to say it, Steve. You're a decent man and I know there can never be anything between us as long as you're married to Nora. But, I had to be sure you knew." She faced the front and stared toward the carport. "I won't say anymore. I won't embarrass you or myself again. Just know that I'll be there if you need me." With that she turned the key and the Corolla came alive.

Steve got out of the car and came around to the driver's window. It was rolled down and he bent to look in at her. "I have things I have to get straightened out. I don't know what's going to happen. Until I do, I can't think of anything else, anyone else, only Sarah. You understand that, don't you?"

"Yes." A tear rolled down her cheek and she reached up with her right hand and wiped it away. A moment later she backed out onto the street. Steve was still standing in the middle of the driveway when the car turned onto the highway and disappeared from sight.

CHAPTER 28

THE HOSPITAL ROOM WAS cold, colder than it normally was, Kathy thought. It would be time for Ray to make his rounds in just a few minutes and she had to know. She couldn't tell if Steve was getting better or not. Ray said his physical condition was improving but he would give Kathy no indication of when he would wake up. Several times over the last few days an eerie sensation had come over her when she sat alone at night. It seemed as if she wasn't alone although no one else was in the room at the time. And it was during these times that the room seemed much colder than usual. Now it was that way again. It even seemed that a cold breeze was blowing down on her shoulders. But there were no vents in the ceiling, no reason for a breeze or a wind to descend on her at odd times. It was crazy.

She heard sounds in the hall and perked up as they came closer.

The door swung open and Ray stuck his head in. "Evening, Kathy?"

"Hello, Ray."

"Anything happening this evening with Steve?"

"He hasn't moved," Kathy whispered.

Ray pulled back the covers and studied Steve's left arm and chest. "Improving," he said quietly. Ray moved his fingers gently across the bruise under Steve's chin. He moved his head back and forth with his right hand while still pressing the protrusion under his chin. "Not much change here." Ray pulled the covers up over Steve's shoulders and stood staring down at his friend.

"How is he, Ray? How is he, really?"

Ray could hear and feel the distress in Kathy's voice. He moved around the bed and sat down in a chair opposite her. "Kathy, physically he's improving every day." He reached over and took both her hands in his. "You know how I feel about Steve. He's my best friend. If there is anything that can be done we're going to do it. If…when he wakes up he'll be fine. It's up to Steve now. He's got to come back to us."

"There's nothing that can be done for him?"

"We're doing everything we can."

Kathy squeezed Ray's hands. "I know you are," she whispered. "I just want my husband back." Tears were rolling down Kathy's cheeks now.

Ray sat there for several moments just holding her hands. After several seconds he squeezed back. "Kat, why don't you go home and get some real rest. You'll feel a lot better tomorrow. The nurses will watch him. I'll make sure of that. They'll call you if anything happens. Go home, Kathy. Go home and check on Tommy. He needs you right now just as much as Steve does."

She nodded. "I will, Ray."

Ray squeezed her hands again and got up. "I'll check on him again before I go home. Now, you get out of here."

Kathy nodded. "I will. I promise."

CHAPTER 29

STEVE HAD BEEN IN the living room since lunch, staring out the picture window and up Dickson Drive. Sarah was home from Mrs. Peterson's and sat in the middle of the floor coloring in the big yellow and black book. It looked amazingly like the one Kathy had bought Tommy the Saturday before the accident.

They had gone to Little Rock to finish their shopping and Kathy couldn't resist buying the book as an extra gift. Now, as he watched Sarah, he thought about Tommy. There had been no Tommy when he saw Kathy in Dallas yesterday. He and Kathy had never married and Tommy had never been born. He was a figment of the dream, not even real in this world. That was hard for him to digest. Steve pushed the recliner back and closed his eyes. He wasn't aware when Sarah got up and tiptoed through the den to her bedroom.

A light drizzle was beginning to patter softly against the picture window. The sound soothed and relaxed Steve's muscles just as Kathy's fingers had rubbed away the tension and anxiety so many times before. Exhaustion, not completely relieved by last night's sleep, reached down and enveloped him. Outside, a brisk wind was beginning to blow down out of the northwest as the promised cold front began to move through the Hot Springs area. For those who were awake, a low rumble of thunder could be heard in the distance. But Steve was unaware of anything around him.

~ ~ ~

Like he had as a child, he found himself falling through endless black space. And, as he fell, he could see those same groping hands reaching out in the darkness. As it had always been, he fell through their fingers as if there was no substance to them. The fall always ended the same way. A giant white feather bed was there to catch him. When he was a child, the dream ended and more than once he found himself awake and in a sweat.

But it was different this time. The feather bed was gone but the dream didn't end. He was in the hospital room again. His body was just below him, not more than an arm's length away. Kathy was there. And there was someone else. The other person, a man, seemed to be a blur. His back was to him and he was leaning over Kathy, saying something to her. Steve's eyes searched the room. Tommy was not there. But something else was. It was hovering over in that dark corner where he had seen it before, just floating there like a wisp of smoke. It seemed to be looking straight at him, pointing toward the body on the bed. But he couldn't be sure and he turned his attention back to Kathy.

She was crying and holding his hand, much the same as in the other dreams. Her mouth was moving and he strained to hear what she was saying. But he couldn't. The man that he couldn't distinguish before had moved behind her and turned so that Steve could see his face. It was Ray. Good old Ray. He must have given up that trip to the Bahamas and stayed to save one more life. Susan would not be happy with him.

And then, as if he had never been there, the man was gone and only Kathy and the body on the bed remained. He looked toward the dark corner. The apparition was still there, still seemingly pointing toward the body. Steve took his eyes from the dark corner and looked at Kathy again. He shouted her name but the only sound was the constant pounding of the rain on the hospital window.

"Daddy, Daddy, wake up, wake up!"

Steve sat up and the recliner came upright. For a moment he wasn't sure where he was. Lightning and thunder came all in one instant in the darkened room. Like in the dream, rain was beating furiously at the window, making it difficult to see the Peterson house across the street.

"Daddy, Daddy. I'm scared." Sarah was tugging at his arm, terror in her voice and tears flowing down her cheeks.

"I'm awake, honey. It's okay. Daddy's awake now."

Her small body was heaving when he lifted her gently into his lap. For a time she held tightly to his neck as he stroked her yellow hair. Finally, she pulled away and looked up in his eyes.

"I was so scared, Daddy."

"I know you were, honey. But there's nothing to be scared of. We're safe from the storm in here."

"It wasn't the storm," she said. She put her fingers to his lips and rubbed them back and forth. "You were screaming. I thought at first you were screaming at me." She rested her head against Steve's chest again. "But you weren't." She paused and looked into his eyes again. "Daddy, who's Kathy? Why were you screaming her name?"

Steve felt a chill as if the temperature in the room had suddenly dropped ten degrees. At the same time he felt chill bumps break out on Sarah's arms.

"I'm cold, Daddy."

"So am I, Sweetheart." He pulled her closer and began rocking in the recliner.

"Daddy, do I know Kathy?"

"No, dear. Daddy knew her a long time ago, a whole world ago, long before you."

"Is she dead, Daddy?"

Steve felt the chill again. Was his Kathy dead? And then he knew. To him she was. But his answer to Sarah was different. "No. But she lives very, very far away now."

"Will I ever meet her?"

"I'm afraid not, darling."

That seemed to satisfy her and she didn't pursue it any longer. Gradually, he felt the bumps on her arms go away, and after a few minutes she slipped from his lap and went back into the den. The sound of the television told him she had forgotten the incident.

Rain was still falling steadily, but the wind had died and the sudden storm had moved off to the southeast. It was getting dark outside and fog was beginning to settle in. Visibility was a little better than it was when the rain was beating down but he could still see only a half block up the street. When the Montego appeared suddenly it was like a phantom ship gliding silently through the mist.

Nora came in and stopped in the doorway that separated the kitchen from the living and dining rooms.

"I suppose I'm in for a tongue-lashing. Well, I can tell you right now, I'm in no mood for it."

Steve only turned the recliner back in the direction of the picture window without speaking.

She waited for nearly a minute before she spoke again. "Say something. Surely, you have something to say."

"Let's drop it, Nora. It isn't worth discussing."

"You mean I'm not worth discussing. Well, let me tell you something, Mr. High and Mighty, you aren't any prize either." Her voice seemed to be rising with every syllable.

"Sarah's in the den. She'll hear you," Steve said.

"Let her hear. If it wasn't for her, I wouldn't be stuck with ...." she gestured wildly at the ceiling. "...Sky King."

Steve walked to the door and closed it firmly. Then he brushed past Nora and returned to stare out the picture window. "Whatever happened to you and...." he started to say him, then realized he was the him or to her he was. "Whatever happened isn't Sarah's fault.

"I suppose it's mine. It's always been mine. If I hadn't shown up eight years ago, wagging her on my hip, you could have finished college, gotten your accounting degree. Don't think I don't know that you blame that on me."

"I don't blame you for anything. It takes two to create life. I knew the chance we were taking and so did you. We're paying for that mistake, both of us. But Sarah has never been part of that payment. She's the only decent thing in this mess." It hadn't taken him long to realize that he was in a loveless marriage even if he hadn't created it. And from what he was learning from Nora, Sarah's father had not created it either. And somehow, he knew this wasn't the first time they had this argument.

"Then maybe we need to call it a day. Maybe you need to leave. You can do it with my blessings," Nora growled.

"And Sarah?"

"What about her?"

"If I go, she goes."

Nora moved closer to him. He could see that she was seething. "Oh, no you don't. If you leave, you leave alone. Nobody's going to accuse me of throwing out my husband and my kid." Their eyes met and she put her hands on her hips and spat the words. "You'd like that to happen, wouldn't you? I can see the headlines now: "Mother throws husband and daughter out of house." Well, forget that. It isn't going to happen." She waited for a response.

"Then I stay," Steve said firmly.

"Well, just suit yourself. But I'll tell you one thing. It's gonna be different around here. I expect to have more freedom and that means you got the kid more than ever. And don't try to slip around and take her away from me. If you do, I'll see to it that you and that little snip, Lisa Carter, won't ever see her again."

"What's Miss Carter got to do with anything?"

Nora threw her head back and burst out laughing. "What's she got to do with anything? Don't play Sir Galahad with me. It won't work." Her laughter turned to a sneer. "What were you two doing at the airport today, taking flying lessons?"

"I've never given Lisa a second thought." At least I don't think I have until today. What Sarah's father has done, he didn't have any idea. But based on his conversation with Lisa, nothing had ever gone on between them.

Nora laughed again. "Oh, but that first thought was a doozy, wasn't it?"

"Let's just drop it, Nora. Nothing good can come of this."

"Ed told me about that little flirt. She's done everything but...."

"That's enough." Steve moved toward Nora and for a second

she thought he might hit her, but he brushed past her and went through the kitchen and den. He could still hear Nora's voice following him into the hall. But he wasn't concerned about her any longer. Sarah had evidently gone to her room and he was thankful for that. Her bedroom door was closed and the record player was going.

Even as loud as Nora had been shouting, it was possible Sarah had not heard most of the argument. He paused at the door and listened. The only sound was the music. He listened for another minute and when he didn't hear anything else, he turned left down the hall toward the guest bedroom, unaware that Sarah had curled up on the bed and was sobbing softly.

CHAPTER 30

BY CHOICE, STEVE MOVED all of his clothes into the guest bedroom. It had been just over twenty-four hours since he had seen Kathy and the memory of her still lingered. As he lay there in the darkness trying to piece together everything that had happened since the accident, he had that same premonition. Something was just in the back of his mind, something he had heard or read somewhere in the past. If he could just remember what it was.

He was getting drowsy, almost asleep. And then it hit him. He sat bolt upright in bed. The light had been turned on. In seconds he was out of the bed and into his robe. The answer was in the bookshelves in the living room. He hurried down the hall and slipped through the den to kneel in front of the shelves. His college annual was right where he had left it. The section with faculty pictures was near the front and he thumbed through them quickly looking for the man. He was not there. He didn't know why and then all of a sudden he did.

Doctor Carl Savage didn't teach at Ouachita. He was across the ravine at Henderson State. Of course, the class he had taken had been at Henderson. The two schools had an agreement. If a student had a conflict with classes he or she could cross the ravine, take that class and receive credit. Steve had been forced to do that in his senior year. And Carl Savage had been the instructor. Savage had explained a strange concept to his psychology class one spring day when Steve had found himself daydreaming about Kathy. At the time it had barely registered. But it was there in the back of his mind.

Steve dropped the annual on the couch and went into the kitchen. He was excited now, more so than he had been since the accident except for his brief encounter with Kathy. If what he remembered about Carl Savage's theory was true, then there just might be a way to.... He let the thought pass and picked up the phone. A moment later he had the information operator.

"What city, please?"

"Arkadelphia."

"What name?"

"Doctor Carl Savage."

"Thank you."

A moment later the familiar voice that reverberated all across the telephone lines came on.

"The number is...."

Steve listened and wrote. The voice repeated the number and he double-checked it. A moment later the connection was broken and he began dialing. With all but the last two numbers dialed, he glanced toward the kitchen window and then the clock. It was the middle of the night. Steve replaced the phone in its cradle and slumped into a chair.

"You wouldn't appreciate a two o'clock wake up call, would you Doctor Savage?" He flipped off the kitchen light and went back into the living room. It was quiet outside now. The storms of late afternoon had moved on, and when he turned off the living room light he could see stars breaking through the scattered clouds. He sat down in the recliner and let his mind drift back to that sunny, spring day and the lecture Carl Savage had given. If only he had paid more attention, he thought. Maybe he was on to something. Maybe. Steve closed his eyes and smiled. Maybe the light had come on.

At seven he got up from the recliner and tiptoed through the den into the hall. He glanced to the right. Nora's door was closed and, he assumed, locked. He opened Sarah's and peeked in. She was on her side resting peacefully with the stuffed animal nestled up under her chin.

He slipped into the bathroom and washed the sleep out of his eyes. When he was finished, he retraced his steps into the den and found the number he had scribbled on the front of the phone book just a few hours before. He dialed, pulled a chair from under the table and sat down. The phone rang three, four, five times before someone picked up.

He heard someone clear their throat and then a woman's voice. "Yes." She had been asleep.

"I'm sorry if I woke you. But could I speak to Doctor Savage, please?"

There was uncomfortable silence from the other end of the line. After what seemed like a minute but could only have been a few seconds, her voice, quiet and somber, came back on.

"Doctor Savage died two years ago." Without hesitating, she continued and her voice seemed to grow in strength. "I'm Mrs. Savage. Is there something I can do for you?"

Steve felt like a load of bricks had just fallen on his head. His ignorance of the situation had come across as insensitive.

"Mrs. Savage, I'm sorry. I didn't know. I was a student of your husband's about eight years ago and I just wanted to speak to him about something he said in class one day. Please accept an apology for my ignorance."

"Of course you didn't know and of course I accept your apology, although it wasn't necessary. But I repeat. Is there anything I can do for you?"

Steve was crestfallen. It was hard to focus on what the woman was saying. "I wish I could say yes, Mrs. Savage. I really do." His voice was nearly a whisper.

"Pardon," the old woman said.

"I'm sorry, Mrs. Savage. I seem to be talking to myself a lot these days. Please forgive the intrusion and accept my condolences. Doctor Savage was one of my favorite instructors." It was a lie. He barely remembered the man. But it might help her through another lonely day. If so, the lie was worth it.

"Might I ask your name, young man?"

"Oh, I am sorry, Mrs. Savage. I'm Steve Pearce and I live in Hot Springs. Again, I'm sorry for the intrusion."

"And again, Mr. Pearce, your apology, while not necessary, is well taken."

After another brief exchange, they said their goodbyes and Steve replaced the phone in its cradle. He leaned back in his chair and stared up at the ceiling. If only the good doctor was still alive. But he wasn't. And there was no record. And then he stopped. It was coming back to him now. In one of his lucid moments that spring day, the doctor did mention something about a letter. Steve grabbed the phone and dialed the Savage number again. It rang only twice this time before Cora Savage picked up.

"Yes." There was just a hint of impatience in her tone.

"Mrs. Savage. It's Steve Pearce again. I don't want to make a pest of myself, but you offered to help me if you could. Does that offer still stand?"

"Of course, Mr. Pearce."

"May I come down and visit with you this morning?"

She hesitated before answering. "I should think that would be all right."

He felt a surge of elation. "I can be in Arkadelphia in two hours if that's not too soon."

"That will be suitable." They said their goodbyes again and Steve hung up. He went into the hall and down to Nora's room. All was quiet. He retraced his steps and looked in on Sarah. She was the same. His body was tingling with excitement when he slipped under the warm shower. He was on the right track. For the first time he felt there was hope. It would start coming together now. He was sure of it.

Sarah was still asleep when he slipped out of the house just after eight. He had knocked softly on Nora's door when he was ready to leave but got no answer. So he wrote her a note and left it on the breakfast table. She would not be happy, but right now he didn't care as long as she didn't take it out on Sarah. His plans were to be at the Savage house before ten o'clock. According to

Cora Savage, her house was on a street that bordered the rear of the Henderson campus. Her husband had been able to walk to work every morning.

At nine thirty, he located the old wood frame house, which was right where the woman said it would be. And from his short memory of Carl Savage, it fit the man's personality perfectly. It had white, horizontal siding with a small front porch and a wooden swing with rusted chains. There were two front doors like many early twentieth century houses had. One generally led to a bedroom and the other to a living room. Cora Savage opened the one that led into the living room.

She was small, probably no more than five foot, with white hair pulled back into a bun on the back of her head. She wore a yellow dress that hung loosely around her waist, reminding Steve of a maternity dress a younger woman might have worn.

"Mr. Pearce?"

Steve nodded as Cora Savage pushed open the old wooden screen door and motioned him inside. "Mrs. Savage, let me apologize again for intruding. I was hoping...."

The woman shook her head. "No need for that. I'm only too happy for company. I don't see many young people anymore. At least not since Carl passed on." Her voice became subdued and Cora Savage looked toward the mantle and a picture of her husband and herself taken a number of years earlier. At second glance there were several pictures from early marriage to what Steve guessed was only shortly before the professor's death.

Cora Savage continued. "Carl used to have a lot of his students in for chats. They would visit till all hours. I didn't understand a lot of what they were saying but I enjoyed the company." She looked at Steve closely as if trying to recall his face. "I must say, I don't recall you. Were you ever here?"

"No, Mrs. Savage. I never was." Steve glanced toward a chair and the old woman's mouth opened slightly.

"I'm forgetting my manners. Do sit down, Mr. Pearce, and tell me what I can do for you."

Steve sank into the comfortable chair and leaned forward on his elbows. "I'm not sure you can do anything, Mrs. Savage. At this point I'm not sure anyone can." Steve hesitated, not sure just how much he should tell this woman. He didn't want her to think he was crazy, but if he was to get any help from her he would probably have to go all the way. She had seated herself on a couch just a few feet away and was intently studying his face.

"You're troubled. My Carl would have recognized it immediately."

"You're very perceptive," Steve said.

"Would you like to tell me what's wrong? Land sakes, I'm not my Carl and I'm sure I can't help but Carl always said that talking about a problem was the first step in setting things right." She turned her head toward the mantle and Steve could see the sadness in her eyes. "He was a very good listener."

Steve waited until she looked back his way. "It's difficult to know where to begin." Again he hesitated but this time Cora continued to meet his gaze. After a moment he began. He told her the whole story from the day of the accident, or as he now believed, two accidents at precisely the same time, until this morning. Cora Savage never blinked, never interrupted him. When he finished and slumped back in his chair he realized for the first time that he was soaked through to his underwear with perspiration.

When she realized he was finished, she got up and looked down at him. "I must fix us something to drink. Will you have hot tea or a soft drink? I have both."

"Whatever you're having." He needed something to replace the body fluids he had expended over the last half hour.

"Hot tea with just a squeeze of lemon for me." She started toward the back of the house. "I do have something cold if you prefer that."

"The hot tea sounds wonderful."

She disappeared through a back door and he got up and crossed the room to the mantle. For the first time he studied the pictures closely. Same Doctor Savage that he remembered. He located the one that most closely paralleled the time he would have been in the professor's class. He looked much the same, except a lot thinner. The man looked ill. Then he remembered.

The Carl Savage whose class he had attended was not this same Carl Savage. And then he wondered. Had this Carl Savage believed the same things that his Carl Savage had? Was it possible that Cora Savage was somewhere in the back of the house calling the police or whoever came to pick up crazy people like him? Steve didn't have to wait long for his answer. As if on cue, he was suddenly aware that she was standing next to his right shoulder.

"He was such a handsome man," she said proudly and handed Steve a cup of hot tea with a slice of lemon floating on top.

"Yes, he's just as I remember him."

Steve felt a few drops of hot tea slosh out of the cup and onto his fingers. He carefully placed the cup back in the saucer and retreated to his chair.

"You mentioned that Carl spoke to your class about a letter." She hesitated a moment and Steve could see that she was staring unseeingly into space. It seemed as if she was lost in her own thoughts, her mind fleeing back to events of the past. After several seconds, her eyes refocused and she smiled at Steve. "Please forgive me. I was recalling the letter, the one you referred to, and the trouble."

Steve sat the cup of tea on a side table and leaned forward. "The trouble," he repeated.

She sat back on the couch and seemed to sink deep into the cushion. In a matter of just a few minutes she seemed to have aged ten years. A slight tremor was building on her lower lip.

"Are you okay, Mrs. Savage?"

She nodded. "Yes. I'm fine."

"You aren't ill?"

"No." She smiled but Steve knew it was forced. "Memories," she said quietly. She closed her eyes for just a second. When she opened them this time the smile was real. "What you've told me has...." She hesitated and a tear ran down her cheek. "I just wish Carl could have been here today." Then, just as suddenly as the smile appeared, a frown creased her brow. "This, what you've told me, would be a cruel joke if it isn't true, Mr. Pearce. You haven't done that, have you?"

Steve was not surprised at her outburst. What he had told Cora Savage was hard for even him to believe. The woman had every right to question his intentions. He had to convince her that he wasn't lying. "Everything I've told you today is the truth, Mrs. Savage. I would never do anything like that."

The smile did not reappear. Instead she looked directly into Steve's eyes, still searching for the truth. "John Hubbard can be a heartless scoundrel. He's proved so in the past. If it hadn't been for him and his derision, Carl might still be...." The frown and accusing eyes softened and the smile returned. "Even he could not be so cruel as to haunt Carl's memory. I'm sorry for my distrust, Mr. Pearce. Please forgive an old woman's suspicions."

"I understand your feelings. But this John Hubbard. Who would he be?"

A psychologist. Well known. Learned. Arrogant." She took a sip of tea and as she moved it away from her mouth she said, "A man I shall always hate." She put the cup back in the saucer and leaned forward on the couch. "You must hear the whole story. It's directly related to your experience. Once you've heard, you must have a copy of the letter, the one Carl told you about in class."

"A copy."

Cora nodded. "The original is quite old. It's stored away in my lock box at the bank. Carl had it translated into English and made a number of copies. I'll give you one of those."

A tingle of excitement ran through Steve's body. It was his first break. He had found a friend, someone who believed him, someone with a vested interest. Cora's eyes narrowed as she began to relate the painful events.

"Four years ago," she began, "Carl made the decision to publish a paper based on the letter and his own research. He named it 'Parallel Realities.' The letter had fascinated him for many years, since that first time he was allowed to read it. The prospect of life

THE LEFT SIDE OF REALITY

existing within our very reach, life that we could never contact, haunted him for years."

"You mentioned research. What other evidence did he have besides the letter?"

Cora shook her head slowly. "Very little written on the subject and only then in a random, haphazard fashion. No, he had no hard evidence, as he called it. But he believed, how my Carl believed. So strongly did he believe, that he wrote to the village in France where the letter originated."

"And." Steve said.

"And he found that this doctor, this Doctor Genet, I believe his name was, had ancestors that still lived there."

"Was he able to communicate with them?"

"Yes. In a fashion. He would have it no other way than to pack a bag and go immediately to France. He was obsessed with his theory." She hesitated and took another sip of tea. "Where was I? Oh, yes. Carl went off to France that summer of 1994, and like the dutiful wife I am, I trotted along behind him. We were gone nearly two weeks. By the time we got back home, Carl had already begun to formulate the paper."

"Did he find more evidence in France?"

"Enough for Carl. Enough for his obsession to grow even more intense. It would be a major breakthrough, he said. A new world, a new experience was within reach. Somehow he was convinced that he and others could bridge the gap from this world to that other reality. The world was filled with brilliant minds. It was his duty to report what he had found and work would begin. They would embrace his theory as if it was their own."

She paused and her eyes moved to the mantle and that last picture before he died. It was the one where he had grown so thin. "My poor, naive Carl. How terribly wrong he was," she whispered. She seemed to retreat within herself and then she was back. "When he presented the paper, they laughed at him. Oh, not so that you could see it. But it was behind his back that they derided him. We both knew it. The loudest dissenter, the one that hurt him the most, was John Hubbard. Carl had been on several committees with him and counted him as a friend. He trusted John Hubbard and allowed him to read the paper before it was presented. The man sent Carl's paper back by messenger with only a stick-on note. The only comment on the note was the word 'Interesting.' But after Carl read his paper, John Hubbard had much more to say. He called Carl an old fool who had outlived his time. It destroyed my Carl."

Tears formed in her eyes and began to slowly roll down her cheeks. She took a handkerchief and brushed them away. "The conference was in St. Louis. By the time we arrived back in Arkadelphia, the news had reached here and the laughter had already begun."

"I'm truly sorry, Mrs. Savage."

"Yes. So am I." She reached for the teacup and took a long sip.

"You said there was other evidence in France."

Cora replaced the cup and nodded. "Yes, a little." She wiped her mouth with a napkin and continued. "It seems the French doctor kept a diary. Much of what he said in the letter was repeated in the diary. It simply confirmed the letter. Until we saw the diary, we could only assume the letter was authentic. But Carl was not satisfied. He took great pains to compare the handwriting. He swore that the same person wrote both the diary and the letter. He compared and found that the events and dates matched. Once he was convinced that the letter was authentic, no one could have stopped him."

"Did he continue teaching?"

Her eyes narrowed and she was in the past again. "No," she finally said. "I encouraged him to but he presented his resignation before the fall semester began." She bit her lip and the tears formed again. "In less than two years, without his work or his students, he was dead." Her words were barely audible.

Steve could only sit there watching her tremble. After a few minutes she looked up and said, "You must have the letter. I'll be back shortly."

She was gone for five minutes. When she returned, she had a

brown manila envelope in her hand. "It's in here." She reached in and pulled out several sheets of paper. "This is a copy but I assure you it's the same as the original to the very letter." She showed it to Steve. "The only thing different from the original is that it's been translated into English."

Steve shook his head. "I don't know what to say."

"Say nothing. Take it and use it as you need. My only wish is that it never leaves your hand. Carl's memory has been besmirched enough already. May I count on your discretion?"

"Yes."

"Would you care to read it before you go. You may still take it with you."

Steve shook his head. "I've taken too much of your time already."

"Nonsense. I have very few visitors these days, an occasional student, a colleague of Carl's now and then. You have been a shining light in my day."

Steve took her hand and felt the tremble again. She seemed about to cry. "I don't know how to thank you, Mrs. Savage. I feel like I've caused you a great deal of anguish. I truly wish I hadn't done that."

"On the contrary, you've given me renewed faith in Carl. Someday, I hope, before I depart this world, Carl Savage will be exonerated. The John Hubbards will be forced to admit his genius. No, young man, you've not hurt me." His hand was still holding hers and she squeezed it and held it to her cheek. "Bless you." She looked at him for a moment. "And may you find your way home and back to your Kathy and Tommy."

Steve put his arms around the little woman and the tingle he felt earlier returned. He held her for just a moment, then gave her one last squeeze and went out to the car. He dropped the envelope on the seat and glanced back toward the house. She was standing just outside the screen door, the fragile body framed by the opening. Cora was smiling now and the extra years that were etched on her face a short time ago seemed to have faded away.

CHAPTER 31

FRIDAY MORNING SARAH WOKE up with a hundred and two degree temperature. Since their confrontation on Monday and his return from Arkadelphia, Nora had left all cooking and caring for Sarah up to Steve. He was giving Sarah two children's Tylenol for the fever when Nora came down the hall and glanced casually into the bedroom.

"She's burning up," he said quietly.

Nora came in and laid her hand on Sarah's forehead. The small blue eyes were dull and listless.

"Is your throat sore?" Nora asked.

Sarah nodded.

"It happens every winter. Nothing new. You know that. Just keep giving her the Tylenol every four hours. She'll be all right."

"Are you going out again?" Steve asked.

"I am. I don't know when I'll be back."

"I'll need the car if Sarah has to go to the doctor."

"She won't. Just keep the pills handy." Nora turned and left the room without another word. A moment later Steve heard the kitchen door slam and there was silence.

Sarah looked up at her father with questioning eyes. "Daddy, is Mommy mad at me because I'm sick?"

Steve brushed the hair back out of his daughter's eyes and smiled. "No, honey. She isn't angry with you. She just isn't herself right now." He bent and put his lips to her hot, dry forehead. There was no sweat yet. If the fever didn't break in the next two hours, he would call the doctor. "Close your eyes and try to sleep. You'll feel better soon. You'll see."

He sat on the side of the bed until her eyes closed and her breathing became even, then slipped out of the room and into the den. The night before, the TV news anchor had predicted an arctic cold front would move through central Arkansas sometime during the morning. As he fed several oak logs into the fireplace, he could see the first indication out the window. It was beginning to look like the same kind of day as that Saturday before Christmas.

Steve checked on Sarah every twenty to thirty minutes, and before two hours had elapsed the sweat began to pop out on her forehead. Just after noon he took her temperature and it was just below a hundred. She wanted to come into the den where he was so he made her a bed on the couch and switched on the television. Her appetite was beginning to return and he found a can of chicken soup in the cabinet and had her a hot lunch by one o'clock. She spent the day on the couch, perfectly happy and feeling better.

Steve retrieved the letter again and read it over half a dozen times. He couldn't find anything that would help him "find his way home," as Cora Savage had put it. He was beginning to think this might be his home. And his only shining light here was Sarah. She had found her way into his heart. When he thought about anyone taking Tommy's place, though, he felt guilty.

~ ~ ~

The first day out of the hospital, Steve had found a small fireproof safe in the master bedroom closet behind his clothes. He checked his key ring and found that the smallest key on the ring fit the safe. When he got back from his visit with Cora Savage he had placed the letter there for safekeeping. Now he returned the letter to the safe and went back into the den. It was two o'clock and when he checked Sarah, her temperature had dropped to ninety-nine. It was nearly normal. It showed in her conduct. She was much more active and was sitting up on the couch watching television and coloring. Nora was right. The pills worked.

He dropped another log on the fire and stoked it until he had a warm blaze. Out the back window, he could see several inches of snow already on the ground. And Nora was not home. In spite of everything, he was beginning to worry about her. The accident had given him a new appreciation of what could happen on a day like this.

~ ~ ~

Mark Hayes was on the last twelve hours of his forty-eight hour shift at the south Hot Springs unit of the fire department. Ever since morning, he had watched the falling snow with concern. His worst day ever was one just like this last February. He had been a fireman for six years and seen a lot of destruction and a few deaths. Every fire had taken a little piece of him. But when someone died, the hurt shook him to the bone. The one last February had taken a massive chunk and left him shaken for weeks. Even now he could think about it and feel tears forming in his eyes.

Snow had been falling that February evening. It was just past seven when the call came. A converted duplex in the Albert Pike area was ablaze. When they arrived, the entire west side of the house was engulfed in flames. A woman, in her mid-thirties, was being restrained by neighbors. Her six-year-old son had been left inside while she ran to the grocery store for cigarettes. Mark, along with Thad Young, broke in a door on the east side of the house and began to work their way through the smoke-filled rooms. They found the boy in a back bedroom, seemingly untouched by the flames. When Mark picked him up his eyes opened and he screamed.

"I hurt." It was all he said, but for Mark it was enough. They had found him in time, or so he thought.

Outside, he carried the child to the ambulance and watched as the EMTs administered oxygen. The child's eyes were closed again and he wasn't moving. The technician checked his pulse. They couldn't find one. They were about to begin CPR when one of the EMTs noticed something black under the child's shoulder. They carefully turned him on his side. When they did, they discovered why the boy was hurting. The whole of his back was charred black. Some of his bones, blackened by the flames, were exposed. The boy had probably died in his arms on the way out of the house. It was all he could do to control himself until he could retreat behind the fire truck. He lost his dinner that night and it took a long time for food to taste right again.

The next day they attempted to piece together what had happened. The mother had left the boy alone in the house while she ran quickly to the store. Because of the cold, she had left a small gas heater burning in the bathroom. The boy was wearing a pair of cotton pajamas. It was thought he must have backed up against the stove and caught himself on fire. Then, while running through the house in an attempt to find relief from the flames, he touched off the main blaze. By the time the boy reached the bedroom and collapsed, the flames had destroyed his back. Mark shuddered. It was a night just like this.

~ ~ ~

The sound of a key in the carport door woke Steve up. He had fallen asleep on the den couch with the television on. As Nora entered the back door, he sat up and glanced at his watch. He had been asleep nearly two hours.

"How's Sarah?" She stopped at the door leading to the hall.

"Her temperature was nearly normal when I put her to bed at eight. She still had a sore throat, but I think she'll be all right now."

Nora nodded and disappeared into the hall. A few minutes later she was back, dressed in a long red nylon robe that hung a couple of inches off the floor. She grabbed two logs, pitched them against the back wall of the fireplace, and began working on the fire. It was starting back up but she wasn't satisfied.

"Hand me those newspapers on the table."

"You don't need to do that. It's hot. It's already beginning to catch," Steve said.

She ignored him and gathered the papers herself. In less than a minute the fire was roaring.

He came up close behind her while she was stoking the fire. When she turned to face him, the heavy odor of liquor was on her breath. "Something?" she asked with a glare.

"You've got a pretty good blaze going. Can you handle it?"

"Don't be ridiculous. Of course I can."

Steve sighed. Nora was drunk but he knew arguing with her would be a lost cause. "I'm going to bed then. I'll look in on Sarah. Will you check her before you go to bed?"

"Yes," she muttered. Her tongue seemed too big for her mouth and her speech was slurred. She waved toward the hall. "Go to bed and give me some peace." She shoved the wire screen in place and stalked into the kitchen.

Sarah was cool when Steve touched her forehead. The fever had been down since the late afternoon, five hours at least. But, if Sarah was anything like Tommy, the fever could rise again during the night. He would check her every couple of hours.

Steve went into the bedroom and turned off the light. The drapes were closed but even before he opened them, he knew the snow was still coming down. Five or six inches were already on the ground. He left the drapes open and sat down in the old recliner that was just to the right of the foot of the bed. It was strange how imagination worked. As he sat down he could have sworn he saw Kathy's reflection in the glass. But it wasn't there now.

He pushed the recliner back and closed his eyes. Despite the fact that he had slept for two hours on the couch, he still found that his eyelids were heavy. In minutes he was dozing. It was sometime later that something woke him, some sound that wasn't normal in the house. He wasn't sure what it was but he listened to see if it would come again. And there it was. Sarah was coughing.

He pushed the recliner back to a sitting position and rubbed his hand across his forehead. His nose was stinging and tears were in his eyes. Swallowing hurt his throat. Another loud burst of coughing from Sarah's bedroom and he was on his feet. Something was wrong. The acrid smell of smoke hit him as soon as he was on his feet.

He flipped the light switch but nothing happened. His door was closed and he reached for the handle to open it. But he hesitated. Something he remembered from a long time ago stopped him. His hand groped for the wooden door panel. It was cool to the touch, safe to open. Heavy gray smoke enveloped him as soon as he opened the door. Nothing was visible in the hall. But he could hear Sarah crying. He reached out for the wall and began moving slowly down the hall toward her room. The door to the den was on his right and Sarah's room on his left.

It was difficult to breathe now and he dropped to his knees and got his head as low as possible. Tears were running furiously down his cheeks, blurring any vision he might have had. After he crawled a few feet he began to feel the heat. It became intense as he reached Sarah's door. If he was right, her door would be cool. The fire should be in the den, from the fireplace. Nora had let it get away. He touched Sarah's door. It was cool and he threw it open and crawled in. The coughing was coming from the bed.

"Sarah, where are you!"

At first, all he heard was a cough. Then he heard the slight whimper of a voice. "Here, Daddy. I'm on the bed."

Steve found her quickly. She was sitting up with her hands clenched tightly over her mouth.

"Get off the bed, honey. Get off and get just as low to the floor as you can. The smoke isn't as bad down here. And take hold of Daddy's arm."

She did as Steve said. The window was their only escape and it had to be broken. The chalkboard had to be between him and the window. Once Sarah was latched onto his arm, he crawled quickly to where he thought it ought to be. "Let go of Daddy for just a second, Sarah. I'm going to break the window." He grabbed the chalkboard, got up and swung it hard into the aluminum and glass panel. It shattered. He began swinging it back and forth at the glass and aluminum until he had a passage. Then he gathered

Sarah up in his arms and dropped her through the hole to the snow-covered ground below.

"Sarah," he yelled, "can you hear me?" The sound of the roof caving in somewhere behind him almost obscured his voice.

She was still coughing but she nodded and the white background of snow allowed him to see her.

"Run to Mrs. Peterson's. Tell her to call the fire department. Tell them our house in on fire. Hurry!"

Steve watched until she disappeared around the front of the house. The few seconds his head was out the window had helped clear his eyes. His throat was still burning but he had stopped coughing momentarily. He grabbed for the bed and found Sarah's blanket. He needed something to wrap around his head, especially his mouth. The blanket covered everything but his eyes. They were already beginning to water again as he made his way back across Sarah's room and into the hall.

Only smoke had reached this side of the house. The fire seemed to be contained in the kitchen and den area. But it wouldn't stay there long. He had only a few precious seconds to find Nora. He made his way to the left toward the back bedroom where he expected Nora would be. Her door was ajar. She always closed it when she went to bed.

"Nora, are you in here?" He called.

There was no answer. He felt his way to the bed. She wasn't there. He had to drop to his knees again. The smoke was overpowering. He crawled back down the hall to the den door and touched the knob. It was impossible to grasp. The blanket from Sarah's bed had given him some relief and he took a part of it and wrapped it around the knob. The heat still penetrated but he was able to hold on to it. He got to his feet, turned the knob and pushed the door. It didn't move. Something was against it. He put his shoulder against it and moved it slightly.

Flames and heat shot around the narrow opening, driving him back against the wall next to Sarah's door. The flames from the den had caught his shirt on fire and he used the blanket to smother it.

Now his lungs seemed to be on fire and his eyes were burning so bad he couldn't see. He started to move to his right, then realized Sarah's door was to his left. He flailed with his left hand until he found the doorway and stumbled through. He began groping for anything that would give him an indication of where he was.

The blanket that had protected his head and mouth was down around his waist. It dropped from his grasp and tangled around his feet. He began to stumble forward toward where he knew Sarah's bed was. He lost his balance and reached out for anything to break his fall. His hands brushed the footboard of the bed but didn't get a firm grip. The full weight of his body, his neck and throat leading the way, came down on the footboard with tremendous force. It was like a massive karate chop to the Adam's apple.

For a moment, he thought he would pass out, but he pushed away from the bed and regained his knees. The window was just a few feet away now and he struggled toward it. The flames were through the den door now and he could feel the oppressive heat licking at the soles of his feet as he crawled toward the window. He reached for the windowsill and somehow managed to pull himself up to the jagged opening. Glass was digging into his hands as he pulled his upper body through the opening. Jagged shards of glass cut into his stomach and chest as he worked himself through the hole. His upper body was overbalanced now and sheer weight drug his legs up and through the opening. He heard a scream, not realizing it was him, as he fell. It was strange but he never felt himself hit the snow. He was conscious, somewhere in a black void, or at least he thought he was.

CHAPTER 32

LISA'S FIRST THOUGHT WHEN she heard the phone ringing was not *again, tell me it's a dream*. It was no dream and she reached out and grabbed the receiver roughly. "Hello."

Jake's voice screamed at her from the other end of the line. "Get up and get your clothes on. Steve's house just burned down. They've taken him and the kid to the hospital."

She was already out of bed, the receiver tucked under her right ear as she slid the gown up over her head. "Are they all right, Dad?"

"Don't know. I'll pick you up in five minutes. Be ready." The line went dead before she could reply.

She slipped on slacks and a sweater and dropped to her knees to locate the shoes that she had kicked under the bed earlier. In less than five minutes she was hurrying down the stairs, pulling the heavy leather coat on as she did. Jake's old truck was pulling up as she came out.

Lisa hardly felt the cold as she crunched through the snow and settled in the cab next to Jake. "What happened?"

He shoved the gearshift into drive and slid away from the curb. "Ain't sure. Some old gal named Peterson called. Said she knew Steve worked for me and thought I should know. Sometime around midnight his kid comes beatin' on her door, yellin' "Fire!" The old gal called the fire department and ambulance." He hesitated and glanced toward Lisa. "Said Steve took a lot of smoke. Thought she heard a fireman say 'maybe too much.'"

Lisa's body went rigid and Jake reached over and patted her knee. "Take it easy, honey."

"I'm okay." She was silent for a second. "What about Nora?"

Jake shook his head. "Don't know." The cigar stub protruded from the middle of his mouth, clenched tightly between his teeth.

~ ~ ~

It was an hour after they arrived before Mark Hayes and Ron Ballanger made their way through what remained of the front door. By that time the inside was gutted and portions of the ceiling over the living room and den had caved in, leaving gaping holes that gave entrance to the still fluttering snowflakes. The bedroom area had been the last to catch fire, but the damage was complete there, too. The sheetrock on the ceiling of the guest bathroom was drooping from the weight of the water and seemed ready to let go any second. Tremendous heat had shattered the large plate glass mirror that hung over the sink and dressing table. In the hall, ceiling tiles had let go in various places, allowing charred insulation to slip through the holes. It gave the impression of moss hanging from the huge cypress trees that infested the southern swamps.

"A bad one," Ron said as he moved through the living room door into what was left of the den.

Mark flashed his light back and forth across the blackened furniture toward the bookshelves and their charred remains.

"Check the other side of the bookcases," Mark said.

While Ron worked his way around the smoldering debris, Mark stepped gingerly into the den and flashed his light toward the fireplace. Brick had fallen away just to the left, leaving a hole in the outer wall. The falling flakes in his beam reminded him of what he saw that night as he carried the boy out of the Albert Pike house. He pushed that out of his mind and let the beam run down the ruined fireplace to where several charred logs still lay on the andirons. The absence of a screen struck him immediately.

He moved the light back and forth until he found the remains of the screen melted into the leg of what used to be a small metal breakfast table. He worked the beam of light back across the floor toward his feet. A gooey mass of melted plastic lay just a couple of feet from the ruined fireplace. It was melted around another charred log.

Ron was at his shoulder. "What's left of an old bean bag chair," he said. "That log must have rolled out and touched off the fire."

Mark nodded his head. "Could be." He stepped over the rubble and examined the kitchen. Except for a portion of the ceiling that had fallen through, it seemed less cluttered than the living room and den.

On the opposite side of the den, Ron was moving his light back and forth over a heap of ceiling tile, insulation and studding that had collapsed and wedged against the door that led to the hall and bedroom area. The beam stopped on a small piece of what looked to be the remains of a woman's slipper. He reached down to pick it up and it came apart in his gloved hand.

"Whatcha got?" Mark asked.

"Woman's slipper, I think."

Together, they flashed back and forth over the mass of rubble. The third time across, Mark stopped his beam and held it steady on what looked to be the end of a broom handle.

"Pull away some of that lumber and insulation."

Ron switched off his light and stepped into Mark's beam. The insulation came away in gobs, exposing a blackened pile of what was once ceiling beams. He was struggling with one that was still smoking when Mark stepped close and pointed the light down into the mess. He nearly gagged. Ron's eyes were following Mark's beam and he threw his hands to his mouth and stumbled into the living room. The retching came moments later.

At the sound of Ron's discomfort, Mark moved away from the sight. The bile was building in his stomach, rushing up into his throat until he could hold it no longer. He poured his guts out on the floor for nearly a minute before he could regain control. When he was finished, he turned to see Ron still spitting out the rotten taste.

"Better get Cap."

Ron turned. "The woman?"

"Probably. What's left of her anyway."

CHAPTER 33

JAKE AND LISA HAD been watching a parade of nurses scurry in and out of the emergency room for over an hour. Most of that time Lisa had spent pacing the corridor while Jake leaned against the wall chewing untiringly on the cigar. Twice he had tramped down the corridor to a silver ashtray on a stand to clear a stream of saliva and tobacco juice from his throat.

"What time is it, Daddy?"

"You done asked me that a dozen times in the last hour."

"Daddy!"

Jake glanced at the watch on his right wrist. "Four forty-five."

"Why don't they tell us something?"

"They will in time. You ain't doin' no good here. Why don't you go into the waiting room and get some sleep? I'll call you if anything happens."

"I can't. I'm too nervous to do anything but pace." She was about to say something else when the big nurse they had seen at the reception desk approached. "Maybe she'll know something." Lisa stepped toward the woman.

As if the woman had read Lisa's mind, she shook her head. "Not yet, Miss. The doctor will be out in a little while. He'll be able to tell you something then." She gave Jake a faint smile, pushed open the emergency room door and disappeared inside.

Lisa's shoulders slumped and she turned to Jake in frustration. He only turned his head to one side and raised his eyebrows.

It was another ten minutes before the door opened again. This time Doctor Banks came out.

Jake pushed away from the wall and confronted the man. "Doc?"

"Ah, Mr. Carter. Good to see you again."

Lisa stepped shoulder to shoulder with her father and the doctor studied her for a moment.

"My daughter, Lisa, Doc."

"Miss...." He paused.

"Carter, doctor, Lisa Carter," she said.

"Miss Carter."

"How are they, doctor?"

"The child is fine. She inhaled some smoke, but she's resting comfortably. We're going to keep her overnight to monitor her condition."

Ted Banks paused, giving Lisa an opportunity to press on.

"And Steve, Mr. Pearce. How is he?"

"That's another matter. We had quite a time there for awhile. Thought we lost him once but he rejoined us about an hour ago, just about four a.m." Ted Banks paused, thinking about the events of the past hour, the absence of a pulse when he had arrived at the emergency room and then all of a sudden the man had started breathing again. He always marveled at how a patient could be on the verge of death and all of a sudden come back. And then there was what the man said. That puzzled him. "I think, now mind you, I said I think, he'll be all right in a few days if there are no complications."

Lisa took her eyes off the doctor and looked toward the door. "Can we see Steve and Sarah?"

"The child, yes. I prefer Mr. Pearce get all the rest he can. But I expect him to make a full recovery." He saw Lisa pucker her lips. "Tell you what. In about fifteen minutes they'll be bringing him out of emergency and transporting him to ICU. You can't go up there with him tonight, but there's no reason why you can't accompany him to the elevator at the end of the hall. And tomorrow you'll be able to visit him in ICU. The child has already been taken to a room."

"The wife, Doc," Jake said. "Have they found her yet? Does

she know about Steve and the girl?"

Ted Banks frowned and folded his arms across his chest. "I assumed you already knew."

"What?" Lisa asked. Already her hand was moving up to her heart.

"Are you close friends, Miss Carter?"

"Only an acquaintance."

"I'm sorry. We received word a few minutes ago. The firemen found someone in the house they think was a woman. The body was burned beyond recognition, but they assume it's Mrs. Pearce. I'm sorry."

Lisa's arms and legs felt rubbery and she was thankful for her father's arm as it slipped around her waist to steady her.

"You all right, baby?"

"Yes, Daddy." For extra support, she put her arm around his shoulder. "Doctor, do they know about Nora—Steve and Sarah, I mean?"

"No, neither one of them is up to that yet. And it might be best if a friend or relative is present when they're told. Of course, Mr. Pearce needs to be told first and then he can make the decision about how to tell the child. But, of course, they don't know for sure if the body belongs to the wife. You understand we must be sure about that."

"Sure, Doc," Jake said. "We understand. But, you said the kid could get out in the morning. Where'll she go, Doc?"

Before Ted could answer, Lisa intervened. "She can go home with me until Steve is able to take care of her." She looked at Jake for support. "I have plenty of room, don't I, Daddy?"

"You sure you're up to that, baby?"

"Yes, Daddy, I am. Sarah needs to be with someone who knows her and cares about her."

"How 'bout that, Doc?"

Doctor Banks nodded. "If Mr. Pearce agrees, I'm sure that will be fine."

He began to walk away from them, then stopped. "Funny thing

Mr. Pearce said when he first regained consciousness."

"Yeah." Jake took out the cigar and watched the doctor roll his eyes toward the ceiling.

"Said it twice."

"Said what, Doc?"

"He said, 'Tell Jake it was ice, ice on the wings. Couldn't keep it in the air.'"

Jake glanced toward Lisa, then back to the doctor. "That all, Doc?"

"No. He said one other thing. Really strange. He was delirious, of course, but he kept asking me if he'd be home for Christmas. It was as if he'd just woke up from the plane crash and the last two weeks had never happened."

Ted looked from Jake to Lisa for a response. When he didn't get one, he turned and continued down the corridor, leaving the two of them staring at his back. A few minutes later the emergency room door swung open and they rolled Steve out. For a time it erased all thoughts of Ted Bank's parting words.

CHAPTER 34

IT WAS JUST AFTER four a.m. when the young nurses aide finished changing the sheets in room 308. Out of habit, she stopped at the doorway to 310 and glanced in at the young man. His condition had not changed since she began her duty on the floor ten days earlier. So young and handsome, she thought. But, completely dependent. In an effort to guard against bedsores, she had helped turn him several times. He had been in the coma for two weeks and she had heard one of the older nurses say that he might never get better. What a shame, she thought.

She was about to move on down the hall when a rattling at the window caused her to glance that way. The wind was increasing, blowing the few remaining flakes horizontally past the glass. She started across the room to close the curtain, tiptoeing as she always did when a patient was sleeping. In this case she wasn't sure why she was tiptoeing. The man needed to wake up.

As she was passing the foot of the bed she found that someone had left the handle that was used to raise and lower the patient's head protruding from the metal frame. The young aide caught her right leg on it and lost her balance for a moment before grabbing the bed for support. The pain just below her knee was sharp, and when she bent to rub it there was a tear in her stockings and a damp spot underneath.

"Darn," she fussed. "Darn, darn, darn, another pair of panty hose ruined." A slight red smudge appeared on her fingers when she held them up and examined them in the light from the hall. She snapped the handle back under the bed and stood up. The pain was diminishing quickly but she still limped when she started toward the lighted hall.

Something, a sound or movement, she wasn't sure what, caused her to turn and look toward the head of the bed. Something was different. His head seemed to be turned toward her. She went around to the right side of the bed and bent over in the half-light to see his face better. As she did, she straightened up quickly. Only her hand, leaping quickly to her mouth, stifled the gasp.

~ ~ ~

Mary Strange heard the shuffling sounds of running feet from her desk at the third floor nurses' station. When she got up and leaned over the counter toward the noise, the young aide was on her before she knew it.

"Mary!" The girl was breathless.

The head nurse came around the counter and caught the girl in full stride. "Calm yourself, Millie. What's wrong?"

"He opened his eyes! Just now! I was in there! He opened his eyes and looked straight up at me!"

"Who?"

"Room 310!"

Mary turned toward Twyla Jackson. The other nurse had approached from the opposite end of the hall and was listening intently.

"You sure, Millie?"

"Yes, ma'am, I'm sure. He was awake."

"Why didn't you press the call button?" Mary was in motion now. "Twyla, look up Doctor Philpot's number and stand by. I'll send back word by Millie. Come on, girl."

It was only a matter of seconds before Mary was bending over Steve. She took one quick glance and turned to the young aide. "Millie, tell Twyla to call Doctor Philpot and tell him to come running. Tell her to tell him that Mr. Pearce in 310 is with us again. Hurry, Millie."

"Yes, ma'am," the girl said and was gone.

~ ~ ~

The emergency appendectomy had kept Ray out past midnight. By the time he had showered and collapsed into bed, it was half past one in the morning. Now, barely forty minutes in bed and off his feet, he was just beginning to doze when the phone rang. He woke just as the second ring ended and fumbled in the darkness until he found the lamp.

Susan raised on one elbow and yawned. "I'll get it, Ray."

"Go back to sleep. At this time of night, it's got to be an emergency of some kind." He threw his legs out of bed and reached for the phone. "I'll end up having to talk anyway." He lifted the phone from its cradle. "Doctor Philpot."

"Doctor, this is nurse Twyla Jackson at the third floor nurses' station."

"Yes, Miss Jackson," he said as he felt Susan turn over and press her body to his back.

"Doctor, Mr. Pearce in 310 has regained consciousness."

"Say that again, Miss Jackson."

"Mr. Pearce has regained consciousness, doctor."

"Are you sure?"

"Yes, sir. Mary Strange is with him now."

Ray was already on his feet, stretching the phone cord to its limits as he moved toward his closet. "Tell her to stay with him. I'll be there in fifteen minutes." He started to hang up, then put the phone back to his ear. "Nurse, call Mrs. Pearce. I sent her home to get some rest. You have her number on Steve's, Mr. Pearce's chart. Tell her to come back to the hospital immediately."

"Shall I tell her why, doctor?"

"Tell her there's been a change in her husband's condition and it might be for the better. Got that?"

"Yes, sir."

Ray hung up and tossed the phone back on the bed. "Hang

that up, Susan."

She was propped on her right elbow. "Is it Steve?"

"By all that's holy," he mumbled." He didn't finish.

"Ray, tell me what happened."

He was zipping his pants. "Mary Strange says that Steve woke up. Just like that." He slipped on his shoes and tied them quickly. "Gotta go, Susan. Go back to sleep."

"Will you call me as soon as you know something?"

"Wake you up?"

"Yes, I want to know."

He nodded and turned out the light. A moment later Susan heard the bedroom door open, then close.

~ ~ ~

It was only the second night since the accident that Kathy had gone home. She didn't want to but Ray had insisted. The first time had been a week ago tonight. Tommy had come down with a high fever and she had come home that night because he was crying for her. The next day the fever broke and she went back to the hospital and had not been home again until tonight. She couldn't sleep that first night and she couldn't sleep tonight. Just past midnight she got up and tiptoed down the steps, past Tommy's room and the guest room her mother was using. She was sitting in Steve's favorite chair, the old brown recliner they had bought that first year of marriage. Somehow, in the old chair, she felt closer to him. She pulled the green afghan tight around her shoulders and shifted her body into a more comfortable position. After an hour, her legs had begun to ache from being doubled beneath her.

As hard as she tried, she couldn't block out what Ray had told her a few days ago. The coma, he said, could last a few days, a few months or for years. Ray couldn't promise anything. The only encouragement he could offer was that Steve's body was improving. When Ray and the nurse left the room that day, Kathy rested her head on Steve's chest and cried. Later she got down on her knees and prayed. It was a position she found herself in more and more since the accident. And God had been there for her. She could feel his presence envelop her.

Now, she ran her fingers over the armrest of the recliner and fought back the tears. She wasn't sure how she could survive without him. How could she tell Tommy that his daddy might never be able to come home? Two years ago, Brenda Sullivan, who was five years older than her, had lost her husband to cancer. When she visited Brenda a month after the funeral her friend couldn't decide if it was good or bad that Phillip had never given her children. Kathy knew the answer to that. No matter what, she would have Tommy. Right now, he was the only light in her dark tunnel.

She was shifting to another position in the recliner when the sudden jingle of the phone caused her to pitch the afghan to the floor. She pushed herself out of the recliner and raced up the five steps to the kitchen. It was in the midst of the third ring when she grabbed it.

"Hello."

"Mrs. Pearce?"

"Yes." She was having a hard time getting her breath. It could be no one but the hospital, and the thought terrified her.

"This is nurse Twyla Jackson on the third floor. There's been a change in your husband's condition and Doctor Philpot says you should come as soon as possible."

Kathy felt her heart skip a beat. "I'll leave as soon as I can get dressed." Before the nurse could say anymore, she hung up and ran for the stairs that led to the upstairs bedrooms. Her mother had heard the phone and was at the top of the landing pulling on her robe when Kathy started up.

"Mother. Something's happened at the hospital. They've told me to hurry." Her voice was quavering.

"I'll go with you," Ann Wilson said. She reached out to comfort her daughter.

"No, Mama." Kathy was fighting back tears now. "Tommy's asleep and it would take too long to get him up and in the car. I'll be okay. Just stay with Tommy." Tears were streaming down her cheeks as she ignored her mother's offered embrace and hurried past her into the bedroom.

It was four twenty-five when Kathy backed out of the carport. She had a passing thought about how lucky they were to have a friend like Leland Corso. The chains he had put on her car that afternoon could make the difference in whether or not she even reached the hospital.

~ ~ ~

The third floor nurses' station and the hospital corridor were both empty when Kathy stepped off the elevator. That was unusual, even for this time of night. As she ran past the station, a nurse came hurriedly out of Steve's room and disappeared into another room across the hall. She was only a few feet from the door to 310 when a grave Ray Philpot walked out with Mary Strange close behind. Kathy had to put on the brakes to keep from running into the both of them.

Ray grabbed her shoulders as she started around him. "Kathy. Wait."

"Ray, is he....did he...." She was frantic and shaking.

"Settle down, Kathy. He's all right. He's awake, out of the coma. Do you understand what I'm saying."

Her eyes were searching the door behind him. "Ray, what happened?"

"He just woke up all of a sudden. He's going to be all right, Kathy."

"He's not going to die?" She asked.

"No. He's much better."

She didn't know whether to laugh or cry. Instead, she collapsed against Ray's chest. Then the tears came. The fears and frustrations of the last two weeks poured out of her as she lay there in Ray's arms. When she finished and pushed away, the front of his shirt was soaked.

"How, Ray? How did it happen?"

"We don't know. Around four o'clock an aide went in to check on him. One second his eyes were closed, the next open. All of a sudden the coma just evaporated."

Kathy looked toward heaven. "Thank you, Lord."

"A lot of prayers went up for him," Ray said.

"I know," she whispered. "Can I see him?"

"Yes. In a minute. But he'll probably be asleep." Her eyes widened and Ray saw the fear. "I said asleep, Kathy. Not in a coma. His vital signs are all moving back in normal range. He's going to have a speech problem for a while because of the injury to his throat. That's the one thing that hasn't improved as much as the rest of his body. I'm not quite sure why. But the inactivity of the last two weeks would be enough to cause him to have a problem talking. He'll get over that in time. He did understand me when I spoke to him.

Kathy looked again toward the door. "You talked to him?"

"I talked. He only nodded."

"Can I go in, now?"

"You can go in, but don't wake him if he's asleep." He looked at her closely. "Did you get any rest while you were home?"

"I couldn't sleep."

Ray turned to Mary. "Have an orderly put a cot back in the room so that she can get some sleep." He looked back at Kathy. "I expect you to lay down. Steve is going to be okay. You need to take care of yourself now."

Kathy was wiping tears from her eyes again. She grasped Ray's arm. "Thank you, Ray. Just, just thank you so much."

Ray just pointed his index finger toward heaven. "Thank Him."

She nodded and reached up and gave him a kiss on the cheek. "Yes. I intend to."

CHAPTER 35

WHEN STEVE OPENED HIS eyes, the only illumination was from a narrow shaft of light that slipped around the edge of the door and stretched along the floor until it fell across the foot of the bed. The drapes were pulled and the only thing he could distinguish was the table that sat between the bed and the door. There was no sound, either in the room or from the hallway.

He moved his tongue back and forth across the roof of his mouth and it seemed the acrid taste of smoke still lingered. He repeated the action and couldn't taste it the second time. His nostrils didn't burn now and there was no feeling that he would break out in a violent coughing spasm.

Coughing reminded him of Sarah and for a moment he panicked. Then he remembered letting her down through the broken window and watching her disappear around the corner of the house. He winced at the memory of the broken window glass tearing at his flesh. He tried to move his hand down toward his damaged stomach but couldn't. His hand and arm seemed like it weighed a ton. There was no life, no strength in his muscles. It was the same for his other arm, and when he tried moving his legs they were like lead weights. Only his right leg responded at all. It felt like his muscles had not been used in weeks. They were dormant. Smoke inhalation would not do that. Loss of blood would weaken him.

With much effort, he moved his hand slowly toward the buzzer pinned to his pillow. It was a major maneuver to find

291

and press it.

~ ~ ~

Mary had been in 310 less than five minutes before. Since Doctor Philpot had left, she had made it her responsibility to check on the young man every fifteen minutes. Most of the night the man's wife had been alert and watching every movement he made. She seemed more excited every time Mary appeared. But the last two times she had been curled up on the cot. The head nurse could understand. The young woman had hardly left her husband's bedside since the auto accident. It was only natural that she could keep the adrenaline flowing only so long before exhaustion finally overtook her.

So, when the light flashed for 310, Mary was up quickly and half running down the hall. When she pushed the door open, light from the hall flooded the little room. Kathy Pearce was still asleep on the cot. The blanket Mary had covered her with a half hour ago was still in place.

She moved to the bed and searched the man's face. His eyes were open but not dull and listless as they had been a few hours before. There were questions in those eyes now. And he was licking his lips, licking at the beads of sweat that were trying to pry their way into his mouth. She took out her handkerchief and rubbed it gently across his forehead, down the cheeks and around his neck. When she finished, she brushed a wisp of hair back from his eyes.

"Everything is all right, Mr. Pearce." As she spoke, she automatically grasped his wrist and began counting pulse beats. When she finished, she laid his arm back across his stomach and smiled down at him. "Your wife is here with you, asleep on the cot over there."

Nora, alive, Steve thought. Thank God for that. But what about Sarah. Was she all right? But he couldn't get his voice to cooperate. The words seemed to be trapped inside him. For one frightening moment he remembered stories about people who had been in fires and the intense heat and smoke had damaged their vocal chords so bad that they could never talk again. But there was no burning sensation, no pain in his throat. All he felt was weakness, fatigue, as if every muscle in his body had abandoned its function.

~ ~ ~

Mary watched his mouth open and close, thought she could see it forming the word daughter. The man was still confused. He had a son and the boy had been to see him on several occasions.

"Don't try to talk," Mary soothed. "You've been through an ordeal, but you're going to be all right now." She smiled and took a towel from the table to wipe at the new dampness forming again on his forehead.

There was something familiar about the woman hovering over him that bothered Steve. He had seen her before. She had been in the dream more than one time. Was he part of the dream now? And there were other nurses scurrying around the bed while Ray bent over him smiling like some kid whose mother woke him up too late to catch the school bus. That was what was wrong now. In the dream, he had always been an observer, watching from somewhere above. But this time, now and in the dream he had just had, he was looking up into Ray's face. The dream had changed. Everything had changed.

Something or someone moved at the foot of the bed. A shadowy figure moved around the bed opposite the nurse. He expected to see Nora's face appear any moment. But, he heard the voice before his eyes focused on the face and his whole body began tingling with emotion.

"Darling." The voice was unmistakable.

He tried to speak and reach for her all at once but no part of his body seemed to work. But it didn't matter. Kathy was on him at once, burying her head in his chest and digging her fingers into the gown that covered his body. The gown, already wet with his own perspiration, was becoming soaked with Kathy's tears. It was a minute, maybe two, before he realized that it wasn't her body alone that was heaving with emotion. And the tears were not only hers. It took tremendous effort and determination, but he finally raised his right arm and draped it heavily over her back. Then, slowly, his fingers began massaging and caressing her until the heaving and crying began to subside.

Mary slipped to the window and peeked around the curtain. Outside, the first light of a new day was beginning to dawn in the eastern sky. The snow—the beautiful, treacherous snow—had stopped. She tiptoed out of the room and pulled the damp handkerchief out of her pocket, dabbing it first at one eye, then the other. By the time she reached the nurses' station there was no indication that she had been anything but the cold and mechanical head nurse they all knew she was.

CHAPTER 36

THE RECUPERATION PROCESS WAS painfully slow. It was three days after Steve recovered from the coma before they got him to his feet and let him try the walker. The first day he made it across the room and back to the bed. He did it three times that day. Gradually, he worked his way out into the hall. The eighth day he walked the length of the hall and back to his room in fifteen minutes.

Kathy brought him a small rubber ball and when he had nothing to do, he squeezed it until his hands and wrists and lower arms would no longer go. Little by little, he could feel his strength returning. On the tenth day they took the walker away and replaced it with a cane. He had his freedom, they told him, to move about in the halls anytime he pleased.

Though his legs were sore and ached constantly, he was determined to get back to his pre-accident condition. If he became disheartened, he had a supporter. Kathy was always by his side to spur him on. Steve learned that her mother had been staying with Tommy since the day after the accident and that Kathy had spent nearly every moment at the hospital. She had never given up. She had never let the doctors and nurses give up. And on Thursday, the eighteenth of January, the day he was to go home, Ray stopped by his room and spelled it out for him.

"We need to talk before you leave," Ray said.

Steve sat down on the edge of the bed with Kathy by his side.

"I want to be sure you know just how much she's done for you," Ray said, nodding toward Kathy. "I told her sometime early on after the accident that comas were unpredictable. But she never stopped believing that you would break out. She was here almost every minute you were in here. I had to make her go home and get some rest and then she fought me all the way. I know she spent a lot of time in prayer. I think we all did. But I looked in this door on more than one occasion and found her down on her knees with her hands clasped around yours. If not for her...." he let his voice trail off and shook his head. "Quite a woman you've got there."

Steve knew. He had seen her in every dream, seen her love and dedication. "I know. She was always there."

"I just wanted you to know what kind of fighter you've got."

"How about you, Ray? What about that vacation you and Susan were going to take before this happened?"

"We put that on the back burner for awhile."

"Susan let you get away with that?"

"Wasn't my choice. She wouldn't talk about going anywhere until you were on your feet again. You really had a lot of people pulling for you, old buddy." Ray tapped him on the shoulder, then looked at Kathy. "Take this guy home. He's taken up space in this hospital way too long." With that, Ray turned and left the room.

Kathy spoke first. "He really worked hard for you, Steve."

"I know he did." He got up from the bed and put his arms around her. "Let's go home."

CHAPTER 37

ANGELA SANDERS WAS BENDING close to the woman's lips, trying to make out the words she was straining to say. Harriet Stephens was only sixty-five but lying there on the bed with her dentures in a cup on a nearby table, she looked much older. The yellowish wrinkled skin heralded a condition that was slowly killing her.

"How is she today, Miss Sanders?" Doctor Reece Phelps had come into the room without the young nurse noticing.

"Very weak. She wants very badly to tell me something, but I can't make it out. It seems like she's saying Jane or Jean. I can't be sure."

The doctor walked to the opposite side of the bed and bent over the woman, his arms straddling her body as he bent close to her lips. "Good morning, Harriet."

She blinked her eyes and tried to speak, but the words were inaudible. Even with his ear poised over her lips, Reece could not make out what she was trying to say. Finally, he stood up and smiled down at her.

"You're looking better this morning," he lied. "How are you feeling?" Without waiting for the reply he knew would not come, he continued. "Is Miss Sanders treating you okay?"

Harriet's eyes blinked again and she smiled toward the nurse.

Doctor Phelps patted her on the shoulder and nodded to Angela. They both knew the situation. Harriet Stephens probably wouldn't last more than three or four days. A shame, Reece thought, a dirty rotten shame.

CHAPTER 38

THE MORNING AFTER STEVE came home from the hospital, Ann Wilson marched down the stairs and announced that she had packed her bags the night before and would leave for Van Buren immediately after breakfast.

Steve looked up from the morning paper. "Mom, you know you're welcome to stay with us as long as you like."

"I know, Steve, and I appreciate that. But, if I stayed another week, we'd be at each other's throats. As much as I love Kathy and she loves me, two women in one house just does not work." She put extra emphasis on the last three words and winked at Steve. "The only reason it worked this last month was because Kathy was always at the hospital. Tommy and I got along famously." Her face became sober. "Since Henry died, I think I've actually become a loner. Two or three days in a crowd is about all I can stand."

Kathy came to the rail and looked down into the den where her mother and Steve were. "Mother, being alone all the time isn't healthy. You know how much I loved Dad, but I think you should, maybe, start dating."

Ann took a deep breath and shook her head. "Not me. I'm one of those women who loves only once." She paused and winked at Steve again. "Besides, I don't want to take the time to train another one." She stood up and walked to the fireplace where she folded her arms and stared into the blaze. The smile of a moment ago was gone. "No one could ever replace Henry," she said and looked back to the railing where Kathy stood watching her. "Not even the daughter I love more than myself."

299

"Mother." Kathy came down the stairs and put her arms around Ann. For several minutes the two women held each other. Only the timer on the oven, announcing that the biscuits were done, caused them to release their hold.

At ten thirty, Ann backed her blue Ford out of the carport and started home to Van Buren. Steve and Kathy stood at the playroom window and watched until her car disappeared over the hill on Carpenter Dam Road.

"I didn't realize she was so lonely until now. But I think I know a little about how she feels. When you were in the coma, I thought I'd lost you. I don't ever want to feel that way again."

Steve gathered her into his arms. "Hey, don't think about it anymore. It's behind us."

"I can't stop thinking about it." She looked back toward the spot where her mother's car had disappeared. "Steve, we need to go see her more often. I know what she said earlier, but that was just her way of saying that she didn't want to be in the way. She really enjoyed being with Tommy and I know she'd like to see him more often."

"Agreed," Steve said.

She looked back at him and there was just a sign of a tear. "I could have been just as lonely as her. I'm not sure I could endure it as well as she has." She kissed him on the cheek and slipped out of his arms. She was wiping her eyes when she disappeared through the door.

He wasn't sure how long he stood there staring out the window with unseeing eyes. Sarah had been on his mind very much these last two weeks. The Sarah he knew was gone to him for good. And Jim and Mona were gone. He was certain of that. But could Sarah be real? Losing her was like cutting a little piece off of himself.

Finally, he slapped his right fist into his left palm and went through the den to the foot of the stairs. There were some answers he needed and no time like the present to look for them.

"Kathy," he called but there was no return answer. "Kathy," he called again.

She came out of their bedroom door. "What's wrong, honey?"

"I have to go somewhere. I'll be back in a couple of hours."

"Do you want me to go with you?"

"Tommy's still asleep. You wait here. I won't be long. Maybe then I'll need you to go somewhere with me."

"All right. But please be careful."

He wasn't sure what he would find when he turned onto Dickson Drive. It was as if he was back in the other life, the other reality again with Nora and Sarah. For a moment he thought of turning around in the first driveway and heading straight back to Kathy and Tommy. But he couldn't. He had to get those answers. And this was the place to start. The red brick house at the end of the street was just as he remembered. But there was no fire damage. The white mailbox at the corner of the driveway said Alfred Jones. Steve stopped the car in front and turned off the engine. He still had a vision of Sarah that first day he had come home. She was over by the little front porch.

When Jim pulled into the driveway, Sarah had come running. She was real then, and just as real now, just as real as Kathy and Tommy. But how was he going to find her?

He glanced at the mailbox across the street. The name Peterson sprang at him from the side of the black box. Clara Peterson. When he looked toward the house, the woman, the same one that Sarah had stayed with, was staring at him through a front window. Their eyes met for several seconds, then the curtain closed and she was gone.

Steve switched on the ignition and muttered under his breath. "If you're out there, I'll find you, Sarah. I promise I'll find you."

Instinctively, he moved back up the street and turned left. There was another stop to be made. He needed to find out how much more of his experience was real.

For days it had been in the back of his mind. Now, as he pulled into the parking lot and looked toward the metal building, he saw the words he expected to see. Even though the yellow pages had already confirmed it, Steve still needed to see it for himself. Carter

Flying Service was a reality. It was there just as it had been on the other side.

He sat there staring toward the building for several minutes. His fingers were locked so tightly around the steering wheel that they seemed to be a part of it. Something held him, kept him from releasing his grip and opening the door. Deep down he knew what it was. The thought of seeing Lisa again was heavy on his mind. Only a week ago, during that time when she was a part of his life, that other life, he knew he could fall in love with her very easy. It was during that time when he thought Kathy was lost to him forever, that he let those thoughts drift through his mind.

And, yet, there was Nora. But as hard as he tried, he never felt any loyalty to Nora. Now, back where he belonged, he didn't know how he would feel if he saw Lisa again. She wouldn't know him any more than Kathy knew him when he made the trip to Dallas. She had another life just as Kathy had. Right now it was answers he needed. Steve closed his eyes and let go of the steering wheel. It was the next step, the next question he needed to answer. He opened the car door and stepped out.

The chilly air hit him immediately. His eyes moved back and forth as he began the fifty-yard stretch across the concrete parking lot to the flying service door. It all seemed to be just as he remembered. The doorknob was icy to his touch and, when the shudder moved up and down his body, he wasn't sure whether the cause was the touch of the knob or the anticipation of what lay on the other side of the entrance.

He pushed the door open and stepped into the small reception area. The room was empty. The door to the back, the one leading to Jake Carter's private office, was barely cracked. For just a second he was back to that day he and Lisa had heard the voices behind that door. Now he heard other voices. One was unmistakable. It was Jake Carter. The other, a woman's voice, was less discernible. But he could tell it wasn't Lisa's.

Steve moved closer to the cracked door. The female voice belonged to an older woman. He moved a proper distance away toward the window where he had a view of the runway. A small Cessna was landing from the southwest. He watched it touch down, then pick up speed. A moment later it was back in the air. A long time ago he had been the one doing touch-and-go landings on that same runway. That had been years ago. When he stopped flying he thought he might miss it, but he didn't. It was his past. He had no desire to return to that past. He was still watching the small plane climb out when he heard the woman enter from the back office.

"Oh," she said when she saw Steve. "I'm sorry. I didn't know anyone was out here."

Steve turned and was amazed. It was Lisa in twenty-five years. She was medium height, slender, and very attractive. Her hair had streaks of gray and fell down her neck just above her shoulders.

"I'm Mrs. Carter. Can I help you?"

"Steve Pearce, Mrs. Carter." He waited to see if his name meant anything to her and realized very quickly that it didn't. "I...." he stammered for a moment, then regained his composure. "I've been thinking about flying lessons. I took a few when I was in high school but never followed through." As he spoke, Jake appeared from the office. The ever-present cigar stub was stuck in the left corner of his mouth.

"Dear, this young man is interested in lessons. Would you like to talk to him?" She turned back to Steve. "Mr. Pearce, this is my husband, Jake Carter."

Steve's eyes met Jake's. For a moment it seemed as if there might be some recognition. He dismissed that with Jake's first question.

"Say your name is Pearce? Ever flown before?"

"No ... I mean, yes. I took a few lessons but it's been maybe ten years."

"Why'd you stop?"

"I don't know. Ran out of time, I guess. I was about to go off to college."

Jake motioned toward his office. "Let's go in here." Steve followed him in. The little room was just as he remembered. Two wooden, straight chairs sat across the desk from the small swivel chair that Jake used. Several rolled-up maps were leaning in a corner behind the desk. In the opposite corner, a small green safe was swung open.

Jake's desk was just as cluttered as he remembered. But the thing that caught his eye almost immediately was the picture of a young woman. She was smiling up at him when he sat down in one of the straight chairs. It had been taken several years ago, probably in high school or just afterward, but it was Lisa.

"You done much flyin' since those high school days?"

"None, really." Steve found it hard to take his eyes off the picture.

"Whatcha do?"

"I'm sorry."

"I said, whatcha do for a livin'?"

"I'm an accountant. I have my own practice in town."

"Hmm," Jake said. "Ain't scared of flyin' are you?"

"I wasn't when I was a kid. Don't think I would be now."

"Did you solo?"

"I was close but I quit about that time."

"Still got your old flight log?"

"Pardon?"

"Your old flight log where you kept up with your hours, how long you were in the air each time you went up. Total hours, that sort of thing."

"I guess I do somewhere."

"Need to find it," Jake said. He opened a drawer and moved some papers around. A moment later he came out with a brochure and handed it to Steve. "Rates are listed in here. I usually start students out in a Cessna 150. High-wing plane that cruises about a hundred knots. You know it?"

"I think that's what I flew before."

"Good. Be some familiarity there."

Steve stared, unseeing, at the brochure. He wanted to point to the picture and ask where Lisa was. But he wouldn't. Just being here right now made him feel guilty.

"Got two pilots. One's my girl." He pointed to the picture. "She's a crackerjack. Better'n her old man, my Lisa is."

Steve looked again at the picture. "She's a pilot?"

Jake nodded. "You bet. Like I said, she's a good one. Some don't like to learn from a female. You got anything ag'in' that?"

"No."

"We can get you started next week?"

Steve looked from the picture to Jake. "Let me think about it and I'll let you know in a day or two. Right now I just wanted to get some prices. You say Li—your daughter, I mean—would be my instructor."

"Don't have to be. My other instructor's a good one, too. Been with me for five years.

Steve's first thought was Ed. "What's his name?"

"Alan Stanley." Jake took the cigar stub out of his mouth and laid it on the corner of his desk. "My son-in-law," he said quietly.

Before he realized it, Steve blurted out. "You mean Lisa's married?" He cringed at his mistake.

The sudden question took Jake by surprise and he sat for a moment staring across the desk at Steve. "You know my Lisa?"

Steve wasn't sure what to say but he thought the truth was best right now. No need to get himself in any deeper. "We met once a long time ago. I remembered her when I saw her picture."

Jake measured him across the desk, then picked up the stub and placed it back in his mouth. "Like I said, you can take lessons from Alan. Probably be better." His voice had suddenly grown cold.

Steve was beginning to feel uncomfortable. He was up from his chair now and moving toward the door. "Like I said, I'll think about it and get back to you."

Jake nodded and the stub moved from one side of his mouth to the other.

Steve retreated through the reception area, nodded to Mrs. Carter and reached for the doorknob. His hand never made contact. The door opened and she came through into the office. A young man was close behind.

"Oh, I'm sorry. I didn't mean to run over you." She smiled as their eyes met.

Steve couldn't speak. She was even more beautiful than he remembered. Her hair was down past her shoulders. She was wearing a leather jacket, faded jeans and a red cotton shirt.

"No problem," Steve finally said. "It was my fault."

For just a moment he tarried, then he nodded to the young man and moved around her and out into the blustery wind. He could feel their eyes boring into his back as he trudged the fifty paces back to the car.

~ ~ ~

Jake had followed Steve into the reception room and watched the confrontation between the man and his daughter. Strange, he thought. The man said he knew Lisa. Why no greeting? When Steve was halfway to his car, Jake put his arm around Lisa's shoulder and drew her tight against him.

"You know that fella?"

She shook her head. "I don't think so. Why, Daddy?"

"Said he met you way back when. Stared real hard at your picture."

Lisa pulled loose from her father and went to the window. Steve was unlocking the front car door. She studied him as best she could from this distance before shrugging her shoulders.

"I don't remember him."

Jake came to the window just as the car began moving. He watched for a moment as the car passed out of the lot and onto the drive that led to the highway. "Strange," he muttered.

As he entered the traffic on Highway 70, Steve reflected on what had just happened. He could understand Jake Carters sudden change in attitude. The little man was watching him through the same window where he had been watching the small plane only minutes ago. And he knew what Jake must be thinking. He, Steve, would be thinking the same thing if he felt Tommy or Sarah was being threatened. But Jake didn't need to worry. Lisa Carter was the past. And she would remain there. Kathy and Tommy were the future, and Sarah, too, the little girl he had to find.

CHAPTER 39

BY THE TIME STEVE pulled into the carport and killed the engine, his mind was made up. If Sarah existed where he had been then she could very well exist here. The problem was finding her. But then, when he did find her, could she ever be his? There would be Nora to contend with. Considering his recent experience with her, that was a meeting he would not look forward to. But if Nora was different, a good mother and Sarah was happy, he could fade away and keep an eye on the child from a distance.

What hurt the most right now was telling Kathy. And she would have to be told. He feared something like this, dropped on her after what she had already gone through, could shake her right down to the soles of her feet. Worse, it could drive a wedge between them that might never be removed. It might destroy her love for him. He wasn't sure he could handle that.

Steve released his grip on the steering wheel, got out of the car and went into the house. Kathy was coming down the stairs with an armful of clothes when he came through the kitchen.

"I've gotten way behind on my housework this past month. As bad as I hate to, I guess there's no time like the present to start catching up."

"Can it wait just a while longer?" Steve asked.

"Why?"

"I want you to go to the farm with me. It's important."

"We haven't been out there in three years. Why do you want to go now?"

Steve met her at the bottom of the stairs and relieved her of the clothes. "It's important and something I have to do and I need you to do it with me. Please, honey. Call Tommy and get your coat on," he said as he started toward the laundry room with the dirty clothes.

"All right." She turned and looked up the stairs. "Tommy."

He came out of his room and looked down toward Kathy. "Yes, Mommy."

"Get your coat on. Daddy's going to take us riding. We're going out to the farm."

Steve put his hands on Kathy's shoulders and turned her around as Tommy disappeared back into his room. "Honey, I'm going to need all the love and understanding you can muster in the next few hours. Are you up to it?"

Her eyes were questioning but her answer came back quickly. "As long as I have you, I'm up to anything."

"Let's go then," Steve said as Tommy came down the steps.

The drive took less than a half hour and Steve wondered why it had been so long since they had made it. Immediately, he could see the differences when they pulled onto the private road that led to the house. With Jim, a few weeks ago, the trees and bushes had been cut back to give clear path all the way through the woods. Now they hung so low over the road that the Chrysler would have been scratched and damaged if they had continued.

Steve stopped the car and pointed ahead. Perhaps thirty yards away a small oak had been blown down by the wind. It was blocking their path to the house.

"It's not far. We'll have to walk from here."

Kathy drew her coat tightly around her small frame. "Why don't Tommy and I wait for you in the car?"

"No, Mommy. I want to go, too. Please." He was leaning over the front seat with his head between them.

Steve reached up and ruffled the boy's hair. "You can, son." Then he looked at Kathy. "I need you to go, Kathy. I have something I need to show you. At least I think I do." He reached over and squeezed her hand and she nodded.

"What are you being so mysterious about? You've got me a little scared."

"No need to be scared, honey. Just bear with me." He looked back at Tommy, who had settled back against the seat again. "I dropped a claw hammer on the floor board back there. Hand it to me, Tommy."

"I'll carry it, Daddy."

"All right, but don't lose it. Daddy needs it when we get to the house."

Tommy jumped from the car and ran up the road. He climbed over the fallen oak and turned to look back at Steve and Kathy. A moment later he was out of sight up the road.

"Wait for us, Tommy," Kathy called.

"I will, Mommy."

She turned her attention back to Steve. "I don't understand. You haven't told me anything yet."

"Just a little while longer. This may or may not be a wild goose chase. If it is, then we'll both sit down and have a good laugh. If not, then...." he stopped mid-sentence and climbed over the tree. Then he took her hand and helped her over.

By the time they reached the clearing in front of the house, they found Tommy trying to beat an old wooden stake into the frozen ground. Steve touched his shoulder as he went by and Tommy dropped the stake and ran ahead of them to the house. The place looked no different than the last time he and Kathy had been here. If anything, it was in even more disrepair.

It was a shame, Steve thought. He should not have let it run down like this. But, after Jim died, he couldn't find the heart to come out here. Too many memories. Still, he was the keeper, the only one left. A little paint, new shingles, fix the steps and the outside could look like new. At least he knew what it could look like with a little loving care. And new windows, it had to have the new windows.

"Tommy, wait for us in the yard. Don't go up on the porch," Steve yelled.

The boy stopped a few feet short of the porch and turned to swing the hammer back and forth as he watched his parents approach. Steve could see that the front door was ajar when he was still twenty yards away.

"Someone's been here," he stopped and surveyed the house from one side to the other. "Let me have the hammer, son." Steve took the hammer and advanced toward the porch.

"Don't go any closer, Steve. Someone might still be in there."

"It's our property. Besides, it could have been a year or more since anyone was here."

Kathy had hung back but Steve noticed that Tommy had slid up beside him. "Wait, son. Let Daddy go in and see if there's anyone in there. You stay out here and take care of Mommy."

Steve tried the first two steps, found them safe, but stepped over the third, which had already begun to rot away. He stepped gingerly onto the porch and shifted his weight from one foot to the other. "It's safe. But that third step is gone. You two wait out here."

Steve pushed the door open and took a wary step inside. He was holding the hammer in his right hand, hidden behind his right leg. The old living room was empty except for litter all over the floor. He took a deep breath and began a room-to-room search. After nearly five minutes he was satisfied and went back to the front door. "No one here."

"Oh, Steve, I was getting scared. Are you sure it's safe?"

"It is. Come on in. But watch that third step."

She got to the third step and Steve reached out and took her hand and she vaulted to the porch. Tommy bounced up the first two steps and Steve bent over and lifted him the rest of the way. Kathy was already peering into the front room.

"Oh, Steve. It's so run down. I had no idea we had let it get like this." She was shaking her head. There was a stack of newspapers against the far wall and a dirty blanket in a heap next to the papers. In one corner were assorted beer cans and liquor bottles. Mixed with the pile of cans were several faded chicken boxes with the picture of an old, white-haired gentleman grinning back at them from the flap.

"Has someone been living here?"

Steve knelt beside the papers and fingered through them. They were mostly the local Hot Springs paper but a few bore the name of the statewide paper out of Little Rock. The dates were from December 22 through February 3 of the year before.

"If these papers are any indication, whoever it was vacated nearly a year ago. Looks like they spent last Christmas here." Steve picked up the blanket and another whiskey bottle fell out. "Probably ran out of juice."

"You think it was kids?"

"Maybe, but I doubt it. Kids would have been in for a one-night stand. Probably wouldn't have brought all these papers." He got up and went to the kitchen door where Tommy was already exploring. More bottles and cans filled the sink. "Whoever it was is long gone."

Kathy was attempting to pull her coat tighter around her. "I hope so."

Steve put his hand on Tommy's shoulder. "Son, why don't you go outside and play in the front yard. Stay close to the house and watch that bad step. Okay?"

Tommy didn't need to be told twice. When Steve heard him run across the porch, he turned back to Kathy.

"Kathy, do you remember the story about my mother's wedding ring?"

"The one she lost before we met?"

"It was the only one she ever owned." Steve moved to the sink and ran his fingers across the rotted sill. "No one ever knew what happened to it. Mother couldn't even remember the last time she had it on."

"I know. She told me."

"Suppose, after all these years, I could show you exactly where that ring is. What would you think?"

She shrugged her shoulders. "That you were psychic, I guess. But you're not. At least I don't think you are."

"Then how would I know?"

She hesitated a moment and her voice became shrill. "Do you know where it is?"

"Let's see if I do." He pointed to a rusted nail that had been driven into the wood framing just above the bottom sash. It held the kitchen window firmly in place. "Dad drove this nail into the wooden track to keep anyone from raising the window from the outside. He meant for it to be a temporary lock until he could fix the regular lock. But he got sick a few days later and he must have forgotten. That's the same nail he drove in all those years ago."

"I see it but I don't see what you're getting at."

Steve placed the claw on the nail and gave a quick jerk. The nail came part way. He adjusted the claw and jerked again. This time it released.

"Suppose I told you that Mother's ring is lodged underneath this window stool, that it has been all these years. It was a plain gold band. It'll be dirty and corroded now." He looked back at her as he leaned over the sink and strained to lift the bottom sash. It didn't want to budge. He took the hammer and slammed it down on the top of the right edge of the bottom sash. Then he did the same to the left. He dropped the hammer on the counter and took hold of the window. This time it moved up a few inches. He tapped both sides of the window frame again, applied pressure and the window raised about a foot. "Now, let's see if I'm crazy."

Kathy moved closer and watched as Steve stuck the claw of the hammer under the outer edge of the windowsill. If the ring was where Jim said it was, he certainly did not want to dislodge it and have it fall through some unseen crack and be lost forever. As he pried on the sill, the wood began coming away in chunks. He maneuvered the claw to the right side of the rotten sill and found a substantial opening to get the claw under. A moment later he heard a dull snap as the stool broke in pieces where it nestled under the side facing. Steve lifted it carefully and dropped it on the cabinet. As he did, Kathy gasped and grabbed his arm.

"Steve." She was pointing to the small area he had uncovered.

Steve's stomach came up into his throat. A small gold band lay poised at the edge of a crack between the side facing and the rotten window stool. It was covered with dust and splinters from his own handiwork of the last few minutes. But it was the ring, his mother's ring. He lifted it gingerly from its hiding place and wiped it clean with his handkerchief. Just as he knew it would be, it was corroded from all those years under the sill. But when he looked more closely, he knew it was the same ring he had seen on the key chain only a few weeks before. Only, he realized, it wasn't really the same ring.

"It's Mother's ring," he announced and handed it to Kathy.

She studied it for several seconds before their eyes met again. "How did you know where to find it?"

Steve turned and pulled the window down on the fragments of the busted sill. "Go find Tommy while I drive this nail back in place and lock the house. We have to talk when we get home."

On the way back, Kathy had taken the ring out of her coat pocket and began working on the corrosion with her fingernails. Some had come off but much was still imbedded in the metal. It would take a special polish to bring back the finish.

There was very little talk on the ride home and Kathy felt an eerie chill begin to build in her body. Even as she worked on the ring, her imagination played games with her. When Steve switched off the car ignition, Kathy hopped out and used her own key to let herself in. She was already building a fire when Steve came through the kitchen and down the den steps.

"Cold?"

"All of a sudden. I can't seem to get warm."

"A chill?"

"Maybe."

Tommy was about to switch on the television when Steve stopped him.

"Son, if you'll go into the playroom until I call you, I'll take you out for an ice cream cone later. Okay?"

"Yes, Daddy." The boy started for the adjoining room. "And,

Tommy, close the door so Mommy and I can talk. I'll come get you when we get through. Okay, son?"

"Yes, Daddy."

Tommy shut the door behind him and a moment later Steve and Kathy could hear the sound of the model train set.

He turned his attention back to Kathy. She was standing in front of the fireplace, her hands clasped behind her back and staring down into the new blaze. She jumped when he touched her on the shoulder.

"I didn't mean to scare you."

"I was a long way off." She seemed stiff to his touch. It was not only his touch that scared her. He knew she had a premonition that what he was about to tell her would not be pleasant.

Steve took her hand and led her toward the couch. "Come sit down." They settled beside each other and Steve took both her hands in his. "I really don't know how to begin. You said a moment ago that you were a long way off." He waited for a response and when she nodded, he continued. "That's where I was during the coma, a long way off."

She had been staring down at their hands and now she looked up at him. "I don't understand what's happening. I don't understand about the ring, how you found it. You said you didn't want to frighten me. But I am frightened. Things like this, things I don't understand frighten me. You've been so mysterious since you came home. That's frightened me. And now you tell me we've got things we need to talk about. That frightens me again."

Steve took her shoulders and turned her toward him. "Honey, I love you. You believe that, don't you?"

"Yes, I think so. I've always thought you did. Now, I...."

"I know you're frightened right now. To be honest with you, I am too. But, I'm asking you to trust me and bear with me. Will you do that?"

"Yes," she said softly.

"What I'm going to tell you will seem completely at odds with everything you've ever believed. I've lived it and I find it unbelievable. Except for you and Tommy, it's all I've been able to think about since I came out of the coma. If you'll let me tell you the whole story without stopping, I'll answer all your questions when I finish, at least all the questions I have answers for right now. Will you let me do that?"

"Yes." Her eyes left his and dropped back to the hands he still held. "I'm scared of what you're going to tell me but I couldn't stand it if you didn't tell me."

"I told you before that I was going to need all your love and understanding, all of it. I meant what I said, every word. Just listen very closely to what I'm going to tell you and know that I love you and Tommy more than anything."

Though they were sitting near the fire and it had grown quite warm in the house, he could still feel her shivering. He gripped her hands a little tighter and began. Slowly, and as carefully as he could, he went back to that Saturday of the accident. He told her about his last thoughts as the Corvette slid sideways into the rear of the pickup, about the log that came hurtling through the side window toward his head. Then he told her about waking up and where he had found himself, in the cockpit of the airplane.

She looked perplexed but held her tongue and let him continue. He told her about that night in the hospital when Jim and Mona had walked into his room. Kathy caught her breath at the mention of Jim and Mona. Still, she didn't interrupt. He told her everything, about Nora and Lisa, about driving to Dallas to find her. Nothing was left out. By the time he finished, her once bright eyes were filled with tears.

"Are you all right?"

She pulled her hands away from him now and pushed her clenched fists down into her lap. "I don't know. I don't know how I am."

"Do you understand what I've told you?"

She rose from the couch and went to stand in front of the fire with her back to him. "Are you saying that while you were in the coma, you dreamed all this, all this you've told me? You dreamed you were married to someone else, that Jim and Mona were still alive."

"Kathy, I didn't dream it. I lived it."

"What you say isn't possible, Steve. You know it isn't."

"Then how did I know about the ring. It was Jim that told me where it had been found. That's why it was so important for you to go with me, to see when and where I found it."

Steve got up and walked over to where she was staring into the fire. He put his hand on her shoulder and squeezed gently. "Honey," he whispered, "I'd feel just like you. I wouldn't believe it either. But I was there. I know it happened. Believe me, it was real."

She turned to face him and there was a mixture of hurt and anguish in her eyes. "Then this Nora Stephens is real, too." Her tone was sharp and the words bit deeply.

"Yes, I'm afraid so." They stared at each other for a moment, the young woman fighting back the tears, the man wanting to take her into his arms and reaffirm his love. After that long moment, he felt compelled to add. "And I think the child, Sarah, is real, too. Kathy, if she is real I have to find her. I have to be sure she's all right. You can understand that, can't you?"

"Then you really had an affair with this Nora? You slept with her?"

She was staring directly into his eyes waiting for the answer. Steve's eyes did not waver but his heart did. For a moment before he answered he felt it might stop. "It happened before I even knew you existed. We went together for a few weeks. I thought I loved her. I found out very quickly that I didn't. I didn't really know what love was until I met you. I loved you then and I love you even more now."

Kathy was biting her lip to hold back the tears. "What is it you want to do?"

"I have to find out if Sarah exists. If she's okay, happy, then I'll leave it at that and walk away. If she isn't...." He shrugged his shoulders and turned to face the flames that seemed to be increasing in intensity with every word.

"And you want me to help you find her, this child of your affair?"

Kathy's normally soft and gentle voice was hard and bitter.

"If you will."

Suddenly, there was hostility in her voice. "How could you ask me to do that? All of these years and you never told me about this other woman. Now, out of the blue, you tell me this fantastic story about some other world, some other reality, as you called it. Then you add a post script about fathering a baby by this other woman." Her eyes were wide and it was everything she could do to keep from screaming.

"Honey, remember Tommy. He's in the next room."

She shook her head and lowered her voice as she did. "Why weren't you honest with me? Why didn't you just tell me about her? This would have been over years ago. Now..."

Steve turned to stare into the fire again. He picked up the andiron and began stoking at the logs. "What would it have accomplished? It was over before my sophomore year in college was half finished. That was nearly a year before I met you. What happened between Nora and me happened only once. I made a mistake and I've regretted it since the moment it happened."

He turned and reached out for her but she drew away. "The last thing in the world I ever wanted to do is hurt you." He moved toward her again, and this time she allowed him to put his hands on her shoulders. "Are you okay?"

"Not really," she snapped. "Should I be?"

"I love you, Kathy. You have to believe that."

"Maybe you just think you love me. You said you thought you loved her."

Steve wanted to take her into his arms, drive the hurt away. But there was no way she would let him do that, at least not right now. She slipped from his grip and retreated to the couch. He watched her for a minute. She sat down with her elbows resting on her legs and her hands clasped together. Her eyes were staring straight ahead at the fire.

He turned and began poking aimlessly at the blaze. How long they both remained that way, he wasn't sure. But, after a time, he felt a light touch on his shoulder and turned to see her looking up at him. Tears were welling in her eyes, eyes that had gone soft again, eyes that all of a sudden seemed lost and lonely.

"Hold me," she whispered.

Steve dropped the poker and drew her tightly against him. She was sobbing quietly, her head buried in his shoulder. They stood like that for several minutes, her holding tightly to him and him stroking the back of her neck. After a time Kathy pushed gently away.

"I'll help you do anything you need to do if you really want me to."

"I do, very much."

She nodded and settled into his arms again. "What you've told me is foreign to everything I've ever believed. You're going to have to give me time to get used to everything you've told me." Suddenly, she pushed away again. "You said I was married to someone else, some preacher a lot older than me."

"That's right."

"And I had a child."

"A little girl," Steve answered.

She pressed against him again. They remained that way until the idea came to him. "Would you like to try an experiment?"

"What? What kind of experiment?"

"Where did you go to church in Tulsa before you transferred to Ouachita?"

She thought for a moment. "First United Baptist. Why?"

Steve released her and went up the few steps to the kitchen phone. "Let's see if this Doctor Gerald Southerland exists?"

"Was that his name, the one I was supposed to be married to?"

"Yes."

He lifted the phone from its hook and began dialing. "Tulsa, Oklahoma, please."

After a few seconds he said. "First United Baptist Church, please." He pointed toward Kathy in the den and held his hand over the receiver. "Pick up the phone down there. I want you to hear this."

The ringing had already begun by the time she placed the receiver to her ear.

"First United Baptist Church," the female voice said.

"Hello, Miss. I would appreciate some information, please. I'm trying to locate a gentleman who may have been your pastor some time in the past. I believe he would have been there in the last ten years."

The woman hesitated. "I'm not sure I can help you. I've only been a member for a little more than a year."

"This would have been before your time. Would there be anyone there who might have been on staff during those years?"

"Perhaps Mrs. Montgomery can help you. She's been here for a long time."

"Could I speak to her?"

"Of course. Wait just a moment and I'll connect you."

Half a minute passed before an older voice came on the line. "I'm Vera Montgomery. Can I help you?"

"I hope so. I'm trying to locate Doctor Gerald Southerland. I understand he served as your pastor there for a while."

"Yes, he did. What would you like to know?"

Steve heard Kathy gasp quietly on the other phone.

"I'm wondering where he went after he left your church?"

He moved to Dallas, Ridgeview Road Baptist Church."

"I see. Do you know if he's still there?"

"I assume he is. I haven't heard otherwise."

"And his wife," Steve continued. "Can you tell me anything about her?"

"I'm sorry, but Doctor Southerland was a widower. His wife died in an automobile accident over ten years ago in Georgia. As far as I know he's never remarried."

"I'm sorry to hear that about his wife. One other question. How long has it been since he moved to Dallas?"

"It must have been six years ago."

"Thank you very much for the information." Steve replaced the phone quickly before the woman could question him and looked toward the den where Kathy was listening. He saw her replace the phone and stare at it for several seconds. He was coming down the den steps by the time she looked toward him.

"Well," he said.

"I don't know. It's all too much, too fast. I have to think about it." She got up from the couch and started toward the steps before turning around to where he had stopped by the fire. "I remember that when I left Tulsa they had a search committee looking for a new preacher. But I don't ever remember meeting him. I was already at Ouachita by then." She shook her head and started up the steps.

"One other question, Kathy."

She turned and looked down at him.

"Did you ever think about leaving Ouachita and going back to Tulsa?"

Kathy laid her hand on the railing and stared down at Steve. "Several times during that first year."

"What stopped you?"

"I met you and fell in love."

Steve nodded and their eyes locked for several seconds before she turned and started up the stairs again. A minute later Steve heard their bedroom door close.

He waited several minutes for her to return. When she didn't, he sighed and opened the playroom door.

"Come on, Tommy. Let's go get that ice cream cone."

CHAPTER 40

ELIZABETH STAPLETON OPENED HER office door and walked down the long hall to the girls' wing of the children's home. At the door to the dormitory room, she paused and listened to the excited voices on the other side. Two would be going away that afternoon and if things worked out for them, the next time they left it could be a lot longer than just the weekend.

The prospect thrilled her. It always had. But when they left she missed them just as she had her own when they grew up and went off to college. But as much as she missed them, she was even happier if she knew they were placed right. That was the important thing, that they be placed with the right family.

She pushed the door open and smiled at the mess. "Children, be quiet a moment. Sheila, Sarah Jane, are you packed and ready to go?"

~ ~ ~

Reece Phelps stuck his head into the office and smiled at the young woman. "Is Ted in?"

"Not right now, Doctor Phelps. But he should be back in about a half hour. Do you want me to page you when he gets here?"

"Not necessary. I just wanted to talk to him about Harriet Stephens."

The woman took her hands off the computer keys and looked intently at the doctor. "How is she today?"

Doctor Phelps held up his hand with the palm facing down

and moved it back and forth. "Holding her own right now. I really can't tell too much difference from yesterday."

"Poor old dear," the woman said.

"Yeah," Reece said and waved as he pushed away from the door. "Tell Ted I'll see him later."

The young woman nodded and went back to her typing.

CHAPTER 41

RAY PHILPOT WAS IN the process of washing his hands when the phone rang. He was about to go home and grab a quick bite before evening rounds at the hospital. He looked warily toward his desk and thought about not answering it. Since his receptionist and nurse was already gone for the day, the answering service would get it if he didn't pick it up by the fourth ring. Instead, he took a deep breath and picked up before the fourth ring.

"Doctor Philpot."

"Ray."

He didn't recognize the female voice immediately.

"It's Kathy Pearce, Ray."

"Hello, Kathy. Good to hear from you. How's our patient?"

"He's out right now. Took Tommy to get an ice cream cone." Ray noticed an edge in the tone of her voice. "Is everything okay?" She didn't answer.

"You still there, Kathy?"

"Yes."

"What's wrong?"

"I'm not sure." Again she hesitated, but this time for only a few seconds. "He told me some fantastic story." Again there was silence for a few seconds. "I'm sorry, Ray, but I don't understand what's going on. Could something have happened to him in the coma, something that affected...." she stopped again. She was about to ask Ray if something could have happened to Steve's mind, but she couldn't bring herself to do it.

"What are you trying to say, Kathy? What did Steve tell you?"

"Ray, I don't know. I just don't know."

"Tell me what's happened."

She took the long telephone cord and pulled it across the den and into the playroom. From here she could see when Steve and Tommy started up the driveway.

Ray's voice caused her to refocus on the phone. "Talk to me, Kathy."

"I'm sorry, Ray. I can't seem to concentrate right now." She took a deep breath and let it out slowly. "Could he have had....could he have had some kind of experience while he was in the coma?"

"I'm not following you, Kathy. What kind of experience are you talking about?"

"He told me about something that happened to him during the time he was in.... Oh, you're going to think we're both crazy and we aren't, neither one of us. Never mind, Ray. I'm sorry I bothered you."

"Kathy." Ray leaned forward unconsciously as if he could reach out to her across the phone lines. "Kathy, wait a minute. Don't hang up. Are you still with me?"

"Yes."

"You say he told you something happened to him during the coma?"

"Yes."

"What?"

"I don't know really." She hesitated, then said. "A dream, maybe." But she knew what Steve had said. He had sworn that it wasn't a dream. He had sworn that it had really happened.

"You say he thinks he had a dream in the coma?"

Then she blurted it out. "No. He said something really happened to him, some out-of-this-world experience. He said it wasn't a dream. And he...." she started to tell him about the ring and the phone call to Tulsa but thought better of it. How could anyone believe him or her? And the phone was not the place to spell out what Steve had told her. "Ray, I'm frightened for him. Could his mind have been affected some way?" she finally asked.

"No, Kathy. No. I'm sure nothing like that has happened. All of his vitals were normal before he left the hospital. But for your peace of mind, why don't you have him come in the first part of the week. I'll have my receptionist clear a spot for him."

Her voice was high-pitched when she answered. "No, Ray. I don't want him to know I called. Please, don't ever tell him."

"All right. Calm down. Tell you what I'll do. He's supposed to come in Wednesday anyway. I'll have Maria, my receptionist, call him Monday morning and set up an early appointment. She can tell him that there's an opening and we can work him in a couple of days early. How'll that be?"

"I wish there was some way you could see him before then."

"Well, I could drop by this evening after rounds. I could tell him it's a social call."

Kathy thought about that for a moment, then shook her head. "He might find that strange, especially the same day he told me about.... No, Ray. I guess the first of the week, Monday, will have to do."

"Okay, Monday it is then. In the meantime you take it easy and don't worry. Steve's fine. The mind can play tricks on a person and I'm sure that's all it is with him. He came pretty close to leaving us. That may be playing on his mind. In no time he'll be the same old Steve. You'll see."

"I suppose," Kathy said. "Thanks, Ray."

"Sure, Kathy. Anytime." Ray replaced the receiver and flipped off the desk lamp after scribbling a note that he would drop on Maria's desk on the way out.

The mind, Ray thought as he opened the outer door and stepped out into the parking lot, can really send one off the deep end. What kind of weird tale, he wondered, had Steve told Kathy to get her so upset?

The sky was overcast and the wind was beginning to blow in from the north as he pulled the collar of his overcoat up over his ears. He hadn't heard the weather report, but from the look of it they could have more snow before morning.

~ ~ ~

Kathy spent most of the afternoon and evening in the bedroom. She had gone over and over Steve's story until her mind was so clogged and confused that she was ready to scream. Finally, to take her mind off what he had told her, she found an old magazine and propped herself on the bed, trying to read. She was sound asleep when Steve touched her on the shoulder.

"Kathy, it's after eight. I've got Tommy in bed. Why don't you get your gown on and crawl under the covers? You need a good night's sleep."

By the time she was finished in the bathroom, Steve had already climbed into the big bed. She slid in and lay there looking up at the black ceiling for nearly fifteen minutes. In the darkness she couldn't see him, but it was evident that he was awake beside her.

"Steve."

"Yes, hon."

"Did you love her?"

Steve turned on his side toward her. "Like I said this afternoon, I thought I did once. But that didn't last long. I never really loved anyone until you."

That seemed to be what she wanted to hear. She turned on her side and snuggled into his arms, laying her head on his chest as she did. He could feel the dampness as her tears buried themselves against his chest. He pulled her close and his hands slowly began to massage her back. After a few minutes she seemed to relax and the tears dried up. They lay there holding each other without a word for nearly a half hour. She finally broke the silence.

"Suppose the child is real," she whispered. "Suppose you find her. What then?"

Steve's answer was quiet but firm. "I'm not sure. I just know I have to try. I can't turn my back on her. If she's okay, if she's safe and happy, then I won't disturb her. But I won't rest until I know."

Kathy sighed and her hand moved up to his face. She rested it there for several seconds before she spoke again. When she did, her voice was soft, like the Kathy he knew.

"I do want to help you find her if she's out there. I really do."

He put his hand under her chin and lifted her lips toward his. "I know you do, darling. I know you do."

~ ~ ~

Steve found himself in the dream again. He was back in that hospital room looking down at himself in bed. But it was different this time. The body on the bed was him, only it was not him. And the people were different. He couldn't make them out at first. And then he saw her. Sarah was sitting next to the bed holding his hand. The body on the bed was the same out-of-shape body he had found himself occupying just a short time ago. But there didn't seem to be any unhappiness in the room. Sarah was laughing and he, the body he had occupied, was smiling. And when he looked closer he saw the other people in the room.

Lisa was sitting in a chair just beside the bed and Jake was leaning against the wall, the ever-present cigar stub protruding from his mouth. But where was Nora? She wasn't there. And then he remembered. He hadn't found her that night in the fire. She wasn't in her bedroom. And he hadn't been able to get into the den because something was wedged behind the door and he couldn't budge it.

Had Nora been on the other side of that door? Was that why he couldn't open the door? Someone else was entering the hospital room, moving toward the bed. It looked like that other doctor, the one that had tended to him before. His name was...

He was falling again through that long black tunnel. Sarah and Lisa and Jake and that other doctor were no longer visible. They were gone and, he feared, so was Nora, maybe forever.

CHAPTER 42

ON MONDAY MORNING STEVE was at the phone as early as possible. By the time Kathy had breakfast on the table, he had already reached the registrar's office at Ouachita. They told him something he probably knew at one time. Nora had come to Ouachita from Texarkana. Sometime during her sophomore year she had dropped out and not returned. No record existed stating she had requested a transcript of her grades any time after that. To Steve that indicated that she had not attended another school. Though he remembered her as a fun-loving woman, Steve also remembered that Nora carried a better than average grade point and would surely have transferred her records if she planned to attend another college.

"Twenty-two hundred Driscoll in Texarkana," he said as he hung up the phone.

Kathy looked up as she was taking the bacon out of the skillet. "Nora's home address?"

"It was eight years ago."

Steve picked up the phone and dialed the number the college had given him. He straightened up in anticipation when a connection was made.

"Hello," the woman's voice came back at him.

"Is this the Harriet Stephens residence?"

"No, it isn't."

"What number have I reached?"

The woman called it back to him and he apologized and hung up. "Someone else has that number."

"Try information. Maybe they moved to another part of town and their prefix had to be changed. And try the Texas side, too."

Steve gave her a thumbs up and began dialing. After several minutes he dropped the phone back in its cradle. No Harriet or Nora on the Arkansas or Texas side of the line.

Kathy was spooning scrambled eggs onto his plate. "Let it rest for a little while. Breakfast is ready."

Steve got up from the kitchen desk and crossed to the table. "There's no record of either of them. They must have moved," he said, and then added, "if they're still alive."

Kathy refilled his half empty coffee cup. "Why don't we drive down to Texarkana? I can get Cora Sanders to pick Tommy up at the bus stop if we aren't back. We can go to their old neighborhood and ask around. Surely, one of the neighbors will know something about them."

Steve looked at his watch. "I was hoping you would say that. We can be there by noon." He reached over and squeezed her hand as she sat down.

~ ~ ~

Elizabeth Stapleton was at her desk bright and early on Monday morning. It had been one of her rare weekends away from the home, and when she was gone it was always a relief to get back. Her first duty that morning, even before unlocking her office door, was to check in on the two girls that had been visiting prospective foster and adoptive parents. Elizabeth was sure both couples were fine people, but she never rested until all the chicks were back in the nest and safe under her wing. Once she was sure, she retreated down the hall to her office. She was going through a half dozen assorted letters and bills when the phone rang.

"Mrs. Stapleton, Mrs. Alfred Carter is on the line."

"Mrs. Carter, oh, yes. Thank you, Holly." Elizabeth pushed a button on the base of the phone. "Mrs. Carter, this is Elizabeth Stapleton. How are you and how was the weekend?"

Elizabeth listened a moment. The smile that had been etched on her face a few moments before slowly turned to a look of concern. "Yes, I understand what you're saying, Mrs. Carter. She is such a sweet child. We've never had a moment's trouble with her." She listened again, nodding as the woman at the other end of the line talked. "This was her second weekend with you." There was more nodding and, unconsciously, she began doodling on a scratch pad. "Yes that is true. Yes, yes. I see." She was listening again. Finally, she nodded again. "She has been examined by a doctor. Evidently, when the accident occurred her leg wasn't set properly. I'm really not sure what happened. But, I do feel that something could be done for her."

Elizabeth stopped doodling and focused on the voice on the other end of the line. After a moment she dropped her pencil on the desk and leaned back in her chair. "I do understand, Mrs. Carter. I wish Sarah didn't have the problem." She listened for a few minutes more, then, "Yes, Mrs. Carter. I do understand how you and your husband feel and we will keep you in mind when another little girl becomes available. Goodbye now." Elizabeth replaced the phone and reached for the intercom button. "Holly, bring in the Carter file, please."

A moment later the young woman knocked and opened the office door. "Here's the file." She crossed to Elizabeth's desk and handed her a folder before returning to the outer door and pausing. "Are the Carters going ahead with the adoption?"

Elizabeth looked up. "They don't want to take on a child with Sarah's physical problems." Elizabeth shook her head. "It's the second rejection because of her leg."

"Oh, my. I'm so sorry for Sarah," Holly said as she pulled the door closed behind her.

~ ~ ~

"That's in the College Hill area," the old man said as he examined the address on the piece of paper Steve held in front of him. "Used to live over in that part of town myself, 'bout twenty years ago."

The man was sitting on a ragged leather couch, leaning forward on a gnarled stick that served as his cane. He was small, no more than five foot six, and wore thick, horn-rimmed glasses. It was an effort for him to stand and hobble across the small room to the map. But he did and traced his finger along an eastward route until it stopped on Driscoll Street.

"Ain't too hard to find. If'n you get lost, just stop. Anyone can tell you how to get to College Hill."

Steve thanked him and went outside where the attendant was still feeding gas into the Chrysler. The meter was just coming up on fifteen dollars. "Make it fifteen even," Steve said and handed him the money.

Twenty minutes later they pulled up in front of the Driscoll street address. It was a small white frame in the middle of the block. An old-fashioned, wooden swing hung on one side of the big front porch and two green metal lawn chairs were turned upside down on the other side. Halfway down the sidewalk, between the car and the house, a rusty red tricycle lay on its side.

Steve reached for the door handle and Kathy caught his arm. "What will you say if Nora's there?" She paused. "And Sarah?"

Steve shrugged his shoulders. "I'm not sure. Play it by ear, I guess." He patted her hand, got out of the car and started up the concrete walk.

By the time he reached the porch he could hear the television blaring. Steve knocked on the door but there was no answer. This time he pounded a little harder. A girl, no older than Tommy and at least half a head shorter, opened the door. A woman who looked to be in her late twenties or early thirties came up behind the child. Her hair was long and unkempt and she was wearing a white, short-sleeve top and short shorts. A diaper-clad baby was balanced on her right hip.

"Yeah?"

"I'm looking for Harriet Stephens. I understand she lived here at one time."

"We been here a year. Ain't never heard of no Stephens." The baby began to cry but the woman ignored it.

Steve backed away from the door and pointed toward the houses on either side. "Your neighbors. Have they lived here long?"

The woman pushed a twig of hair out of her eyes and nodded toward the house on Steve's right. "Old Granny Cartwright might help ya. Word is she's been livin' over there for nearly fifty years."

Steve glanced toward the two-story, gray house. "Cartwright, you say?" He turned back to the door just in time to see it shut and hear the lock click. He stepped off the porch and motioned toward Kathy.

"Lock the car and let's go next door."

He was already pushing the Cartwright doorbell by the time she caught up with him.

"The woman next door says this lady has lived here for fifty years. She should remember Nora and her mother."

It was a full minute before they heard movement inside the house. When the door finally opened, the old woman staring through the screen at them had to be at least ninety. She was wearing a loose-fitting, blue dress that hung on her like a potato sack. It stopped several inches below her knees. But it wasn't long enough to cover the two inches of slip that was visible beneath. Under one arm she carried a large brown Siamese and draped around her neck like a fox fur was an even bigger black and white cat.

The sight caused Steve to forget her name for just a moment. "Uh, Mrs... Cartwright?" he finally asked.

He felt Kathy prod him with her elbow. "I'm Steve Pearce and this is my wife, Kathy. I wonder if we might ask you a few questions?"

"Land sakes, whatever fer?"

"It's about one of your former neighbors and her daughter. Mrs. Harriet Stephens and her daughter, Nora. Do you remember them?"

"Course I 'member um. Lived right over there next door for nigh onto twenty years. What is it you want to know?"

"Could we come in for a minute, Mrs. Cartwright?"

The old woman looked them over carefully before pushing the

ancient screen door open. "Can't be none too careful these days," she said, "what with all the meanness goin' on. But then you seem to be fittin'." When they were in, she turned and dropped the Siamese before starting toward the back of the house. "Pardon the mess. Ain't had no chance to take a broom to the place today. Come on back to the kitchen. I was just a fixin' me a bowl of stew."

Steve and Kathy were barely in the door when the smell hit them. It was no mystery where it came from. There were no fewer than a dozen cats in the big front room. Papers were strewn against an outside wall and a small box filled with sand was in one corner. It only took them a quick glance to realize the cats had missed both the papers and the sand box on numerous occasions. Kathy lost her balance and grabbed Steve's arm as she tried to step around one pile that lay just short of the kitchen door.

The old woman was shooing two more cats off the cabinet as Steve and Kathy entered the kitchen.

"Here now. Git down from there Bootsy and you too, Puff. You know better than that," she said and swung her arm at a big yellow cat as it leaped from the cabinet to what had at one time been a nice kitchen table. The other cat hit the floor running with the yellow cat close behind. Both disappeared quickly into the front room.

"Would you young folks like a bowl of stew?"

Steve was about to say thanks but no thanks but Kathy beat him to it. Her stomach was already churning. "No, thank you, Mrs. Cartwright. We've just eaten," she lied.

Steve got straight to the point. "Mrs. Cartwright, can you tell us where we can find Mrs. Stephens or her daughter, Nora?"

The old woman unwrapped the big black and white cat from her neck and dropped it to the floor. "Now you git along, Charlie." The big cat lazily wandered off toward the front room and Granny began spooning stew into a bowl that Kathy was sure the big yellow cat had its nose in when they entered the kitchen.

"Sure you won't have a bit?" She said, looking toward Kathy. Then without waiting for a reply, she said, "Institutionalized, they said." She stopped and looked toward Steve. "Yep, that's the word they used."

"I beg your pardon," Steve said.

The old woman took a sip of the stew and smiled. Then she dipped the spoon back in the bowl and held it toward Kathy. "Powerful good, dearie. Sure you won't have a taste?"

Kathy could feel the bile rising in her throat. "No, thank you."

The woman looked back at Steve. "They put Harriet in one a them places for drinkers. She's been in um before. Always got out. Don't know about this time, though." Granny slurped down the spoonful of stew she had held out to Kathy and twisted her head with satisfaction.

"What about her daughter?" Steve pressed.

"Her daughter. You mean, Nora?"

"Yes, Nora."

"Dead."

"You mean Nora's dead? Are you sure?"

"Yep. Went to her funeral way back then. Near killed Harriet." She stopped, grabbed a salt shaker and sprinkled it on the stew. "Been dead six, seven, maybe eight years. Ran head on with a truck up near...." she paused, took another sip of stew and smacked her lips. "Up near to Hot Springs, I reckon."

Steve's legs felt rubbery and Kathy must have realized it. She slipped her arm around his waist and squeezed.

"Was she alone?" Steve thought his voice sounded like it was coming out of a barrel.

"Needs a mite more salt," Granny said and sat the shaker back on the table. "Had the baby with her, did Harriet. A wonder the little dear didn't git done in too."

Steve felt a shudder run up and down his body. "What happened to the baby?"

Granny took a slice of bread out of an opened package and began sopping what was left of the stew. "Went off to live with her brother, Harriet and little Jane did."

"You mean Sarah," Steve corrected.

Granny shook her head. "Think her name was Sally Jane or

Sarah Jane. Anyways, they called her Jane."

Steve let all he had learned sift through his brain a moment. "But if Mrs. Stephens is in an institution, what happened to the little girl?"

Granny carried her bowl to the sink and placed it carefully among more than a dozen other various bowls and glasses. As she did, the big yellow cat that was on the cabinet when they had first entered leaped up on the edge of the sink and stuck its nose into what was left of Granny's stew. The old woman took a swipe at the big cat, missed and shook her head.

"Got a letter from Harriet a while back. The brother died and they was puttin' Harriet back in the hospital. Then 'bout a month ago she writ again and said it looked like she was there for keeps. The whiskey done it, I reckon."

"But what about Sarah, I mean Jane? What happened to her?"

"Weren't no mention of her."

Steve could feel sweat breaking out on his neck and back. "You say she was living with her brother?"

"She done moved in with him right after Nora was killed."

"Where?"

"Memphis," Harriet answered. "That's in Tennessee."

"Yes, I know. What hospital did she write you from?"

"Lawsy me. I'm nigh onto ninety-five. I don't recollect all them names."

They followed Granny into the front room where she picked up the four corners of one of the soiled newspapers and started back toward the kitchen.

As she passed them, Kathy touched Steve's arm and pointed toward the door. Her face was ashen. "I'll wait for you in the car."

"It'll be cold out there."

"I know. That sounds wonderful." She was moving quickly as she opened the front door and hurried out onto the porch. Steve watched for a moment, before he followed Granny back into the kitchen.

"Mrs. Cartwright, do you still have the letter?"

"Letter. What letter might that be?"

"The one from Mrs. Stephens telling you she was going back into the hospital."

Granny looked past Steve to the front room. "Your Missy gone?"

"She's been feeling ill. Something she ate. She's waiting for me in the car."

The old woman pulled the blue dress tightly around her neck and gazed at Steve suspiciously. "Shoulda had a bowl of stew." She pointed toward a door at the rear of the kitchen. "I'll see do I still have it. You wait in there in the front room."

It was ten minutes before she returned with an envelope clutched in her right hand. She had put on a red sweater and buttoned it to the top.

"This here has the hospital name on it. I done writ it down in my address book. You can have this."

Steve pulled a single sheet of paper out of the envelope. The name and address of the hospital were prominent across the top. "Thank you, Granny. You're a queen." He glanced once more at the roomful of cats, reached behind him for the knob and hurried out and across the yard to the car. Kathy had her head back against the headrest when he opened the door. Her coat was pulled tightly around her and her eyes were closed when he slid in beside her.

"You okay?"

"I'm not sure." She raised her head and eyed him with mock anger. "Just don't offer to feed me any time soon."

Steve laughed and slipped the key into the ignition. As he moved out into the street, he patted the envelope and letter he had slipped into his shirt pocket.

CHAPTER 43

WHEN HIS YOUNG SPANISH receptionist knocked, Ray Philpot was studying the x-ray of a broken right elbow. A twenty-year-old metal worker had fallen backwards off a ladder, landing elbow first on a concrete floor. The knob had been broken in half and now, a month after removal of the cast, the arm was still frozen in a thirty-degree bend. Extensive therapy had failed to straighten it and Ray was slowly becoming convinced that it would remain that way if some other treatment was not undertaken. He looked up as the young woman came through the door.

"Yes, Maria."

Maria Gonzales was a slender, dark-haired, twenty-three-year-old with just a touch of an accent. Because of that she had trained herself to be very precise with the pronunciation of every word she spoke.

"Doctor Ray, I have called the Pearce home all day. There is still no answer."

Ray glanced at his watch, saw it was time for Maria to go home and flipped the x-ray on the desk.

"That's okay, Maria. You go on home. I'll get in touch with Mr. Pearce later today."

"Yes, Doctor Ray. Goodnight."

"Night, Maria."

When Ray heard the outer office door shut, he picked up the phone and dialed. After half a dozen rings he pushed the disconnect button and dialed his home.

"Doctor Philpot's residence."

"Susan."

"Oh, hi."

"I have to stop by the hospital for a few minutes. Should be home by six or six thirty."

"Dinner at seven, then," his wife replied.

"Fine. Oh, say, you haven't by chance spoken to Kathy Pearce today, have you?"

"Kathy, no. Why?"

"Just wondered. Maria's been trying to set up an early appointment for Steve all day and they haven't been home."

"Anything wrong?"

"No, of course not. Just a routine checkup to see how he's progressing."

"Oh, wait a minute," Susan said. "I was talking to Cora Sanders this aft...."

"Who?"

"Cora Sanders, Ray. They belong to the country club. He's Bill Sanders, the lawyer."

"Oh, yeah. What about her?"

"Well, like I was saying, I was talking to her about three this afternoon, when she suddenly said she had to go. It was time for Tommy Pearce's school bus. She said Steve and Kathy were out of town and she had to pick up Tommy."

"Say where they went or when they'd be back?"

"No."

Ray reached for the disconnect button. "Okay, Susan. I'll see you around six." He pressed the button and dialed his answering service.

"This is Doctor Philpot. I'm leaving my office for the evening. I'll be going from here to the hospital, then home around six."

"Yes, sir."

Ray disconnected again, started to make another try at Steve's number, then hung up and went out his private door to the parking lot.

CHAPTER 44

The sun had set by the time Steve pulled into the carport. He had been on a high all the way from Texarkana. Finding out for sure that Sarah existed had been like a tonic to him. It had not seemed to be the same for Kathy. He could only hope that sooner or later she would come around. But right now he could understand her feelings.

Seconds after they entered the house, Steve was dialing the number in Memphis where Harriett Stephens was hospitalized.

"Markwood Nursing Home." The elderly woman spoke slowly, pronouncing each syllable precisely.

"I'd like to get some information on a patient, a Mrs. Harriett Stephens. Can you...."

"I'm sorry, Sir. I'm not at liberty to give out patient information. You would have to speak to our administrator, Doctor Owens, or his assistant, Miss Tracy Benton."

"May I speak to one of them?"

"I'm sorry, Sir. All administrative offices are closed for the evening. If you call back in the morning, I'm sure one of them will be available to speak to you."

"Would there be anyone there that I could speak to now, a nurse or doctor, maybe?"

"I'm sorry, Sir. All administrative personnel have left for the evening."

"Yes, but...."

"Please call back after nine in the morning. Thank you for calling Markwood Nursing Home."

Before Steve could answer the line went dead. He sat with the phone pressed to his ear for several seconds before it hit him. The woman had hung up on him. Finally, he slammed the phone back in its cradle and slapped the desk top with the flat of his hand.

"What's wrong, Honey?" Kathy was halfway up the stairs when she heard him unleash his temper.

"Can you believe it? Long distance and she hung up in my ear. I was paying for the call. People like that, I'd like to...." He took his hands and made a twisting motion like he was wringing out a wet towel. Then he sat back in the straight chair and shook his head. "All comes down to calling back in the morning."

Kathy came back down the stairs and dropped carefully into his lap, wrapping her arms around his neck as she did. "Then you'll just have to be patient and wait until then." Her voice was soft and sensuous as she bent forward until their lips met. They both jumped when the phone rang.

"Darn. That silly thing scared me half to death," she said as she got up.

Steve slapped her on the bottom and reached for the phone. "Hello."

"Steve, Ray."

"Hi, Ray."

"Where you been? My receptionist has been trying to reach you all day."

"Sorry about that. What's the problem?"

"No problem. I've got some free time day after tomorrow and thought we'd move up the examination. Can you make it?"

"Hmmm. Sure, why not. What time you want me there?"

"Three o'clock okay?"

"I'll be there."

Kathy had moved around behind Steve and was massaging his shoulders, listening to every word her husband was saying. When he hung up, her fingers quit working but stayed on his shoulders.

"What did Ray want?"

Steve leaned back in the chair. "You ever hear of a doctor with free time?"

"Free time?"

"Yeah. He wants to move my appointment up to day after tomorrow."

"Oh."

Something in the way she answered caused Steve to turn and look up into her eyes. They were damp and, without knowing it, her teeth had clamped down on her lower lip. He had seen the expression before. It was the look she always got when she was uncertain Steve would be happy with something she did. She could never hide her guilt from him. He caught her wrist as she released his shoulders and started to turn away.

"Kathy, have you been talking to Ray about what I told you?"

"No." Her voice was barely audible, to Steve a confirmation of guilt.

"Honey, what did you tell him?"

Tears were streaming down her cheeks. "Steve, please."

He stood up and pushed the chair out of the way. As he did, he wrapped his arms around her shoulders and drew her to him. "Kathy, it's all right. It's all right."

"I was afraid for you. When you told me the story of what had happened to you I didn't believe you. I'd heard that strange things can happen to someone who's been in a coma." She pushed away from him and looked up into his face. "Everyone thought you were going to die. Someone even said that your mind might be affected if you did live. I heard someone mention brain damage." Her body began heaving with emotion. "I was so scared. I didn't really believe you were going to die. I didn't believe there would be brain damage. And then you told me what you did and I got scared again, scared for you. Ray was the only one I could turn to, the only one who could help us."

Steve pulled her against him and began massaging the back of her neck. "You've had a terrible time and I'm sorry. But, I'm okay. My mind's okay. I don't want you to worry any longer."

"I know you're okay," she whispered. She pushed away again and looked up into his eyes with a pleading expression. "Please forgive me for doubting you." She paused and Steve could tell she wasn't through. "I don't doubt you any longer. Something did happen to you in that coma. But I know it didn't affect your mind. I don't understand what happened. I may never understand but whatever happened has to be for good, not bad."

She rested her head against his shoulder, finished now. "You asked me to forgive you. There's nothing to forgive, Kathy. I should have realized just how traumatic this would be for you. But it's all true. I think you know it's true now, don't you?"

"Yes. I believe you. And, Steve, you had to tell me. There's nothing else you could have done. I just took it badly at first." She was trembling. "But, I'll be fine now."

"You're cold." He pulled her closer to him.

"Yes, a little. But, I'll be okay now."

CHAPTER 45

TRACY BENTON HAD WORKED at Markwood since college, more than ten years now. She started as the receptionist, then eight years ago she became Ted Owens' private secretary. As the nursing home grew and the position became necessary, the office of assistant to the administrator was created. Tracy was Ted's personal choice.

Although only five foot seven, with the auburn bun pulled tight on the back of her head and reading glasses in place, Tracy bore a striking resemblance to the Wonder Woman character that had been on television a number of years ago. She was going through the mail when the intercom buzzed.

"Yes."

"Miss Benton," the switchboard operator said, "I have a Mr. Steve Pearce on line two. He asked for Doctor Owens. I told him the doctor wasn't in and he asked to speak to you."

"Do you know what it's about, Karen?"

"No, ma'am."

"Thanks. I'll take it." Tracy pushed the flashing red light. "Hello, this is Tracy Benton. How may I help you?"

"Miss Benton, my name is Steve Pearce. I'm trying to locate the mother of a former college acquaintance. I've been in touch with a friend of hers in Texarkana, Arkansas, and she showed me a letter she received from the woman. It bore Markwood's address."

"What's the lady's name?" As she talked, Tracy shifted the mail about, pushing to one side the large amount of junk mail they received daily.

"Harriet Stephens."

Tracy dropped the mail on the desk in front of her and leaned forward in her chair. "Are you calling to inquire about Mrs. Stephen's condition?"

"Yes. But I'm also interested in locating her granddaughter."

Tracy took off her glasses and stuck one stem in the corner of her mouth. "Her granddaughter?"

"Yes. I'm trying to locate her."

"I'm sorry, Mr. Pearce. I...."

"Excuse me, Miss Benton, but the last time someone at your institution said they were sorry, they hung up in my ear."

Tracy Benton giggled. She had heard this before. "Last evening, I'll wager."

"Yes," Steve answered.

"That would be Rose." Tracy put her glasses back on, then took them off and wiped the wet stem with a tissue before replacing them. "I'm sorry about that, Mr. Pearce. But, suppose I take a little different tack. Although I am the assistant administrator, Doctor Owens is the only one with the official authority to reveal a patient's private file. So the information you seek would have to come from him."

"If I come to Memphis, could I see Mrs. Stephens and also speak to your Doctor Owens."

Tracy pushed all the mail to one side of the desk. "If Mrs. Stephens is able to receive visitors at the time you're here, I see no reason why you can't. About Doctor Owens, he's out, but is due back in the morning. And he is very accessible when he's here."

"I appreciate your candor, Miss Benton. One other question, if I might. What are your visiting hours?"

"One four-hour stretch, from two in the afternoon until six. Very rigidly enforced, I might add."

"Thank you, Miss Benton."

"Good day, Mr. Pearce." Tracy replaced the receiver and momentarily turned her attention back to the mail. But without opening another letter she got up and opened the door to Ted

Owens' private office. The cabinet with the patient files stood just to the right of the large mahogany desk that a thankful patient had sent the doctor five years earlier from El Salvador. One of the three keys to those files hung on a chain around her neck. She opened the drawer marked R,S,T and thumbed through the folders until she found Harriet Stephens' file. She scanned down to the blank for next of kin. The typed words - NO KNOWN LIVING RELATIVES - filled the space. She pondered that for a few seconds, then slipped the file back in place, locked the drawer and went back to her office.

~ ~ ~

Steve took a quick sip of coffee as he got up from the kitchen phone. He looked up at Kathy and found his wife watching him intently.

"Well?"

"Harriet Stephens is there," he said. "And I will be by noon tomorrow. I'm going to Memphis in the morning. Visiting hours begin at two and I want to be there in time to meet with the administrator." He got up and started for the stairs.

"Where are you going?"

"I'm going up and pack a bag. I might have to be gone overnight."

"You're not going without me. I'll pack a bag for both of us."

They were halfway up the stairs when Steve stopped. "What about Tommy?"

"Let's take him. It won't hurt him to miss one day of school."

Steve started up again. It was Kathy's turn to stop him. "Steve, what about Ray? Your appointment?"

He stopped again. "I'll call early in the morning and cancel."

Just after nine the next morning Steve was loading the suitcase in the car. Kathy and Tommy had just come out the door and were standing beside the car when they heard the phone.

"I'll get it," she said and hurried into the house before Steve could stop her. Moments later she was back. "It's Ray. Maria told him you cancelled and he wants to talk to you."

"Darn." He stepped past her and hurried to the phone.

"Hello, Ray."

"Steve, what's this about you canceling out this afternoon?"

"Sorry, Ray. Hope it didn't inconvenience you but I've got to be in Memphis this afternoon."

"Can't it wait?"

"Afraid not. Look, Ray. I'm running kind of late. Why don't I call you when I get back?"

"That's a pretty good drive. Sure you're up to it?"

"I'm fine, Ray. Kathy and Tommy are going with me." Steve glanced at his watch and shifted his weight from one foot to the other. He heard Ray take a deep breath and let it out slowly on the other end.

"You say Kathy and Tommy are going with you?"

"Right."

"Okay. But you be careful now and check in with me as soon as you get home. You hear?"

"Will do," Steve said and hung up before Ray could reply.

Kathy and Tommy were standing just outside the back door when he came out.

"What did he say?" Kathy asked.

"Just to be careful. But I think he wanted to say a lot more."

CHAPTER 46

WHEN DOCTOR TED OWENS arrived back at Markwood, he went directly from his car, up the half dozen steps and down the hall to his office. The receptionist was the first to see him.

"Good afternoon, Doctor Owens. How was the conference?"

"Informative, Sandra, informative."

He opened the door that led to Tracy Benton's office and smiled as his assistant looked up.

"Hi, Ted." She got up from behind her desk and met him at the entrance to his office. They stepped through the door marked private and closed it behind them. A moment later she was in his arms.

"Anything earth shattering happen today?" he asked as their lips parted.

"Not really." She nodded back toward her own office. "I've got coffee perking. Interested?"

Ted nodded. "I could use some."

When she came back with a cup and set it at his right hand, he was poring through the two-day accumulation of mail. After a moment he stopped and studied a piece of paper. "Who's this Steve Pearce from Hot Springs?"

She reached down and turned his hand toward her so that she could see the writing. "He called yesterday to inquire about Mrs. Stephens."

"Harriet?"

"Yes, but he seemed to be very interested about a granddaughter that Harriet was supposed to have. I told him he'd have to check with you, that I didn't have the authority to reveal a patient's personal information."

"And?"

"And he asked if he could visit Mrs. Stephens," she said and hesitated. "He also wanted to speak to you if you were here when he arrived."

Ted was drumming rhythmically with the fingers of his right hand on the glass-covered desktop.

"A granddaughter. I don't recall Harriet's records showing a granddaughter. In fact, I thought she was alone except for the brother that died a few months ago."

"Um-hum." Tracy already had the file drawer open and was thumbing through the 'S's. "After I hung up from Mr. Pearce's call, I checked. There's no mention of any granddaughter. And you're right again. No living relatives." She found the Stephens file and opened it in front of Ted.

"Obviously, he must have the wrong Harriet Stephens," Ted said after a moment of studying the file. "You haven't spoken to Harriet, have you?"

"Reece Phelps said she's holding her own, but not lucid very often. She's already lived longer than Reece thought she would."

Ted leaned back in the chair and rested his elbows on the armrests, clasping his hands together in front of his chest as he did. "I like that woman," he said quietly.

"You like everyone, Ted. But I like her, too."

He picked up the piece of paper with Steve's name on it and thrust it toward her. "You say this Steve Pearce wants to see me?"

She nodded and started for the door. "I'm not sure whether he'll be here today, but if and when he shows up I'll buzz you."

Ted nodded without looking up. He was already opening the top letter on the stack of mail.

~ ~ ~

In the early afternoon when the intercom on her desk sounded,

Tracy glanced at her watch without the time really registering. "Yes, Sandra."

"Miss Benton, there's a Mr. and Mrs. Steve Pearce from Hot Springs, Arkansas, here to see Doctor Owens. They said they spoke to you yesterday."

"That's right Sandra. Give me a minute, then send them in."

She pressed Ted Owens' intercom button. "Ted, Mr. and Mrs. Pearce from Hot Springs are here."

"Thanks, Tracy. I'll see them in a couple of minutes."

"Right."

Tracy got up and opened the outer door as Steve and Kathy, along with Tommy, started in. Unconsciously, she reached up and patted the bun atop her head before stretching her hand out to the handsome young man. "Mr. and Mrs. Pearce, I'm Tracy Benton. I talked to you earlier, Mr. Pearce."

Steve grasped the woman's warm hand and released it quickly. "Miss Benton, this is my wife, Kathy, and my son, Tommy."

Tracy took Kathy's hand and smiled. "Mrs. Pearce." Then she smiled down at the boy. "Hello, Tommy."

"Hi."

She turned her attention back to Steve. "I've told Doctor Owens about your call and he's expecting you," she said. Tracy went back to her desk and pushed the intercom button. "Doctor Owens, can you see Mr. and Mrs. Pearce now?"

"Yes, Tracy. Would you show them in, please?"

"Of course."

Tracy moved to the door marked private and opened it. Ted was on his feet and halfway across the office by the time Steve and Kathy were through the door.

"Mr. and Mrs. Pearce, I'm Doctor Owens." He shook hands with Steve and Kathy, then looked quizzically at Tommy. "And who might this young man be?"

Tracy was the first to answer. "This is Tommy, Doctor Owens."

"Hello, Tommy." Ted Owens bent over and stuck his hand toward the child. Tommy reached out and rested his hand in Ted's.

"Hello."

Ted allowed his attention to remain on the boy for several seconds, then released Tommy's hand and looked up at Steve. "Won't you folks have a seat and tell me what we can do for you?"

It took only seconds for Steve to begin. "Doctor, we're very interested in locating Mrs. Stephens' granddaughter. Can you help us?"

"Are either of you related to Mrs. Stephens?"

Steve shook his head. "No. I knew her daughter in college. We dated but other than that, no."

"What is your acquaintance with her now?"

Kathy leaned forward in her chair. "We've never met her, Doctor Owens. But Steve must...." Kathy glanced quickly at Steve. "We feel that we must find her granddaughter."

Ted leaned back in the swivel chair and looked from one to the other. "Before we go any further, I must tell you that Mrs. Stephens' record makes no mention of a granddaughter." He saw the disappointment on Steve's face and quickly added. "But there have been instances when records were wrong."

Kathy reached over and put her hand on Steve's forearm. "You mean the child might be...." she stopped and looked toward her husband.

Ted opened a folder on the desk in front of him. "I simply mean that there is absolutely no mention of a grandchild. I'm afraid the both of you might have been led astray. Possibly, this isn't the Harriet Stephens you're looking for."

"Originally from Texarkana, Arkansas," Steve said.

Ted glanced at the folder. "That's right."

"It's her, doctor. We talked to her next door neighbor and she assured us there was a granddaughter." Steve was fishing an envelope out of his pocket, "She also gave us this. It's a letter Harriet wrote and the return address is your nursing home."

Ted took it, studied it, and handed it back to Steve. "All right, we'll assume this is your Harriet Stephens and that there is a grandchild. If that's so, then I feel obligated to ask you a question."

"Of course," Steve answered.

"What is your interest in the little girl?"

Steve stared at the doctor for a second, then turned and looked at Kathy. Her gaze had remained steady on the doctor. Now she turned and faced her husband. Their eyes met for several seconds before she nodded. Tommy was perched on Steve's lap and she turned now and looked back at the doctor.

"Could Tommy and I be excused?"

Ted knew why Kathy had made the request. "Tell you what, Tommy. How would you like to go out and see Mrs. Butler? She keeps some candy in the top drawer of her desk and I'll bet she would be happy to share it with you."

Tommy's eyes lit up and Ted pressed the intercom button. "Sandra, would you step into my office for a moment?" He released the button without waiting for an answer and looked at Kathy. "Is that all right, Mrs. Pearce?"

Kathy smiled and nodded her head. "Thank you, Doctor Owens."

A moment later the door from the outer office opened and Sandra Butler appeared.

"Sandra, this is Tommy Pearce. I'll bet he'd go for some of that candy you've got stashed in your desk."

The young woman smiled and knelt in front of Tommy. "How about that, Tommy. Do you like chocolate candy?"

"Yes, ma'am." He looked at his mother then back over his shoulder at Steve. "Can I?"

"Sure, son. Go ahead. We'll be out in a few minutes."

When Sandra and Tommy disappeared, Ted turned back to Steve and Kathy. "Sandra has a boy just about Tommy's age. She and Tommy will get along famously." He leaned forward toward Kathy. "I hope I didn't presume too much when I called Mrs. Butler."

"No, doctor. I appreciate what you did."

"Good." Ted leaned back in his chair. "You were about to tell me something relative to the granddaughter."

It was Kathy who spoke. "We.... my husband found out quite

by accident that the child, the little girl, might be his. Before he met me. ..."

Ted held up his hand. "You needn't go any further, Mrs. Pearce." He began rocking in the big chair. "As much as I'd like to help you, the records still show that there is no child."

"Is it possible to speak to Mrs. Stephens?" Steve asked.

"You may see her. But, I'm not sure you'll be able to speak to her."

"Why?"

Ted took a deep breath and let it out slowly. "I don't ordinarily discuss a patient with someone who isn't family." His eyes moved back and forth from Steve to Kathy. "But, this is a little different. Harriet has no one. The best I can tell, you're the closest to a relative or a friend since she came to us six months ago." He drummed his fingers on the typewritten pages in the folder. "Harriet came to us as a common drunk. She'd been in and out of one hospital or another for several years. Dry one day, back on the booze the next."

Ted stopped rocking and closed his eyes for perhaps thirty seconds before continuing. "About six months ago I received a call from a friend, a social worker who knew Harriet. It seems she had landed in jail and was headed for another drying out session. My friend called, asked me to take her in and I consented. She hasn't had very many lucid moments since she's been here. When she arrived, we made some preliminary tests. We were concerned that she might have complications from the years of alcohol abuse. Unfortunately, we were right. I won't go into the details of her illness except to say Harriet is dying." Ted's voice trailed off and he cleared his throat.

"Doctor Phelps, her physician, thinks she has only a few days at the most. Her communication skills, as I've already said, have been very limited since she's been here. They're even more limited now." He held out his hands, palms up. "That's why I'm not sure you'll be able to talk to her."

Steve licked his lips. "I'd still like to try. It might be our best chance to find Sarah."

Ted nodded his head. "Okay. Of course. I'll go up with you." He looked to Tracy, who had been quiet all during the discussion. "Is Doctor Phelps still here?"

"I don't think so. I believe he went over to Memphis General to make rounds."

"Would you mind waiting while we go up to Harriet's room?"

"Of course. I'll be in my office. And if Sandra gets busy, I'll watch after Tommy."

Ted nodded and motioned toward a side door. "Let's go through this door and we won't disturb Tommy." He led the way into the hall. "We're a small home in comparison to many others," he explained. "We try to make up in quality what we lack in quantity." He pushed the second floor button next to the elevator doors and they opened quickly. "Our elevator service, since we have only two floors, is generally very snappy."

In seconds, Steve and Kathy were on and off the elevator and following Ted down another hall. He opened the door to room 230 and peered in.

Harriet Stephens lay on her back, her white hair loose to her shoulders. She was breathing heavily, seemingly asleep. A white-clad nurse was attaching a new glucose bottle to the stand beside the bed. She smiled at Ted and gave Steve and Kathy a curt nod before turning her attention back to the old woman.

"Ted moved around behind the nurse and whispered. "Has she been awake?"

"Just a short time this morning. She kept trying to say a name, then fell asleep again."

"Sarah," Steve said quickly. "Was she saying Sarah?"

The nurse glared at him for a moment, then at the doctor.

"It's all right, Clara. Could you tell what she was saying?"

The nurse shook her head. "It sounded like Jean or Jane. She's so weak and I couldn't make it out."

There was the sound of the hallway door opening and all four looked around to see an even older woman, in her late seventies or early eighties, working her way into the room. She was completely surrounded by the aluminum walker she used to support her fragile body. When she saw Ted her face broke into a toothless grin.

"Doctor Ted," she squealed.

"Hello, Gertie." Ted went over to the woman and put his arm around her shoulders. "How are you feeling today?"

"Oh, tolerable," she answered. She looked across the room at Harriet and frowned, "but not my Harriet," she added sadly.

Ted looked toward Steve and Kathy. "Gertie and Harriet hit it off from the first day Harriet arrived. Gertie's been with us nearly a year now." He squeezed Gertie's shoulder. "Gertie, this is Mr. and Mrs. Pearce. They've come all the way from Hot Springs, Arkansas, to see Harriet and talk to her if they can."

Gertie shook her head. "Ain't nobody gonna be able to talk to her, poor old dear." She began the laboriously slow movement that took her finally to a position beside Harriet's bed. She stood for several minutes staring into her friend's bleached-out face. It was Steve who finally broke the silence.

"Doctor, would it be all right if I asked Gertie some questions?"

"I have no objections, that is, if Gertie doesn't mind."

Steve moved up beside the woman who had taken Harriet's limp hand and seemed to be massaging it tenderly. "Gertie, could I ask you some questions about your friend, Mrs. Stephens?"

Gertie turned slowly toward Ted Owens, saw him smile and nod and turned back to Steve. "I suppose it ain't gonna do no harm."

"Gertie, did Mrs. Stephens ever talk to you about her family?"

"Time or two. She was right proud of that daughter of hers. Got killed in that accident, she did."

"Did she ever mention anything about a granddaughter?"

"Might near killed Harriet when that pretty daughter of hers died. Ran head on into a big truck."

"I'm sure it was terrible for her," Steve said. "But, did she ever say anything to you about her granddaughter, a little girl named Sarah?"

Gertie's face went blank.

Steve pressed on. "Gertie, Harriet has a granddaughter named Sarah. Can you tell me anything about her?"

"Oh, no. There was no Sarah. Least ways she never mentioned that name."

Steve's heart skipped a beat.

"Oh, no. Weren't no Sarah. But that little Jane, she always talked a blue streak about her when she could talk, that is. Couldn't get enough of talking about her." Gertie turned back to her friend and stared down at the motionless body. "Might near killed the poor dear when they took the child away and put her in one of them children's homes." She began massaging Harriet's hand again. "Maybe it is killing her."

Something Jim said not three weeks ago, Jim who was dead again, was rattling around in Steve's head. He called the child Sarah Jane and said the baby, Sarah Jane, had been two months old when Steve and Nora were married.

Steve bent over and kissed the old woman on the cheek. "You've been a great help, Gertie. Bless you."

Ted was standing at Steve's elbow. "You think she's the child you're looking for?"

Steve smiled at Kathy and nodded. "I'm sure it is. Her full given name is Sarah Jane. The last name is probably Stephens." He looked again at Kathy. "I'd almost forgotten that Jim said her name was Sarah Jane. Naturally, I assumed everyone called her Sarah. But Harriet must have preferred Jane, her middle name."

As they waited for the elevator doors to open, Ted turned to Steve. "If you find the girl, I assume you plan to begin adoption proceedings."

Steve glanced at Kathy and she nodded. "Yes." Steve answered.

"Harriet evidently loves that child very much," Ted began. "If or when we find her, I'd like to bring her here where she can be close to her grandmother. It could make Harriet's last days much more pleasant."

They stepped into the elevator and Ted pushed the down button.

"I think that's the only thing to do," Kathy answered.

"Agreed," Steve said.

On the lower floor, they made their way quickly back to Ted's office. Inside, the doctor stopped at Tracy's desk.

"Get me a list of every children's home within fifty miles of Memphis, Tracy. And I'd like you to make some phone calls. Okay?"

"Yes, doctor, right away."

Ted turned to Steve. "In the meantime, I'd like you to give me some references. I need them and I'm sure when we find the girl, you'll have to present them to whatever children's home where she may be living. I'm sure you understand."

"I do, Doctor Owens. I'll give you a list that includes my pastor and my doctor in Hot Springs and anyone else you feel is necessary."

"Good. Now while you're getting that information together, how about some coffee?"

CHAPTER 47

ELIZABETH STAPLETON HAD JUST finished her monthly report to the board of directors and now sat rolling a black ballpoint pen back and forth between the palms of her hands as she reread the four-page memorandum. Except for a few minor changes or deletions, it read much the same as it did last month, even the last six months. One child placed in a foster home, another in the process of adoption. She studied the last page carefully and was about to affix her signature when the intercom sounded.

"Yes."

"Mrs. Stapleton, there's a call for you from a Miss Tracy Benton. She says she's the assistant administrator at Markwood Nursing Home."

"Did she tell you what it was about?"

"No, ma'am. Just that it was important."

"Put her on."

"Yes, ma'am."

A moment later the connection was made.

"Miss Benton, this is Elizabeth Stapleton. What can I do for you?"

"I'm sorry to bother you, Mrs. Stapleton. But your secretary told me you have a Sarah Jane Stephens at your home. We've been trying to locate the child. If she's the right Sarah Jane Stephens, we have her grandmother at our nursing home."

Elizabeth stuck the pen behind her right ear and looked across the room to the files that held the current children's records. "I find it hard to believe that this is the same Sarah Jane, Miss Benton.

The child we have here had only a grandfather living up to a few months ago. He has since passed away leaving the child with no known relatives."

"It's very possible that there was a breakdown in communications somewhere. Our records indicate that our patient, Mrs. Harriet Stephens, didn't have a granddaughter. But we have two different sources that swear that she does."

"I see," Elizabeth said.

"Mrs. Stapleton, let me switch Doctor Owens, our administrator, onto the line. He can give you more information."

"Very well, Miss Benton. Tell the doctor to give me just a minute while I get the child's records from my file."

Ted was in the process of filling his coffee cup for the third time when Tracy knocked.

"Come."

"Doctor," she said coming through the doorway, "I've found a Sarah Jane Stephens. But the children's home says she doesn't have a living relative. They do say she had a grandfather who died recently."

"That could be Harriet's brother," Steve said quickly.

"Maybe. But, let's don't jump to conclusions. Tracy, do you have the home on the phone?"

"On line two. But the administrator, a Mrs. Stapleton, said to give her a few minutes to locate the child's records."

Steve leaned forward and rested his right elbow on Ted's desk. As he did, Kathy reached over from her chair and slipped her right hand in his left. She felt the sweaty palm and squeezed it gently.

"If it's her, we'll know very soon," she whispered.

"It's her," Steve said. "I can feel it. It's her."

Ted cleared his throat and picked up the phone. "Mrs. Stapleton." He waited a moment, then spoke again. "I'm Doctor Owens. Can we speak for a few moments about the child you have in your care, Sarah Jane Stephens?"

After a short pause Ted nodded. Steve wished the doctor would put the conversation on speakerphone but he didn't and Steve sat staring at every move Ted Owens made. Ted opened Harriet

Stephens' file and began studying it line by line.

"Yes, that's the same name we have here for Mrs. Stephens' brother. He would not be the grandfather but the great uncle if what we now understand is true. Our records, as yours evidently are, must be incomplete. Of course, we must do some verifying, but I feel the child is the one we're looking for. Let me get right to the point, Mrs. Stapleton. We would never have been aware of the child's existence if it hadn't been for the young couple that walked into my office this afternoon. As soon as we learned that Sarah did exist, we immediately began a phone search for her. It was important that we contact her quickly since her grandmother's illness is terminal, possibly within the next few days. And we thought that since neither child nor her grandmother had anyone else, they should be together over these next few days. Do you agree?"

Ted listened again, throwing a "um-hum" in every few seconds. When he spoke again, he was looking straight at Steve.

"Mrs. Stapleton, the young couple I spoke of might be interested in adopting Sarah. Are there any complications that would hinder adoption if they should qualify?"

Ted neither spoke, nodded or made any sound for the next minute or two. During that time his eyes left Steve and Kathy and he leaned back in his chair and stared toward the front wall.

Finally he spoke. "Has the child been examined by a specialist?"

He twisted back toward a nervous Steve and eyed him over the receiver. "But not by a specialist. I see." Ted leaned forward in his chair and his eyes seemed to focus on the far wall. "Mrs. Stapleton, I have a good friend who is a specialist. I know if I asked him he would be willing to examine Sarah Jane. Do you have any objection to that?"

After a moment of silence, Ted smiled. "Very good. I'll set up that examination as soon as I can get in touch with Doctor Bates." He looked now at Steve and Kathy. "In the meantime, I have a young couple in my office who would like to meet your young lady. Would that be possible?"

Ted was silent for about a minute. "I understand your concern,

Mrs. Stapleton. I would be just as careful if I were in your position. Suppose I make a suggestion. Suppose I provide you with a list of names of people who will vouch for our institution. You can check us out until you feel comfortable. You'll recognize most of these people and they would be happy to tell you anything you need to know about us. Would that help?"

Ted closed his eyes and leaned back in the chair. "I do understand, Mrs. Stapleton. You do have to be careful. Tell you what. I'm going to have my assistant call your secretary and give her that list of names. You can check us out as much as you need to. When you are comfortable with us, would you call us back and let us know?" He listened again. "We'll call you back in just a few minutes with the names. Thank you again, Mrs. Stapleton." Ted dropped the receiver back in its cradle and looked at Tracy.

"You know the list we need. Pull it up and have Sandra call the children's home and give them what they need."

"Right away, doctor."

He turned to Steve and Kathy. "Now we wait until they call us back."

Steve leaned back in his chair and looked at Kathy. "We've come this far. I guess we can wait a little longer."

It was two hours before the call came. When it was transferred into Ted's office, Steve and Kathy had stepped out into the hall and were moving restlessly up and down the narrow corridor. Tracy Benton opened the door from Doctor Owens' office.

"Mr. and Mrs. Pearce. We've heard from the children's home. Would you come back into Doctor Owens' office?"

They didn't hesitate. Once inside, Ted Owens motioned both of them to their seats. "We've heard from Mrs. Stapleton. She tells me she's comfortable with us and with you. I've made arrangements for you to meet Sarah. It's less than an hour's drive from here and Miss Benton," he motioned toward Tracy, "will be going with you to represent us."

Steve rose quickly from his chair. "When can we go, doctor?"

"How about right now."

Steve reached across the desk. "Thank you, doctor."

"Don't thank me yet. Remember," he said looking from Steve to Kathy, "the decision about Sarah's adoption will be based on what's best for her."

"We both understand that, doctor," Kathy said.

Ted looked at Steve. "Mr. Pearce."

Steve nodded. "She's right, doctor. We both understand that."

~ ~ ~

"Best for her."

"What, Steve?" They were in the back seat of Tracy Benton's Mercury, just pulling into the circular drive at the Harbinger Children's Home. The ride had taken the better part of forty-five minutes and Steve had sat amazingly still and quiet during that time. He had hardly been aware of the freeway as it passed beneath them. His mind had been back there, back in that other world.

Except for Sarah, that world was becoming increasingly distant and more difficult to believe. At times it seemed that it must have been only a dream. He could see why Kathy found it hard to believe. Yet, it had happened. Even though it seemed so far away, it had happened. He was convinced of that. And this child, this Sarah, was the dividend, the reason he had experienced it. He was meant to find her. And now he had. Everything had a purpose. That's why he was convinced that she wouldn't slip from his grasp now. She had once, but never again.

"We're here," Tracy announced.

~ ~ ~

Steve and Kathy stared out the window at the old, two-story, red brick building that loomed before them. Dusk was beginning to fall and, as they watched, a light came on in a second-floor window. A moment later a small face appeared at the window, watched the car roll up the drive, then disappeared as quickly as it had appeared.

In that moment, Steve thought he recognized the face. But it had happened so quickly that he dismissed the thought as his own imagination. As the car came to a stop, he touched Kathy's hand and nodded toward the door.

She opened the door and slid out of the car. As she did she shuddered at what she saw. "Awfully drab," she said looking toward the building. Tommy slipped out next to his mother and latched onto her hand.

Tracy was already out and leading the way up the half dozen steps to the front door. Inside, with Steve, Kathy and Tommy close behind, she strode up to the young woman at the reception desk. "I'm Tracy Benton from Markwood Nursing Home. This is Mr. and Mrs. Pearce and their son, Tommy. Mrs. Stapleton is expecting us."

"Yes, ma'am." She nodded toward a door on Tracy's left. "I'll tell her you're here." She pushed a button and leaned forward. "Mrs. Stapleton, Miss Benton and the Pearces are here."

"Have them come right in."

Elizabeth Stapleton was on her feet and walking around her desk when the four came through the door. She smiled and extended her hand as Tracy led the way across the small office.

"You'd be Miss Benton," Elizabeth said.

"Yes," Tracy said as she grasped the older woman's hand. "And this is Mr. and Mrs. Pearce and their son, Tommy."

Elizabeth shook hands with Steve and Kathy and smiled down at Tommy. Then she motioned toward an old couch and a straight chair. "Please be seated."

She studied Steve and Kathy for several seconds before she spoke again. "Sarah Jane will be along momentarily. While I was waiting for you to arrive I've been able to talk with most of the people your secretary passed along to us. An impressive group of citizens you've provided us with." She paused for a moment then continued. "You and your nursing home have been given a four-star rating by everyone I've spoken to. I'm well satisfied that Doctor Owens and Markwood are everything I've been led to believe."

Steve was getting impatient. "About Sarah."

"Yes, Mr. Pearce. Sarah will be along soon now. She was eating her dinner when your call came in." She stopped and looked from Steve to Kathy and back to Steve. "I understand you've expressed interest in adopting Sarah."

It was Kathy who answered. "Yes." She looked at Steve. "If she's the child my husband knows."

Elizabeth looked back to Steve. "How do you know her, Mr. Pearce?"

Steve took a deep breath. "I knew her a...." he paused. "A long time ago. It seems like another world now."

"Then you knew her long before she came to us."

"Yes," Steve said.

"Then you know she's partially crippled. You know about the accident and her mother."

"I know that her mother was killed in an automobile accident when Sarah was a baby. I know she wears a brace on one leg."

Elizabeth looked at Kathy. "And you, Mrs. Pearce. Have you met the child?"

Kathy instinctively reached out and rested her hand on Steve's. He turned his hand over and let hers nestle in his. Kathy smiled and turned back to Elizabeth. "I've never met Sarah, Mrs. Stapleton. But Steve has told me so much about her that I feel I know her."

"I see." Elizabeth leaned forward and took a pen from her desktop. She made some notes on a pad, then looked back at Steve. "I'm sure Doctor Owens explained to you that the child's best interests and her happiness are our main concern. We have to make every effort to protect her. You do understand that, do you not?"

"Completely," Steve answered as Kathy nodded.

There was a buzz and Elizabeth leaned forward and pushed the intercom button. "Yes."

"Sarah Jane's ready, Mrs. Stapleton. She'll be on the way to your office in just a few minutes."

"Thank you, Anna." Elizabeth got up and pointed to a side door. "She'll be coming down the hall shortly."

She came around her desk and leaned back against it, her body between Steve and Kathy and the door. She looked at Tracy now. "Miss Benton, we're going to let Sarah accompany you back to Markwood. I understand that her grandmother is a resident there and very near death." She waited for Tracy to respond.

"Yes, Mrs. Stapleton. That's true. Mrs. Stephens has been given only days to live. A reunion with her granddaughter could give her last days some ray of sunshine."

"I can understand that. But you do know that Markwood will be responsible for her well-being while she's away from us."

"I do."

"Then I have a release form you need to sign. But before we do that, let's go out in the hall and meet Sarah Jane." Elizabeth started to cross to the door but Steve stood up and touched her arm.

"Would it be all right if Kathy and I met her in the hall." Then he looked down at his son. "And, Tommy, of course."

Elizabeth stopped. "Of course." She moved aside and Steve opened the door to let Kathy step into the hall ahead of him. Tommy followed his mother. For several seconds the three of them stood there until a door opened at the far end of the dimly lit hall. A small blonde girl with a large brown suitcase emerged. A heavyset woman slipped through the door behind her. She looked up the hall toward Steve and then bent over and kissed Sarah on the top of the head. Then she disappeared back into the room and closed the door. When she did the girl picked up the bag and started down the hall toward them.

"Is it her?" Kathy whispered.

"Yes." Steve's voice was trembling as he spoke.

Kathy put her hand on Steve's shoulder and gave him a gentle shove. "Go to her, Steve. Go help your daughter."

He turned and saw tears welling up in his wife's eyes. "We'll all go, all of us."

She nodded and bit her bottom lip as Steve turned back to the child.

He moved slowly toward the small girl. "Sarah."

The girl stopped and stared down the hall toward the strangers.

She watched as they approached, wondering why the woman was crying. Tears were something the child was very familiar with. There had been many lonely, tearful nights since they had taken her grandmother away. And now this woman was crying and she didn't know why.

The man was beside her now and he put his hands on her shoulders and spoke softly.

"Can I carry your suitcase, Sarah?"

Sarah gripped the suitcase tightly for a few seconds and then, gradually, she released it. As she did, Steve knelt and brushed a twig of blonde hair out of her eyes. Then he slipped his arms around the small body and pulled her close. Sarah wasn't sure why, but suddenly there were tears in her eyes. Slowly, her arms came up and circled the man's neck. It seemed the thing to do. And for the first time in months, the loneliness and terror she had felt for so long began to subside. A moment later another set of arms enveloped her as the woman knelt beside her. And then there was the touch of a small hand on her shoulder. She wasn't sure why, but for the first time in a very long time she felt warm—warm and wanted.

The End

Bob Smith grew up in Hot Springs, Arkansas. After graduation from high school, he spent two years at Ouachita Baptist University in Arkadelphia, Arkansas, before joining the Navy. During his time in the Navy he met and married his future wife, Barbara Williams. Upon his discharge from the Navy, he went into the aluminum products business with his father in Hot Springs.

In the early 1980s, Bob sold the business and went back to college at Henderson State University in Arkadelphia, where he received a business degree with a major in accounting. Soon after graduation in 1985, Ouachita Technical College, in Malvern, Arkansas, hired him to teach math and accounting. During those years he commuted to Henderson State in the evenings, where he earned a master's degree in business.

Bob retired from teaching in May 2000. He wrote on and off for a number of years before finally getting serious about it after retirement. Bob and Barbara live in Hot Springs Village, Arkansas, where Bob enjoys golf, writing, and being active in his church. They have two children and six grandchildren. Their son, Greg, and his wife, Sue, live in Fredericksburg, Virginia, and their daughter, Sharon, and her husband, Robert, live in Sherbrooke, Quebec, Canada.

www.ingramcontent.com/pod-product-compliance
Lightning Source LLC
Chambersburg PA
CBHW071205250626
47159CB00001B/209